T0023310

Bonnie Mac's Café

Jill Smith Entrekin

Edited by Amy Bell

FLINTSTAR, LLC

Paisley, Brad. "When I Get Where I'm Going." *Time Well Wasted.* Featured artist: Dolly Parton. Arista Nashville, 2005. en.wikipedia.org/wiki/Time_Well_Wasted.

Wordsworth, William. "Ode: Intimations of Immortality from Recollections of Early Childhood." *Poetry Foundation,* 2023, https://www.poetryfoundation.org/poems/45536/ ode-intimations-of-immortality-from-recollections-of-early-childhood. Accessed 9 October 2023.

Print ISBN: 979-8-35093-076-4

eBook ISBN: 979-8-35093-077-1

Printed in the United States of America on SFI Certified paper.

First Edition

To my cousin Peggy Dumas Hollis, whose resilient spirit and compassionate heart serve as the cornerstone of this story. For all the Trailways bus trips between Macon and Thomaston, the memorable bike adventures that never failed to put us in trouble, and the countless hours of shared giggles, I treasure you, sweet Cuz.

To the memory of my late husband Dana Entrekin, who continues to cheer for me and my writing from his Heavenly perch. The link connecting our souls will never be severed.

PROLOGUE

2008

Grace MacGregor sipped a cup of coffee as she studied the applicants for the third-grade teacher position that would be open in the fall. Since Grace arrived at Pike Elementary School by 5:30 each morning, it was still dark outside. While she could have delegated the job of unlocking the school gates and disarming the alarm to her assistant principal, Grace enjoyed the solitude of the empty building before the rush of the day began.

Just before daybreak, she nursed her second cup of coffee while she and Roosevelt Rucker, her head custodian, turned on lights and unlocked doors. "Y'all did a great job on the lobby floor this weekend, Mr. Roosevelt. It's so shiny I can almost see my reflection." Built shortly after the Civil War, the school had been renovated with alarms and air conditioning in the years Grace had worked there, but its high ceilings and hardwood floors had remained.

"Yes'm, thank you. I appreciate the overtime this weekend, too. I'll still mop it each afternoon, so it'll stay nice and shiny." Roosevelt, a beloved fixture for decades at Pike Elementary, used a long dust mop and wood shavings to catch the dust on the hardwood floors.

Grace made her way to the cafeteria to check on the day's breakfast fare. Almost half of the student population qualified for a subsidized meal. "Estelle, the kitchen smells heavenly. I don't know how you do it on our budget. No wonder so many children come for breakfast."

A heavyset woman with jovial eyes, Estelle was old enough to be Grace's grandmother. She smiled as she handed Grace a cinnamon bun fresh out of the oven. "I know how you love them when they're warm."

By the time early staff began arriving at 6:15, Grace was back in her office to meet with Butch Prosser, a former high school coach turned assistant principal, and the upper grades' counselor Sarah Tucker, whose pregnant belly swelled with each new day. Grace doubted that Sarah would last through these final two weeks of school.

Both the assistant principal and the counselor were serving as chaperones on the fifth-grade field trip to visit the middle school for orientation day. Grace was pleased to see that Sarah was wearing tennis shoes for the half-mile walk to the middle school facility.

"Are you certain we have enough parent chaperones, Mr. Prosser?" While Grace had worked with Butch for ages, she always addressed staff members in a professional manner on school premises.

"We have five parent volunteers along with the fifth-grade staff, so that should be plenty." Butch studied the fifth-grade roster. "I've already designated which teacher will escort one of the four popcorners in the bunch, and I'll oversee their ringleader."

"Popcorner" was a teacher term for students who fed off one another to disrupt the class. Mitchell Waddell, the popcorn ringleader, had seen the walls of Grace's office on more occasions than she could count. Even so, Grace liked Mitchell, who was smart as a whip and full of harmless mischief.

She smiled to herself. "If you have any trouble with Mitchell, remind him of the deal we made." Grace had promised Mitchell that he could read the morning announcements on the last day of school if he did not show up in her office during the entire month of May. So far, Mitchell had upheld his part of the agreement.

At 6:45, Grace stuck her head in the library, where the PTA officers were planning their annual end-of-year luncheon for the staff. Seconds later her walkie talkie crackled with her secretary's voice. "Dr. Mac, you're needed in the office."

"I'll be right there, Mrs. Johnson." Faye Johnson, who had served as Grace's secretary for ten years, had a sixth sense about who truly needed to see the principal. Faye managed the front office like triage on a battlefield, sending the lesser concerns to the assistant principal or one of the school's two counselors so that Grace could handle the critical cases.

The "critical case" this morning was second grader Ruthie Lawson. When Grace reached the front office, little Ruthie stood bawling as Faye handed her tissue after tissue. "I tried to find out what was wrong, but she couldn't stop crying to tell me."

Grace kneeled so she was eye-level with the hysterical child who was gulping for air. "Ruthie, come with me so you can tell me all about it." Within minutes, Ruthie was sitting in Grace's lap as they rocked in the Amish bentwood rocker that sat in the corner of the office. As she relaxed to the rocker's rhythm, the little girl's wails subsided into muffled sobs.

Grace patted her gently. "You want to tell me what happened, Ruthie?"

"The big boys at the bus stop called me a monster. Am I a monster, Dr. Mac?" Grace's beloved nickname was reserved solely for students and staff.

"You are not a monster, pretty girl. Were these boys from our school?" Grace despised bullying and worked diligently to squash it before it mushroomed.

Ruthie ignored the question. "They said I had leprosy, and that if anybody touched me, they'd catch it. What's leprosy, Dr. Mac?"

Grace sighed. She never withheld the truth from a child. "Leprosy is a sickness that makes a person's skin look different from other people—but you do not have leprosy, Ruthie, and before long the scars on your neck and arm will be almost invisible." Little Ruthie, burned in a car accident when she was only four, had already endured numerous skin grafts and still faced several more surgeries.

Ruthie's voice trembled. "When I get big like those mean boys, will I still be ugly?"

"Sweetheart, you are not ugly now. But let me show you something." Grace sat Ruthie on her feet and stood to retrieve a tarnished picture frame and a broken pair of small eyeglasses from the shadow box behind her desk.

She handed the picture frame to Ruthie. It held a school photo of a little girl about Ruthie's size. She wore a patch over one eye and glasses identical to the pair that Grace now had in her hand. "Tell me, Ruthie, what do you think of this little girl?"

Ruthie giggled. "She looks funny with that big bandage over her eye. And her glasses are so ugly. Those mean boys would think she was a monster, too."

Grace smiled. "Well, that little girl was me a long time ago. I had to wear a patch over my eye and these ugly glasses so my eyes could get well. Sometimes people would call me a monster, and it would make me cry, but it also made me brave."

Ruthie gulped. "But you're so beautiful now, Dr. Mac. I want to be beautiful and brave like you."

Grace straightened the child's curly pigtails. "Ruthie Lawson, you are already beautiful and one of the bravest people I know." Ruthie was grinning as she skipped away to class.

The special education bus was one of the last to arrive each morning. Grace always tried to greet the children as they exited the bus. Deb Hardin, the bus driver, had started the job when her autistic son Daniel had been a student. Daniel now worked as a groundskeeper at a golf club in Griffin, but Deb continued her bus route.

"Mawnin', Dr. Mac. Could you help me with the lift? It's stickin' agin." Together the two women managed to get the lift to descend so that the wheelchair-bound children could exit.

Grace had requisitioned the county office for a new bus two years ago. So little money, so much need. She shrugged her shoulders at Deb. "Maybe it will pass in the budget next year."

Grace grinned at Preston Jones, a studious fourth grader with cerebral palsy, who rolled down the ramp on his scooter. "So, what chapter are you on, Preston?" She and Preston were simultaneously reading the Percy Jackson series, modern stories based on Greek myths. They were up to the third installment entitled, *The Titan's Curse*.

"I finished Chapter 10 last night, Dr. Mac. "

Grace held up her hand in a stop position. "Don't you dare tell me what happens, Preston! I'm only on Chapter 8."

The tardy bell was ringing as Grace headed back to the office for the morning announcements. While fourth and fifth graders oversaw the school news, Grace always followed with a character word for the day.

She kept a file of character words and usually settled for whatever was on top. However, today she shuffled through the file until she found a topic which seemed appropriate after her meeting with Ruthie Lawson. "Good morning, students. Today's character word is *compassion*..."

After watching the parade of fifth graders march off to the middle school, with Mitchell Waddell right beside Mr. Prosser, Grace spent the next hour visiting with the third graders. Students were presenting oral reports on safety, and Grace learned the importance of wearing a bicycle helmet, the steps for exiting one's house in case of a fire, and the correct method for rescuing a kitten from a drainage pipe.

Grace returned to her office for the final hour before lunch, when she would circulate through the cafeteria. While there were usually designated teachers on lunch duty, she found lunch an opportune time to listen to students. Today, her presence would be necessary since one counselor and the assistant principal were at the middle school with the fifth graders.

In the quiet hour leading up to lunch, she spent the first few minutes signing various forms that Faye had left in her "Immediate Action" box. Then she returned to the applications for the third-grade position. Grace usually appreciated this time to decompress from the busyness of the morning, but she hated the silence today.

Silence made Grace think, and Grace did not want to think. She reached into her briefcase and retrieved a large manila envelope. The envelope's front was labeled "Bonnie Kaye MacGregor," written in large block letters, the kind teachers taught to first graders who are learning to write the alphabet. She'd decided the document's significance required her daughter's full name instead of "BK," her nickname for most of her life. For the umpteenth time, Grace inventoried the envelope's contents—a life insurance policy, a detailed list of her assets, funeral arrangements, a copy of her will, and the thumb drive.

Just before 2 a.m., Grace had saved her full confession to the thumb drive. It was the final piece of the puzzle. She'd tried to sleep for a couple of hours, but without the Ambien she'd been prescribed a few months ago, she lay awake and stared at the red minutes as they rolled across her digital clock.

When she had last seen her daughter, Grace had yet to come to terms with her decision. During spring break, she had driven to Nashville where BK had a gig at the Bluebird Café, which was highlighting "up and coming" song writers. Maybe it was better that Grace had not finalized her plan because her intuitive daughter hadn't sensed anything awry.

Grace still marveled at her daughter's ability to pick up almost any instrument and begin to play. On that night, BK was featured in a dueling banjo number with a young man who had recently written a song for Keith Urban. Then her daughter donned her acoustic guitar and played her latest piece, a moving ballad that complemented her deep, sultry voice.

Clad in a pair of jeans and a soft, white blouse, her curly auburn hair in a simple ponytail, BK exuded a comfortable sincerity that always stunned her mother. When she finished her performance, BK joined Grace at her VIP table for a glass of wine.

Shortly thereafter, a gentleman in a blue suit and a cowboy hat had approached their table. "How's it going, BK?" No one ever called her by her full name anymore. "I represent Jennifer Nettles, and she might be interested in that ballad you sang. Here's my card; I'll get your information from the manager. You'll be hearing from us."

In her usual unflappable manner, BK had pushed a wisp of hair from her face. "Thanks, it'd be great to work with Jennifer. I love her music."

Back to reality in her office, Grace finally sealed the envelope. "Please forgive me for waiting so long to share these secrets and for not giving you a proper goodbye, sweet daughter."

Grace had made a note on the calendar she shared with her secretary that she would be leaving the premises as soon as the buses rolled this afternoon. She wanted to put the envelope in her safety deposit box at the bank before she lost her nerve.

She was thankful that she had demonstrated no visible symptoms on this school day. She had suffered no dizzy spells or forgotten anyone's name as the morning had progressed. Just yesterday, though, she had dialed the number to the county office, and while it was ringing, she had no idea why or whom she was calling. Though always a list maker, Grace had discovered that lists were not enough. Instead, she had begun to write paragraphs beside each bullet point on her lists in hopes that she would not embarrass herself by drawing a total blank.

She had been wise to tell her new primary physician in Griffin about her insomnia at her six-month checkup. She didn't mention the lapses in memory, the dizzy spells, the confusion that had become commonplace. Although she rarely slept anymore, she'd hoarded enough Ambien for her plan.

Perhaps she should have followed through with the appointment she'd made with a neurologist at Emory in Atlanta. But what could he tell her that she didn't already know? She had watched her precious BonBon descend into the hellish world of dementia. BonBon—so vibrant, so intelligent, so energetic—had slowly and agonizingly lost her senses to the thief that came in the night and stole her piece by piece.

The dementia took its agonizing time to run its course and destroy BonBon's entire being. Grace had no desire to repeat the performance for her daughter. She would wait until the school term ended and teachers had exited for the summer. Then she would swallow her stash of sleeping pills and drift away quietly and effectively.

The phone shook her back into reality. "Dr. Mac, I need your assistance, please."

Grace sensed the panic in her secretary's normally composed voice. "I'll be right out."

As she walked into the outer office, Grace almost bumped into a young man, disheveled in appearance with drooping eyelids. His speech was slurred. "You tha princthipal? I want to check my son outta school. Ish a 'mergency, but your shecretary says I can't do that. Whash that all about? He's my son, for Godsthake!"

Grace took a deep breath and shifted her eyes to Faye, who handed her a student info card. "Well let's see if I can help you." Grace studied the info for Weston Turner, a second grader. His mother was a dental hygienist at an office in Griffin, and the card left explicit instructions, with a copy of a court order, that the boy's father was not allowed to pick up Wes.

Grace inhaled and managed a smile. "You must be Mr. Turner. Is that correct? "

"Yer damn right, I am! And I want my son right now!" The man stumbled closer to Grace.

Grace didn't smell alcohol on his breath but observed that several of his teeth were rotten. She wondered if he could be a meth addict. "Why don't you come into my office, Mr. Turner, and we'll work this out." As she escorted the man towards her office door, Grace nodded at Faye. She knew Faye would alert police as quickly as possible.

The call was not quick enough. As soon as Grace closed her door and turned around, the man was on her. "You bitch. Yer just like my wife." Then he plunged a knife into her gut.

Sliding to the floor, Grace had one thought.

"I won't have to do it myself."

PART ONE

CHAPTER ONE

1957

Bonnie MacGregor was pulling the final pan of tomorrow's mud hens from the oven when she heard the front door's bell jingle. "I'm all out of coffee, Sheriff. And Betsy will kill me if I serve you another piece of pie."

With the warm pan in her oven-mitted hands, Bonnie used her rear end to push through the swinging doors that separated the kitchen from the lunch counter. "Oh, hi there. I thought you were Sheriff Riggins. He's about the only one who comes in this late."

A wisp of a young woman, her threadbare cotton dress soaked and sticking to her thin frame, stood just inside the doorway. Bonnie grabbed a clean dish towel from the counter. "Honey, you're drenched to the bone! Come on in and let's get you dry."

Soggy shoes squished across the floor of the café. It was not until the woman reached the counter that Bonnie spied a child hanging onto the back of her dripping hemline.

"Well now, who do we have here?" Bonnie smiled down at the little girl whose eyes remained glued to the floor.

"She don't talk." The woman snatched the towel from Bonnie and roughly wiped down the little girl's yellow ringlets. "Are you really out of coffee?"

Bonnie handed the young woman another towel and spread two more on the seats of the nearest booth. "I can have coffee ready in a jiffy." Then she turned towards the little girl whose eyes remained downcast. "I bet you would like some hot chocolate; I make mine with whipped cream and sprinkles on top."

The little girl's chin came up. She closed her right eye and cocked her head as if to focus on Bonnie with her left eye. Then she smiled.

After starting the coffee pot, Bonnie poured a cup of milk into a small boiler on the stove. "Tonight's special is chicken and dumplings. How does that sound?"

"How much is one special and maybe a grilled cheese sandwich?" The woman rummaged through a ragged diaper bag that obviously served as her purse.

Bonnie set the steaming beverages on the table. "Honey, it's almost closing time, and I was about to throw out what's left in the pot. Let's say it's on the house tonight." Bonnie scurried through the kitchen's swinging door before the young woman could refuse her charity.

While the woman and child ate in silence, Bonnie washed the empty dumplings pot. Her final chore before closing was to remove any baked items left in the display counter. As she leaned down to pull out an almost empty tray of brownies, she saw the left side of a tiny face pressed against the glass.

Bonnie winked at the face. "Oh dear, I have two brownies left, and I hate to see them go to waste. I've already made a fresh batch for tomorrow. Are you up for dessert?" She turned toward the little girl's mother who was taking a long drag from a freshly lit cigarette.

The young woman breathed smoke out her nostrils as she stood up. "Not for me, but she can have one. The rain's let up a little bit, and I need to make a call. I saw a phone booth on the corner. I'll be right back."

She was gone before Bonnie could offer the use of the café's phone. Bonnie cut the little girl's brownie into bite-sized pieces. "I think I'll join you." She poured herself a cup of coffee and slid the last brownie onto a plate for herself. The little girl devoured her brownie in silence, licked her fingers clean, and curled up on the padded booth bench.

Marie Beasley, the girl's mother, was pure and simple a prostitute. Her pimp Freddy had promised that if she could get rid of the girl and get back to Atlanta before daybreak, she could go with him to California. Freddy said he knew they could make big money on the Sunset Strip, and then maybe Marie could stop hooking.

Marie had intended to drop off her daughter at the Southern Pines Children's Home, less than a mile from Bonnie's Café. But her old piece of junk Pontiac had limped into town on fumes. By the time it sputtered to a stop, there was only one establishment still lit up in the town square. Marie grabbed her little girl and slogged through the driving rain until she reached the front door of Bonnie Mac's Café.

Now that she'd ditched her daughter at the café, Marie waded through puddles to the phone booth and dug through her pockets. She had just enough change to call Freddy and beg him to wait for her. As she hung up and stepped out of the booth, she spied the headlights of an overloaded pickup stopped at the only traffic signal in town. When she waved down the driver, Marie realized he was just a teenager.

Chewing on a toothpick, the young driver stuck his head out the cab's window. "You need some help, ma'am?"

Marie unbuttoned the top button of her dress and leaned her well-endowed bosom against the window. "What I need, sweetie, is a ride to Atlanta."

The boy's ears turned red as he almost swallowed his toothpick. Never once did his eyes stray from Marie's breasts. "Um, I'm hauling these watermelons to the Farmer's Market in Forest Park. I can get you that far."

Marie grinned. "That'll work."

By the time Bonnie had cleared and washed the dessert dishes, the little girl was sound asleep. The child's mother was almost to Griffin before Bonnie realized she wasn't coming back.

Bonnie considered calling the sheriff. The rain had finally abated, and she could see the jail house from her front window. There wasn't a light on in the apartment above the jail where Sheriff Riggins lived with his wife Betsy and their three sons, the youngest only a month old. The sheriff had looked exhausted when he'd stopped by the café an hour earlier for a cup of coffee before making his final rounds. He'd mentioned their newborn was colicky and had kept them up all week.

"I think I can take care of you for one night. I'm sure your mama will be back by morning." Bonnie reassured the sleeping child as she lifted her easily into her arms and carried her through the kitchen and out the back door of the café.

Bonnie crossed the street into a small, neat yard just a stone's throw from the café. She eased up the front steps and onto the porch. The white framed house with its matching picket fence had been willed to Bonnie by Emmett Lyons, the owner and her landlord, when he'd died several years back. Mr. Lyons had been Bonnie's unlikely savior after she lost the diner that she and her husband Oscar had owned in Thomaston.

Twenty-five years earlier, without Bonnie's knowledge, Oscar mortgaged *MacGregor's Diner* and everything they owned to fund his harvest of a new peach variety. There was a drought the first season, and then the new strain of peaches developed a blight the second season. Oscar blew his brains out in the middle of the orchard and left Bonnie holding the bill.

The diner, along with everything else Bonnie owned, was auctioned off on the Thomaston square. Emmett Lyons, a childless widower, purchased the diner and offered Bonnie a job there. A couple of years later, Emmett decided to open a second eatery in Zebulon. He offered Bonnie a partnership if she'd move to Zebulon and run the café. Bonnie was more than happy to escape Thomaston, where she'd grown tired of being a favorite subject of gossip.

Now as she carefully cradled the little girl in her arms, Bonnie used her foot to bump open the screen door, which she left unlatched during the day. She laid the sleeping child on the sofa and covered her with a cotton quilt that had been handmade by her grandmother.

·❧·

It was almost 10 p.m. by the time Ricky Edson and his hitch-hiking lady in distress pulled into one of the open stalls at the State Farmer's Market in Forest Park. Marie gave Ricky a little pat on his thigh and smiled seductively. "Do you think you could take me to the Greyhound Bus station in Atlanta when you're finished unloading? I'll certainly make it worth your while."

Ricky gulped. He had a girlfriend back home in Concord, a little village a few miles west of Zebulon. His girl Misty was flat-chested, and he'd never touched a rack like the one Marie was sporting. He hopped out of the truck and cleared his throat. "I know where the Atlanta bus station is. It won't take me fifteen minutes to unload these melons. "

"I'll just go freshen up, sweetie." Marie grinned provocatively as she slid out of the truck's cab and slinked off to the nearest restroom.

Marie dug through her diaper bag. She'd intended to leave her daughter's few belongings at the children's home, but she'd been in too big of a rush. Besides, a little girl's clothing was perfect camouflage for what lay beneath.

In addition to being a prostitute, Marie was a junkie, and Freddy was not only her pimp but also her supplier. Marie pulled a spoon and a small packet of heroin from the bottom of the bag. After filling the spoon with water from the bathroom faucet, she used her cigarette lighter to warm up the white mixture. She found her needle and syringe buried beneath a ratty, old stuffed dog that her daughter would dearly miss.

"Oh, that feels so good." Marie experienced a better-than-normal rush as the substance flowed through her veins. If the concrete floor had not been so uncomfortable, she would have drifted off and missed her ride. It wouldn't have mattered anyway because Freddy had already left for Los Angeles on the 8 p.m. Greyhound out of Atlanta.

When Marie returned to Ricky's truck, she was high as a kite. She slid over beside him and laid her head on his shoulder. Having never seen anyone high on heroin, the boy mistook her behavior for romance.

"Here we are, ma'am. The Atlanta bus station." As Ricky gently shook Marie to wake her, he saw drool mixed with blood seeping out of the side of her mouth. The boy screamed.

CHAPTER TWO

After a quick shower, Bonnie checked on her guest, now curled into a fetal position and sucking her thumb. As the child slumbered, Bonnie had a chance to study her. She was a pretty little urchin, even though her dress was soiled, and she appeared malnourished. "We can fatten you up in no time," Bonnie breathed softly as she examined the dirty rust rings around the child's neck and ankles.

She stroked the sleeping child's hair. "I wonder what your name is. Your mama never said. How could your mama just up and leave?" Bonnie sighed. "I don't understand God sometimes. He leaves me childless and wanting, then blesses another woman with a child she doesn't want."

In the aftermath of Oscar's untimely death, Bonnie could've had her choice of any single man in three counties, but she'd had no time or desire for courting. When she wasn't lying to herself, Bonnie knew she'd never quit loving Oscar, even though he'd taken the coward's way out of a desperate situation.

While she was still an attractive woman with her tall, slim figure that had never borne a child, Bonnie was nearing 50 now and quite set in her ways. The thought of caring for a man after all these years on her own somewhat repulsed her. She had no stomach for whiskers in her sink and dirty socks on her polished hardwood floors. The mere idea of a man sharing her bathroom, much less her bed, sent chills down her spine.

Bonnie tucked the quilt under the sleeping child's chin. "Don't you worry, honey. The sheriff will get this all figured out in the morning, which isn't far away. We have to be up and back in the café by 5:30 to bake biscuits." She kissed the one clean spot on the child's forehead and tiptoed to bed.

Her clock was set for 5 a.m., an ungodly hour for most, but Bonnie had always been an early riser. The alarm had not yet sounded when she was awakened to a pungent odor. She rolled over to discover a little face peering down out of what was obviously her one good eye. The child didn't make a sound, but tears were streaming down her face, her dirty dress now soaked in her own urine.

"You poor thing. I didn't think about taking you to the bathroom before I put you to bed." Bonnie slid into her slippers and took the child's hand. "Never you mind, sweetheart. We'll get you into a warm bath and all cleaned up."

Bonnie scrubbed the child from top to bottom and washed her matted hair. After toweling her dry and wrapping a second clean towel around her, Bonnie took a comb to the child's hair. "My goodness, I bet your mama has a time with this hair. I hope I'm not hurting you." The little girl stood stock-still, her left eye following Bonnie's every move, as she arduously combed out the tangled curls.

When the job was done, the child reached for her dirty clothes lying in a heap as though she was about to put them on. Bonnie caught her arm. "I tell you what, honey. I think I may have something that fits you in my sewing room." She took the girl's hand and led her into the spare bedroom where she kept her sewing machine.

An expert seamstress, Bonnie volunteered her services for the church's clothes closet by mending any donations before they were given to the area's needy. "Opal Dorsey just dropped off some things her twins had outgrown." Digging through a neatly organized bin labeled *Girls: Sizes 4-6*, Bonnie withdrew a pink shirtwaist dress that barely looked worn and held it up against the silent child. "Perfect! Now let's find you some underwear and a pair of shoes." Bonnie searched two other bins for more wardrobe items.

In the early quiet of the cafe, Bonnie kneaded her biscuit dough in a wooden mixing bowl that had belonged to her grandmother. The little girl sat on a stool at the kitchen's stainless worktable and dug into a bowl of oatmeal sweetened with brown sugar and butter. When she finished, she held her bowl up towards Bonnie. "You certainly can have some more, sweetheart." She dipped another serving into the child's bowl and refilled her glass of milk. "Bonnie never lets her guests go hungry."

Just before 6 a.m., Bonnie turned on the dining room lights, unlocked the front door, and flipped over the door's sign from *Closed* to *Open*. When she turned around, she almost tripped over the child who was standing just behind her skirt. "Goodness, you surprised me. I think you'll just have to be my assistant today." The little girl nodded and offered a timid smile.

As Bonnie headed to the counter, she felt the child grab her hem and follow right behind. "I need to get the coffee started before my first customer arrives. Cooter Renfroe will be here at exactly 6:05, and he likes his coffee hot and strong." Bonnie lifted the child easily and set her on one of the counter stools. "Why don't you fold some napkins for me?" She pulled a large box of paper napkins from behind the counter and showed the child how to fold each one into a triangle.

When the bell on the door jingled a few minutes later, the coffee was perking. "Mornin', Miz Bonnie, coffee ready?" Cooter, dressed in his mailman's uniform, offered his usual greeting and sat on his usual stool, the last one nearest the cash register. The location allowed him to make small talk with every patron who stopped by to pay their bill.

"I've got you a cup on the way." Bonnie poured coffee for Cooter before turning around. When she did, she discovered the entire box of napkins perfectly folded into neat triangles. "You work fast, honey." She smiled at the child as she handed Cooter his coffee. "Your usual, Cooter?"

"Yep." Cooter's usual included eggs sunny side up, two strips of bacon, grits, and hot biscuits with honey. "Who's your little helper today?" As Cooter eyed the little girl, she tucked her head into her dress, slid off the stool, and scurried behind the counter and Bonnie's skirt.

Cooter Renfroe was not only the county's solitary mailman but also one of the biggest gossips this side of Griffin. Bonnie chose her words carefully. "Oh, she's just visiting for the day. Her mama will be back to get her soon."

Cooter peered around Bonnie to get a better look at the little girl. "Well, I ain't ever seen her around here before. Where's she from?"

As Bonnie considered a reply, the oven buzzer went off. She took the child's hand and pushed through the swinging door to the kitchen. "Hot biscuits coming up, Cooter."

Transferring biscuits to a basket and covering them with a cloth napkin, she began to regret not calling the sheriff last night. What if this child's mama showed up and accused Bonnie of kidnapping? She decided it was better to keep the little girl out of sight until she could reach the sheriff.

She lifted the child onto a stool at her stainless worktable. Then she prepared two warm biscuits with butter and homemade strawberry jam for the child and set them on a plate. "Why don't you stay back here, honey. That way nobody will bother you."

Bonnie went to the storage closet and withdrew some crayons and construction paper she used when she taught the primary children's Sunday school class once a month. She placed the items beside the biscuits. "You draw me a pretty picture, okay?" She patted the child on her head and hurried back with Cooter's biscuits.

In her absence, two more customers had arrived. Buddy Sampson sat at his favorite table, which gave him a view of the counter and the front door. Neither a counter stool nor a booth could accommodate Buddy, who tipped the scales at over 300 pounds. He weighed himself periodically at Akins Feed and Seed down in Thomaston because it had a scale for weighing cotton bales. Buddy was a self-proclaimed bachelor and playboy who was always talking about his various girlfriends—none of whom had ever been seen in town since, according to Buddy, every one of them lived at least 60 miles away in the Atlanta area. Buddy's voice possessed a high-pitched, nasal quality that made strangers do a double take when he opened his mouth.

Somewhat disheveled and bleary-eyed, Ouida Clarkston was sitting next to Cooter at the counter. "I am in dire need of coffee." Hers was a deep, raspy voice, the result of years of smoking.

Ouida was recovering from one of her notorious binges. Bonnie had observed the sheriff escort Ouida to the jail across the street two days earlier. She obviously had just been released. Bonnie set a steaming cup in front of her.

Puffing desperately on her first cigarette in almost two days, Ouida dumped a mound of sugar into her coffee. Ouida, whose daddy had made a fortune in the lumber business, was perhaps the richest woman in the county. When she was sober, she spent her days driving around Zebulon and its neighboring communities and stopping to visit with anybody who was home.

When she wasn't socializing or drinking herself into a stupor, Ouida spent her every waking hour sharing whatever information she had gleaned from the people she visited. Though never hateful or harmful, she colored her stories just enough to make them more interesting. Ouida's story-telling abilities made Cooter seem like a gossiping amateur. "You're not going to believe what I just overheard at the sheriff's office."

Cooter's ears perked up. "Whaddya hear?"

Ouida took another deep draw on her cigarette. "You know the Edson family?"

Buddy chimed in. "I had a girlfriend named Luella Edson. She lived up in East Point. I took her to the Theater Under the Stars in Atlanta last year to see Bing Crosby in *White Christmas*. She had the curves, that Luella did. But she wasn't much of a conversationalist, so I broke up with her."

Ouida rolled her eyes. "Buddy, it's called the Fox Theater. Only children refer to it as the Theater Under the Stars. I'm talking about Otis Edson, that farmer in Concord."

Cooter interrupted. "The Edsons are on my rural route. They grow some fine watermelons and the sweetest white corn I ever ate."

"That's the ones." Ouida poured another heap of sugar in the coffee that Bonnie had refreshed. "Well, what I heard was about his son Ricky, the one who plays baseball for Pike County High."

"Yeah, he's a big strapping boy but kinda dumb, I hear. His daddy told me that Ricky's gonna get a full scholarship to the University of Georgia to play starting shortstop next fall." If someone were to strip away all the adjectives from Cooter's description, they still wouldn't have the truth.

As Bonnie served Buddy his pancakes and sausage with a side of biscuits and gravy, Ouida lit another cigarette. "Well, from what I hear, Ricky was playing with something other than a baseball last night."

Cooter was close to foaming at the mouth. "What was he playing with?"

"Not what, but *whom*." Ouida smirked. "The poor boy got taken by a woman of ill repute in our very own town last night."

His mouth full of biscuit, Buddy practically squealed. "A whore in these parts? You're kidding me. You'd have to drive to downtown Atlanta to find a real hooker." Buddy checked himself. "At least that's what I've heard."

Ouida feigned indignant shock. "Buddy, please, there are women present." She flicked an ash from her wrinkled blouse and waited for Cooter to start twitching for more information. "Anyways, Ricky picked her up at the corner right outside of here in the pouring rain last night. He said the girl was drenched to the bone and looked scared to death. "

Bonnie discreetly leaned into the conversation as Ouida continued. "He was on his way to the Farmer's Market, he said, and she asked for a ride. The poor boy claimed he didn't know what kind of woman she was. Well, when he finished unloading his truck, Ricky said he'd drive her downtown to the Atlanta bus station because he didn't want to leave her stranded all alone. But by the time they got to the Greyhound Station, the girl was dead."

The coffee tin Bonnie was about to open slipped out of her hand and rolled across the tile floor. "Dead? What happened to her?"

Ouida pulled her compact and a tube of lipstick from her purse and attempted to repair her face. "I'm not sure about that, but when I was leaving Sheriff Riggins' office, I saw an official looking gentleman in a suit standing beside Ricky. I figure he's an investigator from somewheres, hopefully nearby. Nothing like a handsome man in a suit to get my motor running."

Cooter guffawed. "Just because he's got on a coat and tie don't make him a cop."

Ouida took a long drag on her cigarette then blew it directly at Cooter's face. "For your information, Cooter Renfroe, he had his coat slung over his shoulder and was wearing one of those shoulder holsters with a big gun. He must've brought poor Ricky back to town because I didn't see the Edsons' truck outside. I assume the investigator is retracing the poor woman's final journey."

As much as Bonnie did not want to believe Ouida, whose track record for truth was tenuous at best, she knew in her bones that the dead woman had to be the one who visited her café last night. How would Bonnie ever explain the situation to the sheriff? Before she had time to contemplate her dilemma, Sheriff Riggins walked in with the official-looking stranger in tow.

CHAPTER THREE

Sheriff J. Carl Riggins was a long, lean man, almost 15 years younger than Bonnie. Despite his youth, the sheriff, who had served on Guadalcanal during the war, had a weathered look and a weariness in his eyes, like he'd seen enough horror to last a lifetime.

After the war ended, J. Carl had returned home to marry his high school sweetheart. He'd worked in one of the textile mills down in Thomaston until five years earlier when he ran for the office of sheriff, vacated by his daddy T. Carl Riggins. Sheriff Riggins was the only law in Pike County as there was no money allotted for a deputy. He did employ Josephine Poole, a Negro woman, to clean the jail and cook meals for the few inmates occasionally housed there.

Not one to mince words, Sheriff Riggins nodded at the three patrons and then spoke directly to Bonnie. "This is Detective Rob Benefield with Atlanta PD. There's an old Pontiac with an expired tag parked on the side of Hwy 19 about a quarter of a mile north of here. Do you know who it belongs to?"

All eyes turned towards Bonnie. "Um, I might have an idea, Sheriff. I had a late customer eat supper here last night."

The sheriff approached Bonnie with what appeared to be a police mug shot of a woman. "Was this your customer?"

Bonnie studied the photo carefully. While the woman in the photo was much prettier than the bedraggled young woman with wet hair who had entered the café, she had the same blue eyes and bone structure as the little girl Bonnie was now harboring in her kitchen. "Yes, I think it could be the same woman. Um, Sheriff, can we talk in the kitchen? I need to check on my biscuits."

The sheriff nodded toward the Atlanta cop, who was scribbling something in a small, leather notebook he'd withdrawn from his coat pocket. "Miz Bonnie, why don't you pour Detective Benefield a cup of coffee, and he can question your customers if that's all right with them." Bonnie nodded and quickly served up a steaming cup of coffee to the detective. Knowing full well that Ouida, Cooter, and Buddy would keep the detective occupied, Sheriff Riggins then took Bonnie by the elbow and guided her through the swinging doors.

Engrossed in her artwork, the little girl didn't notice the swing of the door. When she looked up and saw the tall figure with Bonnie, she leapt from her stool and scurried under the table.

Bonnie stooped down and stuck her head under the table far enough to be face to face with the child. "It's okay, honey. Sheriff Riggins is a friend. He's not going to hurt you. Come on out from there, now."

The child slid from under the table and hid behind Bonnie's skirt. Bonnie could feel the little girl's entire body trembling.

J. Carl had sense enough not to crowd the child. He looked directly at Bonnie and spoke gently. "Who's your visitor, Miz Bonnie?"

Bonnie reached behind and took hold of the tiny trembling hand. "She's my new napkin folder, Sheriff Riggins. Her mama had to run an errand last night, so my new friend had a sleepover at my house."

The sheriff raised his eyebrows and then moved closer to the child. Bonnie realized that even if J. Carl stooped, he'd still tower over the child. So, she lifted the girl up and sat her atop the table. Even then, the sheriff had to kneel to get eye to eye with the girl.

He spied the child's art on the table and picked it up. The drawing depicted a lady in an apron much like the one Bonnie wore. The child had drawn a tremendous heart on the front of the lady's apron.

"What a pretty picture. Did you draw this by yourself?" The little girl nodded as she lifted her head and studied the sheriff with her left eye.

Now that he'd broken the ice, J. Carl tried again. "What's your name, sweetheart?" But the child was mute.

J. Carl eyed Bonnie, who shrugged. "Her mama said she doesn't talk." Bonnie poured the child another glass of milk and added a warm biscuit from the oven to her empty plate. "Here you go, honey. You help yourself to that butter and jam on the table. The sheriff and I are going to step outside to get some fresh air. We'll be right back."

Bonnie had barely shut the back door before J. Carl lit into her. "Where did that kid come from? I've never seen her before. What a cluster fu…" The sheriff caught himself. "We got a dead woman in Ricky Edson's truck, and now we've got a mute child in your café. What's going on, Miz Bonnie?"

With every detail she could remember, Bonnie shared the events of the previous night. When she finished, the sheriff was glaring at her. "I know I should have called you, J. Carl. But it was so late, and you looked so tired yesterday. You told me yourself that you and Betsy have been taking turns with the baby since he's had the colic. I figured it could wait until this morning."

J. Carl folded his arms across his chest. "They think the girl's mama, if she is her mama, overdosed on heroin. They found a diaper bag with her driver's license and a bunch of drug paraphernalia. The only indication that she might have been traveling with a child were a pair of little girl's pajamas and a dirty stuffed animal in the bottom of her bag."

Bonnie knew what she'd done had been the right thing to do, so she made no apologies. "So, what happens now?"

J. Carl rubbed his temples. "The body's at Grady Hospital for an autopsy. We should have the results in a couple of days. Benefield's partner is tracking down information on the woman. All we have right now is her name—Marie Beasley. She was twenty-two, but the address on her driver's license was bogus; it belonged to a thrift shop on Lucky Street in downtown Atlanta. So, it could be a while before we can confirm if she was the child's mother and if there's any next of kin. I think the best thing we can do for the little girl is call Southern Pines Children's Home and see if they can take her."

The wheels began to turn in Bonnie's head. "J. Carl, did the detective bring the diaper bag with him?"

J. Carl eyed Bonnie suspiciously. "What's that got to do with the price of tea in China? We need to find this child a place to stay, at least temporarily."

The sheriff's words were lost on Bonnie, who was already headed back into the kitchen. By the time J. Carl caught up with her, Bonnie was on the other side of the swinging doors. "Detective Benefield, would it be possible for me to see the stuffed animal found in the deceased's bag? It might help to shake my memory."

Detective Benefield glanced at Sheriff Riggins, who gave him a go-ahead nod. "I'll be right back, ma'am," and the detective was out the door.

Ouida was the first to speak. "Now why did you go and do that, Bonnie? The detective was about to take my statement." As if Ouida had a statement to make. She pulled out her compact to check her lipstick with her blood-shot eyes.

Sheriff Riggins took over. "Okay folks, I'm declaring the café as part of an ongoing police investigation, and everyone needs to leave."

Buddy began a high-pitched protest. "But—but I haven't even finished my biscuits, Sheriff. And Bonnie's Tuesday supper special is always meatloaf and mashed potatoes with gravy. What am I gonna eat if she's not open this evening?"

Sheriff Riggins flipped Bonnie's *Open* sign to *Closed* before addressing her three patrons. "Let me explain. This is a police jurisdiction right now. If you have a statement to make regarding the situation, you can wait over at the jail, but it might be a while."

Cooter headed for the door. "I already told the detective everything I know." He was quivering like a frantic Chihuahua to spread the news on his delivery route.

Bonnie wrapped Buddy's biscuits in some foil and held up her hand when he tried to pay. "It's on the house, today. I'm sure I'll be open for supper this evening." Mollified, Buddy cradled his biscuits and waddled towards the door.

Ouida snuffed out her cigarette and zipped up her purse. "Sheriff, I have a hair appointment in 15 minutes, but please tell Detective Benefield that he can stop by Hazel's Beauty Shop if he has any questions for me."

Left alone with just the sheriff, Bonnie expertly juggled scrambling three eggs while frying up some fresh bacon on the griddle. "The detective looks hungry. I bet he was up all night." Just as she placed the hot food onto a plate, the detective returned carrying a dirty, ragged stuffed dog with one of its ears hanging by what seemed a single thread.

"Something smells good." Detective Benefield eyed the plate as Bonnie slid it towards him. "Is this for me?"

Bonnie poured him a fresh cup of coffee. "It certainly is, and I hope you like grits." She spooned a large serving from a steaming pot into a bowl and topped it with a generous helping of butter.

The detective was salivating. "Yes ma'am. I haven't had a thing to eat since a couple of Varsity dogs just before I started my shift last night."

Bonnie couldn't take her eyes off the ragged little puppy. "You enjoy, detective. I've got some fresh biscuits baking in the oven. Um, I'll just go check on them in the kitchen, and I'll put the…the evidence back there so it will be out of the way."

Sheriff Riggins' face was filled with amusement as he followed Bonnie for a second time through the swinging doors to where the child still sat drawing at the table. "Miz Bonnie, you know you're just digging yourself a deeper hole, don't you?"

Bonnie shrugged. "Well, if I can solve a piece of the puzzle, maybe you'll go easy on me." She held up the stuffed puppy to the child. "Honey, does this belong to you?"

The little girl's face, now sporting a milk mustache, broke into a smile. She reached out with fingers sticky from strawberry jam and hugged the toy to her thin body.

Sheriff Riggins seized the opportunity to question the child. Once again, he squatted down so that he could be eye level with her. "I bet you like to sleep with that puppy every night."

When the child nodded timidly, he continued. "Where do you usually sleep?" The child shrugged her shoulders as she stroked the ragged animal. "Sweetheart, don't be afraid. We're just trying to find your family so that you can go home. I have a grandmother who lives in Atlanta. Do you? Or maybe you live with your daddy?" The little girl clutched the puppy tighter to her chest as silent tears rolled down her cheeks.

In one fell swoop, Bonnie had the child, puppy and all, in her arms. "It's okay, honey. Don't you cry. Bonnie's right here." It was Bonnie's turn to glare. "That's enough, J. Carl!"

As the sheriff straightened up and Bonnie comforted the child, Detective Benefield pushed through the swinging doors. "Sheriff, you need to get out of here. There's a crowd gathering on the sidewalk, and some reporter banging on the door..." He stopped mid-sentence as his eyes took in the scene.

The detective recovered quickly. "What the hell? Uh, excuse my French, ma'am, but the little girl's the spittin' image of the—the..."

J. Carl interrupted the detective before the child could understand what was happening. "Is the reporter a small guy with a crew cut? That'd be Leon Smith from the *Thomaston Times*. News travels fast around here. "

Bonnie tried some humor. "I bet Ouida called the Thomaston paper. Cooter and Buddy are too tight to spring for a long-distance call."

The sheriff ushered Detective Benefield back into the dining room. "I'll explain all this to you at the jailhouse."

Bonnie rocked the little girl in her arms until the child relaxed and fell asleep, still clutching the soiled stuffed animal. "Sweet, innocent baby girl. You didn't ask for any of this, did you? Bonnie's not going to leave you until the sheriff gets this all figured out. I promise."

CHAPTER FOUR

Bonnie tucked her little guest away at her house under the competent care of Vicki Fordham, the preacher's 16-year-old daughter who worked in the church's newborn-to-toddler Sunday school class. Vicki had arrived with an armful of puzzles and books she'd borrowed from the church nursery. "I thought we might need some entertainment, Miz Bonnie." She was right since Bonnie had not a single toy in the house. The child took readily to Vicki and her bag of tempting tricks, leaving Bonnie time to run some errands.

Bonnie's first stop was Cotney's General Store on the square. Eugenia Cotney, a spinster in her late 60s, was the only Cotney remaining in the family business that she'd helped run since she was just a girl. Bonnie had known Miss Eugenia her entire life and had never seen the woman without her hair up in a bun and a pencil sticking through it like a Christmas tree ornament. When Bonnie approached the cash register with sugared cereal and Popsicles, Eugenia winked. "Got a sweet tooth, Bonnie?"

Miss Eugenia, along with every business owner on the square, was well aware of Bonnie's little guest. Bonnie didn't take the bait. Instead, she accepted her change with a nod. "A little sugar now and again is good for the soul, don't you think, Miss Eugenia? "

Bonnie's second stop was a few doors down at Wheatley's Dime Store. She filled a basket with coloring books and crayons, a *Candy Land* boardgame, some modeling clay, a half dozen *Little Golden* storybooks, and a soft, stuffed teddy bear. Luckily, the cashier was Ludlow Wheatley's daughter, who was too busy smacking on her gum and reading the latest *True Romance* magazine to notice or care what Bonnie had purchased.

The sheriff's office rounded out Bonnie's afternoon errands. J. Carl sat hunched over a typewriter employing the "hunt and peck" method while typing a form in triplicate.

After offering Bonnie the chair across from him, J. Carl shared the latest updates. "Okay, here's what we have at this point. Marie Beasley was a local junkie and prostitute who'd been busted a few times by Atlanta Vice. Detective Benefield's partner ran down another working girl who had known Marie. She claims that Marie never went to a hospital when she was pregnant and delivered the baby in an apartment on Fairlie Street. She also claimed that Marie never even named the child. When Marie was working the street or getting high, she'd leave the girl with anybody who'd watch her. Sometimes she'd bring her clients to the apartment while the child was there." J. Carl paused to rub his temples. "Some life for a kid, huh?"

Bonnie was near tears. "She doesn't have a name? No wonder the poor thing doesn't talk."

"I called Southern Pines and talked to Superintendent Hogan. They have a waiting list right now for four and five-year-olds. I'd reckon the little girl's about five, wouldn't you?" J. Carl sounded as though he had a lump in his throat. "Superintendent Langston suggested we get the child a complete physical when Dr. Hunt's in town."

Bonnie didn't hesitate. "I could take her to see Dr. Hunt tomorrow afternoon as soon as the lunch crowd is gone." Since most of her patrons attended Wednesday night choir practice or prayer meeting, Bonnie took Wednesday afternoons off.

J. Carl looked grateful. "That'd be a big help, Miz Bonnie." He cleared his throat. "And since you've already developed a rapport with the child, it'd be a shame to move her somewhere else right now. Don't you agree?"

Bonnie smiled for the first time all day. "I totally agree, Sheriff. There's no reason to upset her little apple cart. She's settled in right now with Vicki

Fordham. When I left the house, they were putting together a Mother Goose puzzle."

⁂

Bonnie Mac's Café reopened at 5 that evening, just in time for the supper crowd. There wasn't a single empty table or stool in the café for Bonnie's Blue Plate special. Fortunately, she'd had enough sense to prepare two extra meatloaves and double her usual batch of mashed potatoes. She'd even called in Ashley Myles, who waited tables for Bonnie on occasion.

Ashley was a pretty brunette who worked well under pressure. She could handle demanding customers, remember everybody's order, balance several plates on a tray, and smile simultaneously. Ashley usually preferred working the lunch crowd when local businessmen gathered to eat. They were good tippers.

It was neither Bonnie's cooking nor Ashley's sweet smile that had drawn the crowd out on a weeknight. A dead prostitute and an abandoned child made for better entertainment than a movie at the Imperial Theater in Griffin.

Ouida Clarkston, freshly coiffed and dressed as if she were ready to attend a tea party, joined Buddy Sampson at his regular table. While Buddy seemed content to enjoy his usual Tuesday dinner fare, Ouida chain-smoked and carried on about Detective Benefield as if he were Dick Tracy.

Pinkney Sylvester and Urliss Sloane had locked up the *S & S Grocery and Tractors* at 6:01 p.m. and grabbed the last table in the café. They generously offered the other two seats at their table to the Barnett brothers.

The Barnett brothers worked next door to each other on the west side of the square. Campbell "Bushy" Barnett was the town's only fulltime firefighter, thus its fire chief. He ran the Zebulon Fire Department, which was manned by volunteers in the event of a fire. While Bushy was a soft-spoken

Southern gentleman, his brother Brooxie, the best car mechanic in the tri-county area, was what citizens referred to as "a card."

No one ever knew what might come out of Brooxie's mouth. Several old codgers with little else to do sat around Brooxie's Garage just so they could hear what he would say next. Brooxie's comments became less than benign when he had a snoot full of the Old Granddad Whiskey, which he kept in one of his toolboxes. He never drank at home because his wife Floretta was a teetotaler. Brooxie referred to his wife as "Sanctified Flo," at least when she wasn't around.

Just a week earlier as Miz Bitsy Crawford and Miz Mavis Gilbert had been riding their bicycles on the sidewalk by his garage, Brooxie had stuck his head out from under a car and accused the ladies of breaking the law. When the ladies offered Brooxie a look of consternation, he'd explained, "You're pedaling pussy, aren't you?" The next day Brooxie was sporting a black eye, compliments of Raymond Crawford, Miz Bitsy's husband.

Bonnie's mouth fell open when Miss Eugenia Cotney climbed atop a stool at the counter. Miss Eugenia was tight as Dick's hat band and never paid to eat anywhere. She only dined in her own kitchen or at the Women's Missionary Circle's monthly covered dish supper.

"I'm just too worn out to cook tonight," Miss Eugenia explained as she placed her purse on the stool beside her. "Idalee's joining me as soon as she locks up the library." Idalee Hazelwood, who spent her days shushing children and dusting books in the library, was Zebulon's second old maid.

Leon Smith from the *Thomaston Times* also sat at the counter nursing a cup of coffee in hopes that he'd get a statement from Bonnie. As she huffed back and forth from the dining room to the kitchen, she finally took time to acknowledge Leon, who quickly produced a pen and a small notebook. "Could you just tell me a bit about the child?" The clink of silverware and the din of conversation ceased.

Bonnie leaned over the counter and refreshed Leon's coffee. "She's a beautiful little girl who's had a bad time of it. At present, that's all the sheriff will allow me to say on the matter. Now who needs a coffee refill?"

Leon paid his bill and smiled at Bonnie. "I'll be back tomorrow." Bonnie had to appreciate his journalistic tenacity.

Cooter Renfroe, freshly shaven and in a clean Sunday shirt, had shown up early with his wife Fannie Mae to assure his favorite counter stool. Two hours later, they were still sitting at the counter and holding court with every customer who came to the cash register. When Bonnie overheard Fannie Mae referring to the child as "poor white trash," she slammed the cash register shut and announced loudly that she was out of coffee and dessert and would be closing in five minutes.

While Bonnie scrubbed out the meatloaf pans, Ashley wiped down the now empty tables. "Thanks for calling me, Miz Bonnie." She pulled a wad of silver from both pockets of her apron. "This is the most I've ever made waiting tables. If the café stays this busy, I can quit my job at the cannery."

Pike County was home to three canneries, all owned by Jefferson Edmunds. They processed turnips and pimentos in the fall and winter months and peaches in the summer. Mr. Edmunds was the only businessman in the county to hire coloreds to work the processing line, but not a single white person ever complained about his hiring policies. Without Edmunds Cannery, the prospects of employment in Pike County for both coloreds and whites would dwindle considerably.

Bonnie usually paid Ashley hourly minimum wage to supplement her tips. Tonight, she added an extra couple of dollars. "I would hold on to your canning job with the peach crop about to come in, Ashley. I have a feeling this influx of customers is a temporary situation."

By the time Bonnie climbed the porch steps to her front door, there was only one light burning in the living room. Vicki was half asleep on the sofa. "I put her to bed about an hour ago. She was worn slap out, Miz Bonnie." Vicki wouldn't take a fee for her services. "No thanks, Miz Bonnie. This will be part of my tithe for the month. And I can help you out anytime you need me."

Bonnie was touched by the teenager's kindness. As she watched Vicki walk the block to her house, she whispered a prayer. "Lord, don't let that sweet Christian girl catch the nosy disease that seems to be spreading like an epidemic in this town."

Then she tiptoed in the sewing room to check on her charge. The old iron bed that had been in Bonnie's family for several generations swallowed its tiny guest. The newly purchased teddy bear, still wearing its price tag, lay at the foot of the bed. Just as she'd been the night before, the child was curled in a fetal position, but this time she was clutching the tattered stuffed puppy Bonnie had retrieved from her mama's diaper bag.

CHAPTER FIVE

As Bonnie dried the last of the lunch dishes, Vicki Fordham, with her tiny charge in tow, knocked on the café's back door. The little girl gripped Vicki's skirt tightly in one hand while clutching her dirty puppy in the other. Freshly bathed and dressed in a blue jumper, the child sported curly pigtails with matching blue bows.

Bonnie grinned. "Now don't you look precious. Opal Dorsey will be proud to see her twins' hand-me-downs put to good use. And look at those darling piggy tails. Vicki, how in the world did you tame that curly hair?"

Vicki beamed. "It took me a while to get the tangles out, but she sat really still for me. I found the ribbon in your sewing basket. I hope you don't mind."

Bonnie hugged Vicki and handed her a box filled with food. "I know Wednesdays are busy for your mama what with her playing the piano at choir practice and then staying for prayer meeting. I thought she might enjoy not having to cook tonight. "

Vicki sniffed appreciatively. "I love your chicken pot pie, Miz Bonnie!" She lifted the cover on a pastry box. "Those mud hens are still warm. Daddy calls them brown sugar heaven. I'll have to fight him for them."

⚜

Dr. Hunt's office was on the east side of the square next door to Cotney's General Store. Fortunately, as Bonnie strolled down the sidewalk with the little girl, they didn't encounter any curious pedestrians—although Bonnie spotted Miss Eugenia pretending to rearrange the window's display as she peeked out at the child.

When they checked in with the receptionist, there were only two patients ahead of them. One was the very pregnant Betsy Fain, who had been "with child" practically non-stop for the last decade. Three little boys climbed all over the empty chairs in the waiting room despite Betsy's efforts to control them.

Betsy patted her swollen belly and grinned up at Bonnie. "The doctor thinks it may be twins! Farley and I are hoping for girls this time." Bonnie nodded and thought that Farley Fain, who bought and shipped pecans for a living, had better pray for a good pecan crop.

Worth Bickley, dressed in dirty overalls, sat opposite Betsy. A handkerchief wrapped around his left hand was slowly turning from white to red. The eldest Fain child, wearing a holster with a cap pistol strapped to his belt, was fascinated. "Look, Mama! Mr. Worth's bleeding. Did you get shot, Mr. Worth?"

Worth, whose farm was just down the road in Meansville, grunted. "No, son. I got tangled up with my goldarned tractor." When Dr. Hunt's nurse called Worth back, he mumbled as his hand leaked a trail of blood across the tile floor. "That Dadblamed piece of junk tractor. Just wait till I get my hands on Urliss Sloane. He said the thing was fixed. Dadburn tractor!"

Although she didn't move from her chair, the little girl closed her right eye so that she could get a better look at Mr. Worth and his bleeding hand. Silent but seemingly amused, she followed the blood trail with her good eye.

Betsy Fain drew the child's attention back. "I heard you had a little visitor, Miz Bonnie. She sure is a cute thing and so quiet." The child clutched her puppy closer and eased her free hand into Bonnie's open one. Betsy's boys were now turning the empty waiting room chairs into a fort and fussing over who would be the cowboys and who would be the Injuns.

Before Bonnie had to do any explaining, the nurse called Betsy back. As she heaved herself out of the chair, she scolded the boys. "Put those chairs back like you found them, or I'll have Dr. Hunt give each of you a great big shot!" The boys scurried around quickly replacing the chairs and then followed Betsy like three little chicks behind a waddling duck.

Thirty minutes later when the child's examination was complete, Nurse Naomi swept Bonnie's charge away to select a lollipop. Bonnie sat in front of Dr. Hunt's desk and watched him study the child's chart. She had only needed Dr. Hunt's services on two occasions: once when she had strep throat and another when she'd required stitches for her little finger, which got in the way of a knife as she sliced up onions.

Dr. Hunt divided his practice between Zebulon and Thomaston, where he and his family lived. He was a country doctor, who could deliver a baby, set a broken bone, or remove an appendix. A slight man with a blonde crew cut, his relaxed nature had a calming effect upon his patients. Before he'd finished examining the little girl, he had her giggling, but even Dr. Hunt couldn't get the child to speak.

He slowly closed the chart and peered over his reading glasses. "She's got three serious problems, Miz Bonnie. She's suffering from malnutrition and some vitamin deficiency. I'm going to start her on a multiple vitamin and count on you to fatten her up with that good cooking of yours."

Bonnie relaxed. "She's eating everything I put in front of her. I'll make sure she gets plenty of vegetables and lots of milk."

Dr. Hunt nodded in agreement. "The second thing is her lack of speech. I don't see any physical abnormality that would prevent her from speaking. I read the sheriff's report about the child's background. I think it's an emotional problem, and in time, if she trusts someone enough, she'll start to talk."

Bonnie sighed in relief. "And the third thing?"

Dr. Hunt himself sighed. "Have you noticed her closing her right eye and turning to look at things with her left eye?"

Bonnie nodded. "Is she cross-eyed?"

Dr. Hunt shook his head. "I think the problem is more complex than that. The muscles in her eyes don't seem to work properly, so she can't control her eye movement. That's why she closes one eye. She's attempting to compensate so she can focus better. Probably everything she looks at is blurry and distorted."

Bonnie's heart ached for the little girl. "Can the problem be corrected?"

"There's a specialist at Emory who's made some progress with this kind of problem." Dr. Hunt scribbled the Atlanta doctor's information on a prescription pad and tore off the sheet for Bonnie. "You need to get her in to see him as soon as possible. "

Bonnie studied the information. "A specialist like this is going to be expensive, isn't he?"

Dr. Hunt grimaced. "I'm afraid so, Miz Bonnie. The sheriff said the child was on the waiting list for Southern Pines." When Bonnie nodded again, the doctor continued. "Don't get me wrong, Miz Bonnie. The children's home is a well-run and loving haven for children in need, but it is supported by private citizens. I'm not certain how equipped the home is to undertake the financial burden of such a serious problem. I think it would be wise for someone, preferably someone with the means to finance the child's needs, to adopt the child."

Bonnie and the little girl spent the remainder of the afternoon in the café's kitchen. She helped the child pour the dry ingredients for her brownies into her large glass mixing bowl. The whir of the electric mixer drowned out Bonnie's worries and the child's inhibitions.

By the time they had the last batch of the next day's cookies baking, the little girl had abandoned her puppy to lick the cookie batter bowl. Covered in batter from her forehead to her chin, the child smiled at Bonnie as she licked her fingers. "You've been passed from pillar to post enough, haven't you, little one?" The child grinned again and melted Bonnie's heart.

Bonnie took a wet cloth and sponged cookie batter from the child's face. "That's good stuff, isn't it?" The child nodded her head in agreement. Bonnie lifted a pan of brownies from the cooling rack. "Let's get these brownies frosted so we can close up." After shoveling some frosting onto a spatula, she placed it in the child's hand, which she then covered with her own. "If you're going to live here, you can learn how to help."

Barely touching her supper, the child dozed off at the kitchen table. As Bonnie dressed her in a pair of the Dorsey twins' pajamas, she kept up a steady prattle. "I guess I let you fill up on sweets and spoiled your appetite. That's all right. Everybody needs spoiling occasionally."

She tucked the little girl in bed. "Now you're as snug as a doodle bug in a rug." The little girl giggled. "My mama used to call me doodle bug. How about I call you that until we get you an official name?"

"My mama also taught me a bedtime prayer," Bonnie added. She folded the child's tiny hands together and whispered over her. "Now I lay me down to sleep, I pray the Lord my soul to keep. May angels watch me through the night and wake me with the morning light."

Bonnie stroked the child's hair until she drifted off to sleep. Then she leaned over and kissed the child on her forehead. "Sleep tight, little doodle bug."

CHAPTER SIX

A month later, Bonnie sat in the Zebulon law office of Calhoun and Brownlee. She had secured a late afternoon appointment, which gave her enough time to finish her baking for the next day, scoot home to change from her grease-splattered uniform, and hand the little girl over to Vicki Fordham, who'd become a godsend for Bonnie. She had no idea what she would do when Vicki started back to school in a few weeks.

Bonnie reasoned with herself as she whispered under her breath, "First things first," to the pecking of the receptionist's typewriter. While this was her second appointment with the attorney, Bonnie didn't really know Derwood Brownlee outside of serving him lunch in the café on various occasions when Pike County court was in session. Mr. Brownlee had been hired by Johnson Calhoun a couple of years ago when Colonel Calhoun was elected to the state legislature. Johnson Calhoun had earned his title of "colonel" after battling honorably in the courtroom for 30 years.

Bonnie wished the colonel with his decades of experience had been in town for her legal matter, but Johnson spent most of his time at his Thomaston law office when the state legislature wasn't in session. He'd turned over all his Pike County cases to his new attorney. While Derwood Brownlee was young, Bonnie tried to console herself with the belief that he was obviously capable. Derwood's experience for the most part came from defending moonshiners in the county. However, he'd gained some notoriety last summer when he saved a colored woman from death row.

Poor Hattie Cook did kill her husband, but Derwood won her a reprieve from the death penalty by arguing that she had been physically, emotionally, and mentally battered by her husband Henry Cook. Henry, who beat Hattie on a regular basis, was a follower of black magic. While Hattie could take the beatings, Henry kept threatening her with a voodoo doll that shared an eerie resemblance to his wife. One morning Hattie awakened to find the doll, punctured with needles throughout its straw body, lying inches from her face on her pillow. Just as usual, Hattie fried up Henry a pan of bacon and eggs, and while he was eating, she threw a can of hot, bubbling lard all over him. Henry succumbed to his burns within twenty-four hours.

Certainly, if Derwood Brownlee could save a murderess from the gas chamber, he could handle an adoption case. Bonnie was ready to fight for the child who had become so dear to her.

The two of them had fallen into a routine over the past weeks. They awakened before daybreak and headed to the café. After watching patiently as Bonnie mixed up and rolled out her biscuit dough, the child applied the biscuit cutter to create large, doughy circles.

While the biscuits cooked, the two would share a quiet breakfast. Bonnie was pleased that the child couldn't seem to get enough of her grits. By the time the biscuits were done, Cooter Renfroe would be waiting at the front door. Bonnie would slather a warm biscuit with butter and jam and pour another glass of milk for the child, who was quite content to remain at the worktable in the kitchen with her breakfast and a coloring book.

The café's regular customers had grown accustomed to seeing the child scurry behind the counter and tug Bonnie's skirt if she needed something. "What is it, Doodle Bug?" Bonnie had grown adept at tending to the child between flipping eggs on the griddle.

One such morning, Ouida stubbed out her cigarette and said, "I think she needs to go potty. Come on, sweetheart, I'll take you." Studying Ouida with her one good eye, the child shyly but obediently placed her hand in Ouida's outstretched one. As they walked to the bathroom, Bonnie observed

Ouida running her hand through the child's unruly hair. "After breakfast, I'm taking you over to Hazel's Salon and see if she can shape up these curls."

One day Cooter brought the child a postcard featuring a picture of a Palomino horse on its front. "I believe that's Flicka from the T.V. show. Would you like to have it?" The child grinned shyly as she accepted the postcard from Cooter.

However, it was Buddy Sampson who captivated the child. She seemed fascinated by this big man with the tiny voice. "I think Miz Bonnie should let me take the two of you to the Loew's in Atlanta to see *The Wizard of Oz*. The Loew's is running the film to celebrate its 15th birthday. "

Buddy winked at the child. "I bet you've never been to the movies." The child shook her head no as Buddy continued. "*The Wizard* should be your first movie. It's got a lion and a scarecrow, and a man made of tin." The little girl's jaw dropped. "And that's not all, sweetie. There's a wicked witch and a good witch, whose name is Glenda. That Glenda witch, now she's a real looker and reminds me of a girlfriend I once had named Glenda. She lived in Decatur. That dame was bewitching."

Ouida blew smoke rings into the air. "Hush up, Buddy. She's a child. She doesn't need to hear about your imaginary exploits. But I wouldn't mind seeing *The Wizard of Oz* with y'all."

So, the following Wednesday after the café was closed, Buddy drove the three females to the Loew's in downtown Atlanta. For all his talk, it was probably the first time that Buddy had truly had a car full of gals. The child watched the entire movie with her hand over her right eye, and hers were the only dry eyes in the entourage by the movie's end.

Whenever Bonnie and her charge passed Cotney's General Store, Eugenia Cotney no longer peeked out the window. Instead, she'd come to the door and call out. "Why don't y'all come in from that heat for a while? The child needs a Popsicle." The little girl always grinned and chose the banana flavor.

One evening just at closing time, Brooxie Barnett, still in his mechanic's jumpsuit, ambled into the café. Appearing somewhat sober for the time of day, Brooxie grinned sheepishly. "Miz Bonnie, I ran across something I thought the child might enjoy." He stepped outside and returned with a red tricycle that looked as though it had come straight off the floor of Bankhead's Hardware. "I found this at the junkyard when I was looking for a fender that would fit an old Ford I'm working on. I touched it up with a little paint and some oil here and there, and it works like new." As Bonnie mopped the floor that night, the child followed behind her on her new mode of transportation.

The child's favorite place in town to visit was the Zebulon Library, where she and Bonnie would spend an hour or so after lunch each day. If Bonnie tired of quietly reading aloud, Idalee Hazelwood would appear from behind the circulation desk and take over. More than a few times, Idalee insisted that the little girl stay a bit longer so Bonnie could get started on her evening meal at the café. "Honey, I believe if you could see with both eyes, you would be reading on your own," Idalee would whisper to the child in her librarian voice.

Bonnie agreed with Idalee that the child was quite intelligent. She was hopeful that the eye specialist they were scheduled to see in a couple of weeks could correct her vision problem. The initial appointment would deplete most of Bonnie's savings, but she was determined that her Doodle Bug would get the best care possible, even if she had to mortgage the house and the café to pay for it.

Lost in her thoughts, Bonnie was surprised to see the young lawyer suddenly standing at the doorway of his office. He was a big fella who looked as though he'd be more comfortable in a football uniform than the coat and tie he wore. He smiled at Bonnie. "Come on in, Miz Bonnie. I'm sorry I kept you waiting." The two had agreed to use their first names when they'd met a month earlier.

At that initial meeting, Derwood had indicated the adoption would probably be just a matter of paperwork. Judge Thomas Handley, tough but fair, had awarded Bonnie temporary custody of the child until the adoption process could be completed. While Bonnie was no legal expert, she felt assured that the child would be hers by Christmas.

Derwood waited for Bonnie to be seated before he took his own seat. "We may have a problem, Miz Bonnie. Someone else has petitioned the judge to adopt the child."

Bonnie's heart fell into her stomach. "Who?"

Derwood shuffled some papers on his desk as he gathered the gumption to answer. "Do you know Talmadge and Louvenia Loosier over in Concord?"

Of course, Bonnie knew the Loosiers. They were the richest, most influential landowners in Pike County. In addition to a dairy farm that supplied milk to Pike and surrounding counties, a peach orchard that covered several acres, and another vast acreage planted in pecan trees, Talmadge Loosier also owned the Bank of Concord.

Bonnie gulped. "But they have a child. Their little boy must be about eight now. Why do they need another child?"

Derwood shook his head. "It's not Talmadge but his wife Louvenia that wants the child. I've heard she's big into charity, and she seems to think…" Derwood paused and shuffled some papers to get Louvenia's exact words. "Here it is. She said that the child is a worthy undertaking for her."

Bonnie was livid. "An undertaking? That sounds like Louvenia Loosier."

Derwood looked up from his papers. "What do you mean, Miz Bonnie?"

"You're new to Pike County, Derwood, but I've lived in this area all my life. Louvenia Loosier is a *do-gooder* with strings attached. She likes to take on charitable projects that will put her in the limelight. One of my café's regulars sings in the Baptist Church choir. She told me that the Loosiers purchased a new organ and new choir robes with the understanding that Louvenia would be the featured soloist at the Christmas and Easter services. The woman is tone deaf, but she got her way."

Derwood folded his hands on his desk. "If you want to fight, Miz Bonnie, I'll fight for you. But I must tell you, it's going to be an uphill battle. The Loosiers will argue that the child needs a mother and a father. They'll also show that they have the financial means to provide for the child's medical needs."

Bonnie began clutching at straws. "There are plenty of children at Southern Pines who need the love of two parents. The Loosiers could have their pick."

Derwood shook his head. "I did some research on that very idea. Southern Pines has a policy that only family members can adopt a child from the home."

Bonnie knew that Derwood was correct. On rare occasions, a family member would come to reclaim her child, or a distant relative would show up and take the child. For the most part, however, the residents lived out their childhoods at the home.

Derwood cleared his throat. "Judge Handley has ordered a hearing for next week to determine whether you or the Loosiers should proceed with the adoption process. What do you want to do, Miz Bonnie?"

She didn't hesitate. "I want to fight."

The hearing was set for Monday at 9 a.m. in Judge Handley's quarters. The judge had determined that he would hear arguments from the lawyers only, so neither Bonnie nor the Loosiers were present.

Word of the hearing traveled through Zebulon like a whirling dervish. Bonnie had Vicki sleep over on Sunday night. That way the child could stay home and wouldn't be subjected to the café's gossip.

That morning, every regular along with several new faces crowded in the café and nursed cups of coffee as they awaited the judge's verdict. Leon

Smith from the Thomaston paper had stood patiently near the counter until Cooter Renfroe surrendered his stool to start his mail route.

Bonnie was glad for the business, more for the distraction than the money. She stood behind the counter with a pot of steaming coffee. "Need a refill, Mr. Smith?"

Leon grinned and held out his cup. "I'm pulling for you, Miz Bonnie."

Bonnie's hands shook as she filled Leon's cup. "I appreciate that."

A journalist who believed in doing his homework, Leon was sincere in his hopes for Bonnie. What he couldn't and didn't tell Bonnie was what he'd uncovered about the Loosiers. He had discovered some unsettling information about their son.

Talmadge Leverett Loosier, III, who went by Beau, was a nine-year-old terror. His behavior was not that of a normal boy his age. Instead of breaking windows with a mishit baseball or getting into a scrap with a buddy, Beau Loosier took mischief to another level. He had been suspended from Concord Elementary half a dozen times for a variety of acts that rang of a seriously deep-seated emotional problem.

Leon had questioned the boy's third grade teacher, who had since transferred to an elementary school in Thomaston. The teacher related that one day she had relegated Beau to stand in the hall outside the classroom after he pitched a tantrum because he couldn't master one of the week's spelling words. The boy sneaked down to the empty teachers' lounge and defecated on the floor.

On another occasion, Beau hid behind a tree during recess. When a little girl approached, he knocked her down, lifted her skirt, and was pulling down her underpants when the teacher caught him. Beau claimed that the girl had fallen, and he was just helping her up.

Leon had followed up on a lead about some vandalism at the Concord Baptist Church earlier in the summer. Beau, who always accompanied his mother to choir practice, would wander the church's grounds while the choir rehearsed. The morning after one of those rehearsals, the janitor discovered that the framed paintings of Christ in each Sunday school room had been defaced with the foulest words Leon had ever read.

While Derwood Brownlee was privy to Beau's behavior, the judge threw out the information as unsubstantiated and irrelevant to the argument at hand. Judge Handley could not overlook the fact that the Loosiers were a couple with the means to care for the needs of the little girl. On the other hand, he also maintained that the child, who had already suffered so much, should be in a happy, loving environment, which Bonnie was providing. In the end, Judge Handley's ruling called for a compromise.

When Derwood entered the café, Bonnie could see by the slump of his shoulders that the ruling was not in their favor. She and Derwood retreated to the empty kitchen while the café's clientele held their collective breath.

"I'm sorry, Miz Bonnie. The judge wants to give the Loosiers a chance with the child. He has ordered the child to be released to their custody for a trial visit. I'm to escort her over to the courthouse at 4 p.m. Then, at the end of the week, Judge Handley will make his final ruling."

Bonnie's eyes brimmed with tears. "I know you did your best, Derwood. I'll get her things packed. But promise me one thing."

"What's that, Miz Bonnie?"

Bonnie grabbed both of his hands and held them tightly. "You won't give up on us."

Derwood's voice shook slightly. "Yes ma'am. I swear, I won't."

CHAPTER SEVEN

Bonnie did her best to explain to the child what was happening. "Doodle Bug, there are some very nice people, the Loosiers, who want you to pay them a visit. You'll have so much fun at their house. They have a dairy farm, so you'll get to see how they milk cows. I bet Miz Loosier will even have you some new toys."

While the child seemed to understand, she clutched her ragged puppy with one hand and clung to Bonnie's skirt with the other as the Loosiers drove up to the courthouse. Louvenia climbed out of the front seat with a big balloon in her hand. "Now, aren't you the cutest thing! I bet you like balloons!"

Before Bonnie even had a chance for a goodbye kiss, Louvenia grabbed the child's hand and escorted her to the backseat of the Loosiers' station wagon. "Beau, say hello to our little visitor. You two are going to have a great time!"

Beau Loosier glared sullenly as the little girl, holding her big pink balloon, sat beside him. When the car reached the outskirts of town, Beau quietly pulled a sharpened pencil from his pocket, reached behind the child's head, and popped her balloon. The sudden, unexpected sound so frightened the child that she gasped and began to sob.

When Louvenia turned around to observe what had happened, Beau shrugged his shoulders. "I don't know what she did. It just popped."

Beau was a disappointment to his parents, especially Louvenia. She had suffered a miserable pregnancy and a horrendous, two-day delivery that left her unable to conceive again. The Loosiers' son had never been an easy child. Fussy and colicky throughout his infancy, as the boy grew into a toddler, he was distant and irritable.

By the time he was of school age, Beau had alienated any playmate who lived in the area, including his own cousin. The boy's aunt refused to visit after Beau knocked her five-year-old daughter off the backyard gym set while she was swinging. Of course, Beau, who had been pushing little Cousin Betsy in the swing, claimed she fell out accidentally. Betsy required several stitches on her busted chin and swore that Beau had purposely pushed her off the swing.

Louvenia owned a green parakeet named Petey who lived in a cage on the screened porch. Hoping that her son would bond with the bird, Louvenia gave Beau the responsibility of feeding Petey. One morning as she lifted the cover from Petey's cage, she discovered the bird dead. Mr. Loosier pushed back from his morning coffee and ran to his hysterical wife. "What did the boy do this time?"

Beau appeared astonished at the bird's demise. "Poor Petey! He was such a good little bird." Beau knew his parents would never find the Coca Cola bottle that he had shattered and ground into tiny bits, which he'd been adding to Petey's seed each day.

And then there'd been the incident with the rabbit. After Beau and his father built a rabbit hutch together for a Cub Scout project, Louvenia surprised them with a floppy-eared bunny from the pet store. One day Mr. Loosier discovered the door to the hutch had been left open. "Beau, did you have Bugsy out today? He's gone."

Beau appeared remorseful. "Oh gee, Dad, I guess I forgot to close it when I changed his water." Beau's father just shrugged his shoulders as Beau giggled under his breath. He'd enjoyed watching Bugsy squirm when he hung the rabbit from a noose a mile into the woods behind the pecan orchard. As the rabbit quivered for its final breath, Beau felt a rush of ecstasy like he'd never experienced.

Louvenia Loosier longed desperately for a normal child, a normal family. If Beau just had a little sister, Louvenia believed that her son would grow into a loving brother.

By the time Louvenia had settled the little girl into a guest room, supper was ready. The Loosiers took their evening meal in the formal dining room where their maid Cookie, dressed in a grey uniform and starched apron, stood ready to serve them.

Cookie, carrying a huge platter of fried chicken, circled the table so that each diner could select a piece of chicken with the large serving fork. When she arrived at the little girl's seat, the child shook timidly. "I bet you'd enjoy a drumstick, wouldn't you, sweetheart?" Cookie smiled lovingly as she placed a perfectly fried chicken leg on the child's plate.

While Mr. Loosier immersed himself in the *Atlanta Journal*, and Beau stared into another dimension as he chewed, Louvenia tried to make conversation with the child. "You have the prettiest blonde curls, sweetheart. Once we get those eyes fixed, you are going to look like a little China doll. Don't you agree, boys?"

Mr. Loosier looked up from the sports section and nodded his assent while Beau played with the gravy in his mashed potatoes. Louvenia tried again. "Beau, after we have dessert, you should take our guest to the basement and show off your train set." When the boy didn't acknowledge his mother, she sighed. "Beau, did you hear me?"

Lost in his plotting of how to rid himself of the little girl, Beau looked at his mother with cold eyes. "I don't want her touching my things." Then he caught himself and turned on the charm. "Forgive me, Mama, but I have a stomachache. I want to go to bed. May I be excused?"

Louvenia foolishly fell for his act. "I'll have Cookie stir up some baking soda and water for you, dear." The little girl felt a chill run over her as Beau left the room.

While the master bedroom was on the main floor, the remaining bedrooms, including Beau's, were upstairs. Louvenia tucked the little girl into a bed far too large for her. "I'll leave a light on in the hall bath, honey. If you need anything, just knock on Beau's door, and he'll come and get me."

The child had no intention of knocking on Beau's door. She sensed the evil in the boy, and she smelled the fear it created in her body. She recognized that smell from not so long ago as she would lie on her pallet in the corner of a dark, dingy closet while men came and went from her mother's bed. Just as she'd done on those long nights, she clutched her puppy and willed herself to stay awake for fear that some harm might come to her. Finally, sleep overcame her, and she drifted away.

Seconds later, it seemed, the little girl awakened as she felt a tug on her hair. Where was she? What was happening? Her eyes adjusted to the dark, and she sensed someone in the room with her.

The child realized it was Beau, wielding a large pair of scissors. He smiled at her. "Don't worry. I'm almost finished. Let's see what Mama thinks about your pretty curls now. It's a good thing you can't scream."

A few hours later when Louvenia came to wake the little girl, she discovered the child's beautiful blonde locks strewn all over the bedroom floor. While the child couldn't scream, Louvenia sure could.

☙

Bonnie was pouring Buddy Sampson's third cup of coffee when Talmadge Loosier burst into the café. The man wore a look of distress, and Bonnie's heart fell into her stomach. She forced herself to remain calm as she walked towards the cash register where Mr. Loosier stood silently with his hat in his hands.

"Miz Bonnie, could I have a moment in private with you?"

Bonnie nodded and led Talmadge to the kitchen as the eyes of every café patron followed them. Once there, Bonnie could no longer control her fear. "What's wrong? Is she hurt? Where is she?"

Talmadge was perspiring. "She's not hurt, but there was a situation at our house overnight. Umm, you'll understand when you see her, Miz Bonnie. She's safe in the judge's quarters at the courthouse. I, um, I mean Louvenia and I want you to know that we are withdrawing our petition to adopt the child as long as you don't press any charges."

Bonnie was wild-eyed. "Charges? For what? "

Talmadge had replaced his hat. "You'll understand when you see the child. I'm so sorry for all of this. I tried to dissuade Louvenia from pushing the adoption, but she's stubborn. The judge will explain it all to you. If it's okay, I'll go out the back way."

Bonnie tore off her apron as Talmadge slunk out the back into the alley. She pushed through the swinging doors into a dining room of curious patrons. "Breakfast is on the house this morning. Now, I need everybody to leave."

Ouida Clarkston stubbed out her cigarette. "Go on, honey. I'll close up for you."

Breathless by the time she reached the courthouse, Bonnie took a moment to gather her wits. "Lord, please let that sweet baby be all right."

Judge Handley's secretary ushered Bonnie right in. The little girl, her precious golden locks shorn almost to her scalp, clutched her ragged puppy as she sat quivering in an overstuffed chair.

When she saw Bonnie, the child's fear evaporated, and her tiny body relaxed. Then she spoke her first word: "BonBon!" She ran into Bonnie's outstretched arms.

Bonnie enveloped the precious child. "Don't you worry, sweet thing, you're home now."

CHAPTER EIGHT

For the next few weeks, the child couldn't go into the café without somebody asking her to say something. She'd always had the ability to talk. She just chose not to because Marie slapped her almost every time she uttered a word.

The child learned quickly not to call Marie "Mama" or else she got smacked, and Marie would yell, "When are you gonna learn it pisses me off when you call me that?! Call me Marie, you stupid girl."

The child wouldn't have known Marie was her mama if their apartment neighbor Miss Camilla Parsons hadn't told her. Marie didn't have a single lady friend except for Miss Camilla (or *Old Lady Parsons* as she called the woman behind her back). When Marie wanted to go out, she'd drag the child across the hall and spit-clean her face before she knocked on the door. "Miss Camilla, could you watch the kid for just a little while, just long enough for me to go get my hair done?" Miss Camilla always gave in, and the child was glad because they played Old Maid cards, and Miss Camilla gave her a Coca Cola to drink.

Marie sure was annoyed when Miss Camilla up and died. She and the child watched the paramedics carry the old woman down the stairs on a stretcher. She was all covered up with a sheet. Marie just shook her head and muttered under her breath. "Damn, damn, damn. Now what am I gonna do?"

Marie locked the child in the closet when a "date" came over for a party," which was most every night. All of Marie's visitors were men. She and her date always had their party in the bed, which didn't seem like a good place to the child. Most nights the child could hear Marie and a man laughing and rolling around in the bed. Sometimes the man would yell out, "I'm coming, I'm coming!" The child never understood why he'd say that since he was already here.

Marie rarely had the same date twice. Except for a man named Elroy Peavey. He showed up every Thursday night. With her ear against the closet door, the child heard him say that Miz Peavey thought Thursday was his poker night. Marie just giggled. "Oh Elroy, I guess you need to buy us a deck of cards and some poker chips." Mr. Peavey laughed and laughed, and then it got quiet except for some moaning from Mr. Peavey. The child reckoned he got a stomachache from laughing so hard.

Since the child usually slept in the same bed with Marie, a blanket and a pillow remained on the closet floor in case Marie's friend decided to spend the night. One night after all the moaning stopped, the child heard Marie's visitor snoring. She had to pee so bad she thought she would explode. The child tapped on the closet door from her side and whispered, "Marie, I need to pee." The man's snoring drowned out the child's pleas. The only thing she could find to pee in was a box that held Marie's fancy hat that Mr. Peavey had bought her for Christmas. The child got the worse whoopin' of her life the next day. From then on, Marie kept a pot and some toilet paper in the closet.

There was one man who came by at least three times a week. His name was Freddy, but Marie didn't call him a date. She called him her boyfriend. Boyfriends were different from dates, the child figured. Freddy and Marie would have a party in the bed, but then he'd hang around longer than her dates did.

Instead of paying Marie like all the other men did, Freddy would go through Marie's billfold and take out some of her money. He called it his "share." On days when Marie didn't have much money, Freddy would get mad. It was those times that the child didn't mind staying in the closet.

While she couldn't see what was going on, the child could hear Freddy hollering. "You stupid bitch! Where's the rest of the cash from this weekend? I know you're holding out on me."

Marie would start sniffling. "Honest to God, honey, you know I wouldn't do that. I had to pay the light bill, and we didn't have a bit of food in the house. Come on back to bed and let me rub your back. You're so tense today."

Sometimes Freddy would give in to Marie, but other times he'd scream and throw things. On the worst nights, pressing her ear against the door, the child could hear his hand slap against Marie's face and Marie whimper. The child knew how a slap like that felt and despised Freddy for hurting Marie.

When Freddy started talking about moving away, Marie begged to go with him. They must've thought the child was asleep in the closet, but she heard them making plans. "Don't worry about her, Freddy. I got an idea." The child fell asleep before she could hear Marie's idea.

Anyways, when BonBon asked her why she hadn't been talking, the child just shrugged her shoulders. BonBon hadn't locked the child in the closet a single time since she came to live with her. The child reckoned BonBon wouldn't understand Marie's bed parties. "I don't know. I guess I ain't got nothing to say."

"You *don't* have *anything* to say, honey." BonBon was always trying to change the way the child talked.

Just before Christmas, the child got a name. Since Marie was dead like Miss Camilla, the child got "*a-dotted*" by BonBon. She guessed it was called "*a-dotted*" because all BonBon had to do was sign on a dotted line of some papers in Mr. Brownlee's office, and then BonBon was the child's mama.

BonBon decided the child shouldn't call her "Mama" since she already had a mama even if she was dead now. The child didn't tell her that Marie never even claimed her as a daughter, much less gave her a name. Anyway, she liked calling her new mama BonBon because she was as sweet as the chocolate candy Mr. Buddy brought back from one of his trips to Atlanta.

He called them chocolate Bonbons. He said he'd bought them for his new girlfriend, but she was on a diet, so he thought the child might like them. Miss Ouida laughed so hard she got choked on her cigarette smoke, and BonBon giggled. The child didn't care because that candy was delicious, almost as sweet as her very own BonBon.

Since Christmas Eve fell on a Sunday that year, BonBon and Preacher Fordham decided it was the perfect time to christen the child. BonBon explained that getting christened was a very special event because it would make her a child of Jesus. She'd been learning all about Mr. Jesus in Sunday school. On some Sundays, BonBon was her teacher, and she played the piano so the children could sing songs about Mr. Jesus. The child learned that Mr. Jesus especially loved little children— "red and yellow, black and white, they are precious in his sight." She figured BonBon would marry Mr. Jesus so that he could be her daddy if she was gonna be his child.

Preacher Fordham explained that he would sprinkle some holy water on the child's head to make her name official. She didn't really understand how the water would get on her head if it had holes in it, but BonBon was so excited that she didn't bother her with too many questions.

BonBon made her the prettiest white dress with something called a crinoline to wear underneath. That crinoline was the scratchiest thing, but she figured she could bear it for BonBon's sake. BonBon also took the child to the beauty parlor since some of her hair had grown back. Miss Hazel trimmed it up into what she called a curly pixie. BonBon had read the child a book about fairies that were called pixies, so she reckoned Miss Hazel thought she was a fairy, too.

Miss Ouida drove to a place she called the Red Goose store in Thomaston and bought the child a pair of red shoes just like the ones Dorothy had in *The Wizard of Oz*. When BonBon rolled her eyes at the color, Miss Ouida winked at the child. "She needs something Christmassy for this big occasion." The child smiled, but she wished she could have seen that goose laying those red shoes.

That Sunday, at the end of the singing and preaching, Preacher Fordham called the child and BonBon up to the front of the church. In no time, the preacher sprinkled some warm water on her head, drew a plus sign on her forehead, and called the child by her new name—Sunday Grace MacGregor.

BonBon had chosen the name because she wanted the child to remember that she was named on a Sunday and that she would always remain in God's grace. She said that God was Jesus' daddy, so Grace figured God knew what he was doing.

As the warm water dripped down Grace's face, Preacher Fordham asked everyone to bow their heads as he raised his arms and said a prayer over Sunday Grace and Bonnie MacGregor. Grace squinted downward with her good eye so she could see her shiny red shoes. Dorothy was right, she thought. There's no place like home.

CHAPTER NINE

On New Year's Day, just three miles down the road from Bonnie's Café, six-year-old Charlie Callahan was finding a new home of another sort. Charlie stared at his ragged PF Flyers as he listened to his granny explain her plight to Reverend Hogan, the superintendent of Southern Pines Children's Home.

"I done ever thing I could for Charlie since the accident, Reverend. But my arthritis done got the best of me. I had to quit my job at Carter's factory. My fingers can't work the sewing machine no more." Charlie glanced down at his granny's gnarled fingers as she began to sob. "God knows I've tried, but the boy needs better than I can give him."

While Reverend Hogan had already heard her story when she'd completed the paperwork just before Christmas, he understood that she needed to talk. He pulled a fresh linen handkerchief from his pocket and handed it to Charlie's grandmother. "And there's no other family who can help, Miz Callahan?"

She shook her head. "My oldest son Danny died at Pearl Harbor, and then I lost my boy Bill—Charlie's daddy—last year in the accident. Charlie's mama was an only child." She wiped the tears that wandered down her wrinkled face. "Charlie was a baby when his other grandmamma died. I'm his onlyest family left since the fire."

At the word "fire," Charlie began to tremble. While he'd learned to shut out the image of the house in flames, he could still hear Mama screaming for

Daddy to get the baby. Worse than those sounds that rarely left his ears, the stench of charred flesh always remained in his nostrils.

"Charlie, did you hear me?" Reverend Hogan, his hand outstretched, was standing over the boy. "Why don't I show you around?"

"B-b-but I w-w-wanna stay w-w-with Gr-Gr-Granny!" The stuttering, which had begun after the fire, grew worse when Charlie was agitated.

Charlie clung to his granny as she tried to peel him away. "Don't you remember, we've talked about this, Charlie? You'll have new clothes to wear and good food to eat and lots of children to play with. And I'll come to visit ever week, I promise." Granny ran her arthritic fingers through Charlie's sandy hair and pushed down the lump in her throat. "Now, you run along with Reverend Hogan, and I'll see you next weekend."

Southern Pines Children's Home was built shortly after World War II. The conception of civic-minded businessmen in the Tri-City area, the home was originally established as a safe and loving haven for children whose fathers had died in the war and whose mothers, for one reason or another, were unable to care for their children. Just two years earlier, the original frame house had been replaced with a large brick facility that served as a dorm for forty or so children. The Reverend and his family lived in a roomy apartment that anchored one end of the facility.

Reverend Hogan was a gentle, godly man and a genius at making frightened children feel at ease. Taking Charlie's small hand in his large one, the Reverend ushered the child out of the office and down a long corridor with shiny tile floors. "This side of our home is for all the boys. I hear you like baseball, Charlie. So does Mr. George; he and his wife Miz Peg are going to be your house parents. Mr. George pitched for the Atlanta Crackers for a while back in the day. And by the way, you can call me 'Rev' like everybody else does."

Charlie stared at his dirty shoelaces as Reverend Hogan guided him down the long hallway to the boys' dorm. "We'll get you settled in, and then you can join the rest of the kids in the rec room. They're taking down the Christmas decorations."

Reverend Hogan opened a door into a large room with beds lining both sides. All but one of the beds were made up in brightly plaid blankets, and each bed had a trunk at its foot. Some of the trunks displayed store-bought toys, the likes of which Charlie had only dreamed about.

Charlie's wide eyes were not missed by the Reverend. "The fellas had a windfall from Santa." As he stopped at the only bed stripped of any linens, a rather round lady with twinkling eyes entered with her arms full.

"You must be Charlie Callahan. I'm Miz Peg, your house mother. Sorry I didn't get your bed made before you arrived, but I wanted you to choose. Do you like the blue plaid or the red plaid blanket?"

Charlie's bottom lip trembled. What he really wanted was his worn quilt that was on his bed back at Granny's. "I g-g-guess the r-r-red."

Miz Peg seemed accustomed to sad little boys. "Good choice, Charlie. I've always been partial to red plaid, especially around Christmas. Oh, and speaking of Christmas, I believe if you open that trunk at the foot of the bed, you'll find that Santa was expecting you."

Charlie stared at the trunk in disbelief. All he'd gotten at Granny's house was a stocking with a candy cane and a pair of socks. Miz Peg nudged him forward. "Go ahead, honey. There's nothing inside that will bite you." Charlie slowly lifted the lid and peered at his loot. Two new shirts, a pair of tennis shoes, Billy the Kid blue jeans, underwear, and socks. Underneath the clothes lay the best surprise—a spanking new catcher's mitt.

Charlie swallowed. "Is this all m-m-mine?"

The Reverend laughed a huge belly laugh. "Merry Christmas, Charlie! I'll leave you with Miz Peg to get you all settled in, and I'll see you at supper. I hope you like pork chops, turnip greens, and black-eyed peas with her pan-fried cornbread. Our cook Minnie's been working all afternoon in the kitchen. I think I smelled banana pudding for dessert. We ring in the New Year the traditional way."

By the time Charlie and Miz Peg got his bed made and his few personal items stashed away, he heard laughter from the hallway. Miz Peg straightened Charlie's new blanket. "That'll be the boys coming back to wash up before supper."

The door burst open as a gaggle of boys ranging in ages from five to eight tumbled into the room. A redheaded, snaggletooth kid plopped down on the bed beside Charlie and grinned. "Hi. I'm Tommy Davis. You'll be sleeping right next to me. I hope you like baseball. We need a catcher real bad."

CHAPTER TEN

"Sunday Grace MacGregor, if you don't hold still and let me get this hair combed, I'm going to tan your hide!" While BonBon was always threatening, she had never followed through. Grace squirmed and wiggled while BonBon ran the brush through her tangled curls.

"Ouch, BonBon, that's enough! My hair looks fine. I'm just going to regular school, not Sunday school." Grace dreaded Sunday mornings when BonBon would spend thirty minutes trying to tame her curls into what she called a presentable ponytail.

On this school morning, BonBon finally gave up and tied matching bows around two pigtails. "Now, hold still while I put your patch on." She applied a clean patch to Grace's left eye and then handed her a pair of glasses with orange frames. "Hurry up now, you don't want to miss the bus this morning. I need to get back to the café and help Vern with the late breakfast crowd. Then I can get started on my meatloaf for tonight's Blue Plate special."

Right after Grace started school, BonBon hired some morning help for the café. She called Mr. Vern Martin her right hand. Mr. Vern was a cook in the Navy for 25 years. He'd moved back to nearby Concord five years ago to look after his mama, who was the oldest lady Grace had ever seen. When his mama finally died, Mr. Vern came to BonBon looking for a job. Grace loved to watch him flip a pancake with one hand and crack eggs at the same time with the other.

Grace tracked BonBon with her uncovered eye. "Why does Mr. Vern have pictures of ladies on his arms?"

BonBon sighed as she handed Grace her lunch box. "Those pictures are called tattoos, and when did you see them?"

"Saturday morning when he spilled milk all over his shirt. I was in the kitchen eating my pancakes, and he came in to change. One of those ladies didn't have no shirt on, and the other lady was showing her panties."

"Grace, you cannot use 'didn't' and 'no' in the same sentence." Before BonBon could give Grace an answer about the tattoos, they heard the school bus rounding the corner. "Don't forget that it's Tuesday, and I'll be picking you and Charlie up after his speech lesson. You can sit in Miz Brown's class and get your homework done while you wait on him." BonBon gave Grace a peck on the cheek and patted her behind. "Now skedaddle!"

Instead of riding the bus home on Tuesdays and Thursdays, Grace waited on her best friend Charlie Callahan to finish his speech therapy class. She'd first met Charlie in Vacation Bible School at the Methodist Church the summer after Mr. Jesus became her daddy. Charlie and all his friends from a place called a Children's Home rode the bus every day to Bible school.

Charlie was in Primary 2, and she was in Primary 1, so they had different Bible school teachers. But all the kids came together in the fellowship hall for arts and crafts. Grace was sitting all by herself at a table painting a crib with Mr. Jesus in it when he was a baby. She'd stopped sitting with the other kids after she heard them giggling and calling her "Popeye" and "one-eyed monster."

Dr. Holliman in Atlanta had put a patch over Grace's left eye, which was stupid to her because it was the good one. He said it would make her right eye work harder. She begged BonBon to remove the patch just for Bible school, but BonBon insisted that Grace had to wear it all the time if she wanted her eyes to get stronger. On top of her patch, Grace was forced to wear the ugliest glasses she'd ever seen. No wonder everybody called her a monster.

On that particular day, Grace was trying to paint some eyes on Mr. Baby Jesus when she was interrupted by a voice she didn't recognize. "C-c-c-can I s-s-sit here?"

Grace didn't look up. It was hard enough to paint little bitty eyes when she had to do it with her bad eye. "Sure, if you don't mind sitting with a one-eyed monster."

"I d-d-don't mind c-c-cause everybody c-c-calls me a stupid st-st-stutterer."

Grace raised her head and saw a boy with big hazel eyes and a red shirt. "I guess you're at the right table then. What's your name and why haven't I seen you in Sunday school?"

"Charlie C-C-C-Callahan. I-l-live at the Ch-Ch-Ch-Children's Home."

Grace nodded. When she had helped BonBon make Easter cookies and tried to eat one, she got her hand slapped away. "Those are for the children at Southern Pines Children's Home."

Grace licked icing off her fingers. "What kind of place is that?"

BonBon handed her a wet towel. "Wash your face, Gracie. Southern Pines Children's Home is a place for children to live if their parents can't take care of them."

Gracie wiped her mouth and fingers with the wet towel. "Oh, kinda like Marie didn't take care of me."

BonBon raised her eyebrows. "Well, yes. Not all parents die like Marie did. Sometimes they are sick or can't provide for their children. Then Southern Pines takes a child in to care for them until their parents or a relative can take them home."

"What's a relative?"

BonBon wiped some more sticky off Grace's face. "A relative is someone like an aunt or an uncle or maybe a grandmother."

"Oh, I see. Like Mr. Buddy and Miss Ouida. Is that right, BonBon?" BonBon went to the sink and washed her hands. When she turned around there were tears in her eyes.

"What's wrong? Did you get icing in your eyes?"

She just smiled. "I guess I did. To answer your question, a relative is a person who loves you very much, just like Mr. Buddy and Miss Ouida."

Grace studied Charlie Callahan as he picked up a paint brush. "Is your mama sick, or are you waiting on a relative to pick you up?"

Charlie didn't look up. "My mama and daddy is d-d-dead, and my g-g-granny is t-t-too sick to keep me."

Grace hardly ever thought of Marie anymore because BonBon was her mama now. She knew if something happened to BonBon, she wouldn't have to stay at Southern Pines long. Miss Ouida or Mr. Buddy would take her. Now she had discovered somebody that didn't have nobody to love him. "You wanna use my blue for Mr. Baby Jesus' eyes?"

Charlie and Grace had been best friends ever since. When real school started, the only time they saw each other was at recess since he was in the third grade, and she was in second.

When Charlie started staying after school for speech lessons with Mrs. Davison, the bus to Southern Pines couldn't wait on him, so BonBon volunteered to drive him to the Children's Home every afternoon. That was two years ago. Now Grace was in fourth grade and Charlie was just ahead of her in the fifth.

Charlie let Grace watch over his baseball glove and ball while he was at his speech lesson. She always waited on the school playground so she could toss his baseball and try to catch it in his glove. If there were other kids around, she'd retrieve her baseball bat from its hiding place so they could play a little "roll the bat." Coach Dawkins was the only person allowed to have a baseball bat inside the school building after some dumb kid broke his tooth on one that he was swinging in the hall one day. Grace kept her bat hidden inside a hollow tree by the creek in the woods that edged the school yard.

The only time Charlie and Grace didn't get treated like freaks was when kids were choosing up teams to play ball. Even Eddie Wilkes, who loved to torment the two, would stop his name-calling to have them on his team.

At any other time, Eddie was the worst about making fun of Grace's ugly, orange-framed glasses. Grace got so tired of being called Four Eyes and Bug Eyes that she determined to destroy her glasses. Once she put them in her back pocket and then had Charlie push her down a rocky hill on a piece of cardboard. Another time she *accidentally* dropped them right underneath her Pogo stick when she was bouncing.

One day Geetah, the toothless colored man who slept in the hull of a car in the Negro part of town, was cutting BonBon's grass. When he stopped to get some water from the hose, Grace hid her glasses underneath the mower. Geetah rolled the mower right over them and crunched them to bits.

A few minutes later, Grace saw Geetah standing at the back door of the café with what was left of her glasses. He was trying to explain to BonBon. "Lawd have mercy, Miz Bonnie, I sho' don't mean to do that!"

Grace felt bad because everybody loved Geetah. BonBon cooked him special soft food that he could gum since he didn't have teeth. Cars would toot at him when he was walking down the street. Geetah would always throw up his hand and yell, "Git on down the road!"

Grace was skulking around the backyard when BonBon came home from the café. When she poked her head out the screen door, BonBon easily read the guilt written all over Grace's face. "Miss Sunday Grace MacGregor, get in this house right now!" She was furious, so Grace didn't even try to lie.

"I knew you had to be sabotaging your eyeglasses. But blaming it on sweet old Geetah just takes the cake. That poor man was shaking all over."

Grace got several swats on her rear with the fly swatter and her baseball bat confiscated for an entire week. Then BonBon marched her over to Mr.

Banks Sutton's gas station where Geetah pumped gas and washed windshields. "Go on, Grace, tell Geetah."

"I dropped my glasses on purpose, Geetah. It was my fault. I'm sorry."

Geetah gave her a gummy grin and raised his hand. "It's okay, little miss. Git on down the road!"

Ever since Geetah forgave her, Grace stopped trying to destroy her glasses, no matter how much other kids taunted her. Anyway, Eddie's usual "Popeye" and "Stutter Chuck" for the two best friends were forgotten on the playing field. Grace was the best girl player in both her class and Charlie's class. When Grace did get a hit, she could run the bases faster than most of the boys. Coach Dawkins called Charlie a real slugger because when he connected with the ball, it sailed over everybody in the outfield.

Today, though, there was nobody around, so Grace contented herself with throwing the ball as high as she could and trying to catch it. While she wasn't good at catching a ball with only one eye to see it, her friend Charlie never missed. She was better at hitting because it only took one eye to see the ball come across the plate. Since she'd started moving the patch from the right to the left eye every other week, she'd learned to bat both right-handed and left-handed. Coach Dawkins said she was quite a switch hitter.

After Dr. Holliman told BonBon that baseball was a good exercise for strengthening Grace's eyes, she forgave all the dirt tracked in the house after a game. Grace's one skill that BonBon hated, however, was her ability to sit atop the handle of the bat. She had a little bottom that balanced just right on the round part of the handle. If BonBon saw Grace's balancing act, she always fussed. "Gracie MacGregor, you are going to hurt yourself one of these days!"

By the time Charlie was released from his lesson, his ball was red from being dropped in the dirt so many times. He sneaked up behind Grace. "Nobody to p-p-play with to-d-d-day?" She didn't think the speech lessons were helping him much.

Grace handed over his ball and glove. "Nah. Sorry about getting your ball dirty." Charlie just grinned and wiped the ball down with his t-shirt.

The two walked around to the front of the school and stood at their designated pickup spot. A few minutes later, Miss Ouida pulled up in her big green Cadillac. She rolled down her electric window and blew smoke out. "You two hop in. Bonnie's waiting on a repairman to fix the café's refrigerator. So, you got me as your chauffeur today."

Charlie looked at Grace with wide eyes. "What's a ch-ch-chauffeur?"

She giggled. "It's a fancy name for a driver. It was one of BonBon's Word Power words in this month's *Reader's Digest.* Come on. Miss Ouida always takes me to do something fun when she picks me up from school."

Miss Ouida flicked her cigarette butt out the window. As the kids climbed in, Grace whispered to Charlie, "Be glad Mr. Buddy didn't pick us up. His car is lopsided."

Charlie frowned. "Whaddya mean, l-l-lopsided?"

She giggled. "He's so fat that his car leans to the driver's side, and every time I get in the back seat on the right side, I slide to the left." Charlie laughed.

"What are you two carrying on about?" Miss Ouida raised her eyebrows in the rearview mirror. "I thought I heard you say something about Buddy."

Grace glared at Charlie to stop laughing. "I was just wondering why he didn't pick us up."

Miss Ouida sighed. "Honey, it's March 20th. The man is up to his eyeballs in tax returns. You won't see him again until April 16th."

While she wasn't sure what tax returns were, Grace knew Mr. Buddy counted up money for his job. Miss Ouida said he counted his money all the way to the bank.

Miss Ouida was circling the square looking for a parking place. "Let's get an ice cream cone at City Pharmacy, then we'll walk down to the firehouse. Chief Barnett has something to show y'all."

Charlie settled on a strawberry cone while Grace ordered her usual vanilla. The two licked their ice creams as they followed behind Miss Ouida. Charlie was so busy eating that he bumped into one of the Fain twins who was holding onto his older brother's hand as they headed into their daddy's pecan store. "Sorry, M-M-Mike."

The older brother grabbed the twin out of Charlie's way. "He's Matty, not Mikey. It's okay, no harm done." Nobody could tell those twins apart.

They followed Miss Ouida past Sully and Sloane's Grocery and then Mr. Waddell's Grocery. Grace never understood why there were two grocery stores side by side, but BonBon always went to both of them when she had coupons. She explained that good Zebulonites gave all the businesses a fair chance.

Just past Waddell's was the Firehouse. It was run by Chief Bushy. The chief had white hair and white bushy eyebrows. If he grew a white beard, he would look just like Santa Claus. His last name was really Barnett, but all the kids in Pike County called him Chief Bushy.

When Charlie saw Chief Bushy polishing the windows of Zebulon's fire truck, his eyes got big as saucers. "W-w-wow, I ain't n-n-never seen a real f-f-fire truck up close! Except that n-n-night wh-wh-wh…" Charlie didn't have to finish his thought.

The chief and Ouida shared a knowing glance. Everyone in town knew how Charlie had lost his family. Chief Bushy squatted down and smiled at the little boy. "Well, come on over here, son. You want to sit in it?" He lifted Charlie up in the driver's seat and let him press the button that made the siren sound.

Charlie was grinning from ear to ear when he climbed out. "It's your t-t-turn, Gracie."

"That's okay. I get to do it all the time." Grace turned her unpatched eye towards the chief. "Chief Bushy, has Misty had her kittens yet?"

The chief grinned. "I thought you'd never ask. Come on back to the kitchen."

The kids followed him to the back of the firehouse and into the kitchen. Chief pointed to a large pasteboard box by the stove. "Gracie, peek down in that box there."

Inside was Misty with five of the furriest little things Grace had ever seen. "They're beautiful! Can I hold one?"

Chief rubbed Misty's ears. "If her mama will let you."

Misty and Grace were old friends, and the mama cat meowed like she was giving permission. Grace picked up an orange and white striped ball of fur and let its rough tongue lick the ice cream off her fingers. "I want this one. When can I take it home?" BonBon had already agreed that Grace could have a kitten if she promised to care for it.

Miss Ouida handed another kitten to Charlie. "Hold your horses, Gracie. You must wait until they are at least six weeks old."

"Six weeks? That's forever!"

The Chief patted Grace's head. "You can come by every day and check on them."

Miss Ouida had to threaten the kids with a switch to get them to leave. "Right now, you two! We have to get Charlie home before they serve supper." While Miss Ouida would never take a switch to either of them, Grace didn't want Charlie to get in trouble at Southern Pines.

CHAPTER ELEVEN

Six weeks went by faster than Grace ever expected. Every recess was spent on the baseball field where Coach Dawkins would organize a game. Since Charlie and Grace's classes shared the same recess, they got to play together. Grace was growing better and better at hitting, and Charlie rarely missed catching a ball that came his way in left field.

The day finally arrived when Grace could bring Cheeto home. She and Charlie had been sharing a bag of Cheetos when Grace decided that was the perfect name for her orange cat.

"Gracie, if you don't sit still, we'll never finish." BonBon had her in the tub scrubbing her face with Lava soap. She was convinced it was the only soap that worked.

"But you're hurting me, BonBon. I know my face must be clean by now."

BonBon had removed Grace's eyepatch and was scrubbing the rust rings around the eye where her patch had been all week. "Child, I'm going to have to use a Brillo pad if you don't stop getting so dirty." She paused long enough to study Grace's face. "Now, it looks like I got it all. Rinse off good, and let's get you a new patch over your other eye. You can walk down to the firehouse by yourself. I've got to get over to the café and start my chicken and dumplings."

When Grace returned home with her new kitty, BonBon had already fixed up an old peach crate with a blanket for Cheeto. Even though Grace begged to have the cat sleep in her room, BonBon insisted that Cheeto was used to a kitchen, so that's where they'd keep her. Grace poured some water and some kitten food in the two little bowls she'd bought with her allowance at Miz Cotney's store. Miz Cotney had thrown in some kitty litter for half off, and Grace found a plastic container in the attic to use for a litter box.

She was still playing with Cheeto an hour later when BonBon came into the kitchen with a tray from the café. "I knew you wouldn't want to leave that kitten for your own supper. Wash your hands, then sit down and eat while it's still warm."

As soon as her plate was clean, Grace jumped up and headed back to her kitten. "Not so fast, young lady. I've got time for us to do your exercises. Sit down and take off your patch."

"Oh, come on, BonBon. Can't we skip tonight? I bet you need to get back to the café. Chicken and dumplings is always your busy night."

BonBon pulled out the eye exercise cards from a kitchen drawer where she kept important stuff. "Vern has everything under control at the café. Sit down, Gracie, and let's get this done. We want to tell Dr. Holliman that you're doing your homework when we go to Atlanta next Friday. He's scheduled your next surgery for June."

Grace had lost count of the number of surgeries she'd had since she was five. When she asked Dr. Holliman if she was cross-eyed like all her classmates said, he explained that because her eyes weren't attached like they should be, she couldn't control her eye movement. The result made her appear cross-eyed even though she wasn't.

A few months ago, just before her last surgery, Grace asked Dr. Holliman what he'd be doing to her eyes during the procedure. He always answered her questions like Grace was an adult. "I'll be pulling your eyeball out of its socket. Then I will make a tiny cut with a tiny scalpel to the white part of your eye. After that I can attach your muscles like they should be and put your eyeball back where it belongs." When tears began to trickle down Grace's cheeks, Dr. Holliman took her hand. "Don't you worry, sweetheart, you'll be sound asleep and won't feel a thing."

BonBon never let Grace miss a single morning or evening from her eye exercises. Grace groaned as BonBon made her cover one eye with a card. "Another surgery in June? But you promised me a birthday party at the Lion's Club Youth Center this year." Since BonBon didn't know the actual date Grace was born, she'd let the child choose a month and a day. Grace settled on June 5 because she'd always be out of school for summer, and the weather would be warm enough for an outdoor birthday party.

BonBon handed Grace a card. "Now cover your left eye and stop complaining. The surgery is the third week in June and won't interfere with your birthday."

"Good. At least I won't have bloody eyes for my party." After each surgery, the whites of her eyes were blood red for at least two weeks, and she had to allow the stitches in the corner of each eye to dissolve. During that time, Grace couldn't run or play ball or even ride her bicycle. After the last surgery, BonBon threatened to tie Grace to a stool in the café if she didn't stay still. "How much money is this next surgery gonna cost?"

BonBon held up a prism for Grace to watch with her uncovered eye. "You don't need to worry about the cost. Your only worry is to do what Dr. Holliman tells you to do. Now move that card to the other eye."

"I haven't seen Mr. Bates and Mr. Taylor stop by with a paper sack." Grace knew they delivered a sack full of money to BonBon every time there was a surgery coming up.

"Keep your eye on the prism and stop squirming. We've got almost a month before your surgery. The Lions Club won't forget about you. They always come through."

Still, Grace could see worry in BonBon's eyes. "I bet if you'd known how much my eyes were gonna cost, you'd have sent me to live at Southern Pines."

BonBon almost dropped the prism. "Gracie, I loved you from the very moment I first saw you, and I fought to get you and keep you. If I had to rob a bank to pay for your eyes, I would do it!"

Grace giggled. "You better go to Griffin to rob a bank. Mr. English at the Zebulon Bank would recognize you for sure."

BonBon twirled around. "I'd draw myself a pencil mustache and bushy black eyebrows. I'd shave my head and wear a man's suit. I'd give the teller a hand-written note so she wouldn't recognize my voice."

BonBon grinned and then turned serious. "You are my child, my sweet Sunday Grace, my everything. I'd give my life for you." She pulled Grace into a big hug. "Now let's get these exercises done."

◆

Grace was relieved when Mr. Bates and Mr. Taylor came through with a fresh bag of money from the Lions Club. BonBon didn't have to rob a bank after all.

Shortly after Grace's 11th birthday, Mr. Buddy was sitting at his usual table in the diner. "So, Miss Gracie, I guess you're about to go back under the knife, aren't you?"

Miss Ouida choked on her cigarette as she slapped Mr. Buddy on the arm. "Don't say that to the child." She straightened Grace's pigtail. "Don't you mind him, Gracie. Men can be so rude, crude, and uncouth."

BonBon poured both Ouida and Buddy another cup of coffee. "Dr. Holliman has hopes that this will be the last one. Wouldn't that be a nice late birthday present, Grace? Now run home and feed Cheeto and change her litter box."

Grace dragged her feet towards the kitchen and through the café's back door. She'd given up on this surgery being the last one. She figured she'd be wearing a patch and ugly orange glasses the rest of her life.

She was wrong. In late August just before school started, Grace heard the words she'd only dreamed of hearing. "Well, well, Miss Grace, your eyes are functioning beautifully. No more patches, no more glasses, and no more surgeries. You have 20/20 vision."

Grace leaped from the examination chair and started to dance. "Did you hear that, BonBon? My eyes are all fixed!"

BonBon's own eyes glistened. "Are you sure, Dr. Holliman? What about her exercises?"

The doctor grinned. "She needs to see me every six months, but her eye exercising days are finished."

Since Dr. Holliman's Atlanta office was right across the street from Rich's Department Store, BonBon decided they needed to celebrate. Compared to the stores in Zebulon and even Griffin, Rich's was huge. They rode the moving stairs up to the middle floor. BonBon grasped Grace's hand as she headed towards a narrow hallway. "This is the Crystal Bridge. If you look out the window, you can see Forsyth Street beneath us."

Grace peered through the glass, and sure enough, there was a street with cars moving underneath them. "The bridge connects the south of the building to the north of the building," BonBon explained as they kept walking. "We're on the mezzanine now. They serve great sandwiches here."

Grace ate the best chicken salad sandwich she'd ever had. With her mouth full, she lied to BonBon. "It's almost as good as yours!"

The two strolled through the book department for almost an hour. Grace had never seen so many brand-new books with slick paper covers over them. "These sure are pretty books. All the books in Zebulon's library are worn on the outside and have yellowed pages. Why don't the ones in our library have shiny covers?"

BonBon smiled. "The shiny covers are called jackets. The books in our library had jackets when they were new, but after people borrow them over and over, the jackets get torn." BonBon smiled again. "You can pick out one book to purchase. Make sure it's one you'll enjoy for a long time."

Grace settled on a book about the history of baseball. "Charlie and I can read this one together."

They recrossed the Crystal Bridge and once again took the moving stairs that BonBon called an "escalator" up to the department for girls. "How about some new clothes for school? I think you've grown about an inch this summer, and all your dresses are going to be too short."

BonBon ushered Grace into a dressing room, and before long, they were each carrying a Rich's bag with store bought clothes for Grace. While she'd never minded wearing the Dorsey twins' hand-me-downs, Grace was proud to say nobody had ever worn the clothes in her bag or read her book with the shiny jacket.

That night as Grace was changing for bed, BonBon knocked on her door. "Gracie, I have one more surprise for you." She pulled a tiny box from her pocket and handed it to Grace. "I've been saving it for a special occasion."

Opening the box Grace discovered a fine gold chain with a tiny cross dangling from it. "Wow, it's beautiful, BonBon!"

Bonnie lifted the necklace from its box. "This is about the only heirloom I have to offer you. My mama gave it to me when I got baptized at the age of ten. I was waiting until you had a better understanding of the resurrection before giving it to you."

Gracie giggled. "I guess I've come a long way since thinking 'Mr. Jesus' was married to you." While Grace lifted her hair, BonBon fastened the necklace around her neck. "Thank you, BonBon."

"Just remember that you wear the seal of the Cross. You may be tempted or troubled through your life, but you'll always belong to Jesus." She kissed Gracie atop her head. "I know you're a little too old for tucking in, but maybe just this once?"

She responded with a nod and crawled into bed. As BonBon pulled the quilt up to her little chin, Grace touched the small cross at her neck and started reciting her bedtime prayer. At the end, she whispered, "Thank you, God, that I belong to BonBon as well as to you."

CHAPTER TWELVE

Grace was disappointed that Charlie wasn't in church the following Sunday. She was anxious to tell him the good news about her eyes. Now that Charlie was 12, he had graduated from Cub Scouts to Boy Scouts. His troop was at Camp Thunder in nearby Molena for the entire week.

While Grace contented herself with studying her new book on baseball and helping BonBon with the baking, Charlie was spending his days swamping canoes, swimming, learning to shoot a bow and arrow, and practicing orienteering, which he'd learned was a fancy name for discovering paths through the woods. He hoped to earn at least four merit badges during the week.

Reverend Hogan served as the Scout Master of the troop, which included not only boys from the children's home, but also several from Charlie's class at school. Charlie was happy to have Tommy Davis as his tent mate since they slept side by side at Southern Pines. Their tent, nothing more than a tiny hut with a steeped canvas roof, was just large enough for two cots.

The final night at camp focused on Indian lore. Each scout created a loin cloth from a towel held on by a leather strap they'd made in leather working earlier in the week. While Charlie tightened the strap around his waist, Tommy tugged at his loin cloth. "This looks stupid. I hate it that we can't wear underwear underneath. I hope nothing falls out."

Charlie laughed. "You ain't got n-n-nothing big enough to fall out. Besides, it's just us f-f-fellas." Charlie blushed when he thought about Gracie seeing him dressed in the embarrassing Indian getup.

The entire troop, shirtless and barefoot, sat around the campfire as Scout Master Hogan led them in some Indian songs they'd learned that week. Afterwards, the Reverend announced, "Well scouts, I'm headed back to Southern Pines so I can be there for Sunday service. Tomorrow afternoon will be Family Day when you'll each receive the merit badges you've earned." Charlie grimaced at the thought of Family Day. His granny was in a wheelchair now and wouldn't be able to make the trip.

Charlie almost missed what the Rev said next. "Tonight, your counselors will be in charge. I think they have some rather interesting activities planned to keep you entertained." The counselors, high school scouts who had been in the program for years, began to snicker. Rev shot them a serious look. "Let's remember that we're all a brotherhood. Travis McDonald, since you're the oldest and an Eagle Scout, I expect you to keep everyone safe. Counselors George Harris and BC Stinson will help keep order."

Travis put on a serious face. "Yessir" was all he could manage before he and the other two counselors started giggling again.

The scouts were dismissed to return to their tents. Tommy tugged off his loin cloth and shimmied into his underwear and shorts as fast as he could. "I'm glad that's over. I think I got some pine straw up my crack." He tugged at the waist of his britches and leaned his head backwards to check.

Charlie pulled on a t-shirt. "Don't be so s-s-sure the night is over. I heard T-T-Travis and the other counselors whispering about a h-h-hike to search for M-M-Midnight Myra." The legendary Midnight Myra supposedly lived nearby and roamed the camp at night. Other scouts over the years claimed to have seen the old lady in a tattered white gown with her long silver hair blowing in the breeze.

Tommy's eyes grew wide. "Travis said she killed her husband, cut him up, and put pieces of him in pickle jars. Do your think that's true?"

"Aw, that's just st-st-stupid talk to sc-sc-scare us." Charlie managed a nervous laugh. "Why d-d-don't we try to get s-s-some sleep."

Tommy tossed and turned for at least 30 minutes before his breathing grew slow and steady. Charlie lay with his eyes wide open and his flashlight in his hand. If Midnight Myra came calling, he'd be ready.

The two campers were startled awake by the piercing sound of a whistle and then the unmistakable voice of Travis MacDonald. "Everybody up and at 'em. Get your sneakers on and meet at the campfire. We're taking a midnight hike."

Tommy's voice quivered as he crawled around the tent. "I can't find my other shoe."

Charlie shined his flashlight under Tommy's cot. "There it is. H-h-hurry up. We don't want them to l-l-leave us."

Other scouts were already staggering to the campfire by the time the two of them arrived. The three counselors, all sporting mischievous grins, stood side by side.

Travis cleared his throat. "A week at Camp Thunder is not complete without a hike to Midnight Myra's dwelling. Leave your flashlights here. You will have to depend on your night vision and your orienteering skills to travel." The frightened scouts groaned. "Don't worry; the three of us have flashlights, and we know the way. You will walk in twos with your tent mate. And remember to stay alert. We don't want to lose a scout to Myra."

Tommy grabbed Charlie's hand. "I don't like this one bit. Where do you think they're taking us?"

"I g-g-guess we'll find out s-s-soon enough. J-j-just stick close to me, T-T-Tommy. I won't let anything h-h-happen to you." Charlie felt responsible for his best friend, whose small, thin body and ginger hair had earned him the nickname "Shrimpy."

The group made a slow journey through the campsite and then started down an unfamiliar trail. Travis led the hike while the other two counselors brought up the rear.

Travis kept up a constant chatter about Midnight Myra. "She's lived near the camp for 50 years. People claim she killed her husband, cut him into little pieces, and pickled him. The sheriff could never find those pickle jars, so she got away with it." Travis shone his flashlight up a hill. "But just over that ridge is an old family cemetery."

Tommy whispered to Charlie, "I thought we were going to her house, not a graveyard. I ain't ever stepped foot in a graveyard at night. That's when spirits come out."

"He's j-j-just trying to scare us, T-T-Tommy. You st-st-stay close to me." As the scouts climbed the ridge, Tommy held Charlie's hand in a vise grip.

Just as Travis had promised, a small clearing appeared over the ridge. A weather-beaten fence surrounded several gravestones. "This is where Midnight Myra buries all her victims." Travis waved his flashlight over the graves until the beam of his light stopped at one. "And this grave holds nothing but the heart of Midnight Myra's husband."

Jerry Partridge, one of the braver scouts, raised a question. "I thought she pickled her husband."

BC shone his light directly in Jerry's face. "Midnight Myra pickled everything but her old man's heart. She buried it. Ain't that right, Travis?"

Travis nodded his head in agreement. "Yep, BC's telling the truth. Now here's the deal, scouts. To pass your final test of the week, all you have to do is go inside the fence and lay your ear to the ground in front of her husband's headstone." He waved his light back to the grave. "If you listen real closely, you'll hear her old man's heart beating." Travis smiled at the campers. "Now, who's going first?"

As the line of scouts stalled, Jerry interrupted again. "How do you know it's Midnight Myra's husband? I don't see a name on the headstone."

BC laughed. "That old hag is ugly but not stupid enough to put his name on the tombstone. It's him all right. I heard his heart beat myself when I was your age. Now who's gonna be brave enough to step inside the gate?"

Charlie wrenched his hand from Tommy's grip. "Let's g-g-get this over w-w-with. I'll go f-f-first."

He headed to the front of the line with Tommy at his heels. "I'm going with you, Charlie." Tommy's entire body shook as he took Charlie's hand.

Travis pointed his flashlight at the two boys. "Okay, Callahan and Davis, now we're talking. This is where we separate the men from the boys." Then he waved the beam toward a rickety gate. "Just one more thing before you go in. Midnight Myra has a strong dislike for anyone disturbing her graves. Hopefully, she's at home asleep, but she could be out and about. So be ready to run if you hear her. Okay, fellow scouts, let's give these two some encouragement. How about that Indian chant you learned this week? Get 'em started, George."

From the rear of the line, George Harris began to chant. "A-woony-koony-cha, A-woony." Then the other scouts joined in. "Ay i-yi, yippee ay, ki amos; A- woo, A-deemi kechee."

Travis pointed to Charlie and Tommy. "On the count of three. One-two-three..."

It was Charlie's chance to be known as something other than a stutterer. They were inside the gate and at the grave in seconds.

"Just get on your knees, put your ear to the ground, and listen." Travis urged. "Shh, everybody. Be quiet so they can hear the heartbeat."

Charlie studied the fright in Tommy's eyes. "C-c-come on, Tommy. They'll n-n-never call you Sh-Sh-Shrimpy again."

Just as the pair put their ears to the ground, a thrashing, crashing sound came from behind them. Charlie looked up to see a huge, white-clad woman with long silver hair heading out of the bushes towards them. She carried a hatchet and cackled in an ear-piercing shrill, "Get out of my graveyard, or you'll be next!"

Travis screamed, "It's Midnight Myra! Run for your lives!"

Scouts took off in every direction, but Myra headed straight through the gate. Charlie and Tommy were caught dead to rights with no place to run. "J-j-just stay d-d-down, Tommy, and c-c-cover your head." The trembling captives made themselves as small as possible.

Midnight Myra leaned over and snatched them up in one arm. "Charlie Callahan and Tommy Davis," she whispered. "You two will have a story to tell when you get back to the children's home." She pulled a flashlight from her white robe and illuminated her face. But it wasn't a she; it was a he.

Charlie stared in disbelief. "R-r-rev? Is that you?'

Reverend Hogan set the boys down on their feet. He smiled at them. "I'm proud of your bravery. Everybody else took off."

"Golly, I thought I was dead for sure." Tommy's voice was slowly returning to normal. "You scared the living daylights out of me, Rev."

The Rev pulled off the silver wig and grinned. "Now listen, fellas. Midnight Myra has been a Camp Thunder legend for 50 years. I aim to keep it that way, but I need your help. It will be our little secret. Can I count on y'all?"

Charlie held up two fingers in a Scout's salute. "Wh-wh-whaddya say, Tommy?"

Without hesitation Tommy's fingers went up. "Scout's honor," they vowed in unison.

Rev made sure the two got back to camp. At the edge of the campsite, he patted them both on their shoulders. "I'll see you at Family Day tomorrow. Now go on and enjoy the glory." Then he faded back into the dark woods.

The rest of the scouts, still frightened and confused, were sitting by the campfire. Travis was the first to see them. "Look, they made it back safely! Let's give them a cheer. Hip Hip Hooray! Hip Hip Hooray!"

When the chanting finally ended, Charlie and Tommy went back to their tent. They fell on their cots giggling. "Rev m-m-made an ugly old l-l-lady, didn't he?" Charlie snickered.

Then Tommy got serious. "Hey Charlie, thanks for sticking by me out there. You're a whole lot more than just a stutterer."

Charlie grinned. "And I d-d-don't think anybody will be c-c-calling you Shrimpy from n-n-now on."

Within seconds both boys were sleeping soundly. Midnight Myra wasn't the only legend that night.

The next afternoon, by the time all the campers had finished lunch, rolled up their sleeping bags, and policed the campsite, the Rev was back. "It looks like we have a record crowd gathering at the pavilion for Family Day. Let's line up and look sharp."

Charlie dreaded the ceremony with no one to cheer for him. But to his surprise, he spotted Gracie and Miz Bonnie sitting in the front row. Gracie smiled and gave him a little wave. Charlie's heart skipped a beat when he saw how pretty she looked in a pale green Sunday dress and matching headband around her soft blonde curls. Something was different about her, though. He couldn't put his finger on what it was.

The Rev handed out badges one after another, and Charlie's name was called three times for separate badges. He was disappointed that he hadn't hit his goal of four badges but guessed there was always next year.

Then Rev made an announcement. "We scouts have a special badge that is given only under exceptional circumstances. This year I am proud to announce that two scouts in Troop 155 will receive the Camp Thunder Courage badge for showing unusual valor during a midnight hike last night. Will Charlie Callahan and Tommy Davis step forward."

The entire troop including Travis MacDonald and his two cronies stood and applauded. The Rev continued. "Courage cannot be measured in size and strength but in one's heart. These two young men demonstrated that they have what it takes when put through a secret initiation among scouts who visit Camp Thunder."

While Tommy was quickly surrounded by his aunt, uncle, and five small cousins, Charlie took in the moment all by himself. Until he felt a tap on his shoulder and turned around to see Gracie's grin. "You gonna tell me what you did to become a hero?"

Charlie offered a rare smile and shrugged his shoulders. "S-s-sorry, it's a scout s-s-secret." Suddenly, he realized what was different about Gracie. "You're n-n-not wearing gl-gl-glasses. Wow, I never r-r-realized how bl-bl-blue your eyes are!"

Gracie just grinned. It was the best day of Charlie's 12 years on earth.

Two weeks later, Charlie was shaken awake from a deep sleep. When he opened his eyes, the Rev was sitting beside him. "Charlie, sorry to wake you up so early." The Rev handed Charlie his bathrobe. "Let's talk in the hall so we won't bother the other fellas."

Rubbing sleep from his eyes, Charlie followed Reverend Hogan into the hallway. "Charlie, I have some sad news. Your granny passed away an hour ago."

Charlie drew in a breath, and his lips began to quiver. "She's d-d-dead? But I j-j-just saw her S-S-Saturday, and she seemed f-f-fine. How c-c-can she be d-d-dead?"

The Rev wrapped his arm around Charlie's shoulders. "Dr. Hunt said your granny's heart just gave out."

Tears trickled down Charlie's face. "Did she s-s-suffer? I w-w-want to see her."

Doc Hunt said she died peacefully in her sleep. He squeezed Charlie tightly and led him back to bed. "It's an hour before sunrise. You try to get some sleep, and I'll take you to the funeral home in the morning."

There was no sleep for Charlie, though. He lay staring at the ceiling as he realized he was the only Callahan left. He'd never felt so alone.

The following days floated by with Charlie in a daze. He stood stonily in a new, stiff shirt and necktie as people paraded by his granny's casket and shook his hand. When Miz Bonnie and Gracie each hugged him, Charlie's throat constricted as he stifled a sob.

His granny was buried beside the rest of Charlie's family. Charlie stood staring at the fresh mound of red clay until everyone but Reverend Hogan had left. The Rev rested a hand on Charlie's shoulder. "Son, I can't begin to know how you feel, but I can offer a prayer." The two bowed their heads. "Dear Lord, bless this sweet woman's soul as she gathers with all her loved ones in her Heavenly home. Bless this young man's soul as he continues to travel his earthly journey. Remind Charlie that he never walks alone because You are right beside him. Amen."

When the two returned to the children's home, the Rev took Charlie into his office where he handed him a metal box. "Doc Hunt found this by your granny's bedside. He thought you'd want to have it."

Charlie stared at the box. Although still intact, the box had charred spots all over it. He choked back tears. "I r-r-remember this box. Mama used to st-st-store special things and p-p-pictures in it, b-b-but I thought it b-b-burned up in the fire."

The Rev smiled. "Well, I guess the metal is fireproof. It's yours now, son."

Charlie tucked the box under his bed, changed into a t-shirt, and headed to the dining hall. Later that night when the lights were out and everyone else had fallen asleep, Charlie slipped the box from its hiding place.

With his Boy Scout flashlight, he studied the contents of the box. On the very top was a photo taken the Easter Sunday before the house burned. Charlie stood between his pregnant mother, her beautiful eyes gleaming, and his daddy, puffed up with pride. His baby sister was born two weeks later. There were a few pictures of Charlie when he was just a toddler on a tricycle and in his highchair and even one of his parents on their wedding day. How young and pretty his mama was! There was one single photo of his baby sister the day they brought her home from the hospital. They had named her Rose because Charlie's mama said her little lips looked like a tiny rosebud.

Also in the box were several medals of commendation that Charlie's daddy had earned in the Navy during World War II, as well as his discharge papers and his dog tags. At the bottom of the stack was a small pocketknife that had belonged to his daddy. Charlie remembered hearing his daddy explain that the knife had been passed down through three generations of Callahan men and that it would belong to Charlie when he turned 12.

Charlie opened the knife and ran it across his palm. It needed sharpening, but it still worked. The children's home had a shop where they sharpened tools for gardening. He could sharpen the knife tomorrow. Until then he placed it under his pillow—and for the first time since his granny died, Charlie breathed deeply.

Charlie bowed his head and whispered. "Lord, I pr-pr-promise to h-h-honor those before me by being the b-b-best Callahan man I can be. Please h-h-help me, sweet Jesus."

PART TWO

CHAPTER THIRTEEN

By the time he started seventh grade, Charlie's body was muscled and tanned from his outdoor chores in Pinewood's vegetable garden and countless hours on the baseball field. An accomplished baseball player with an impressive batting average on the junior high team, Charlie's reputation had reached the eyes and ears of the high school coach. He'd grown out his crewcut, and his sandy hair swept over his eyebrows. Although he usually held a serious expression, Charlie sported dimples when he flashed the occasional smile—something that only happened in Grace's presence. Her lively energy reflected as a sparkle in Charlie's hazel eyes.

Grace had experienced her own metamorphosis. Her baby fat had been replaced by graceful curves in all the right places. She'd learned to tame her unruly hair into soft golden curls. After the agony of so many surgeries, her cerulean blue eyes gleamed underneath long, velvet lashes. Her cheeks and the bridge of her nose were sprinkled with freckles that accentuated her flawless, peach complexion. While she enjoyed watching Charlie play baseball, her interests had turned to books of all kinds, and she was never without something to read. She was Miss Idalee's number one patron of the library.

Despite all his obvious physical changes, Charlie still stuttered, and Grace still waited for him during his speech therapy with Miz Harriet Davison twice a week. On days that Charlie was in a speech lesson, Grace would head to their favorite spot by the creek in the woods. The two of them had discovered it last year when Gracie missed a ball that Charlie hit high and hard.

When the two went searching for the ball, they found it resting against a huge mimosa tree with limbs that spread across the creek. Charlie studied the remains of a fire nearby. Cigarette butts and beer cans littered the dirt by the creek. "I've h-h-heard about this place. High school b-b-boys hang out here at night to sm-sm-smoke and drink b-b-beer."

Grace had already climbed the mimosa to a smooth branch that was worn into a natural seat. "We can claim it for afternoons, can't we? Come on up, Charlie. There's room for you next to me."

On warm days when there was no one else to play ball, the two would wander to their special spot. They shared their deepest secrets sitting in the mimosa. One day Grace described her life before BonBon.

Charlie was wide-eyed. "You m-m-mean your mama never even g-g-gave you a name?"

Grace sighed. "BonBon said it was because she was sick from the drugs she put in her body, but I think Marie was just plain mean. She didn't want me in her way. I guess she did one thing right—she left me with BonBon. Was your mama mean, Charlie?"

Charlie grew thoughtful. "No, she was the b-b-best mama in the world. She made the world's greatest fried ch-ch-chicken, even better than what M-M-Minnie cooks at the h-h-home. I m-m-miss her some days."

Grace grabbed Charlie's hand and squeezed it. "BonBon told me there was a fire. What happened?"

Charlie's eyes took on a faraway look. "It'd been c-c-cold that night, and Pa had left the gas h-h-heater running in their b-b-bedroom. Mama was worried that my baby s-s-sister would get a cold. She had the c-c-croup and kept coughing. I was sleeping in the front b-b-bedroom, so Mama brought me an extra qu-qu-quilt. She covered me up and said the same p-p-prayer she said every night: 'May the Lord w-w-watch over you and me until we m-m-meet again.' That's the last t-t-time I ever saw h-h-her."

"The next thing I r-r-remember was the sm-sm-smell of smoke and Pa's voice scr-scr-screaming for me to g-g-get out. But the smoke was so th-th-thick that I c-c-couldn't see a thing. I crawled to the h-h-hall, but it was full of fl-fl-flames. I r-r-remembered from Cub Scouts to close a door against f-f-fire. So, I crawled back in my r-r-room, closed the door, and f-f-felt my way to the w-w-window.

"Then I r-r-remember the s-s-siren and a bl-bl-blanket on my shoulders. I never saw any of th-th-them again. And n-n-now that my granny's g-g-gone, I'm the only one l-l-left. I d-d-don't know why God let me l-l-live." Tears streamed down Charlie's cheeks.

Gracie squeezed his hand tighter. "I know why God let you live, Charlie Callahan."

Charlie turned toward her with questioning eyes as Grace continued. "God knew I needed a best friend, a friend who understands the empty part of my heart."

Charlie managed a weak smile. "I g-g-guess we share that s-s-same emptiness."

Then Grace leaned in and kissed Charlie. They held hands in silence as a soft wind whispered through the mimosa.

⁂

Even though the creek was just barely out of sight of the school grounds, BonBon had warned Grace not to go that far by herself. "As long as Charlie is with you, it's okay, but you shouldn't be out there alone," she admonished.

One warm April day with nothing else to do while she waited on Charlie, Grace ventured to the creek alone. "What she don't know won't hurt her," she thought—a mantra Grace had heard Mr. Brooxie say every time he mentioned his wife, Miz Sanctified Flo.

Her back against their beloved mimosa tree, Grace was deep into the final chapter of *Mrs. Mike*. The wild dogwoods swayed gently, and the bubbling creek kept her company.

Her perfect afternoon was suddenly interrupted by the whiff of cigarette smoke. A funny feeling crept up Grace's spine, but she was too late to react.

Beau Loosier and two boys she didn't know were suddenly standing over her. "So, if it isn't little Miss Grace MacGregor. I see your hair grew back. It's right pretty, ain't it, boys?"

Grace shuddered as Beau's friends laughed. Her legs shook as she stood up with her back against the tree. Although she hadn't seen Beau since the day he cut her hair, there was a smell that Grace would never forget. She realized it was her own scent; she knew it was fear.

Grace's voice quivered. "Look, I don't want any trouble. I'm waiting on my friend, and I'll just walk back up to the school and let y'all have this place."

Grace turned to go, but Beau grabbed her arm. His eyes were cruel, and his breath smelled of whiskey, just like the kind that Mr. Brooxie drank. One of Beau's friends was turning up a slim-necked bottle half full of a dark liquid.

Beau twisted her arm as he explored her body with his eyes. "What's your hurry, Gracie? You sure have grown up since I saw you last. Let's have a little fun."

She tried to pull away, but his grip was iron. She pleaded. "Just let me go, Beau. I won't say a word about this if you just let me go."

Beau laughed. Then he took his free hand and yanked off Grace's shirt. "Lookie there, boys. She's got tits!" His buddies laughed. "Let's see what she's got at the other end."

Grace squirmed and kicked Beau. "Got a little temper, don't you? Jimmy, hold her arms." A pizza-faced boy with greasy hair pinned Grace's arms behind her back as Beau reached under her skirt and snatched down her panties.

Grace's entire body shook as she realized what was happening. "Please don't, please don't. Just let me go."

Beau pushed her to the ground as the pimply boy pried her legs apart. Terrified, Grace watched Beau unzip his pants. She closed her eyes and bit her lip as he climbed on top of her. She felt something hard pressing against her private parts, but then Beau stopped.

"She's too small down there. Jack, hand me the booze." Through the slits of her eyes, Grace watched Beau guzzle the remaining liquid from the long-necked bottle. He wiped his mouth with his shirt sleeve. Then he moved the bottle towards her privates. "This should open her up."

Grace tried to scream, but Beau covered her mouth with one hand as he worked the bottle with his other. The pain was excruciating. Then everything went dark. The next thing Grace knew, someone was slapping her, and something warm was oozing down her leg. "Wake up, you little whore."

She opened her eyes to see Beau Loosier's soulless gaze inches from her face. "You listen, and you listen good. You tell anybody about this, and you'll be sorry. I'll come back and kill your precious BonBon." He grabbed Grace's hair and pulled her face even closer. "You understand me, you stinkin' bitch?"

She nodded, but Beau twisted her hair in his hands. "No, I want to hear you say it."

Grace gritted her teeth to keep them from chattering. "I won't tell a soul. I promise."

Beau released her hair and laughed. "I'm taking these cute little pink panties for a souvenir. And wait a minute…" He snatched the fine gold chain from Grace's neck and tucked it into the pocket of his jeans, tossing the cross onto her chest. "You can have the stupid cross. It'll be a reminder that God can't protect you from me." Then he spat in Grace's face. "If you ever tell, I'll be back. Come on, boys. Let's get outta here."

Clutching the tiny gold cross in her fist, Grace rolled on her side, pulled her knees to her stomach, and sobbed.

⚜

Ten minutes later, Charlie stood over Grace. Taking in her shirtless body and the blood on her skirt, his heart sunk to his stomach. He shook her gently.

"What h-h-happened, Gracie? Who d-d-did this to you?" Grace continued to sob. Charlie found her blouse hanging on a nearby bush. "H-h-here, let's g-g-get you dressed." He gently pulled her arms through the sleeves and buttoned her up. Then he pulled his handkerchief from his pocket. "B-b-blow your nose, Gracie. It's all r-r-right now; I'm h-h-here. It's all right."

Grace sat up and blew her nose as instructed. She wrapped her trembling arms around Charlie's neck. "It hurts so bad. What am I gonna tell BonBon? I promised I wouldn't come out here without you. What am I gonna do?"

Charlie removed his shirt and wrapped it around Grace's shoulders. Then he pulled off his white t-shirt and soaked it in the creek. He sponged Grace's face and then her bloody thighs. "Shh, it's g-g-gonna be all right. Can you t-t-tell me what happened? Who d-d-did this to you?"

But Grace remained mute. Her tears streamed down her face as her body shook. Charlie engulfed her in his arms until she finally relaxed. "Okay, let's g-g-get you up. Do you think you can w-w-walk?"

Grace nodded as Charlie pulled her to her feet. "It's almost time for Miz B-B-Bonnie to get here. She'll be l-l-looking for us. You can t-t-tell her all about it, and she'll c-c-call the sheriff."

Grace suddenly came to life. "No! No! No! We're not telling BonBon; do you hear me? It's our secret, Charlie." She grabbed his arm. "Promise me. You cannot tell her. You have to swear it, or I'll never speak to you again!"

"Okay. Okay. W-w-whatever you want, Grace. It will be our secret, I p-p-promise." He held Grace's wobbly body close to his. "But you're pale as a g-g-ghost and shaking like a l-l-leaf." He touched her face. "There's a w-w-welt on your cheek, too. What in the w-w-world are we gonna tell Miz Bonnie?"

Grace took a ragged breath and wiped her nose once more. "Get my baseball bat from the tree where we hide it. We'll tell her I was sitting on it, lost my balance, and the bottom of the handle went up in me."

Charlie retrieved the bat and grimaced. "D-D-Do you think she'll b-b-believe that story?"

Taking his bloody t-shirt, Grace rubbed some of the blood on the bottom of the bat. "I know she will. She's fussed at me for ages about sitting on it." She gave Charlie a stern look. "Are you sure you can lie for me, Charlie?"

He wiped his brow with his sleeve, took a deep breath, and finally nodded. "And I'll n-n-never leave you alone again. I'll p-p-protect you always." He held her so close that Grace could barely breathe. "I love you, Gracie. I love you m-m-more than anything in this w-w-world."

"Oh Charlie, you can't love me now." Just like Marie, her dead mother, Grace knew she was damaged beyond repair.

She smoothed her hair then picked up her books. "We have to pretend that I just had an accident with the bat. Then BonBon won't be suspicious."

Charlie used his wet t-shirt to wipe a spot of the blood off her skirt. When he did, he noticed that the insides of Grace's thighs were turning blue. "I g-g-guess you c-c-could have gotten those b-b-bruises when you f-f-fell off the bat." He balled up his bloody t-shirt and threw it in the bushes.

Grace squared her shoulders. "Okay, let's go." She walked toward the school with Charlie on her heels.

When the two emerged from the woods, Ouida Clarkston was just pulling into the school parking lot. Grace breathed deeply. "Good, it's Miss Ouida. Ever since she got that new Lincoln, she's been offering to drive me wherever I need to go. This will give me time to get my story straight in my head."

Ouida flicked ashes out her window. "You two hop in for the smoothest ride you've ever had." Then she did a doubletake. "Lord, have mercy!

What happened to you, Grace?" She climbed out of the front seat to get a better look.

Grace's eyes filled with tears, but the words would not come. Charlie helped her into the back seat. "Um, she h-h-had a l-l-little accident, Miss Ouida. I th-th-think she needs to lie d-d-down."

Miss Ouida opened the trunk and pulled out a blanket. "Cover her with this, Charlie. You can sit up front with me."

Once they were all in the car, Miss Ouida, hands shaking, lit another cigarette. "So, what in heaven's name happened, Charlie?"

Charlie was still holding the baseball bat. He swallowed. "Well, I d-d-didn't see it happen, but she said she was sitting on t-t-top of the b-b-bat, lost her b-b-balance and the bat w-w-went, it w-w-went up, you k-k-know."

"Oh no, how horrible! Bless your sweet heart, Gracie. Let me get you home so Bonnie can take care of you."

The usual five-minute trip took less than three as Ouida raced to Bonnie's house. "Charlie, run over to the café and tell Bonnie what happened. I don't want her to see Gracie like this. I'll get her inside and into a warm bath."

Charlie did as he was told. By the time Bonnie banged through the front door to the house, Ouida had Grace soaking in a tub of warm water. Charlie waited on the front porch.

Now, it was Bonnie's turn to shake all over. "Gracie, Gracie! Oh honey, are you okay? She knelt by the tub and saw that the water had turned pinkish. "Ouida, can you drive Charlie home? I'll take care of Gracie now."

As soon as Ouida left, Grace burst into tears again. "I'm sorry I didn't listen to you. It hurts so much, BonBon!"

Bonnie helped her from the tub and wrapped a soft towel around her. "Listen to me about what, honey?"

Grace hesitated. Could she lie to BonBon about what happened? Then she heard Beau's threat. She buried her face in Bonnie's shoulder. "The bat. I was sitting on the bat and lost my balance. Then it jammed up in me."

"Sweet Jesus, you poor thing. We need to get you over to Doc Hunt's before he closes for the night. Thank goodness it's his day to be in town." She dried Grace off and helped her into some clean clothes.

Grace shivered. "You're not mad at me, BonBon?"

Bonnie hugged her closely. "The most important thing right now is making certain that you are okay. I can be mad later."

⚜

BonBon held her hand as Grace shivered on the examining table. "Now, honey, Dr. Hunt is going to examine your vaginal area. It may be a little uncomfortable, but he must see if there's any damage. Do you understand?"

Biting her lip, Grace nodded. She couldn't see Dr. Hunt from her angle. "Now, Miss Gracie, I need you to bend your knees and spread your legs." Instead, Grace squeezed her legs tightly together as tears filled her eyes.

"It's okay, sweetheart. Just look at me." With tears in her own eyes, BonBon leaned over her. "After all the eye surgeries you've had, I know how brave you are. Dr. Hunt isn't going to hurt you, I promise." She brushed the blonde curls from Grace's forehead. "You just close your eyes and find a pretty place to go in your mind."

Grace obeyed. She closed her eyes and tried to find that pretty place. But all she saw was Beau Loosier's snarling lips. She could smell the whiskey again and feel his dirty hands roaming all over her body. She screamed.

In the end, Dr. Hunt had to sedate Grace to complete his examination. Nurse Naomi stayed with her while Bonnie followed the doctor into his office. He closed the door behind them. "The good news, Miz Bonnie, is that I see no permanent damage. She has some tears on the interior of her vagina, which are consistent with something rupturing her. It will take a while for the tears to heal, but once they do, she should be just fine, physically."

Bonnie breathed for the first time in the last two hours. "Thank God there's no permanent physical damage. But…" She burst into tears.

Doc Hunt handed her a tissue. "There, there, Miz Bonnie. It's okay."

"But what if something else happened? I've never seen her so frightened. Do you think she's telling the truth? I mean she has started developing. She had her first period six months ago. Maybe she and Charlie were exploring each other, and something happened?"

"Now, let's don't borrow trouble, Bonnie. The injuries look like they were caused by the penetration of an inanimate object, not by the other, if you know what I mean." He pulled out an ink pen. "I'll write a prescription for the pain. I think Grace's outburst was the result of the kind of examination I had to do. That can be quite traumatic for a girl her age. Here's a second script for a very mild sedative in case she suffers another outburst. Hopefully, you won't need it."

CHAPTER FOURTEEN

Charlie did his best to keep both his promises to Grace. Whenever Bonnie questioned him, he stuck to his story about the baseball bat causing Grace's injury. More importantly, he made sure that Grace was never, ever alone. Grace refused to tell him the name of her assailant, and Charlie learned not to pry. When he did, Gracie would grow extremely agitated and remain mute.

After the incident, Grace's personality seemed to change overnight. Gone were her easy laugh and insatiable curiosity about the world, and her bright blue eyes took on a dull darkness. She rarely stopped by the café to visit with the regulars, choosing instead to wait for BonBon to bring her dinner to the house.

By the following fall, as Charlie headed to high school and Grace entered eighth grade, she showed no signs of improvement. BonBon tried everything to coax her precious girl back to her old self. One evening around dinnertime, BonBon burst into the house and beamed at Gracie, who was sitting at the kitchen table. "Guess who's at the café?" Grace just shrugged. "It's your old babysitter Vicki Fordham! She starts her master's degree program at the University next week. Why don't you come over and have dinner with her? She's been asking about you."

Gracie had once followed Vicki's college career at the University of Georgia with enthusiasm. She shrugged again. "I really need to get a shower,

BonBon. Maybe next time." She picked up Cheeto and headed upstairs to her room.

Bonnie sighed. That cat was Gracie's best friend these days. Bonnie had learned not to push too much. If she did, she discovered that Gracie pulled away even more. She'd talked to Dr. Hunt about the drastic change in Grace's behavior. "Give her space and time," he advised. "Adolescence is hard enough without the trauma she experienced."

On the days when Charlie had speech therapy after school, Grace started hanging out in the high school gym where her PE teacher had an office. Miss Margie Hughes had grown up in Macon, where she was an all-city tennis player in the 1950s. After graduating from Wesleyan College with a degree in physical education, she left Macon and, for some unknown reason, settled in the small town of Zebulon. She soon after became a member of the Pike County faculty. Since Pike's school system was small, the junior and senior high schools shared a gym, and Miss Hughes served as the girls' PE teacher for both. In her mid-30s now, she was attractive with a small, compact body and a curly pixie haircut that framed her face perfectly.

Miss Hughes' diminutive stature was deceiving. Armed with a feisty personality, competitive spirit, and genuine compassion for her students, she'd built a successful athletic program for Pike County's junior and high school girls. Every girl with even an ounce of athletic ability wanted to be on one of Miss Hughes' teams.

Grace would try to make herself invisible in the darkest corner of the gym. She kept her nose buried in a library book so she didn't have to make conversation with Miss Hughes or any of the female basketball players, who often stopped by to shoot baskets or visit with their beloved coach.

One afternoon, Grace was so intensely focused on her book, she was oblivious to the fact that Miss Hughes was standing over her until the coach spoke. "Whatcha reading, Grace? It must be good. You haven't looked up for 30 minutes."

So taken aback by the intrusion, Grace gave a tiny shudder. She recovered quickly. "Yes ma'am. It's *To Kill a Mockingbird* by Harper Lee."

Miss Hughes smiled. "One of my favorites. Which character do you like best?" When Grace didn't answer, the coach continued. "I was partial to Dill Harris. He can tell a good tale, can't he? Could you tear away from the story long enough to help me rack some balls?"

Grace sighed and closed her book. She willed the gym door to open with a member of Miss Hughes' team who'd jump at the opportunity to assist their coach. No such luck. She sighed again. "Yes ma'am. I can help."

As Grace trotted around the gym floor corralling basketballs and placing them on a rolling rack, Miss Hughes chatted away. "I've watched you when we play volleyball in PE. You'd make a great addition to our high school JV team next fall. You interested?"

Grace shrugged her shoulders. She barely had the energy to brush her hair these days much less serve a volleyball over a net.

"Well, think about it. And while you're thinking about it, I'm putting together a girls' softball league at the Rec Center for the summer. Coach Dawkins told me you were a switch hitter and a great fielder. We could really use you on the summer league. We're still trying to come up with a name since this will be Pike County's first girls' softball team. I bet you're good at names with all the reading you do. You think you could jot down some possible ideas for me? I'd truly appreciate your help. While I love to read, I'm better at serving or hitting a ball than I am at writing."

Before Grace could come up with an excuse, Charlie stuck his head in the door. "Gracie, I'm d-d-done. You r-r-ready to go?"

Saved from making any decisions, Grace handed Miss Hughes the last ball. "I'll think about it, Miss Hughes, but I doubt I'll have time for your summer league."

Miss Hughes just smiled. "We don't start until June 4. Give it some thought, Grace. We need you."

Charlie was waiting for Gracie when she got to the lobby. "W-w-what was that all about?"

Gracie sighed. "Nothing really. Miss Hughes wants me to play on her softball team this summer."

Charlie whistled. "A girls' l-l-league? That's great. They h-h-have one in Griffin and in T-T-Thomaston, but I n-n-never thought we'd get one h-h-here. You're g-g-gonna play, aren't you?"

"I doubt it. BonBon will be keeping me busy in the café this summer. Anyways, I haven't hit a softball since before…before…you know." Grace's eyes brimmed with tears.

Charlie grabbed her free hand. "D-D-Don't cry, Gracie. N-N-Nobody will ever h-h-hurt you again." He hung his head. "B-B-But I c-c-can't be around all the t-t-time when school l-l-lets out. I'm g-g-getting a j-j-job at the p-p-peach packing p-p-plant this summer."

Grace snatched her hand back. "A *job*? But what about *us*? What if… if…something happens again, and you're not around?" She burst into tears and took off running.

Charlie was faster and caught up with her easily. He gently held her by the shoulders and turned her to face him. "Gr-Gr-Gracie, stop. I g-g-gotta work this s-s-summer. I'll be s-s-sixteen soon and the Rev says if I w-w-work, the h-h-home will match my income. That w-w-way I can make enough to b-b-buy a used c-c-car. I c-c-can take you on a real d-d-date then."

Grace swallowed. "A date? In a car with you?" She sniffled. "Do you even know how to drive a car, Charlie?"

Charlie grinned. "I w-w-will by my b-b-birthday. Mr. Brooxie has promised to t-t-teach me how to ch-ch-change the oil and to dr-dr-drive a car."

"Mr. Brooxie Barnett? I hope you plan to take your lessons in the mornings before he gets into his bottle of Old Grandad." She giggled and allowed Charlie to engulf her in a hug. "Charlie, I can't live without you."

Charlie kissed her atop her blonde head. "You n-n-never will have to l-l-live without m-m-me." Then they headed to the parking lot where BonBon was waiting.

♠

As the school year crept to an end, Miss Hughes persisted in her campaign to sign Grace up for the softball team. Grace couldn't seem to hide from her.

One afternoon Grace had barely settled into her usual corner of the gym when Miss Hughes approached her with a catalogue attached to her ever-present clipboard. "Hi Grace. I need some advice. Which of these uniforms do you like best? I need to order them by the end of next week so they'll be here before our softball season begins." She stuck the catalogue right under Grace's nose. "And by the way, have you come up with any names for our team?"

Grace had no choice but to study the pictures. "I like the blue one with white lettering. I did write down a couple of possible names." Grace pulled a composition folder from beneath her books and opened it to a page with lots of scribbles.

Miss Hughes grinned. "Oh good! I see you've been brainstorming. What did you come up with?"

Grace's face colored as she snatched out the page and quickly folded it. "I doubt they'll work. They're probably stupid."

Miss Hughes held out her hand. "Come on, let me have a look. They can't be that bad. At least you have some ideas. I keep drawing a blank."

Reluctantly, Grace handed over the sheet and quickly tucked her head back into her library book. Miss Hughes studied the names. "Hmmm. Some of these are promising. I like the Pike Fillies and Pike Pumas. Both are fast creatures. Which one do you like best?"

Grace felt both embarrassed and proud. "You really think those names are good?"

"They're not just good. They're perfect. We want our name to sound threatening to our opponent. I'm leaning toward the Pike Pumas. A puma is quick and ferocious but also a beautiful, intelligent animal like you and my other players. I can just see that in white letters on the back of your blue uniform."

"*My* uniform?" Grace could somehow see it herself. An all-girl team with the best female athletes in the county. But would BonBon approve? "I don't know, Miss Hughes. I'd have to ask BonBon if she could spare me from the café this summer. She's expecting me to help out."

Miss Hughes smiled. "Funny you mentioned your mom, Grace. I ran into her at Cotney's just yesterday. I told her what a great asset you would be for our team, and she agreed wholeheartedly. I don't think it will be a problem as long as you want to play." She hesitated and then grinned at Grace. "You'd make a heckuva catcher."

Grace felt her face heat up again. How did Miss Hughes know that her favorite position was catcher? "I've never played on a real team. I can't imagine I'd be good enough."

"Listen to me, Grace. Let's replace *I can't* with *I can try*. Besides, you've been playing ball in the schoolyard since second grade. You are so ready to be a Pike Puma. What do you say?"

For the first time in quite a while, Grace's eyes began to shine. "I think I'd like to play, Miss Hughes."

"That's great! I can't wait to tell the other players we have a real catcher." Miss Hughes pulled a sheet from her clipboard. "You just need to complete this form and get it back to me by the end of the week, Grace."

Grace took the form and grabbed a pencil from her purse. "Um, Miss Hughes, just one thing. My friends call me Gracie."

Miss Hughes smiled. "Got it. And you can call me Coach."

CHAPTER FIFTEEN

That summer, the Pike County Pumas quickly grew into a formidable softball team. Since most team members worked summertime jobs during the day, practices were held in the evening—right when Bonnie was up to her eyeballs with the supper crowd. So, Miss Ouida and Mr. Buddy volunteered to take turns dropping Gracie off at the Pike County Ballpark. The two had instantly become Gracie's biggest fans, and they often fought over who'd get to drive her.

Usually, they'd both end up coming so they could stay and watch the practice. One such night, perched on the front row of the stands, Ouida puffed on a cigarette while Buddy munched on a bag of pork rinds. Between bites Buddy waved smoke out of his eyes. "You know those cancer sticks are gonna kill you one of these days?"

Ouida blew a smoke ring in the dusk. "Hrmph! No worse than all that fried, salty mess you're putting in your body, Buddy Sampson. When's the last time you could see your feet?"

But when Gracie came to bat, the grumbling stopped. Ouida squashed out her cigarette and turned her attention to the home plate. "Come on, Gracie, hit it over the fence!" Buddy whistled loudly between his fingers. On the first pitch, Gracie whacked the ball into the outfield, giving her plenty of time to race to second base. Ouida squealed with excitement, and as Buddy jumped up to cheer, he almost fell off the stands.

⚜

Grace MacGregor began to shine again that summer. She'd discovered a comfortable camaraderie with her fellow Pumas and was starting to realize her potential as an athlete under Coach Hughes' direction. By August, the Pike County Pumas had battled their way to a coveted spot in the Tri-County finals.

Early each morning, Grace could be found making coffee and taking orders in the café. BonBon spent most of her time in the kitchen baking biscuits and prepping for the evening meal while Vern flipped eggs and fried bacon on the griddle.

One sunny morning, sitting in his usual spot at the counter, Cooter Renfroe had his head buried in the Thomaston Times. "Hey, y'all listen to this from Charles Gordy's sports page," he announced to the breakfast regulars.

> *The Tri-County softball tournament should be quite a battle of the lady sluggers this year. With Thomaston Twister heavy hitters Lindy Blackstone and Cheryl Smith, the newly formed Pike County Pumas will have their work cut out for them. The Pumas do have some outstanding fielders in Katie Palmer and Peggy Mason along with the ready glove and consistent hitting of their catcher Grace Callahan.*

"How about that, Gracie? You made the sports page!"

Buddy poured ketchup on his eggs. "Just wait until that Thomaston team gets a look at Gracie with a bat. Charles Gordy will be writing about a true slugger then!"

Ouida, sitting with Buddy at his favorite table, blew smoke rings from her first cigarette of the day. "Gracie, has Coach Hughes decided who'll pitch against the Twisters?"

Grace topped off Cooter's coffee. "I'm not sure if it will be Chrissy Jones or Phyllis Arnold. They're both good. But first, we gotta play the Griffin team, and they have a couple of tough pitchers."

"Shoot!" Ouida interrupted. "Y'all tore them up last time you played. The Pumas are a cinch for the finals with Thomaston. You just take care of those hands and keep swinging hard, Gracie. We'll need a couple of homeruns when we get to the finals."

While she enjoyed the attention, Gracie found herself blushing. She never imagined that she'd see her name on the sports page of the *Thomaston Times*. She couldn't wait to show the article to Charlie, who'd be picking her up this evening to take her to the movies in Griffin.

BonBon had insisted that Gracie wait until she turned 15 before she could go on a real date. After her birthday last month, she'd been allowed to ride around the square with Charlie in his hand-me-down 1956 Chevy. Mr. Brooxie had bought the old car for what he called a "song" after haggling for an entire afternoon with a used dealer who finally gave into a cheap sell. Once school started back, Charlie had agreed to work afternoons in Mr. Brooxie's shop to pay for the car.

Mr. Brooxie and Charlie had scoured every junkyard from Zebulon to Atlanta for the parts they needed to make the vehicle drive worthy. Charlie's peach packing savings, coupled with the promised money from the children's home, paid for all the parts. Every Sunday afternoon, the two of them could be found in Brooxie's shop working on the car.

After BonBon observed Charlie's driving ability and was assured by Brooxie that the car was in excellent running condition, she finally agreed that Charlie could take Gracie on a proper date. Tonight, they were going to see *Cool Hand Luke* at the Imperial Theater in Griffin.

Gracie was glad that she only had to work in the café through lunch. Since Coach Hughes gave the girls Fridays off from practice, she'd have the afternoon to get ready for her first real date.

Mid-afternoon while Gracie rolled her long blonde hair onto huge curlers in front of the bathroom mirror, Bonnie stood in the doorway watching. She had to be back in the café shortly to start cooking for the Friday crowd. It was always her busiest evening. Bonnie's Blue Plate special on Friday nights always included country fried steak with mashed potatoes and gravy, pinto beans, coleslaw, homemade rolls, and her famous strawberry shortcake.

Bonnie folded her arms as she laid down the law to Gracie. "You know the café will be teeming with hungry customers until we close tonight. So, Charlie needs to come there to pick you up."

Gracie sighed. "How embarrassing! Everybody will be looking at us and knowing we're going on a date."

"Grace MacGregor, the two of you have been joined at the hip for years, so I doubt they'll pay much attention. Now, are you wearing the dotted Swiss sundress or the one with the pink rickrack?"

Gracie hesitated. "I haven't decided. Which one do you like the best?"

BonBon studied the two dresses hanging on the closet door. "The blue dotted Swiss looks beautiful with your eyes. And your new white flats will be perfect." She smiled at Gracie. "I can't believe my little girl is old enough to date. Now don't overdo the mascara."

Gracie sighed again. "I won't, BonBon."

Bonnie started out the door. "Oh, and one more thing. If that young man gets fresh with you, he'll answer to me and all the regulars at the café."

"Oh gosh!" Gracie groaned. "I think Charlie could take Miss Ouida and Mr. Cooter."

"But not Buddy; he'd just sit on the boy and flatten him." BonBon's remark got a giggle out of Gracie. "Just have a good time and say hello to that blue-eyed actor Paul Newman for me." She kissed Gracie atop her wet curlers and headed for the café.

Charlie showed up right at 6:00, the busiest time in the café. Gracie peeked out through the small window in the kitchen's swinging door. He had on a new madras shirt and khaki pants. He looked muscled and tanned, and his hair was bleached from working in the sun at the packing shed the past two months. Her heart did a flip flop as he brushed his bangs away from his eyes.

Bonnie, carrying a heavy pan, suddenly bumped her rear end through the door and almost knocked Gracie down. "Oh Gracie, you look so pretty! There's a young man waiting quite nervously at the cash register. Have fun but remember that curfew is 10:30. After that, I'll turn you into a pumpkin and not let you out of my sight until you're 21."

When Gracie stepped into the dining room, she felt the stares of every patron upon her. But the only eyes she saw belonged to Charlie. He grinned from ear to ear and seemed oblivious that half the town was gawking at him. "You l-l-look amazing, Gracie. R-R-Ready to go?" Charlie grabbed her hand, and they were off.

CHAPTER SIXTEEN

The following weekend, most Pike County residents made their way to Griffin Municipal Park to see the Pumas play in the semi-finals against the Griffin Golden Eagles. As soon as the breakfast crowd headed for the field, so did Bonnie. She left a sign on the door to let folks know the café was closed for lunch but would reopen for dinner. She hoped there'd be a hungry crowd after the game.

Charles Gordy's sports column on Thursday had given a recap of the tournaments thus far.

> *After easily defeating the Williamson Whirlwinds last week with Chrissy Jones' pitching talent and two out-of-the-park homers by Grace MacGregor, the Pike Pumas face the Griffin Golden Eagles in a series of three games on Saturday. Whichever team wins two will continue to the finals. The Thomaston Twisters still lead the pack with heavy hitting from its outfielders Bev Scroggins and Liz Shriver. Once again, the Twisters have the home-field advantage against the Meansville Mosquitoes, who squeaked by the Concord Clashers with one run in the ninth inning last week.*

After a quick warmup, Coach Hughes called the team to a huddle before they took the field. "Okay Pumas, this is a big one. Gracie, you keep your eye on Phyllis' pitching and let her know when she needs to change up. Just play your game, ladies, and we'll be in the finals next weekend." The girls huddled together for a quick prayer and then headed to their positions.

Within a couple of hours, each team had won a game in hard fought battles. By mid-afternoon the temperature had risen to a steamy 90 degrees. Katie Mason, the Pumas' right fielder, had twisted her ankle after fighting for a pop-up flyball. She was nursing it with a bag of ice as she sat on the bench, but everyone could see that her ankle was too swollen for her to play the last game.

As Coach Hughes handed out paper cups of water, she made some changes to the lineup. "Phyllis, your arm is tired, and we'll need you next week when we make it to the finals. Chrissie, you'll pitch this final game." Then the coach turned to her catcher. "Gracie, you're the best fielder we have left. I'm going to put Suzie behind the plate and you in right field. That number 24 is going to hit it your way every time, Gracie. Don't miss it."

Gracie's heart made a flip flop as she took her glove and headed to right field. She heard Miss Ouida in the stands behind her. "What's going on? Gracie's our catcher!" Then Mr. Buddy let out his customary whistle.

By the bottom of the ninth inning, with the sun beating down, both teams were scoreless. Gracie had caught several fly balls in the field but couldn't get a hit to save her life. The Pumas took the field for the last time. Things went well with two easy outs, but then Chrissie gave up two hits.

With runners on first and second, the Eagles' best hitter, Gail Jarvis, came to the plate. Coach Hughes called a timeout and signaled the entire team to gather at the pitcher's mound.

Griffin's number 24, Gail, was a big girl who could slaughter a softball. "Okay, ladies, we're running out of time, and our best bet is a double play. We know Jarvis is a lefty and almost always hits to right field. Problem is she can't run. Chrissie, I want you to pitch her high and inside. Hopefully, she will pop it up right to you, Gracie. It'll be up to you to make the double play. You gotta get it to Diane at first base as fast as you can." Gracie's hands shook as she nodded, and the Pumas returned to their positions.

The first pitch was low and outside, and number 24 didn't take the bait. When the umpire shouted, "Ball!" the batter actually smirked at Chrissie. Behind the batter, Suzie gave Chrissie the high and outside sign. This time Chrissie's aim was accurate, and number 24 hit the highest popup Gracie had ever seen. She squinted at the sun but kept her eyes on the ball. When it landed in her glove, Gracie wasted no time hurtling the ball like a bullet to Diane, her first baseman. The runner, who was headed to second, never had a chance to make it back to first before Diane tagged the base.

As the Pike County crowd went wild, the Pumas trotted in for their final time at bat. Coach Hughes patted her on the back, but Gracie barely noticed. She was too busy silently thanking Dr. Holliman for her 20/20 vision.

The Pumas' reserve catcher Suzie Clayton was the first at bat. She connected on the second pitch and drove the ball past second base where the center fielder fumbled. Suzi made it to first base as the crowd roared.

Now it was Gracie's turn. Coach Hughes took her by the shoulders and grinned. "Okay, Gracie, just envision all those balls you hit over the fence when you played with the boys on Coach Dawkins' field. Hit it out of the ballpark."

Gracie's heart thundered as she headed to the plate. While the crowd continued to clamor, Gracie shut the noise out except for one voice she could hear so distinctly. It was Charlie's. "You got this, Gracie." As soon as her bat connected with the first pitch, Gracie knew it was going to sail. And sail it did, all the way over the scoreboard.

The entire Puma team ate a free celebratory meal at Bonnie Mac's Café that night. Exhausted and full after a second helping of BonBon's apple pie, Gracie fell asleep at the work counter in the kitchen.

The café finally empty, Bonnie pushed through the kitchen door with the last stack of dirty dishes. She'd sent Vern home, but Charlie had stayed behind to serve as her dishwasher. "Charlie, why don't you escort Gracie home while I finish cleaning up the kitchen?"

Still in her dirty uniform, Gracie grinned at Charlie when they reached her front door. "I guess I'm a mess to look at!"

Charlie held her face in his hands. "The most b-b-beautiful m-m-mess I've ever s-s-seen." Then he kissed her softly before he headed back down the steps.

CHAPTER SEVENTEEN

Sunday morning arrived way too soon. "If I have to call you one more time, Sunday Grace, I'll be in there to snatch the covers off you!" BonBon was relentless. No matter what the circumstances, the MacGregors never missed worship on the Lord's Day.

After dragging herself out of bed, Gracie managed to get ready and survive church, only nodding off once during the sermon. She felt like a zombie by the time they made it back home. While most families came home to a big Sunday spread after church, it was the one day of the week that BonBon didn't cook. Sunday lunch usually consisted of a grilled cheese sandwich and a bowl of soup. When Gracie almost dropped her face in her tomato soup, BonBon ordered her back to bed.

"That's where I wanted to stay in the first place," Gracie grumbled as she crawled under the covers. With Cheeto cuddled beside her, she read for a while until she drifted off to sleep.

Meanwhile, Charlie waited on Mr. Brooxie to show up at the garage. They planned to install a radio in Charlie's Chevy since the old one hadn't worked in years. Charlie had found the radio in a junkyard on his way home from the packing shed last week. Mr. Brooxie had long ago given Charlie a key, so he unlocked the overhead door and drove inside. The interior was sweltering. Charlie switched on the large fan and left the door open for ventilation.

Mr. Brooxie was never on time. Charlie figured he was shaking off his Saturday night hangover. While he waited, Charlie used the mechanic's creeper to slide underneath his Chevy and study its chassis. He had sensed some shaking when he drove to the ballgame yesterday.

Charlie hadn't heard Mr. Brooxie come in, but he saw a pair of boots standing by the car. "I was just checking the chassis. It's got a little shimmy." He slid out from under the car and stared up at a stranger. "Oh hi. S-S-Sorry, but the g-g-garage isn't open on S-S-Sundays."

The stranger was tall and slim with long hair and a cigarette dangling from his mouth. "Then what are you doing here if you're not open? And where's Brooxie?"

Charlie stood up and pulled a cloth from his pocket to wipe the grease from his hands. "He'll b-b-be along in a f-f-few minutes. Mr. Brooxie h-h-helps me with my c-c-car on S-S-Sunday afternoons w-w-when the shop's closed."

The fellow threw down his cigarette and crushed the butt into the floor. "And I bet for the right price, he'll take a look at my car today."

Charlie gaped at the red muscle car parked outside then picked up the butt and threw it in the trash can. "I d-d-doubt it. Mr. Brooxie s-s-says Sunday is for r-r-rest and recreation. B-B-But if you c-c-come back tomorrow, he'll be gl-gl-glad to help you."

The stranger studied Charlie's face. "You sound kinda like Elmer Fudd!" When Charlie blushed, the stranger snickered. "I saw you at the softball game yesterday. You were hugging Grace MacGregor after the game."

"That's r-r-right!" Charlie grinned. "Gracie is my g-g-girlfriend and a heckuva b-b-ball player." Charlie took a better look at the stranger. "I've n-n-never seen you around h-h-here. How do y-y-you know her?"

The stranger lit another cigarette, pulled a flask from his jeans pocket, and took a long swig. Finally, he spoke. "Gracie and I go way, way back, but I've been out of town for a while. Will you tell her hello for me?"

Charlie didn't like this guy. The best thing he could do was to get rid of him before Brooxie arrived. If they'd both had a snoot full, it could lead to a drunken fight. "Okay, I'll t-t-tell Gracie that. And you can c-c-come by t-t-tomorrow if you n-n-need to see Mr. Brooxie about your c-c-car." Charlie eased outside and began to pull down the overhead door.

The stranger crushed another butt on the floor with his boot and followed Charlie out of the garage. "I'll do that. Just remember to tell Gracie hello for me."

"W-W-Will do. I n-n-never caught your name."

The stranger snickered again. "Beau. Beau Loosier."

Shortly after Beau left, Mr. Brooxie pulled up bleary-eyed and disheveled. "Howdy Charlie. Just give me a minute." He shuffled to a cabinet in his office, pulled out a bottle of Pepto Bismol, and chugged down half of it. "Had a rough night, and Sanctified Flo woke me up when she was getting ready for church. I don't know why that woman can't be quiet the one morning I get to sleep in." He noticed the cigarette butt on the floor. "Somebody else been here?"

Charlie picked up the warm butt and discarded it in the trash. "S-S-Sorry about that. Yes, some g-g-guy who w-w-wanted you to work on his car. You sh-sh-should have seen it—a s-s-souped-up 442."

Mr. Brooxie scratched his head as he opened his toolbox. "Not many of those around here. Too expensive."

"Yep, I d-d-don't think he l-l-lives here. I told h-h-him to come back t-t-tomorrow when you're open. He s-s-said his name was B-B-Beau Loosier."

Charlie heard a screwdriver hit the ground as Brooxie turned around. "Beau Loosier, you say. I can't believe that sorry S-O-B has the guts to show his face in this town. Even if he washed his face, combed his hair, and brushed his teeth, I still wouldn't let him kiss my ass!"

Charlie was used to Mr. Brooxie's outbursts. "I really d-d-didn't like him either. S-S-Somehow, he knows Gracie. H-H-He asked me to t-t-tell her hello."

Mr. Brooxie's bloodshot eyes almost popped out of his head. He grabbed Charlie by the arm. "Son, whatever you do, don't tell Gracie or Miz Bonnie that you saw Beau Loosier. And if you ever see him in town again, you go straight to the sheriff, you hear?"

By the end of the afternoon, they had the radio installed in Charlie's car, and it was picking up the Thomaston and Griffin stations. "Thanks for y-y-your help, Mr. Br-Br-Brooxie."

"No problem, son. I enjoy working on it with you." His voice was gruff as he studied Charlie. "Don't forget your promise. No mention of Beau Loosier to either of the MacGregor gals."

When Charlie stopped by Gracie's house to take her for ice cream, Miss Bonnie answered the door. "She's been out like a light all afternoon, Charlie. I think we need to let her rest. I'll tell her you stopped by."

On Charlie's drive back to the children's home, the thought of Mr. Brooxie's words made his brain itch. Beau Loosier was someone from Gracie and Miss Bonnie's past. Had he hurt them in some way? Why was he back in town? Charlie had to find out, and he knew who could tell him.

CHAPTER EIGHTEEN

Early Monday morning, a rested and bright-eyed Gracie already had coffee perking when Cooter Renfroe sat down at the counter. "How's our semi-final champion doing this morning? I thought you'd be on the courthouse steps signing autographs."

Gracie just grinned. "Your usual, Mr. Cooter?" He nodded, and Vern started cracking eggs on the griddle as Bonnie pushed through the swinging doors with warm biscuits.

Five minutes later Mr. Buddy and Miss Ouida were seated at their usual table and already arguing about the hottest day in Pike County. Miss Ouida lit her second cigarette. "It hasn't hit 100 degrees since 1955. I remember because I was still married at the time."

Mr. Buddy heehawed. "That was the shortest marriage in the history of Pike County! Gracie, I think I'll have a side of country ham instead of bacon today. And how about some extra butter with my grits."

"You need more butter like you need another hole in your head!" Miss Ouida pulled a bottle of aspirin from her purse. "Just black coffee and a plain biscuit for me, Gracie. Give Buddy my butter."

Gracie didn't understand why the two always sat together because all they ever did was argue. When she'd asked BonBon about it, she had given a mysterious explanation. "That's just how some folks show they care about each other."

Gracie hoped she and Charlie would never argue that way. She'd missed seeing him the evening before. By the time she was awake enough for BonBon to tell her, it was after hours at the Home. Charlie went to the peach packing shed before daybreak, and she'd be at softball practice when he got off work. She could still feel his lips on hers from Saturday night.

BonBon tapped her on the shoulder. "Gracie, did you hear me? We have customers. Where are you? In Never-Never Land?"

Miss Ouida giggled. "She's daydreaming about that boyfriend of hers, aren't you, Miss Starry Eyes!"

Gracie blushed. There were two new tables filled with hungry customers. She pulled her order pad from her apron pocket and went to work.

As soon as Charlie got off work, he headed out to Ouida Clarkton's place. After a failed marriage when she was much younger, Ouida had returned to the country home which had belonged to her family for generations. Just a few miles outside of town, a long driveway, bordered by huge oak trees, ended at an antebellum house with white columns and a wraparound porch.

Miss Ouida was sitting in a rocker fanning herself and sipping from a tall glass of some liquid concoction that Charlie did not recognize. "Well, Charlie Callahan! What brings you out here on this hot day? Get on up on the porch where it's cooler."

Charlie climbed the steps. "H-H-Howdy, Miss Ouida. I h-h-hope I'm not in-in-interrupting anything."

Ouida took a long draw on her cigarette. "Not at all. Just having my afternoon toddy before I go to dinner at the café. Would you like a drink?"

Charlie gazed at her cocktail glass and swallowed. "Um. No th-th-thank you."

Ouida grinned. "I have some lemonade in the refrigerator. How about some of that?"

"Yes m-m-ma'am. I'd l-l-like that."

Ouida patted the rocker beside her for Charlie to sit as she headed inside for the lemonade. She returned in no time with a tall glass just like hers. "This was fresh squeezed just this morning. I hate that frozen concentrate stuff."

Charlie took a small, tentative taste. "That is fr-fr-fresh. Thanks."

The two rocked for a few minutes enjoying their beverages. Ouida broke the ice. "Charlie, I know you didn't drive out here for a cold drink. Is there something on your mind?"

"Y-Y-Yes ma'am. I w-w-want to know about B-B-Beau Loosier."

Ouida's eyebrows shot up. "How do you know him?"

"He st-st-stopped by the g-g-garage yesterday. He s-s-said he knew Gr-Gr-Gracie. I d-d-didn't like h-h-him at all."

"I'm not surprised." Ouida lit a cigarette. "He's not a likeable character. He's nothing but a hoodlum."

"So, h-h-how does he kn-kn-know Gracie?" Ouida didn't respond. "Pl-Pl-Please Miss Ouida, I n-n-need to make s-s-sure Gracie is s-s-safe."

Ouida stopped rocking. "What makes you think she's not safe, Charlie? Has Beau been bothering her?"

"Not that I kn-kn-know of. It was just the w-w-way he smirked when h-h-he said her n-n-name. I g-g-got a bad f-f-feeling." Charlie's eyes turned dark with an anger Ouida had never seen.

She sighed. "I guess you know that Gracie is adopted." Charlie nodded. "Well, when Gracie first came to Zebulon, Beau's parents tried to adopt her away from Bonnie. She had already formed a bond with the child, but the Loosiers had plenty of money, and Bonnie didn't. They argued that Gracie would have two parents with a loving home and a big brother. Some brother! Beau was a nine-year-old devil."

Ouida proceeded to tell Charlie the story of Gracie's one horrible night with the Loosiers. "At the end of the summer that year, Beau Loosier was sent to a boarding school in Virginia. Nobody saw him again until a few summers back when he turned sixteen. Do you know old Geetah?"

Charlie nodded. "Yes m-m-ma'am. I see him p-p-pumping gas for customers at Mr. Sutton's station and w-w-walking with his little bl-bl-black dog Sparky."

Ouida drained her glass. "Well, he had another dog before Sparky. It was a scrawny mongrel that Geetah called Tagalong because that dog followed Geetah everywhere. I was, um, staying overnight at the jail one Saturday night when somebody started beating on the door and screaming. It was late, and the sheriff had already gone to bed. It took him a few minutes to be roused up and come downstairs to the jailhouse. I was scared to death somebody was dying. Sheriff Riggins opened the door to find poor Geetah bawling on the steps.

"I heard the entire conversation through Geetah's hiccupping. 'Sheriff, that Mr. Beau Loosier done took my Tagalong. I begged him to stop, but he was drunk and done took my poor dog anyway.'

"I heard the sheriff buckling his belt with his gun and holster. 'Where'd he take your dog, Geetah?'

"Geetah was sobbing. 'Out the county road is all I sees.'

"After that, the door closed, and the sheriff was gone. About an hour later, I heard him come back in, and he was talking to someone. He sounded real angry. He said, 'Sit down, Beau, and keep your drunk mouth shut.'

"I heard him dial the phone and ask for Talmadge, Beau's daddy. He told Talmadge he had Beau at the jail and was charging him with drunk and disorderly conduct and the inhumane treatment of an animal. He said Beau had taken old Geetah's dog and drove off with it. He'd apparently caught up with Beau about a mile down County Road where he was pouring gas all over that dog. Beau lit a match just before Sheriff Riggins got to him. The only thing the sheriff could do at that point was put the poor dog out of its misery. And after hearing all that, Talmadge thought he could just come pick up Beau. I heard the sheriff say, 'No sir, you can't pick him up tonight. He needs to sleep it off. You'll have to wait until Monday to post bail.'

"Then, I heard the sheriff handcuff Beau, and he came back and let me out of the cell. 'Miss Ouida, if you're sober enough to drive, why don't you go on home. And go out the back door.'

"I was sorry I didn't get to see that drunk hoodlum in handcuffs. Come Monday, he was out on bail. Word was that the sheriff banned Beau from the city limits of Zebulon. I heard Mr. Loosier shipped him back to Virginia to attend summer school. The next day, Mr. Loosier came by the gas station with a little black puppy for Geetah and a $100 bill. Geetah told Banks Sutton it was blood money, and he wouldn't spend it. Instead, he donated it to Mount Hope Baptist Church, the one a block off the square. As far as I know, and I know most things about our little town, Beau Loosier has not been seen in Zebulon until you saw him yesterday."

By the time Ouida finished her story, Charlie had tears streaming down his face. "Oh honey, I didn't mean to make you sad."

Charlie wiped his face with the back of his hand. "I'm not s-s-sad, Miss Ouida. I'm m-m-mad. And I don't think y-y-yesterday was the first t-t-time Beau Loosier has b-b-been back."

"What do you mean?'

Charlie clinched his hands as he hesitated.

Ouida pushed. "What are you talking about, Charlie?"

"I've been so st-st-stupid, Miss Ouida. Why did I p-p-promise her? Why didn't I t-t-tell someone?"

"Promise who? Tell what? Maybe it's not too late to tell," Ouida pleaded.

Charlie covered his face with his hands. "I th-th-think Beau Loosier was here l-l-last Spring. I th-th-think he h-h-hurt Gracie."

Ouida paled. "What do you mean? How did he hurt Gracie?"

Then Charlie spilled the beans. "You re-re-remember the afternoon you p-p-picked us up, and Gracie was hurt and bl-bl-bleeding on her...you know where. She s-s-said she'd injured h-h-herself on the baseball b-b-bat. It w-w-wasn't the bat that h-h-hurt her. It was s-s-someone. She w-w-wouldn't tell me who, and she sw-sw-swore me to secrecy."

Ouida's face paled. "Bless that sweet, innocent child! I've a mind to call Talmadge Loosier and the sheriff right now!" She started from her seat.

Charlie intercepted her on the way to the door. "N-N-No, Miss Ouida. It's too l-l-late, and Gracie is fi-fi-finally getting back to n-n-normal. She doesn't n-n-need to revisit that day. And besides, I'm j-j-just guessing that it was B-B-Beau. She s-s-said there was m-m-more than one guy."

Ouida began to tremble. "I cannot bear the thought of sweet Gracie suffering anymore damage. The child was abandoned by her own mother, for God's sake. Wasn't that enough?" Then she took a deep breath. "Okay, okay. I guess you're right, Charlie. We don't need to add to Gracie's trauma, and the news would devastate Bonnie, too." She sat back down and lit another cigarette. "So, what can we do?"

Charlie's eyes glinted with determination. "We can m-m-make sure Beau L-L-Loosier doesn't get within a m-m-mile of Gracie. Miss Ouida, do you th-th-think you could call Sheriff Ri-Ri-Riggins and let him know B-B-Beau has been around t-t-town?"

Ouida took a long drag from her cigarette. "I can do better than that. I'll stop by the sheriff's office before I go to the café for supper." She patted Charlie on the shoulder. "You head on home before you miss your own supper. We'll make sure that Beau Loosier stays miles from Zebulon and away from our Gracie."

Charlie stood up, and to Ouida's surprise, he hugged her. "I kn-kn-knew I could c-c-count on you, Miss Ouida. I've always ad-ad-admired your toughness. You can even k-k-keep Mr. Buddy in line, and h-h-he outweighs you by about 300 p-p-pounds."

Ouida almost choked on cigarette smoke she was laughing so hard.

CHAPTER NINETEEN

"Gracie, I've set the timer for when the brownies need to come out of the oven. When it goes off, put them on the rack to cool for at least 15 minutes." Bonnie washed her hands and removed her apron. "I can't believe Opal Dorsey bought all the brownies I baked last night. She said they were having an end of summer party for the twins." Since it was Wednesday and the café closed after the lunch crowd, there was no supper to prepare.

Bonnie was hurrying to get down to the Upson County Hospital for a visit with Eugenia Cotney, who had broken her hip earlier in the week. "Eugenia should never have been on a stepladder stocking shelves in the store. That's why she hired Tommy Davis as her stock boy, but Eugenia is so set in her ways about every item being in its right place." She offered a frazzled smile to Gracie. "I'll be back in time to get you to softball practice, I promise."

Gracie finished washing the mixing bowl. "Don't worry, BonBon. If you're running late, I can call Coach Hughes to pick me up. Oh, and did you see Cheeto this morning? She didn't eat her breakfast. I thought maybe she came begging Vern for a bowl of milk."

Bonnie headed for the back door. "I don't remember seeing her, but I bet she's around here somewhere. She likes to wander down to the firehouse. Check with Chief Bushy."

"You're probably right. The chief always keeps a treat for her in his pocket. Give Miss Cotney a hug from me." Gracie watched BonBon scurry out the kitchen's back door to her car.

Just as she placed the brownie pan on a cooling rack, Gracie heard the café door's bell jingle. She sighed, realizing she'd forgotten to lock the door and turn the sign over to Closed.

Wiping her hands on a towel, she pushed through the swinging doors into the dining room. "Sorry, we're closed until tomorrow morning." A greasy-haired young man sporting a toothpick in his mouth stood just inside the door. Something about him made Gracie's heart hit her stomach. Her voice shook. "You have to leave. The café is closed."

As the young man moved closer to the counter, Gracie realized who he was. She could remember the feel of his iron hands holding her down while Beau forced himself on her. She tried to back into the kitchen, but her legs felt like they were in cement.

He grinned at her. "I ain't here to buy anything. I just brought you a present from an old friend." He laid a small cardboard box on the counter, giggled under his breath, and then sauntered out the door.

For what seemed like an hour, Gracie couldn't move. Finally, her pulse returned to normal, and she touched the box. An envelope addressed to her was taped to the box's top. She slowly opened the envelope and unfolded the note inside.

"Hello Grace. Long time, no see. I'm back in town and checking up on you. I hope you're keeping your promise. You don't want your precious BonBon to end up like the gift in this box. Remember, don't tell, or BonBon will be next."

Grace's hands trembled as she opened the box. Inside lay a bloodied cat's tail with orange and white stripes. She knew immediately that the tail belonged to Cheeto. Grace slid to the floor behind the counter as she vomited.

She lay there quivering in her disgrace for more than an hour until she heard the door's bell jingle again. "Gracie, you back in the kitchen?" It was Miss Ouida. "I ran into BonBon at the hospital and told her I'd get you to practice. What is that awful smell?" Ouida peeked over the counter. "My Lord, child. You've been sick!"

Ouida hurried to the kitchen sink and wet a dish towel. She kneeled in front of Gracie and sponged her face. "Honey, do I need to call Doc Hunt?"

Gracie shook her head. "No ma'am. I'm okay."

Miss Ouida helped Gracie to her feet. "Honey, you're trembling all over. I hope you haven't come down with something." Gracie burst into tears. Ouida wrapped her arms around her. "What is it, sweetheart. What's wrong?" But Grace remained mute.

Ouida spied the box on the counter. "What's this?" Gracie tried to grab it, but Ouida was too quick. She opened the lid to the sight of the severed cat's tail. "Sweet Jesus! Who would do such a thing? Oh Gracie, you poor baby. Let's get you and this mess cleaned up."

Grace was too weak to do anything but obey. She slid the note into her back pocket while Ouida was wiping up the floor.

Ouida waited while Gracie showered and got dressed for practice. "Honey, are you sure you feel like going?"

"I'm fine," she lied. "But I need you to do something for me."

Ouida took Gracie's hand. "Of course. Anything, sweet girl."

Gracie swallowed. "I want you and Charlie to find Cheeto and give her a proper burial. Charlie will know where to look."

"Okay, honey, we can do that." Ouida stroked Gracie's damp hair.

"There's one more thing. Miss Ouida, I need you to promise not to tell BonBon about any of this. It will upset her too much."

Ouida raised her eyebrows. "But honey, she needs to know."

Gracie pushed away. "No! No! No! She can't know, Miss Ouida. You must promise."

Ouida studied Gracie's frightened eyes. "Okay, it will be our secret. I promise."

"D-D-Did Gracie say who d-d-delivered the b-b-box, Miss Ouida?" Charlie and Ouida had searched the alley behind the café as well as Miss Bonnie's yard with no sign of what was left of Cheeto.

"No. When I asked her where the box came from, she turned white as a ghost and started shaking." Ouida watched Charlie's jaw clench with tension. "I'm sorry I didn't get more information from Gracie. She was such a mess, and I didn't want to make matters worse."

As they stood in Bonnie's backyard, Charlie grimaced. "I th-th-think I know who did this." He opened the door to the tool shed and searched for a shovel. "And I kn-kn-know where to l-l-look for Cheeto."

Ouida was right behind him. "Well, I'm going with you."

Grabbing the shovel from the back seat, Charlie insisted that Miss Ouida sit in her car in the school parking lot. "You don't n-n-need to see this, M-M-Miss Ouida. I'll t-t-take care of it."

The sun was going down as he made his way to the creek where all of Gracie's misery had begun. Poor Cheeto was hanging limply from a limb of the mimosa tree, the same tree where Charlie and Gracie had sat and talked many warm afternoons.

Charlie untied the lifeless cat and wrapped her in an old towel that Miss Ouida had retrieved from the trunk of her car. He walked into a wooded area, dug a hole, and buried sweet Cheeto.

Once he was finished, Charlie squared his shoulders and shouted into the trees. "Beau Loosier, you ain't long for the living." Charlie didn't stutter a single word.

CHAPTER TWENTY

There was standing room only at Thomaston's Silvertown Ballpark when the Pike County Pumas took the field against the Thomaston Twisters the following Saturday. As Gracie donned her catcher's mask, she felt a bit shaky. She wasn't certain if her jitters were about the game or the events of the past week. She shook it off.

With Ouida, Buddy, BonBon, and Charlie sitting together in the stands, Gracie had her very own cheering squad. Miss Ouida had remained true to her promise, and Charlie had concocted a story that he'd found Cheeto's remains down the road a piece where she'd been hit by a car. BonBon had bought it as the truth.

Ouida had made a second visit to Sheriff Riggins about Beau. "I promise, Miss Ouida, I haven't seen him or his car since Charlie Callahan spotted him at the garage a couple of Sundays ago. I'm keeping my eyes on alert for any sign of him." Ouida seemed pacified.

The Pumas made quick work of getting three outs against the Twisters and headed in for their first time at bat. Gracie was the leadoff hitter. After two strikes, she backed away from the plate, closed her eyes, and took a deep breath. The next pitch was right in her sweet spot, and Gracie hammered it for a triple. The crowd went mad as the Pumas' next batter Katie Mason hit a soft liner to left field, and Gracie had the time and speed to make it home.

By the top of the ninth inning, the teams were tied 3-3. With two outs, the Twisters' star hitter Bev Scoggins got a homerun and gave Thomaston a one-point lead. The next Twister struck out. Now it was up to the Pumas to rally for the win.

Coach Hughes huddled with the players. "Gracie is fifth in the batting lineup. If we can get one or two runners on base, I think she has a homerun in her today. Whaddya think, Gracie?" Gracie offered a weak smile and nodded.

After two quick outs, Katie Palmer hit a double. Then Peggy Mason made it to first on a line drive past third base. The game now fell on Gracie's shoulders. As she made her way to the plate, Gracie heard someone yell her name from the left side of the fence. It was a voice she could never forget. Hidden from view of the stands but directly in her vision as she glanced towards the left stood Beau Loosier.

Gracie backed away from the plate and rubbed some dirt on her trembling hands. Her legs felt like jelly. When the first ball flew past her, all she saw was the sneer on Beau's face. Gracie didn't even swing at the other strikes. She just stood frozen at the plate.

Even though Coach Hughes said she was proud that their young team had made it so far in their first season, Gracie shouldered the weight of their loss as though it was hers alone. The drive home to Zebulon seemed endless.

Charlie pulled up behind BonBon's car as soon as they reached the house. "Miss Bonnie, c-c-can I t-t-take Gracie out for an i-i-ice cream?"

Bonnie appreciated Charlie's timing. While she doubted the café would see as big a crowd as she had anticipated, she still had to help Vern get their Saturday night special cooked.

Gracie wasn't as pleased as BonBon. She dragged herself out of the car and lifted sad eyes towards Charlie. "Give me a few minutes to wash up and change. Then I'll meet you in the café."

Charlie followed Miss Bonnie into the back door of the kitchen. "Charlie, I hope you can improve her mood. Gracie thinks she lost the whole thing by herself. She did seem so distracted her final time at bat. Maybe she was just worn out by then."

Charlie knew differently. He'd left the stands before Gracie's last time at bat to stand by the fence behind home plate. When Gracie stepped away from the plate for a moment, Charlie could tell by her body language that something was wrong. He followed her gaze to the left and caught a glimpse of Beau Loosier. Charlie took off in Beau's direction, but the creep seemed to vanish in thin air. Charlie heard tires squeal in the gravel parking lot and watched Beau's red 442 skid away. He clenched and unclenched his fists as he walked back to the field.

Thirty minutes later Gracie appeared in the café's kitchen. She was too ashamed to walk out into the dining room where so many of her biggest supporters were now mumbling about the loss between bites of meatloaf.

When BonBon pushed through the swinging doors with a tray of dirty dishes, she found Grace slumped at the table. "There you are! My goodness, that ballpark red dirt washed off just fine. You look real pretty, sweetheart. Charlie's been nursing a glass of sweet tea. Now don't keep that boy waiting any longer."

Wearing a soft pink sundress and a pinched smile, Grace hesitated. "BonBon, would you ask Charlie to come in the kitchen so we can go out the back door? I don't feel like facing everybody right now."

Bonnie turned from the sink to face her. "My sweet child, nobody blames you for the loss today. There were eight other players who shared that responsibility. That's why it's called a team."

A single tear slipped from Grace's eye and dropped on her pink dress. BonBon pulled her close. "Wait here, honey. I'll get Charlie. Don't stay out too late. You're worn out. You'll feel better after a good night's sleep." Bonnie kissed her cheek and pushed through the swinging doors.

As soon as they were down the street and away from the café, Gracie burst into tears. Charlie turned onto the Meansville Highway, drove a couple of miles, and stopped in front of Mr. Mallory's peach packing shed. The season had ended as of yesterday, and the place was empty. He gently pulled

Gracie out of the car, gathered her in his arms, and carried her to a picnic table under a huge oak.

Gracie sobbed. "We should have won. It's my fault. I froze. I just froze when I saw…" She hesitated.

Charlie handed her his handkerchief. "When y-y-you saw B-B-Beau Loosier."

"What? How do you know Beau Loosier?" Her eyes filled with fear.

"He's the one who h-h-hurt you last y-y-year, isn't he? H-H-He's the one who k-k-killed Cheeto, too. Why d-d-didn't you t-t-tell me, Gracie?" Charlie engulfed her in his arms as Gracie sobbed into his shoulder.

"I couldn't tell you the truth. I can't tell anybody. He'll hurt BonBon if I do. I can't let him hurt BonBon." Gracie gulped for air.

Charlie's jaw tensed as he held Gracie by her shoulders so he could see her face. "What do you m-m-mean he'll hurt Miz B-B-Bonnie? Did that b-b-bastard threaten you, Gracie?"

Her body shivered as her eyes grew wide with terror. Charlie drew her into him. "You're okay, Gr-Gr-Gracie. I'm h-h-here with you. You're s-s-safe, I promise. Just tell me what h-h-happened."

Gracie took a deep breath. "There were three of them at the creek. One of them held me down while Beau tore off my underwear. He couldn't get himself in me. He said I was…I was too small." Her eyes glazed over as if in a trance. "One of the others handed Beau a bottle of liquor. Beau drank the rest of it, and then he started to put the bottle inside me." She gasped in pain. "It hurt so bad I passed out. When I woke up Beau was standing over me, and his, his stuff, you know, was running down my legs." A shudder ran through Gracie's body. "Beau said if I told anyone, he would come back and kill BonBon."

Charlie held Gracie to his chest. His jaw worked as he seethed in fury. He waited until he was under control to speak. "Did B-B-Beau bring

Ch-Ch-Cheeto's tail to you at the c-c-café? Maybe s-s-somebody saw him and could t-t-testify against him. We n-n-need evidence to put this b-b-bastard away."

Gracie's sobs had turned to sniffles. "No, it was his friend, the one who held me down. I knew him the minute he walked through the door. He gave me the box with a note from Beau."

Charlie's eyes lit up. "A n-n-note? Did you k-k-keep it, Gracie? That could be h-h-hard evidence."

Gracie pulled away and ran to Charlie's car. "It's in my purse. I didn't want to leave it anywhere at home where BonBon might find it." She retrieved the note and handed it to Charlie.

"Th-th-this is a r-r-real threat against BonBon. I th-th-think it's good ev-ev-evidence to take to the Sheriff." Charlie folded the note to put in his back pocket, but Gracie snatched it from him and tore it into shreds.

"Nooo, Charlie! I don't want to get the sheriff involved. It will make matters worse. The Loosiers own most of this county. Not to mention that BonBon would be devastated if she knew what Beau did to me. NO! We can't let BonBon know any of this. You promised me you would keep my secret!" Gracie's eyes glowed with sad determination.

Charlie shook his head. "Okay, I d-d-did promise you, Gracie." He held her in his arms again. "B-B-But you didn't l-l-lose the g-g-game today. You g-g-got spooked by B-B-Beau. That's wh-wh-what happened." Gracie looked up with questioning eyes as Charlie continued. "I s-s-saw you l-l-looking towards the f-f-fence, and then I saw h-h-him. The b-b-bastard don't have the g-g-guts to sh-sh-show his f-f-face in Pike County, so h-h-he came to the g-g-game in Thomaston to sc-sc-scare you. But d-d-don't you w-w-worry. If h-h-he ever sh-sh-shows his ugly f-f-face here, I'll k-k-kill him."

"Beau Loosier knows better than to show up in town." Gracie finally relaxed in Charlie's arms. "I'm glad you know it was Beau who hurt me. I promise I'll never hide anything from you again. But we have to keep the truth from BonBon."

Charlie kissed her forehead. "I c-c-can keep your s-s-secret, Gracie."
And he did.

⚫

The following week, Gracie found herself in Miz Viona Durham's freshman
homeroom. Miz Durham was stylishly dressed in a straight skirt with a
printed blouse sporting tucks down the front. Her hair was coiffed in a French
twist, and when she opened her mouth, she oozed Southern charm.

"Welcome to high school, freshmen. Do you realize that as the Class
of 1970, you will be the first graduating class of the next decade?" She smiled
kindly as she pulled out a stack of schedules. "Of course, that's four years away,
so let's get started on your freshman year."

When Miz Durham handed out the class schedules, Gracie discovered
that she'd be serving as a student aide to Coach Hughes for the last period of
the day. She dreaded facing her after the shame of their loss to the Twisters.

As she fiddled with her new locker combination, Gracie jerked when
she felt a hand on her shoulder. "Hi b-b-beautiful." Charlie grinned at her.
"What's y-y-your schedule l-l-look like?" She sighed as she handed it to him
to peruse. "Oh n-n-no, you have Old L-L-Lady Stanford for s-s-social studies.
She's so old, sh-sh-she came with the b-b-building."

Gracie snatched back the schedule. "She can't be that bad. You passed
her class, didn't you?"

"B-B-Barely with your h-h-help." Charlie took her hand as he studied
her schedule. "Why so gr-gr-grumpy? We h-h-have the same lunch p-p-pe-
riod, and I h-h-have PE when you're C-C-Coach Hughes' aide."

As they walked toward their respective classes, Gracie sighed again.
"I'm not ready to face Coach Hughes after blowing the game for us last week."

Charlie squeezed her hand. "It w-w-wasn't your f-f-fault, Gracie. And
you pr-pr-promised you'd f-f-forget all about it. Here's y-y-your English cl-cl-
class. I'll s-s-see you at l-l-lunch, okay?"

Gracie had Miz Runelle Meeks for first period English. At least she knew Miz Meeks from church. She managed to squeeze Charlie's hand back. "Okay. I'm glad you're in the gym sixth period. I'll need moral support."

Charlie brushed the hair from his eyes and offered up a lopsided grin. "I g-g-got your back, b-b-beautiful!" As he rushed to beat the tardy bell, he thought of the promise they'd made to forget all about the incident with Beau Loosier. He wanted Gracie to forget, but he never could or would. Charlie's sole purpose was to watch over the girl he loved, and no one, especially Beau, would ever hurt his Gracie again.

When Gracie arrived in the gym sixth period, she practically bumped into Coach Hughes. "Gracie, come into my office for a minute."

Gracie's heart sank. How could she ever explain why she froze her last time at bat and lost the game for the Pumas? She trudged slowly into Coach Hughes' office.

Coach closed the door behind them. "Uh oh," Grace thought. "Here it comes."

Instead of the expected lecture, Coach Hughes handed Grace a brown paper package. "This is the uniform for my teacher aides. It's white instead of the regular blue that the other girls wear in gym class. I got you the same size as your softball uniform so it should fit."

Gracie remained speechless as Coach Hughes continued. "Gracie, you're the first freshman I've ever chosen to be an aide. I hope you will consider it an honor. You're so responsible and have such leadership potential, I thought it would be a good position for you."

A tear splattered on the package in Gracie's hands. "I am honored, Coach, but I'm not sure I'm worthy to be your assistant after losing Saturday's game." More tears splashed down her face.

Coach Hughes put Gracie in a bear hug. "Gracie MacGregor, there were nine players on that field last Saturday. Nine players, not one! Do you hear me? We are a team. We win together, and we lose together. So, stop beating yourself up, and go dress out. I'll need you to get these freshman girls ready to play volleyball. Most of them have never even held a volleyball, much less served one over a net."

Feeling a ton of bricks fly off her shoulders, Gracie headed to the girls' locker room to change. As she pulled the lanyard holding a whistle over her head, she grinned for the first time in a while. She vowed to be the best teacher assistant Coach Hughes had ever had.

CHAPTER TWENTY-ONE

The Pike County Pumas redeemed themselves by winning the Tri-County Softball Championship for the next three summers in a row. Charlie Callahan received his diploma from Pike County High School with little fanfare in 1969. Charlie, who was now 18, also received his independence and walking papers from Southern Pines Children's Home.

Brooxie Barnett offered Charlie a rent-free room above the garage along with a parttime job as a mechanic. In his spare time, Charlie worked on an old '59 Ford truck that had been sitting on blocks for years behind Brooxie's shop. When he got it running, Charlie started his own business hauling Pike County farmers' produce to the Georgia Farmer's Market in Forest Park.

One early morning while Charlie was visiting Gracie in the café's kitchen before the breakfast crowd arrived, he overheard Miz Bonnie complaining. "I swear, Vern, these eggs are not as fresh as they should be."

Vern shrugged his shoulders. "I'm sorry, Miz Bonnie. I can either get to the café at 5 a.m. to start breakfast or drive out to the Colwell's place to get the freshest eggs."

Charlie interrupted. "I g-g-got an idea. I d-d-don't start w-w-work at the garage un-un-until 7:30. For a s-s-small fee, I can t-t-take my truck out to C-C-Colwell's and pick up fr-fr-fresh eggs every morning. I c-c-can also g-g-get you the freshest p-p-produce that you n-n-need."

"That's a perfect idea, Charlie. Let's talk business." While the two of them put their heads together, Gracie heard the front door's bell jingle. "That will be Mr. Cooter wanting his coffee. Mr. Vern, you better get the griddle warming up." And another day at Bonnie Mac's Café began.

By October Gracie had fallen into a routine as a senior at Pike County High. Always arriving early, she'd head straight to Coach Hughes' office where Coach would be sipping coffee and going over her lesson plans for the day.

Gracie loved these quiet times before the day truly started. She quickly discovered that Coach was a good confidante, and although Gracie never told her about Beau Loosier, she talked about everything else with a freedom she lacked with BonBon.

One morning Coach was reading the social page of the *Thomaston Times*. "Well, I'll be. One of my former students is getting married. Do you know Vicki Fordham?"

Gracie grinned. "She used to babysit me when I was little. Who's she marrying?'

Coach studied the announcement. "Hmm, a young man from Decatur, Georgia. He graduated from the University of Georgia, so I guess they met there. It says here they'll make their home in Decatur. Vicki's own dad, Preacher Fordham, will be officiating the wedding. That should be interesting…he'll walk her down the aisle and then stay, I guess." Coach sipped her coffee.

Gracie realized that this was the perfect opportunity to ask a question that had been worrying her. "Why aren't you married, Coach?"

Coach set down her coffee cup and got a faraway look. "I was engaged to my high school sweetheart, Robert Watson. He went by Robert, but he let me call him Robbie. He gave me a ring just weeks after we graduated. I was headed to West Georgia College, and he was headed to the Marines. His was one of the last units to ship out to Korea in the winter of 1953. It was early March when I got the news. A thousand soldiers in the First Marine Division were killed by the Chinese when they crossed the UN front line. My Robbie was one of them.

"I thought I would die without him. I crawled into my dorm bed and stayed for three days. My roommate finally dragged me out, stood me under a cold shower, and made me eat something." Coach seemed to return to the present. "It was a long time ago, I know, but there won't be another." She reached inside her blouse and pulled out a tiny silver chain. On it hung a diamond engagement ring. She smiled wistfully. "He's always with me."

In the early Spring of 1970, Gracie spent a Sunday afternoon with BonBon in her attic. What started out as a search for items to donate to the church rummage sale turned into a treasure hunt of BonBon's life before Gracie.

As Gracie rummaged through an old cedar chest, she discovered several silk dresses with tiny shoulder straps and tassels fringed along the hem. "Are these yours, BonBon?"

Bonnie laughed. "No, those belonged to my grandmother Mary Moore. She was a flapper in the '20s. My own mother wanted to throw them out when Gramma died, but I hid them in a box under my bed."

Gracie held up a dress to herself and stared at an old mirror leaning against the wall. "With a few alterations, I could wear this to the prom."

"Over my dead body!" Bonnie snatched the skimpy dress from Gracie as she continued. "Gramma Mary was quite a card. She was married three times. When she came to visit us, she would hide in the bathroom and smoke cigarettes.

"Now *these* belonged to me. I used to wear them to church in the '50s." BonBon withdrew several hats in a variety of shapes and sizes, some with veils and some with flowers.

Donning a big-brimmed straw hat, Gracie dove deeper into the cedar chest. "Look BonBon, I found your high school yearbook!" Gracie thumbed through the pages looking for the photos of the senior class. "Wasn't your maiden name Jones?" BonBon nodded. "Look, here you are. 'Bonnie Louise Jones: National Honor Society, Homecoming Court, FHA, and Latin Club.' I didn't know you took Latin."

BonBon grinned. "Ah yes, the ancient language. Not sure it's done me much good in real life." She studied the photo. "And I'm certainly not sure I even remember that girl."

Gracie giggled. "You haven't changed very much, BonBon. You're still beautiful." She thumbed through until she got to the "M" page. "I found him." She gazed at the photo of BonBon's husband, Oscar Urliss MacGregor. What an awful name."

"He was named after both of his grandfathers." BonBon smiled at the photo. "Urliss was his paternal grandfather—he came to America on a boat from Ireland. Oscar was his mother's father."

Bonnie's Oscar had dark hair but light eyes in the black and white photo. "What color were his eyes, BonBon? I can't tell in this picture."

She smiled wistfully. "They were hazel. Sometimes his eyes looked almost gold and other times they looked green. It depended on what he was wearing. He was quite handsome."

Gracie noticed the quiver in BonBon's voice. "You still miss him, don't you?"

"Sometimes." Bonnie cleared her throat. "But that was long ago, and I've made a wonderful life with you, Gracie. I wouldn't change that for anything."

"Not even if you could have Oscar back? You could've had children of your own." Gracie closed the book.

Bonnie breathed deeply before answering. "Perhaps, but Oscar chose to leave me just like your mother did, Gracie. While both of them made choices we can't understand, we need to forgive them and be thankful for the life you and I have together."

This time Gracie's voice shook. "Have you forgiven Oscar?"

"Yes, I did that a long time ago. What about you, Gracie. Have you forgiven your mother?"

Gracie hesitated. "I'm working on it, BonBon. I still don't understand how a mother could just abandon her child like she did me."

Bonnie put her arm around Gracie's shoulder. "Honey, she was sick with the drugs in her body. I think deep down she knew you would be better off with someone who could love and care for you."

Gracie sniffled. "I guess so, but how could she just throw me away?"

Bonnie pulled Gracie to her feet and surrounded her with a bear hug. "If it hadn't been for her leaving you here, I never would've had the chance to be a mother." She brushed away a stray hair that had slipped from Gracie's ponytail. "While you may think she threw you away, I'm so blessed that you landed in my arms."

CHAPTER TWENTY-TWO

The following Saturday morning, as Gracie washed a stack of breakfast plates, Miss Ouida and Mr. Buddy showed up in the kitchen grinning like two Cheshire cats. Gracie wiped her hands on a towel. "What's up with you two?"

Ouida blew smoke rings in the air. "Buddy and I are giving you an early graduation gift."

Mr. Buddy chimed in. "It would be my pleasure to drive you and Ouida to Rich's Department Store next Wednesday afternoon to purchase you a prom dress. Afterwards, we will have dinner at Miss Pitty Pat's Porch and then catch a movie at the Lowe's Grand on Peachtree Street."

Gracie's eyes grew big as she danced around the kitchen. "Oh wow! Since I can't afford a new one, I'd planned to wear the same dress I wore last spring."

"Last year's fashion will not do!" Ouida interrupted. "Our Gracie MacGregor deserves to look ravishing for her senior walk. I was thinking something sky blue might work gloriously with your hair and eyes."

Gracie was speechless, but Buddy wasn't. "Since you're out for spring break next week, your chariot will await you at 9 a.m. on Wednesday. I just need to have a healthy breakfast here before we go."

Ouida heehawed. "Buddy Simpson, your idea of a healthy breakfast is enough grease to choke a pig."

The next Wednesday morning, when Charlie delivered fresh eggs to the café before daybreak, he found Bonnie already making coffee. "Charlie, I do appreciate your helping out today. With Gracie's shopping trip and most of Pike County headed to Macon for the state baseball finals, I'm truly short-handed. At least I'm just serving breakfast and lunch today. You know I don't serve dinner on Wednesdays. Anyway, thank you for your help."

Charlie grinned. "No pr-pr-problem, Miz B-B-Bonnie."

"I don't think we'll have much of a lunch crowd with everybody gone to Macon, so Vern and I can handle lunch. But I'll need help getting ready for tomorrow's special—fried chicken. Could you please drive out to Colwell's farm and pick up a dozen fresh chickens?"

As Charlie nodded, Bonnie explained the job. Before bringing the chickens back to the café, she wanted Charlie to watch Mr. Colwell wring each bird's neck, plunge its lifeless body into a huge boiler of hot water, and then pluck the feathers. That way she was assured the freshest fryers.

Bonnie refilled the salt and pepper shakers on the counter. "Then, I was hoping you could help me cut up the chicken when you get back. That way they'll be ready to fry up on Thursday."

"I c-c-can do that." Charlie stacked egg cartons in the refrigerator.

By 8:30 Wednesday morning, the café was buzzing with folks headed out to Macon for the baseball game. Even Brooxie Barnett had closed his shop for the occasion. Appearing somewhat hungover from his nightly libations, Brooxie sat in his usual spot at the café counter and poured a heaping spoon-ful of sugar into his coffee. "I missed my nephew's homerun in the region playoffs. I ain't missing this one," he grumbled to Cooter Renfroe, who had just strolled up to the cash register.

Cooter stuck a toothpick in his mouth and paid his bill. "Sure glad the rain finally stopped. Spring Creek was so swollen on Monday, it flooded the bridge on Dripping Rock Road in Molena. I couldn't get across to deliver the mail yesterday."

Shortly before 9:00, Gracie appeared in the kitchen. Charlie had just pushed through the doors with a stack of dirty plates. "There's my f-f-favorite gal." Gracie had chosen a short navy skirt with a pink oxford blouse for her shopping adventure. Her hair, which sported a matching pink headband, curled softly around her shoulders. "You c-c-could be a m-m-model for Rich's instead of a c-c-customer." Charlie kissed her softly on the cheek as he headed to the sink.

Gracie giggled. "We're going to see *MASH* at the Lowe's Grand. It was that or *Love Story*. I decided to save *Love Story* for when it comes to Griffin so we can see it together. Besides, watching a romantic movie with Mr. Buddy would be embarrassing."

Bonnie rushed through the doors. "Gracie, they're here for you. Buddy has on a tie and even washed his car." She straightened Gracie's collar. "You look so cute. Please don't pick out a dress that costs a fortune. Even though I realize the two of them could afford it, such behavior on your part would be tacky. Now skedaddle."

Charlie, his hands in soap suds, winked over his shoulder. "H-H-Have fun!" and Gracie was gone.

CHAPTER TWENTY-THREE

By late afternoon Bonnie Mac's Café was cleaned, closed, and quiet. Bonnie's arthritis had kicked in, and with Vern taking the afternoon off to go to the game, she was glad she'd asked Charlie to stay and help her cut up the chickens. While Charlie unloaded the truck in the alley behind the café, Bonnie went out front to unwrap a package Cooter had delivered at lunch.

Charlie picked up the last crate of chickens and began to carry it through the back door to the kitchen. Suddenly, someone grabbed Charlie from behind and stuck something sharp to his neck.

"Don't even try to get away or I'll slice right through your throat." Beau Loosier, holding a switchblade against Charlie's neck and using his other hand to grab Charlie's hair, backed his prey into the kitchen.

When they reached Bonnie's stainless worktable, now covered in dead chickens, Beau twisted Charlie around. "Perfect! Another big chicken to cut up. Put your hands on the table so I can see them."

When Charlie hesitated, Beau pricked his neck with the tip of the blade. "So, where's your little girlfriend? I've been looking for her ever since school let out."

"I-I d-d-don't know. Besides, if I d-d-did know, I w-w-wouldn't tell a slime b-b-bag like you!"

Beau snatched Charlie's head back by his hair. "Bullshit! You know exactly where she is. You follow her around like a puppy, you stuttering sissy. I bet you can't even get your little dick up." Charlie bowed his back in an attempt to free himself, but as he did, Beau inched the blade's tip farther into his neck. Charlie grew still as he felt blood trickle down to his shirt collar.

Beau leaned closer and spoke into Charlie's ear. "You don't mind if I get a little piece of that action, do you? If you actually *can* get it up, you get to tap that thing all the time. Just remember that I'm the one who loosened it up for you. That was almost five years ago, and I've been missing that sweet stuff. I started remembering how ripe she was for picking when she was 13 and figured it was time for me to give her another taste of a real man. You know, a little graduation gift."

As Charlie started to thrash about, Beau pushed in the blade deeper. Charlie felt a jolt of pain followed by a gush of warmth streaming down his neck. "Another half inch and I'll hit your jugular. I've butchered enough animals to know just how to make it a slow death. Blood spurts out with each beat of your heart until there's just no blood left. Once you're gone, sweet little Gracie will be all mine."

Charlie's knees grew weak with dizziness. He willed himself not to black out. Suddenly, there was a whoosh and then a loud crack. And then just as suddenly, Beau's hands loosened from Charlie's neck. A moment later, Charlie heard something hit the floor behind him with a thud.

Grabbing the wound in his neck with one hand and the table's top with the other, Charlie slowly turned around. Bonnie stood over Beau, who was face down on the floor. Her freshly sharpened meat cleaver was stuck to the hilt in the back of Beau's head.

As she stared down at the puddle of blood slowly pooling up under Beau's head, Bonnie appeared to be in a trancelike state, almost as if she was outside of her own body. Charlie watched in disbelief as she planted her foot in the middle of Beau's back and grabbed the cleaver handle with both hands. She grunted quietly as she pulled with all her might, slowly rocking the cleaver back and forth, eventually unwedging it from his skull. Once it was out, she gingerly stepped away from the body and studied the bloody blade. "It's a good thing I sent this off to be sharpened," she said in an oddly calm tone. "Cooter just delivered the package this afternoon." She turned her eyes to Beau's pale, lifeless face. "I heard everything that monster said."

Then Bonnie straightened her shoulders and jumped into survival mode. She grabbed a fresh towel from the sink and pressed it to Charlie's bloody neck. "Come on, Charlie, sit down on the stool before you faint."

Charlie was too weak to hold himself up on the stool. "Don't call the sheriff. We have to keep Gracie's secret. I promised." Then he slid onto the floor and lost consciousness.

When Charlie woke up, he was lying on the kitchen floor with a blanket over him and a pillow under his head. He reached up to scratch his neck and felt stitches in it. Bonnie was wiping the worktable down with soap and water, and somebody else, in wingtip shoes, was mopping the floor around him.

"Looks like our patient's coming to." The legs belonging to the wingtips bent down in front of Charlie. "Try not to scratch those stitches, son. We don't want that cut to open back up. It's a good thing I was still at the office instead of on my way home to Thomaston, or you could've bled to death."

Placing his stethoscope in his ears, Dr. Hunt pumped up a blood pressure cuff that was already around Charlie's arm and listened as he released the built-up pressure. "BP's back to normal. Now, you two promise me to be more careful when you're working with knives. Another quarter inch and you would have hit his jugular, Miz Bonnie."

Bonnie's face lost all its color. "I feel so bad. You know how I always talk with my hands. I just didn't know that Charlie was standing right behind me when I was waving that knife in the air."

Dr. Hunt grinned down at Charlie. "Next time she has a knife in her hand while she's talking, I advise you to duck. Miz Bonnie, give the boy a couple of aspirins and send him home. He'll be good as new by tomorrow. Son, come by my office in two weeks so I can remove those stitches." Dr. Hunt packed his bag and headed out the back door.

Charlie sat up as BonBon, still pale as a ghost, handed him two aspirins and a glass of water. He now had a view of the entire room. He spotted the handle of the meat cleaver sticking out from a sink of soapy water. "Where's Beau?"

Bonnie put her finger to her lips. "Shhh." She waited until she heard the roar of Dr. Hunt's car engine before explaining. "I dragged him into the storage closet. We've got to get him out of here before Gracie gets home."

At the mention of Gracie's name, Charlie came to life. He pulled himself up from the floor and headed out the back door of the kitchen. It didn't take him long to discover an old beat-up Ford hidden behind the dumpster. He checked the ignition for keys. When he didn't find them, he hurried back into the kitchen.

Bonnie was leaning against the counter in a daze. All the energy she'd expended was gone now, and she seemed to shrivel up before his eyes. Charlie walked into the storage closet and cringed at the grisly scene inside. There was a blood-soaked tablecloth wrapped tightly around Beau's head, and a stream of crimson flowed from it to the floor drain in the center of the closet. Charlie looked away and searched Beau's pockets where he found a set of Ford keys. "These must belong to the car hidden behind the dumpster," he said as he showed Bonnie the keys. "Beau wasn't in his 442."

Bonnie began to shake uncontrollably as tears splashed down her cheeks. "Dear God, what have I done?"

Charlie picked up the blanket that had been covering him and threw it around Bonnie. "It's okay, Miz Bonnie. You saved my life, that's what you did. Now you just sit down here, and I'm going to fix you a glass of your sweet tea. Then I'm going to move this body somewhere it will never be found."

As Bonnie sipped the iced tea, her heartbeat slowed, and her eyes took focus. "We must get him out of here before Gracie gets home. What are we going to do, Charlie?"

"Don't worry, Miz Bonnie, I have a plan." He headed out the back door and removed a tarp from his pickup truck. Back inside, Charlie laid the tarp beside Beau's body and rolled the body onto it. "I need your help, Miss Bonnie."

Together, Charlie and Bonnie dragged Beau's body out to the car behind the dumpster. In life, Beau Loosier had been thin and wiry. But to Bonnie and Charlie now, as they panted and groaned with effort, hauling his lifeless heap felt a lot like heaving a ton of bricks. But somehow, probably because of the adrenaline rushing through their veins, they conjured up the Herculean strength to lift the body of Talmadge Leverett Loosier, III into the trunk of the old Ford.

Charlie returned to the kitchen, filled a bucket with warm soapy water, and mopped the floor of the storage closet. Once the kitchen was back in order, he could tell that Bonnie was about to collapse. She struggled for words. "What are we going to do with him?"

"I know where to take him, Miz Bonnie. Nobody will ever find him either. Don't you worry. I got this."

As Charlie patted Bonnie on the shoulder, her eyes pooled with tears again. "Oh my God, what have I done?" she moaned.

"It's what *we've* done, Miz Bonnie. And we did it to protect Gracie. God only knows how many other poor girls have suffered because of this pathetic human being. He'll never be a threat to anybody, ever again."

Bonnie followed Charlie out into the alley. As he climbed behind the wheel of the Ford, he smiled weakly at her. "Now you go on home so you'll be there for Gracie. She'll be dying to show off her prom dress and tell you what she had for dinner at Pitty Pat's Porch."

Bonnie nodded like an obedient child as she headed back inside. It wasn't until she trudged up the steps to her house that she realized Charlie had not stuttered a single time since Beau Loosier's death.

She ran a hot bath and soaked in it until the water turned tepid. She was still shivering as she dressed in her night clothes. She turned toward her bed and hit her knees. "Dear Lord, I know I have committed a deadly sin. I know that one day I will pay the price for it. And please don't blame Charlie. That young man has been through enough of his own, but he is living a godly life for you. I'm not certain that Beau Loosier truly knew you as his savior, Lord, but I pray that he did and is in Heaven with you right now. If he is with you, may his sins be forgiven. Teach me how to forgive him and to forgive myself. Amen."

Bonnie crawled into bed and fell into an exhausted sleep. It was after midnight when she heard a car door slam in the driveway. "BonBon, are you still up?" The sound of Gracie's precious voice filled her with peace.

At that very moment, Charlie was pulling the old Ford onto the dirt road leading to Camp Thunder. Dripping Rock Road served as a dam for the camp's lake. Cooter Renfroe had been correct in his description of the flooding in the area. Although the waters had receded, the lake itself was brimming higher than Charlie had ever seen it. He couldn't have asked for a better situation to complete his chore.

Charlie drove the car to the middle of the bridge and turned the front tires so that they were teetering over the lake. Removing Beau's lifeless body from the trunk by himself was an arduous task. Grunting with effort, Charlie dragged the corpse to the front seat, unfolded the tarp, and heaved Beau into the driver's seat.

Sweating profusely from his labors, Charlie sat on the ground and leaned against the front tire. The night sky was clear for the first time in days. Charlie studied the stars and allowed his breathing to return to normal.

He wondered aloud. "Lord, why did it have to come to this? Was there something I could have done to prevent his death and at the same time, save Gracie from him? He was evil, Lord. He would've killed both me and Miz Bonnie tonight in her kitchen. If I don't hide his body, Miz Bonnie will go to jail, and I can't have that on my conscience. So, I'm doing what I gotta do. But I know it's a sin, Lord, and you can punish me however you see fit."

Charlie pulled himself up and opened the car door. He put the car in gear, then moved to the rear and put all his weight into pushing the vehicle. The car rolled into the lake without too much effort from Charlie. He watched it slide into the muddy water and begin to sink. He didn't breathe easily until the vehicle was completely submerged and the bubbles had evaporated.

CHAPTER TWENTY-FOUR

The following Saturday morning, Vern was frying eggs on the griddle while Bonnie refilled customers' coffee cups. Cooter Renfroe sat reading the Thomaston Times on his usual stool at the café counter. "Well, I'll be. Listen to this." Cooter read aloud.

> *Pike County Sheriff J. Carl Riggins has issued an all-points bulletin for 23-year-old Beau Loosier. Beau's parents, Mr. and Mrs. Talmadge Loosier, were last with their son at dinner on Tuesday evening. They have not seen him since. Spalding County officials located Beau's vehicle, a red 442 Oldsmobile, in the back parking lot of the Imperial Theater in Griffin. At this time, officials do not consider any foul play but are looking for anyone who may have seen Beau Loosier since Tuesday night.*

Ouida lit her third cigarette for the day. "I hope that SOB is on a slow boat to China. Watch out, Bonnie, you're spilling coffee everywhere!"

Bonnie, hands trembling uncontrollably, grabbed a cloth to clean up the counter. "Sorry about that, Ouida. I guess I wasn't paying attention."

Ouida added some cream to her coffee. "Honey, are you okay? Your hands are shaking."

"I'm fine," Bonnie lied. "I guess I'm a little weary from getting Grace ready for tonight's prom. We were up late making some alterations to her dress."

Ouida sipped her coffee. "I tried to get Gracie to have her dress altered at Rich's, but she insisted that was too expensive. I'm sorry the task landed on you."

The color slowly returned to Bonnie's face. "Oh, it was just a quick hem, Ouida. Besides, that would have meant another trip to Atlanta for you and Buddy to pick the dress up."

Busy sopping his biscuit in red eye gravy, Buddy chimed in from his nearby table. "I never mind going to Atlanta. Besides, that sales lady in the dress department was giving me the eye."

Ouida hooted. "Buddy Simpson, you think you're God's gift to every female that looks your way. That sales gal was making nice to you because she figured you for the fat wallet. She was hoping to score a big commission."

Buddy wiped his mouth. "Well, maybe I'll just drive up to Atlanta and see if she'd like to go out with me. That'd shut you up, Ouida Clarkston."

Bonnie relaxed as talk of Beau Loosier was forgotten. She and Charlie hadn't spoken since the events of Wednesday. She'd suffered sleepless nights since then. What had Charlie done with Beau's body? She wasn't sure she wanted to know and doubted that Charlie would tell her if she asked.

After Charlie had watched the last bubbles disappear into the lake that fateful night, he knew he had to get back to town without being spotted by any potential witnesses. He'd had enough sense to bring a flashlight, which was useful as he traveled every back road in the county to wind his way back to town. The night sky was beginning to brighten by the time he made it to his apartment over Brooxie's garage. As he stood under the steaming water of a shower, Charlie let the tears fall, but not for Beau. He cried for Miz Bonnie as he prayed that she would keep their secret.

Bonnie was relieved to have the distraction of helping Gracie get ready for the prom. She'd left Vern in charge of the café so she could give Gracie all her attention.

Gracie sat in front of the bathroom mirror in her robe. "BonBon, I can't decide whether to wear my hair up or leave it down. What do you think?"

Bonnie stood behind her and pulled Gracie's long blonde curls atop her head. "I like it both ways. You decide." She handed Gracie a soft blue ribbon just the color of her dress. "Actually, if you pull it away from your face with the ribbon, your blue eyes will really sparkle against your dress."

Gracie nodded. "Charlie likes it around my shoulders." She grinned at Bonnie. "I can't believe this is the last big event before I graduate."

"Make the most of it, sweet girl. Once you graduate and start to college, life will change." Bonnie tied the ribbon at the nape of Gracie's neck. "And about college. If Georgia Tech offers you a full scholarship, you'd be crazy not to accept it."

Gracie had been accepted to Georgia Tech as well as the University of Georgia, but she'd had little to say about either school. "I'll think about it after tonight. Okay, BonBon?"

Bonnie smiled. "You're right. This is a special night, and I want you to enjoy every moment. Just one more thing. An early graduation gift." She handed a tiny box to Gracie. Inside lay the heirloom gold cross suspended on a new gold chain, even finer quality than the original one. "I know you haven't worn the cross since you lost the chain."

For a moment, Gracie remained speechless. She'd never explained to BonBon what had happened to the chain. As the horrific memory of Beau Loosier stuffing the chain in his pocket started to surface, Gracie pushed it back down like she'd done so many times before. She managed a smile. "It will be perfect with my dress," she said as she allowed BonBon to attach the chain around her neck.

As always, Gracie had an audience at the café waiting for her to emerge in all her glory. Her blue satin dress had a fitted bodice and a flowing skirt that looked like whipped cream. Charlie, equally handsome in his new suit, stood smiling and speechless by the front counter.

Ouida was the first to utter a word. "You are stunning, Gracie MacGregor! Simply stunning!" Gracie blushed as the entire café applauded.

Pike County High School's gym had been transformed into a ballroom for the special night. Every flower garden in the county had been raided for blooms to bedeck the room. There were trails of purple wisteria hanging from the ceiling along with the fragrance of roses and magnolias softly permeating the air.

Charlie gave Gracie his arm to escort her into the gym. He couldn't take his eyes off her. "You're the prettiest girl here tonight, and I'm the luckiest guy." He squeezed her hand tightly as he led her to the dance floor. The first song played was *I Just Can't Help Believin'* by B.J. Thomas. "And I can't believe you're mine, my precious Grace MacGregor."

Gracie grinned up at Charlie. "I'm doggone lucky myself, Charlie Callahan. You look so handsome, and there's something different about you tonight. I can't put my finger on it."

Charlie held her closely. "Then put your head on my shoulder instead."

"Wait a minute. I know what it is. You're not stuttering!" Gracie lifted her astonished blue eyes and gazed into Charlie's. "You haven't stuttered a single time tonight."

Charlie swept her across the dance floor. "I guess all Miz Davison's speech lessons finally paid off."

Alfonzo Britt's band the SOAB's (Sons of Alfonzo Britt) from Thomaston knew every 60s hit and played them all. When Alfonzo performed his famous rendition of James Brown's *I Feel Good*, the dance floor started to steam.

Charlie pulled his handkerchief from his pocket and wiped his sweaty face. "It's hot in here. If you've had enough, why don't we go for a drive?"

Gracie downed a cup of too sweet punch. "I'm ready. I could use something better to drink than this sticky punch, and BonBon gave me a later curfew. I don't have to be home until midnight."

They drove through the county with the windows down so they could feel the cool night air. Charlie pulled Gracie close to him. "I've got some Cokes at the apartment if you're still thirsty."

Gracie had never been to Charlie's apartment, but the time felt right. "Okay, that sounds good."

The downstairs garage was dark except for an outside security light. Charlie opened one of the overhead doors and pulled his car inside. He helped Gracie out and led her to a staircase towards the back. "Hold on to me. Don't trip on your dress." He pulled on a chain attached to a bulb that lit up the stairs.

Gracie giggled. "Lead on, my captain."

There wasn't much to his apartment, but Charlie had made it a home. His kitchen consisted of a small refrigerator, a stove top, and a sink. "Sit down, my lady, and I'll get us something cold to drink." He pulled out one of the two metal chairs at a small round table.

Gracie was quiet while she sipped on her Coke and studied Charlie's tiny living quarters. The rest of the apartment was one big room that served as both his living area and bedroom. There was a small bathroom in the corner.

"I got the sofa at a garage sale in Molena. Mr. Brooxie already had a bed up here. He told me that he used to sleep here when he'd had too much to drink and didn't want to listen to his wife bitching at him." Gracie raised her eyebrows, and Charlie laughed. "His words, not mine."

Charlie moved to a small table with a record player that Miz Ouida and Mr. Buddy had given him for graduation. "What about something calmer than James Brown?" He pulled a 45 record from its sleeve. "This one's an oldie, but it always reminds me of you."

It was Little Anthony and the Imperials singing *I Think I'm Going out of My Head*. Charlie pulled Gracie from her chair, held her closely, and danced her across the small kitchen floor. "I love you, Gracie. I realized that when you came to visit on my last day at Camp Thunder years ago. I thought I'd never see anyone more beautiful than you were that day. But I was wrong."

Gracie looked puzzled until he continued. "I was wrong because every time I see you, I find you prettier than the time before. And tonight, I can barely breathe when I look at you."

Charlie pulled her into him and kissed her with a passion that Gracie had never felt before. "Gracie, I want you so much. I've never pushed you because I wanted you to be ready, and I won't push you now."

She'd been afraid for so long, ever since Beau Loosier took from her what wasn't his to take. The tension never left her—that frightening vulnerability that prevented her from letting go.

Charlie sensed her go rigid in his arms. "Gracie, you don't have to be afraid anymore. I promise you that Beau Loosier will never ever hurt you again."

His words rang with a confidence that Grace had never heard before. Maybe it was his newfound ability to speak without a stutter or the fact that he was a man now, living on his own. Whatever was different in his words and in his touch resonated through Gracie's whole being.

For the first time since that horrible day with Beau at the creek, Gracie completely let go. She was limp in Charlie's arms as he carried her to his bed. "Don't be afraid, sweetheart. We won't do anything you don't want to do."

Gracie whispered softly as she turned her back to Charlie. "Unzip my dress." Charlie gasped when he saw what was beneath.

How glad she was that Miss Ouida had sneaked her over to the lingerie department while Mr. Buddy had sauntered over to peruse the books in Rich's. Explaining that every young woman should feel beautiful from the inside out, Miss Ouida had selected a baby blue strapless satin bra and a pair of lace panties.

Charlie quickly stripped down to his underwear and lay beside her. He began kissing her softly as he moved down her body. When he reached her belly button, Gracie shivered in excitement.

For the next hour, they explored every inch of each other's body, caressing and kissing and giggling. Charlie never tried to enter her. "I know you're not ready for that. It's okay, Gracie. You'll know when it's time. Until then, I'm happy just holding you."

At the stroke of midnight, Gracie stood at her front door for one last kiss. "I love you, Charlie Callahan. Now let me get inside before I turn into a pumpkin."

The house was dark except for a single light burning over the kitchen sink. Gracie tiptoed to the faucet and quietly poured a glass of water. She found BonBon sound asleep at the kitchen table, her head lying on the front page of yesterday's *Thomaston Times*. As she gently pulled the paper away, Bonnie woke with a start. "Gracie, you're home. What time is it? How was the prom?"

"It's after midnight, BonBon. Come on, let's get you to bed." Bonnie didn't argue as Gracie guided her to the bedroom. If she hadn't been so exhausted, Bonnie would have laughed with amusement as Gracie tucked her in.

Wandering back to the kitchen for her glass of water, Gracie found the newspaper on the floor. She wished she hadn't as soon as she read the headlines about Beau Loosier. Was he gone for good? Was he off hurting another 13-year-old girl? Would he be back?

As long as there was a possibility that he could come back, Beau was still a threat to her and to BonBon. The euphoria of her night with Charlie shattered as she felt Beau's evil creep into her blood once again.

PART THREE

CHAPTER TWENTY-FIVE

Pike County's Class of 1970 graduation took place beneath the stars of a glorious June night on the school's football field. With the poise of an 18-year-old woman ready to conquer the world, Grace MacGregor—who had wrapped up her senior year at the top of her class—delivered the valedictorian speech.

"Graduates, you may now turn your tassels," she announced and was met with a standing ovation from her fellow classmates and all the spectators. No one cheered louder than Charlie, except maybe for Buddy Simpson, who clanged a cowbell he'd brought along for the event.

Ouida Clarkston, cranky from her need for nicotine, grabbed the bell from Buddy's hands. "If you bang that thing one more time, I'm going to bang it against your head."

Charlie couldn't help but giggle. As the stands began to empty, the field was overrun with family and friends celebrating their graduates. Beaming with pride, Bonnie wiped a tear from her eye as she and Charlie slowly worked their way out of the stands.

"Miz Bonnie, I know you need to get down to the café," Charlie said. "I'll wade through this crowd and fetch Gracie, and we'll get there as soon as we can."

Bonnie Mac's Café was bedecked with streamers and balloons for Gracie's graduation party. It seemed like half of Zebulon was packed into the café to celebrate her special day. Clad in a creamy pink sundress, much shorter than Bonnie preferred, Gracie made her entrance on the arm of Charlie Callahan, who was grinning from ear to ear.

Between meals for their regular customers over the last few days, Bonnie and Vern had toiled tirelessly making finger food for the party. Vern had raised his eyebrows as he watched Bonnie stuff small wieners into her homemade crescent roll dough.

She pulled a pan of the rolls from the oven. "Try one, Vern. It's a new recipe I found in *Better Homes and Gardens* magazine. They're called pigs in a blanket."

Vern obliged her then smiled. "Miz Bonnie, those are good!"

Besides Bonnie's newest recipe, there were chicken salad, egg salad, and pimento cheese sandwiches on crustless white bread, meatballs cooked in grape jelly, cheese fondue served with veggies and toasted French bread, Bonnie's candied pecans, and Gracie's favorite—cheese straws.

Vern carried out tray after tray, placing them on a large table covered in a crisp, white tablecloth. The table's centerpiece featured a towering vase of roses in Pike County's school colors of red and white.

Ouida, with Buddy carrying a huge bakery box right behind her, sneaked in through the back door to the kitchen where Bonnie was pulling a hot pan of her pigs in a blanket from the oven. Ouida pointed to an empty spot on Bonnie's stainless worktable. "Put the box there, Buddy. Be careful! We don't want the icing to get smudged."

Buddy obeyed as he sniffed the air. "Those smell heavenly, Bonnie. I do detect the aroma of pork!" He swiped a couple of warm ones from the pan before Bonnie could remove them.

Ouida sighed. "Go on out and stuff your face, Buddy. I think Bonnie and I can handle the cake." Buddy bowed and grinned as he pushed through the swinging doors.

Bonnie watched as Ouida opened the huge white box. "Ouida, the roses you and Buddy sprang for were certainly enough. I can't believe you insisted on buying the cake, too."

Ouida unfolded both sides of the box. "You had your hands full with all this food you've prepared. Bringing dessert was the least we could do." She grinned. "And look! Fred Kitchens packed it just right so that the icing didn't get smudged. He knows his cakes."

Since there was no bakery in Zebulon, Buddy had driven Ouida to Thomaston to pick up the cake. Covered in white icing and outlined with red flowers, the huge sheet cake had *Congratulations Grace* scripted across it. Ouida grinned. "Do you think this will be enough to feed that crowd?"

"You and Buddy have been so kind to Grace." Then Bonnie burst into tears.

"What on earth, honey?! Are you okay?" Ouida put an arm around Bonnie's shoulder.

Bonnie grabbed a clean dish towel and wiped her face. "I'm just so filled with emotion today. It seems like only yesterday when that scrawny little five-year-old was abandoned in my café. Now she's 18 and all grown up. I'm not sure I've done the best I could raising her."

"Whatever do you mean, Bonnie? That child could have ended up spending her days in a rat-infested Atlanta apartment, or even worse, with the Loosier family and that crazy son of theirs."

Bonnie flinched at the mention of Beau. "That boy was evil incarnate."

Ouida eyed her sharply. "Bonnie MacGregor, I've never heard you say a mean word about anybody. But I agree. Beau Loosier doesn't belong on this earth, and I pray we never see him again."

Bonnie's voice quivered. "I don't think he'll be back." She squared her shoulders and changed the subject. "I'm so proud of Gracie but, at the same time, so disappointed that she would not accept either of the scholarships from Tech and the University she was offered."

"I wondered about that myself," Ouida lit a cigarette. "Did she give you a reason?

"Oh, she made all kinds of excuses. She said she wasn't interested in being an engineer, so she didn't see a reason to go to Georgia Tech. She claims she wants to be a teacher, and she's been accepted to Tift College for Women in Forsyth."

"Gracie would make a good teacher." Ouida blew smoke rings in the air. "I know the University of Georgia offers a reputable teaching degree."

Bonnie stacked dishes for the cake. "That's what I told her. She says Athens is too far from here and if she goes to Tift, she can drive back and forth each day. It's only 30 miles. At least that's the reason she gave me."

"Hmmm. I can think of another reason. He's tall with a crooked smile and green eyes that light up when he stares at your daughter. Let's get this cake out to all those hungry celebrants!" Ouida picked up the cake and headed through the swinging doors.

Ouida's assumption was somewhat correct. Grace couldn't bear the thought of not seeing Charlie every day. More importantly, Beau Loosier's threats to hurt BonBon never strayed far from Gracie's thoughts. She didn't intend to leave her precious BonBon alone without protection. Grace knew Charlie would keep an eye on BonBon while she was away during the day for classes. But she wanted to be home each night to watch over the woman who had been both her savior and her protector all these years.

Once the celebration was over, Charlie offered to clean up the kitchen, but Bonnie would have none of it. "Vern and I don't need any assistance. You take Grace and enjoy what's left of this lovely night." She turned to Gracie, still radiant with excitement. "I guess now that you're 18 and a graduate, I can't enforce a curfew on you. Just let me know when you get home."

"I won't be too late, BonBon. I'm exhausted. After being all nervous about my speech and then eating so much, I won't last long." Gracie started out the door with Charlie but turned around and ran to Bonnie, wrapped her arms around her, and gave her a big hug. "Thank you, BonBon, for everything."

Bonnie's eyes filled with tears. "You *are* my everything, Grace." She cleared her throat. "Now you two don't get into any trouble. Nothing good ever happens after midnight."

CHAPTER TWENTY-SIX

Two weeks before Gracie started college, Ouida decided a shopping trip to Atlanta was in order. "Now don't you start your arguments, Bonnie MacGregor. Buying our Gracie some new clothes for school brings such joy to me."

"And me, too," Buddy added between bites of his biscuit. "Besides, I might run into that saleslady who helped us last spring."

Ouida blew smoke in Buddy's face. "Buddy Sampson, the only reason that woman would show any interest in you would be for your bank account."

"That's okay. I've got plenty of it to wine and dine her all over Atlanta." Buddy poured more sugar in his coffee. "And me and Ouida got plenty between us to take Gracie on a shopping spree. So, let us have our fun, Bonnie."

Bonnie threw up her hands. "You two spoil that child." She hushed when the kitchen doors swung open. Grace appeared wearing a sleeveless blue shift covered in daisies with a matching headband holding back her long, blonde hair.

Ouida smiled. "You are such a lovely young woman, Gracie." She winked at Bonnie. "You are definitely not a child anymore." The three set off for Buddy's car while Bonnie headed to the kitchen with the last of the breakfast dishes.

A few minutes later, Charlie came through the kitchen's back door. "Hi Miz Bonnie. I brought your Chevy back and parked it in your driveway." He handed Bonnie the keys. "Sorry, I'm already dirty with grease." He turned on the sink and soaped up his hands. "I guess the shoppers are on their way to Atlanta."

Bonnie tucked the keys in her pocket. "They just left. What did Brooxie say about the car?" After years of wear and tear, the transmission on her 1960 Impala had been acting up. "I want it running smoothly so Gracie can safely drive back and forth to school each day."

Charlie dried his hands. "Mr. Brooxie says the transmission is okay to drive around town, but he doesn't recommend putting a lot of miles on it." Bonnie frowned. "Miz Bonnie, don't get upset. Mr. Brooxie and I have a plan."

Bonnie folded her arms and raised her eyebrows. "Just listen, Miz Bonnie, before you say no. Last month Mr. Brooxie and I went to the car auction in Griffin. We bought a 1964 Dodge Dart for a song. It's a stick on the column so I'll have to teach Gracie how to use a clutch, but you know she's a quick learner. We've replaced the spark plugs and put in a new radiator, and that little car sings. Mr. Brooxie says you can't tear up one of those Darts."

Bonnie sighed. "And how much is that car going to cost me?"

"Not one dime. Mr. Brooxie and I want it to be our graduation gift for Gracie." Bonnie shook her head. "Come on, Miz Bonnie, you'll be able to keep your car here and not worry about Gracie on the road. I think you and I agree that our biggest concern is keeping Gracie safe."

Bonnie's eyes glistened with tears. "You're right. We want to keep her safe." They had not spoken about Beau Loosier since the night Charlie drove away with his body. In fact, this was the first time that Bonnie and Charlie had been alone so they could discuss it. "And about Gracie's safety…"

Charlie wouldn't go there, though. "I know what you're thinking about, Miz Bonnie. Just don't ask me any questions. The less you know, the better." He placed his hand on Bonnie's shoulder. "We made a pact to keep Gracie safe, and that's what we're doing. Let's promise that we'll never speak of Beau Loosier again."

Bonnie wiped her cheeks with her apron. "Agreed." Then she cleared her throat. "And Grace can have the car, but you have to teach her how to drive a straight stick. I haven't used a clutch in years."

Charlie grinned and hugged her. "I'm headed to Griffin to pick up some parts for Chief Bushy's old Chrysler. I don't know why he won't buy a new one, but he says as long as Brooxie can keep it running, he's happy with that old jalopy."

While Charlie did need to pick up some parts in Griffin, he didn't share his ulterior motive for the trip. After stopping at Spalding Auto Parts, he headed two blocks over to the Army Recruiting Office.

"Son, with the war still raging in Vietnam, it's only a matter of time before you're drafted," Sgt. Bledsoe asserted as he straightened a stack of papers on his desk. "You'll have a better chance of choosing your future if you go ahead and join up." Sgt. Bledsoe was good at his job. "With your experience in auto mechanics, you'll be a cinch for working on aircraft after some training. When you get out, you could easily get a job with one of the major airlines."

Charlie saw through the sergeant's sales pitch, but he'd made up his mind before he'd even set foot in the recruiting office. He knew he wasn't college material. He'd barely made the grades to graduate from high school. The Army would give him the skills to make a better life for Gracie. By the time she graduated with a teaching degree, he'd be finished with his military duty and have the experience to get a good paying job. Maybe he'd even buy the auto shop when Brooxie retired.

While Charlie had his life all worked out, he'd overlooked the fact that it would be difficult to convince Gracie. The next Saturday night while they were in his apartment, Charlie sprung his news on her. He wasn't ready for Gracie's reaction.

"You're joining the Army?!" Gracie was livid. "What in the world are you thinking, Charlie Callahan? Don't you watch the news? Young men are dying by the hundreds in Vietnam. And I don't care what you say. As soon as you finish your training, the Army will send you over there to die, too."

Charlie wrapped his arms around Gracie's quivering shoulders. "Baby girl, calm down. I don't even report until late October. Who knows? By the time I finish my training, the war could be over. I do watch the news, and the peace talks are still going on in Paris."

"Yeah, and they've been going on for two years. They could go on for another 20." Gracie sobbed into Charlie's chest. "I can't lose you, Charlie. I just can't."

"You're not going to lose me, Gracie. The recruiter says with my experience, they'll have me working a job in mechanics."

Gracie sniffled. "I bet. In the South China Sea!" She snuggled up to Charlie. "I guess you'll look handsome in a uniform." Then she straightened up and looked deep into his hazel eyes. "But don't expect me to marry you and watch you go to Southeast Asia and die. I won't be a child widow!"

"Who said anything about marriage?" Charlie's lopsided grin never failed to win her over. His tone changed. "Gracie, I have to do this for us, don't you see? If I'm going to marry a college graduate, I want to have something more than an hourly wage job. The Army is my best ticket to success."

As Charlie caressed her, Gracie sighed. The argument was over, at least for the time being.

CHAPTER TWENTY-SEVEN

The first Monday in September, Grace sat at the café counter stirring heaps of milk and sugar into her coffee. "I guess you college gals like your coffee sweet," laughed Cooter Renfroe, perched on his usual stool by the cash register. He gave Bonnie a wink when she stopped by with the coffee pot. "Just black for me. I'm sweet enough."

Grace giggled as Bonnie set a plate of eggs, grits, and bacon before her. "You need to start this first day with a good breakfast."

"I'm too nervous to eat." Grace picked at her food. She was dressed in a plaid A-line skirt with a pale green blouse, compliments of her shopping trip with Ouida and Buddy. Her matching green knee socks and Weejuns loafers, a surprise splurge from Bonnie, had come from Neal Logue's Department Store in Thomaston.

While Vern flipped eggs at the griddle, Bonnie freshened Ouida and Buddy's coffee. Ouida lit her second cigarette of the morning. "Where's Charlie? Isn't he going to see his gal off?"

Grace sipped her milky-sweet coffee. "He's meeting me in BonBon's driveway. He wants to go over my driving instructions one more time." She rolled her eyes. For the past two weeks, Charlie had trained Grace in the art of driving with a clutch. After several outings of her bumping and jumping down some backroads, she'd finally gotten the hang of it.

"And he'll be there in five minutes, Gracie. I don't want you to be late your first day." Bonnie came around the counter and gave her a hug. "Please drive carefully. You are precious cargo."

"We'll be waiting to hear you talk some college when you get home this evening," Buddy added as he poured syrup on his second biscuit. "I'll be right here because it's chicken and dumplings night."

"Buddy Sampson, you're here every night!" Ouida turned to Grace. "You will be the prettiest and smartest collegiate at Tift, sweet Gracie."

Grace smiled and headed through the swinging doors. When she walked across the street, Charlie was already leaning against her baby blue Dodge Dart. "Hi, beautiful! Ooh, I like that short skirt."

"I'm glad you do. I didn't think BonBon was going to let me out the door in it. All the girls are wearing them like this. She can be such a fuddy dud sometimes."

Charlie offered her his lopsided grin. "Aww, she's just protective of you. Come here, my pretty college girl." He opened his arms for Gracie and pulled her close. "Now remember, clutch before gas, clutch before brake."

She snuggled under his chin. "I've got it. I had a good teacher. You gonna miss me today?"

Charlie kissed Gracie atop her head. "I doubt it. I'll get to flirt with all the old biddies who eat lunch in the café." They both giggled. "Actually, I have a busy day at the shop and gotta drive to Griffin to pick up some parts for Mrs. Fain's station wagon. She can't live without that car with all those kids."

Gracie looked at her watch. "I need to go. My first class starts at 9:00. I should be home by 5:00. Will you be back from Griffin by then?"

Charlie turned Gracie's chin up and kissed her gently. "You betcha, gorgeous! Now let me see you back out of the driveway without that car jumping." He watched Grace execute reverse with expertise and waved to her as she headed down the street.

Tift College, an all-women's Baptist school, sat right off Interstate 75 in Tift County. From the highway, drivers could see a huge wrought iron arch, which served as the entrance to the small campus. Across the arch were the words TIFT COLLEGE. At least that's what it was supposed to say. As Grace drove through the arch on her very first day, she saw that the *F* was missing from *TIFT*. She laughed out loud as she changed gears for the Dart to climb uphill.

Gracie didn't laugh for long as she took her seat in her first class, Religion 101. Since Tift was a Baptist College, all students were required to take religion courses. Dr. Gore wasted no time in getting class started. "I apologize for the lettering on our archway this morning. Forsyth is populated with some unscrupulous and foolish young men whose antics are a blemish on our campus. Now let's move on to the syllabus for this course."

For the next hour, Gracie tried to keep up with taking notes as Dr. Gore rattled on in a fast monotone that grated on her nerves. By the end of the hour, her hand was cramping. As the students filed out of class, a cute brunette muttered under her breath, "Now I know why they call him Dr. Bore!" When Gracie giggled, the girl said, "Hi, I'm Marcy Harper. I thought I met all of yinz at the freshman dorm meeting last night."

Gracie massaged the muscles in her writing hand. "I'm Grace MacGregor. I'm not in a dorm. I'll be commuting to campus every day."

"Oh wow! You have a car?" She turned to two other girls behind them. "Hey ladies, jeet yet? Grace, these are some of my dormmates. Maybe we can get off campus for lunch. I've been craving a cheesesteak since I left Pennsylvania."

Gracie wasn't sure what a cheesesteak was, but she was fascinated by Marcy's northeastern accent and the curious slang she used. "What's your next class?" she asked Marcy. "I have Dr. Middleton for Introduction to Education."

"So, you're an education major? Me too. That's all there is to study here unless you're going to be a Southern Baptist missionary. We're in luck. I have

Dr. Middleton for my next class." Marcy locked arms with Grace. "Come on, I'll show you the way."

By the time Grace headed home in the late afternoon, her head was spinning. She'd spent a chunk of her savings at the campus bookstore on all the assigned textbooks and had enough assignments to keep her busy all evening. She laughed for the second time as she drove under the archway with its missing F. With nothing but females on campus, *TIT* College seemed appropriate to her.

The café was already jammed with the supper crowd when Grace entered through the kitchen's back door. Bonnie scurried through the swinging doors with an armload of dirty dishes. "You're home! I can't wait to hear all about your first day, but right now I could use your help. The Women of Faith Missionary Circle decided to have dinner here tonight, and I haven't come up for air." Gracie smiled, grabbed an apron, and went to work.

By the end of the week, Grace had fallen into a routine. She left home by 7:00 each morning and didn't return until after 5:00. She'd spend the next two hours helping in the café and then head across the street to study. It was well past midnight before she turned out her bedroom light.

Saturday morning, the usual breakfast clientele had come and gone before Grace showed up in the café. Face glowing and eyes bright after a few extra hours of sleep, she poured her usual half cup of coffee and then topped it with milk and sugar.

Ouida, nursing a third cup of coffee, smiled. "There's our college beauty! How was your first week?"

Gracie sat down at the counter. "A little overwhelming, but I'm getting the hang of it."

Buddy slathered syrup on a biscuit. "I remember when I went to Massey Business College in Atlanta for my accounting degree. I was lost for a month. You're smart, Gracie; you'll figure it out in no time."

Grace smiled at the thought of Buddy Simpson as a college student. "I guess that's when you learned your way around Atlanta."

"Yep. It wasn't any time before me and some of the other fellas were driving over to Agnes Scott College where all the girls were. On Saturdays my buddy George and I would load up my '46 Chevy Fleetmaster with as many girls as could fit in it and head to the Varsity. I was a hundred pounds lighter then and quite the lady's man. Now, those were the days."

Ouida lit another cigarette. "And if you don't quit eating so many biscuits, the rest of those days are numbered."

"Oh, hush up. Those cancer sticks will take you out first, Ouida Clarkston!" Buddy pulled himself up from the table and waddled to the register to pay his bill. "Don't study too hard, Gracie. I'm off to attend to some tax issues with a client up in Griffin, but I'll be back in time for supper, Miz Bonnie."

As he shuffled out, Buddy almost bumped into Charlie who was walking in. Charlie's eyes lit up when he saw Gracie at the counter. "Hi, beautiful! I was hoping I'd catch up with you this morning." He kissed her on the cheek.

Gracie brushed Charlie's bangs off his forehead. "I'm sorry I haven't returned your calls. I've fallen asleep every night in my clothes with a book on my lap."

Charlie grabbed her hand. "It's a beautiful September day, and you need some fresh air. Miz Bonnie volunteered to pack us a lunch so we could have a picnic."

As if on cue, Bonnie pushed through the swinging doors carrying a wicker picnic basket. "Gracie, you need a break from the books. There's plenty to eat in the basket along with a thermos of sweet tea. I don't want to lay eyes on you before dark. Now skedaddle!"

Charlie took the basket in one arm and offered Grace his other. "Where are we going?" she asked. "Do I need to change?" Gracie was dressed in bell bottom jeans and a white peasant blouse covered in embroidered flowers.

As they headed to his truck, Charlie grinned. "Our destination is a surprise. And your outfit is perfect. I really dig those jeans, or rather what's in them."

Grace punched him softly in the arm. "You'll get to enjoy these jeans on the weekends. I had planned to wear them to school, but Tift has strict dress code rules. Only skirts or pantsuits are allowed. Marcy even told me if she has on shorts after classes, she has to wear a trench coat to the bookstore!"

"I kinda like having you in those jeans all to myself." Charlie grinned mischievously. "Who's Marcy?"

Grace filled him in on her classes, her strait-laced professors, and her new friend. "And you should hear Marcy's accent. She says 'yinz' for 'y'all' and 'Jeet' for 'Did you eat?' She's from Pennsylvania and loves something she calls a cheesesteak."

Charlie headed south on the highway. "Who would mess up a good steak with cheese?"

"Actually, it's a sandwich with thinly sliced steak and melted cheese. We looked all over Forsyth for a restaurant with cheesesteak on the menu but had no luck. Maybe I can get Vern to concoct one for her."

Grace spent the rest of the drive entertaining Charlie with stories about the missing *F* in the college's sign. "The girls say anytime classes are not in session and they return, the *F* is gone. It's a tradition with all the teenage boys in the county. Marcy called them rednecks."

"Ain't nothing wrong with being called a redneck," Charlie laughed. "I've been called worse." As they passed the Children's Home, Charlie honked his horn. "Seems like I've been gone from there for years."

Gracie scooted closer to Charlie. "When are you going to tell me where we're going?"

"You'll see soon enough." They drove through Molena. Just south of Concord, Charlie pulled over onto a dirt area that had been worn down by other vehicles. There was a beat-up Chevy truck parked in the dirt. Always a gentleman, Charlie climbed out and then opened Grace's door. "We're here."

Charlie pulled the picnic basket and an old quilt from the bed of the truck and took Gracie's hand. "Down here is Flat Shoals Creek. Reverend Hogan used to bring us here on picnics every spring. We'd get up early on Saturday morning to dig worms before we set out on the bus. Then Rev would bring along some fishing poles, and we'd have the entire afternoon to fish and wade around in the water. Minnie, the home's cook, always packed the best lunches, too."

Gracie followed him down a narrow dirt path until they reached the creek. There were a couple of old men in overalls packing up their fishing gear. "It's all you'rn. Done got too hot for us." One of the men held up a string of fish and grinned. "I guess we done caught enough for supper."

"You see those flat rocks out in the middle? We can wade over there and set up our picnic." Charlie set the basket and quilt on the ground and then sat down beside them. He removed his shoes and began rolling up his jeans.

Gracie followed suit. Charlie grabbed her hand with his free one as they crossed through the shallow water to the rocks. The setting was perfect. The September sky was cloudless and bright blue. The two sat cross-legged on the quilt and feasted on cold fried chicken, deviled eggs, and pimento cheese sandwiches.

When they finished, Charlie dug into the bottom of the basket. "Look, Miz Bonnie packed dessert." He sniffed the foil package. "Oh yes siree, they're her famous mud hens!"

Grace lay back in the warm September sun. "None for me. I'm stuffed. This is just what I needed." She smiled up at him. "You know you're sweeter than sugar to me. I think I'm going to call you Shug."

Charlie grinned. "Only you can call me that. I don't want the fellas at the garage to think I got sugar in my blood." Lying down beside her, Charlie brushed a strand of hair behind Grace's ear. "You are the most beautiful creature on this earth." He leaned over and kissed her deeply. "I love you, Gracie."

Grace caught a small hitch in his voice. She raised up on her elbow and studied his serious hazel eyes. "What's wrong, Charlie?"

Charlie sighed. "I can't hide anything from you." Then he took a deep breath. "I got my orders earlier this week. I report to Fort Bragg in two weeks."

Grace swallowed back the lump in her throat. "Where's Fort Bragg?"

"North Carolina. I'll be there for eight weeks of basic training. Then they'll send me somewhere else for AIT."

Tears trickled down Grace's cheeks. "What's AIT?"

Charlie pulled her into his chest. "It stands for Advanced Individual Training. The recruiter says I'll be in the Armor Division—hopefully, in the Maintenance Battalion, where I'd be working on tanks. And I wouldn't be in harm's way."

"Hopefully? That means you don't know for sure if you'll be in harm's way or not." Grace began to sob.

"Baby girl, don't cry." Charlie lifted her chin and wiped her tears with his handkerchief. "It's going to be all right, Gracie. No matter where I go, as long as I have you waiting for me, I'll come home."

They lay together in each other's arms until the sun set over the water. The drive home was a quiet one.

CHAPTER TWENTY-EIGHT

With Grace commuting to Tift daily and Charlie finishing up an engine overhaul at Brooxie's Garage, the next two weeks seemed to evaporate. Charlie was scheduled to report to the recruiting office in Griffin at the crack of dawn on Saturday. Grace cut all her classes that Friday so she and Charlie could spend the entire day together.

Since it was a sunny, cool October day, the two decided to drive to Stone Mountain. Once again Bonnie packed them a picnic basket. She carried it over to the house to add a tablecloth from the linen closet.

She found Grace upstairs still in her nightgown. "Grace, why aren't you dressed? You'd better take a jacket. It will be cold on top of the mountain." Her eyes still swollen from crying most of the night, Grace sat in front of the bathroom mirror trying to repair them. "Oh honey, bless your heart. Let me fix you an ice compress. That will help the swelling."

When Bonnie returned, Grace collapsed into her arms. "I can't do this, BonBon. I'm not strong enough."

"Sweet daughter of mine, you are stronger than you think." Bonnie pressed the cold bag to Gracie's face. "And you're not alone. You've got me and Ouida and Buddy." She handed Grace a tissue. "Now blow that runny nose."

Grace obeyed then looked up with teary blue eyes. "I know I've got all y'all, BonBon, but what if I never see him again? What if he gets killed?"

BonBon wrapped her arm around Grace's shoulder. "Nobody's going to get killed at Fort Bragg. Now you quit borrowing trouble, sweet girl. You need to give Charlie a happy sendoff, not a teary one." She lifted Grace's chin and stared into her face. "Can you do that for him?"

"I guess so." Gracie sighed. "Will you help me pick out what to wear today? I just can't make up my mind."

They chose a pair of tan corduroy bell bottoms and a soft blue pullover. Bonnie watched as Grace began to brush her hair. "Why don't you let me braid it for you? That will keep the wind from blowing it all over the place." Grace sat obediently while Bonnie gathered her long blonde locks into a French braid down the middle of her back. She smiled. "Just like when you were a little girl."

"Sometimes I wish I was still a little girl without a care in the world— besides what kind of dessert I'd find you baking when I got home from school." Grace stared at BonBon through the mirror.

"Sweetheart, I'd love to tell you that life is always easy, but you already know that's not true. It's been my experience that during my lowest times, the Good Lord has always held me up. Now you put on some of that sweet perfume Ouida gave you for your birthday and hold that pretty head high. You got a fella waiting to spend a day with his beautiful gal." Bonnie pulled softly on Gracie's braid and noticed a hint of a smile in Gracie's eyes.

Down the street at Brooxie's Garage, Charlie was saying his farewells to his employer. "I don't know how to thank you for all you've done for me, Mr. Brooxie."

"Son, you're a grown man going into the United States Army. I think it's time you dropped the mister."

Charlie grinned. "Okay, then. Thanks for not leasing the apartment while I'm gone, Brooxie. It will be good to have a home to come back to."

"It's yours as long as you want it, Charlie. And you've got a job here whenever you get back, too. You're the best damn mechanic around these parts. Well, besides me." They both chuckled.

Then Brooxie turned serious. "When I went to basic training, my drill sergeant was a real son of a bitch. I figure most of 'em are. But you listen to every word he says. What I learned from that mean bastard saved me more than once when I landed in Normandy."

"Yessir, I'll remember that." While they worked on cars together, Charlie had been privy to many of Brooxie's war stories, some too risqué for him to repeat in mixed company.

"Stay away from the poker sharks. There's always some cheaters in every platoon. And when you go on leave, watch yourself in the bars. You don't want to end up an old drunk like me." There was a hint of remorse in Brooxie's voice.

"Oh, and speaking of bars, I've got you a little going away present." Brooxie pulled a tall bottle from the refrigerator in his office and handed it to Charlie. "This here is Cold Duck. It's a sparkling red wine, kinda fruity tasting. I thought you and Gracie might want to have a little farewell celebration."

Charlie's eyes grew wide. "Wow! Thanks, Mr...uh, I mean Brooxie."

Brooxie lowered his voice. "This'll be our secret. We don't want Miz Bonnie or Sanctified Flo to find out about it. Now, I got a lube job to finish and a carburetor to replace. You two have a good time today. The garage will probably be closed when you get back this evening. So, let's say our good-byes now."

Charlie offered his hand, but Brooxie grabbed him in a hug. "You're one fine young man, Charlie Callahan. God be with you!"

Charlie was drinking coffee at the counter when Bonnie and Gracie made it to the café. Gracie's eyes were bright even though her smile felt forced. "You ready to go, Shug?"

Charlie brushed the hair from his eyes and grinned. "You betcha, gorgeous! Thanks for the picnic, Miz Bonnie. We'll be home by dark." With that, they were off.

For once both Ouida and Buddy remained silent until the couple were in Charlie's truck. Ouida snuffed out her cigarette. "That child's heart is breaking."

"Which one?" Buddy's voice shook.

"Buddy Simpson, I've never seen you choked up before! Are you crying?" Ouida eyed him curiously.

Buddy coughed. "Of course not! This wind's just been bothering my eyes all day. How about another cup of coffee, Bonnie." He wiped his eyes on his napkin. "Did Gracie call the boy 'Shug'? I hope none of Charlie's fellow recruits get wind of that pet name. He'll never hear the end of it through basic training."

With Brooxie's help, Charlie kept his '56 Chevy running like a fine-tuned machine. They'd recently added new speakers for the radio, and the tunes from Atlanta's WQXI blared as they traveled Hwy 41 towards Atlanta. Having Charlie beside her gave Gracie's mood a boost, and she sang along with each song.

When the old Chevy rounded the curve on Hwy 78 and Stone Mountain came into view, Charlie hit the horn. "There it is! Reckon what the Indians must've thought the first time they saw this huge granite rock. Did you know Vice President Agnew was here in May for the dedication of the carving?"

Gracie laughed, "And look, it's still not finished." There was scaffolding attached to the side of the mountain.

Once they were inside the park, Charlie pointed to a line for the Skylift. "We'll have to wait if you want to ride to the top."

"Are you kidding me, Shug? Not this tomboy!" Gracie took off up the walking path with Charlie right behind her.

When he reached her, Charlie grabbed Gracie's hand and pulled her to him. "I'm glad you don't look like a tomboy anymore." He kissed her briefly. "Okay, you take the lead until you get tired."

Gracie didn't tire, and they reached the summit hand in hand. "I'm glad BonBon told me to bring my jacket." Gracie buttoned up her peacoat. "Aren't you cold?"

Charlie put his arm around her and pulled her as close as he could. "Not as long as I have you to snuggle up to."

She lay her head on his shoulder, her blue eyes sparkling. "The view is perfect today. The sky is so clear, it shimmers!"

Charlie shot her his lopsided grin. "You're the one that shimmers, baby girl." Gracie brushed Charlie's windblown hair from his eyes. Charlie chuckled. "You better enjoy that long hair because come Monday, it'll be gone."

Gracie's eyes dimmed. "Please don't remind me."

Charlie squeezed her tightly and changed the subject quickly. "Wanna race down?" He took off as Gracie squealed behind him.

Both the café and Brooxie's garage were dark when the two made it back to Zebulon. Gracie had fallen asleep on Charlie's shoulder. He nudged her awake as he pulled his car into the garage. "Come on, baby girl, let's get you inside where it's warmer."

Gracie struggled to open her eyes. "We're back already? How long did I sleep?"

Charlie chuckled as he pulled her from the car. "Most of the way. Come on up. I have a surprise waiting."

By the time she climbed the stairs to Charlie's apartment, Gracie was wide awake. "A surprise, you say! I think I've had enough surprises from you in the past month." She sat down grumpily on the couch while Charlie pulled two jelly glasses from his one cabinet and the Cold Duck from the fridge.

Gracie's eyes grew big. "What bootlegger sold you that, Charlie Callahan?"

Charlie tore off the foil and fiddled with the top. "Actually, it was a going-away gift from Brooxie."

"I should have known. What kind of drink is it anyway?" At that very moment the top popped off and a pink bubbly liquid sprayed both of them in the face.

Gracie got so tickled she slid off the couch, and Charlie slid down beside her. He kissed her face. "It tastes pretty good. Try some." He leaned his chin towards her lips for her to sample.

Charlie filled the glasses to the brim. "Now let's make a toast. I'll go first. To the girl who stole my heart and kept it: No matter where I am, you'll always be my Baby Girl. Now, take a big sip."

Gracie obliged. "That doesn't taste like Mr. Brooxie smells after he's been nipping." She giggled. "I guess it's my time to toast. To my sweet soldier boy: I'll keep the fire in my heart burning for you. But I'll really be pissed if you don't come home. Now drink!" She guzzled the bubbly liquid from her glass.

"Grace MacGregor, I've never heard such a word come from your pretty mouth." They both giggled and finished their glasses.

"My tongue is numb. Does that mean I'm drunk?"

Charlie took her glass. "Naw, just a little tipsy. But I think we've both had enough. I don't want you to pass out or throw up on our last night together."

Gracie gazed at him with serious blue eyes. "Neither do I. Take me to bed, Charlie Callahan."

"Gracie, are you sure? It's not the wine talking, is it? I don't want to take advantage…"

She put her arms around his neck. "I've been dreaming of this for a while. I'm ready to make love."

Charlie lifted her in his arms and carried her to his bed.

A bright autumn Friday disintegrated into a dark, stormy Saturday. Grace pulled her Dart up to the garage door at Brooxie's before daybreak. The gray clouds suited her gray heart.

Charlie was waiting with a small duffel bag. He threw it in the back seat. "The recruiter said we don't really need any clothing. I packed a few personal things—my glove and ball, and a couple of framed photos."

Grace was determined to be positive. "Two framed photos? Hmmm, who's the other girlfriend?" She grinned at him and caught his hand. "Give me a kiss. There'll be too many people watching when we get to Griffin."

Charlie didn't argue. He held her in his arms and kissed her until neither could breathe. "It's only two months. Then I'll get leave before I head to AIT."

Even though she tried to stop them, tears spilled from Gracie's eyes during the short drive to Griffin. There was an Army bus waiting in front of the recruitment office with several young men milling around. "I don't want to watch you board that bus. It will feel too final. Let's just say our goodbyes now."

"Okay, I understand, Gracie." Charlie held her face in his hands. "Just one last look at my gorgeous girl before I go." He kissed her gently. Charlie pulled his bag from the backseat, shut the car door, walked into the recruitment office, and was gone.

Just as Gracie pulled away, the sky opened up with a hard, cold rain.

CHAPTER TWENTY-NINE

Charlie's first week at Fort Bragg, North Carolina consisted of hurrying up and waiting as all the new recruits were processed. He stood in line for what felt like the umpteenth time to receive his uniform, which included Army-issued "skivvies," as the military called underwear. Later that day, Charlie's arm grew increasingly sore as he made his way down yet another line to receive a myriad of shots, each injected with what looked like a starter pistol.

Brooxie had been right about one thing. Charlie's drill sergeant was a real son of a bitch. A tall black man with steel blue eyes, Sergeant Cato had served two tours of duty in Vietnam and had the scars and medals to prove it.

Pope Air Force Base was right next to Fort Bragg, and during training, recruits often saw transport planes taking off nearby. Sergeant Cato always had a remark about the planes. "Look up there, soldiers. That's a C-130 filled with the 82nd Airborne headed straight for Vietnam. All you cherries better listen to everything I teach you or you'll die in those jungles."

After living at the Home for so long, Charlie was comfortable sharing barracks with a dozen other men. The latrine was another story. Back at the Home, at least they had stalls for the toilets. Here, the toilets were lined up, side by side. When he had to relieve his bowels, Charlie often found himself touching hairy legs with the fella on the toilet next to him.

One soldier in Charlie's squad had a real hangup about the side-by-side toilets. Pete Thornton, the palest white boy Charlie had ever seen, had ridden the bus from Griffin with him. Before he boarded the bus, the boy's mother was crying and fussing all over her son in front of the recruiting office. Charlie, along with all the other recruits, heard Mama refer to her son as "Sweetie Petey."

Of course, the name stuck. Charlie knew that a group of fellas could be merciless, and they were. Every time Private Thornton headed to the latrine, several of the recruits would march behind him and chant in unison: "Sweetie Petey off to beat his meaty!"

Thornton avoided the latrine as much as possible. One night Charlie heard groaning and then a loud clunk. He jumped out of his bunk to discover Pete Thornton, his skin whiter than white, rolling on the floor in agony. Someone called a medic, and Thornton was taken to the infirmary. The poor guy hadn't taken a dump since arriving at Fort Bragg.

Thornton returned in time for the morning's formation. When Charlie asked how he was feeling, Thornton managed a weak smile. "They cleaned me out, and my stomach feels better." His voice quivered. "I was always teased about being pale back home, but the teasing in the barracks is torture."

Charlie wrapped his arm around the boy's shoulder. "Don't let these hard tails get to you. I bet if you ignore them, they'll give up on the teasing. Next time you need to hit the latrine, I'll go with you and stand watch."

Charlie learned to keep his newly shorn head down and to follow orders without hesitating. His obedience and physical capabilities earned him the rank of squad leader. His fellow soldiers respected Charlie's title except for a roughneck everyone called Moose. His real name was Morgan Maddox, and he'd grown up on the mean streets of Brooklyn, New York.

Moose lived in his own little world and often paid no heed to orders. He was always the last one up at reverie, never made his bed according to military regulations, and had to be reminded almost daily to tuck in his shirt. The rest of the squad, especially Charlie as squad leader, paid the price for Moose's indifference.

Most mornings when they lined up for formation, Sergeant Cato would be screaming, "Who's missing, Callahan? If you can't get every sorry ass out here on time, I'll find me a better squad leader. I hate sorriness, you hear me? We're going to run a mile before we head to the mess hall. Maybe that'll remind you that this ain't no nursery school."

In hopes of coercing Moose into following the rules, Charlie made every effort to befriend him. One night before lights out, Charlie tried to engage him in conversation. "Hey Moose, my gal back home just sent me a box of brownies. You want one?"

Leaning down from his top bunk where he'd been studying a *Playboy* magazine, Moose grabbed the entire box with one paw. "Don't mind if I do."

Charlie was furious. "Take a couple then give it back, Moose."

Moose didn't budge. Instead, he stuffed as many brownies in his mouth as he could fit. "If your girlfriend's pussy is as good as her brownies, I'd like a taste of her."

In a split second, Charlie snatched Moose off his bunk and put him in a stranglehold. While Moose was big, Charlie was quicker and stronger.

The entire squad encircled Charlie and Moose. "Take him down, Callahan! Take that lazy SOB down!"

While Moose flung punches at his back, Charlie never loosened his hold on Moose's neck. Charlie whispered in his ear, "You gonna take that back about my girlfriend, or I'm gonna choke the life out of you."

As Charlie's grip grew tighter, Moose's face turned crimson, and his eyes started to bulge. "Okay, okay! I take it back." His voice squeaked from lack of air.

Charlie loosened his grip a little but didn't let go. "I want an apology, too." Taking advantage of the looser grip, Moose socked Charlie in the head. Charlie re-tightened his grip.

Moose gasped for air. "All right, I'm sorry. And you can have your brownies back. Just let me go."

Charlie wasn't finished. "One more thing, you lazy piece of crap. The next time you make us late for reverie or show up with your shirt untucked, I'm going to finish the job." Charlie relaxed his grip and shoved Moose against the bunk. "And that bed better be made up perfectly in the morning."

Seconds later, Sergeant Cato entered the barracks. "Everybody up and dressed in two minutes. We're taking a night hike. And there better not be any stragglers if you want to be back in time for breakfast!"

As soldiers scurried in all directions, Sergeant Cato sidled up to Charlie and muttered softly. "It's about time you took control of that yellow-bellied troublemaker. Good work, Callahan."

As squad leader, Charlie had a tiny bedroom off to the side of the open barracks. Every night, he spent his few spare minutes before lights out writing a quick note to Gracie. He rarely told her about the strenuous training and never about the sergeant's promise that they'd all ship out to Vietnam. While he wasn't afraid, he worried that any mention of a tour in 'Nam would destroy Gracie.

Back in Zebulon, Gracie kept a plentiful supply of airmail paper and stamps. Every single morning without fail, she stopped by the café and handed Cooter Renfroe a letter for Charlie.

"I bet Private Callahan gets more mail than any other soldier in Fort Bragg," Cooter commented one morning as he placed the envelope in his mailbag. "Don't worry, Gracie, I'll make sure it gets posted today."

"I hope you told 'Shug' that we all miss him." Buddy guffawed as he poured sugar in his coffee. Just as he raised his cup for a sip, Ouida punched him in the arm. "Ouida, what do you think you're doing? You done made me dribble coffee on my new tie."

Ouida blew smoke in his face. "Do not make fun of her pet name for Charlie. Next time I'll do more than ruin your tie."

Buddy hung his head and sipped what was left of his coffee.

One evening as Grace returned from school, she found a large manila envelope postmarked "Fort Bragg" waiting on the kitchen table. She tore it open with excitement. Inside was a 5 x 7 photograph of Private Charles Callahan sporting his military uniform and almost bald head. "Oh, my sweet Shug, your beautiful hair is gone."

After the café closed that night, Bonnie discovered Grace sound asleep at the kitchen table, her cheek resting on Charlie's photograph. "Gracie, wake up. I brought you some supper. It's chicken and dumplings. Come on, honey, you need to eat. You don't want to be skin and bones when Charlie comes home."

"Look what they did to his hair, BonBon! He looks so thin and forlorn. He's not even smiling. That place must be awful." Grace burst into tears.

Bonnie enfolded Gracie in her arms. "He's okay, sweet girl. The military doesn't like them to smile in these photos." Bonnie studied the picture. "But I can still see that shine in those green eyes of his. Take a look."

Grace sat up and studied the photograph again. "Yes, I guess you're right. His eyes are the same." She blew her nose on a napkin. "And his hair will grow back."

Bonnie grinned. "And as soon as he's home, I'll fatten him up with all his favorites. Now, come on and eat a little."

Grace obeyed and picked at her dinner enough to satisfy BonBon. "I have homework and a letter to write." She trudged up the stairs with Charlie's picture in her hand.

The following Tuesday, Gracie sat in the college courtyard eating a sandwich and gossiping with Marcy Harper and Bev Scroggins. The three had become quick friends since they shared almost all the same classes.

At the beginning of the quarter, Gracie had been paired with Bev to complete a project for their religion class. Bev had eyed Gracie oddly. "Don't I know you? I'm sure we've met before."

Gracie suddenly realized they had played softball on opposing teams. "You were that heavy hitter from the Thomaston Twisters, weren't you?"

Bev grinned. "And you were the catcher for the Pike County Pumas! I guess we look different without our softball uniforms." It turned out that Bev also happened to be Marcy's roommate. "I'm glad to have a Southern friend to balance out my roommate's Yankee ways," Bev told Gracie.

Since then, the three had shared coffee, class notes, and lunches daily. On this chilly afternoon, Bev crunched a chip as she said, "It's almost getting too cold to sit outside."

Gracie shivered. "I know. I need to start wearing my peacoat."

"Yinz are such wusses! Yinz wouldn't make it a day in Pennsylvania. We sunbathe on days like this." Marcy was still wearing short sleeves.

"Well, you Yankees are idiots." Bev buttoned up her sweater. "Gracie, do you have your notes from Dr. Gore's Monday lecture on Moses and the Ten Commandments? I was half asleep in class in yesterday."

Marcy laughed. "And tell Grace *why* you were asleep in class yesterday."

Bev's cheeks colored as she looked up from under her lashes. "We went to Underground Atlanta this weekend and had us a good ole time, didn't we?"

"Yep, and you were still tipsy on Monday morning." Marcy shook her head. "I told you those two-for-one cocktails were gonna kill you, but you wouldn't listen."

"Oh, hush up, Marcy! I don't have a wooden leg like you, and I'd never had a Tom Collins, much less any alcohol, before Saturday night." Bev turned to Gracie. "You should go with us this weekend, Gracie. Underground is unbelievable. There's a bar called Muhlenbrink's Saloon, and a fella named Piano Red who can kill on the piano."

"You really should come with us." Marcy began to badger Gracie. "All you do is study and write letters to that soldier boy of yours. It'll do you good to have a little fun."

Gracie wasn't sold. "I don't know. I usually help out in the café on weekends, and I have lots of laundry to do and that English 101 paper to finish."

Bev chimed in. "All work and no play will make Grace MacGregor as boring as Dr. Gore Bore! I'm sure Miz Bonnie wouldn't mind if you took a weekend off. You could pack a bag and spend the entire weekend with us in the dorm. That way if you're hungover on Sunday, she'll never know."

The two wouldn't give up until Grace caved. "Okay, I guess I could use a change in my monotonous existence."

The following Saturday afternoon, the three girls climbed into Bev's Volkswagen and headed to Atlanta. The November air had turned blustery, but it didn't keep them from walking the Underground Atlanta tracks lined with bars and eateries.

"One day we'll have the funds to try the fondue at Dante's Down the Hatch." Marcy pointed to a set of steps leading downstairs to a busy establishment.

"That's way over my budget. Let's get a slice of pizza at Jocko's." Bev led the way. "Grace, it's good to have some food on your stomach before you start drinking."

Grace was amused. "Just how are you going to get a cocktail since we're only 19?"

"Never fear!" Marcy opened her wallet and pulled out an ID with her picture and a birthdate indicating that she was 21. "Back home I have a friend who has a friend who knows a counterfeiter. Stick with me, and I'll buy drinks for all three of us."

By the time the girls made it to Muhlenbrink's, the place was standing room only. Somehow Marcy wormed her way to the bar with the other two right behind her.

Winking at Grace, Marcy laid her ID on the bar and ordered three Tom Collins. The bartender barely glanced at her license. "Okay, you two, ante up. I can't afford to pay for your drinks." Marcy handed each girl two glasses. "It's almost 7. We just made the two-for-one cutoff. Drink slowly so these will last unless yinz got lots of cash."

The girls wriggled their way closer to the piano. "Look, those folks are leaving. Let's grab their table." Bev hurried ahead and almost knocked down a young man who was headed for the same table. "This one's for me and my friends. Sorry!"

The young man, brown eyes dancing, smiled at the girls. "Certainly, you three Sheilas wouldn't deny this old Bluey the extra chair."

Bev's eyes grew big. "You talk funny. Where you from, fella? Not a single one of us gals are named Sheila, and you certainly aren't blue!"

"A Sheila is a pretty girl where I'm from, and we redheads are often nicknamed Blueys." He smiled charmingly. "I'm from down unda."

Grace couldn't help herself. "Down under where?"

He threw his head back and laughed. His hair was the color of ginger, his eyes as brown as molasses, and his teeth pearly white. "That would be Australia."

His chocolate eyes seemed to bore into Gracie's blue ones. "Well, we Southerners are known for our hospitality," Grace said. "And since you are so far from home, it would be impolite not to offer you this extra seat." She wasn't sure if the two sips of alcohol had made her sound so coy, but the fella sat down.

Just as the four of them got settled at their table, Piano Red and his band started their second set. Grace was glad it was too loud to make conversation. There was something about the redheaded Aussie that caused her heart to beat a little too fast.

By the time the set was over, both Marcy and Bev had finished both of their cocktails. "Want another one, Gracie, or are you still good?"

Grace hadn't even finished her first one. She remembered how quickly she'd gotten tipsy on Cold Duck that night with Charlie when she ended up leading him to bed. "I'm good. Thanks."

Bev hopped up beside Marcy. "I'll go with you. I need to find the little girls' room."

Before Grace could join her two friends, they had disappeared into the crowd. She sipped her drink awkwardly to avoid looking into the Australian's eyes again.

He seemed quite at ease as he took a swallow of beer from a sweaty mug. "So, is your cocktail too strong? These American beers are like drinking water compared to the beer back home."

Gracie didn't want to be impolite. "I'm not much of a drinker. With the way my friends are guzzling, I'll probably be driving them home."

"Where's home for you ladies?" He smiled warmly.

"We all attend Tift College in Forsyth, Georgia. It's about 85 miles down I-75 South."

"That's not far from Macon, is it not? I'm planning to make my way down there soon. I hear Macon is the home of the Allman Brothers. I love their music."

Gracie found her voice. "So, are you a musician?"

Mischief played in his eyes. "Not exactly. I play a little guitar in my spare time."

"And what brought you to America? Are you researching the history of rock and roll?" She sipped her drink.

"I wish I had the time to do that. I'm in the foreign exchange program at Emory. I'm studying to be a cardiologist. I'm Hugh Lockett, by the way."

"Grace MacGregor. Should I call you Dr. Lockett?"

Again, he leaned back with an amused laugh. "No, please no. Dr. Lockett would be my father back in Darlinghurst. Please to meet you, Grace MacGregor." He offered his hand, and she took it. "You may have the bluest eyes I've ever seen!"

Just as Gracie began to blush and stammer, her friends returned. Marcy was practically dragging Bev. "I hate to break up this lovely party, but this Cinderella is about to turn into a pumpkin. Gracie, I'm glad you know how to drive a straight stick because Bev is in no condition to get behind the wheel."

Hugh stood up as the three girls gathered their coats and purses. "Perhaps I'll see you lovely Sheilas again." While he directed his words to all three of them, his eyes were on Gracie's.

Marcy spoke up. "You can't miss Tift College. The college's sign is right on I-75 South. Look us up if you're ever down that way."

Grace was glad she'd left her second Tom Collins untouched. Both her friends were snoring by the time she reached the interstate. The quiet drive back to Forsyth gave her time to think about the unusual man with his funny accent and laughing brown eyes. She'd never met anyone like him. As a matter of fact, she'd never even taken notice of any other male besides Charlie.

CHAPTER THIRTY

A few days before Christmas, Private Charlie Callahan ducked into Brooxie's Garage in hopes that no one would see him. His company had been released a day early after they graduated from Basic Training. During the long bus ride to Griffin, he talked Pete Thornton into driving him to Zebulon so he could surprise Grace.

Pete was more than willing. Once Charlie had taken Pete under his wing, the teasing from the other recruits had eased. Pete's parents were waiting at the bus depot in Griffin when the two arrived. Pete's mother grabbed him in her arms. "My Sweetie Petey is home!"

"Aww, Mom. Don't call me that. I'm a grown man!'

"He sure is, Gladys. Let's drop that nickname. How you doing, son?" A tall man with Pete's same coloring, or lack thereof, put an arm around his son's shoulder. Then he smiled at Charlie. "And this must be your squad leader." He extended a huge paw to Charlie. "Thanks for keeping an eye out for our boy."

Charlie offered his hand. "No problem, Mr. Thornton. And I appreciate that y'all are offering me a ride to Zebulon."

Mr. Thornton pulled a set of keys from his pocket. "And you two soldiers will be riding in style." He turned to his son. "Since you couldn't get home for your birthday, here's your belated gift."

Behind the Thornton's station wagon sat a blue 1970 Mustang convertible. Charlie knew from conversations with Pete that his dad owned the Ford dealership in Griffin. At the sight of the beautiful car, Pete let out an excited whistle. After thanking his dad and carefully inspecting his new ride, Pete gladly drove Charlie home, chatting excitedly the whole way.

By the time Charlie made it home, the garage was empty except for Brooxie, tucked underneath his brother's old Chrysler. Charlie could hear him muttering. "This goldarned piece of junk. It's time Bushy bought a new automobile!"

Still dressed in his uniform, Charlie stood next to the car and cleared his throat. "Sorry, I didn't hear you come in," Brooxie grunted as he slid out from under the car. When he bumped into a pair of black boots, he said, "What can I do you for, mister?"

Charlie guffawed. "It's me, Brooxie!"

"Well, I'll be a horse's patoot! Charlie Callahan! What the hell? I thought you weren't due back until tomorrow. That's all Gracie's talked about for the last week." Brooxie wiped grease from his palms and grabbed Charlie's outstretched hand. "The garage ain't been the same without you."

Charlie couldn't stop grinning. "It's good to be home."

Brooxie backed up and took him in. "Boy, you ain't nothing but feet, peter, and muscle! How's the Army treating you?"

"I can't complain. I got through Basic by following your advice. I had a tough drill sergeant, but he taught me how to stay alive through just about anything. I've got until after Christmas before I report to AIT." Charlie rubbed the top of his cropped head.

Brooxie laughed. "That hair will grow back soon enough. And where they sendin' you for AIT?"

"I'm headed to armor school in Fort Knox, Kentucky. I scored the highest in mechanics in my class. The instructor said I'd make a good armor mechanic. I told him I owe everything I know to the best mechanic in the state of Georgia."

Brooxie blushed and quickly changed the subject. "Fort Knox, you say? Maybe you can bring me a couple bars of gold when you come home on leave."

"I hope I'll be able to come home occasionally. I can drive my personal vehicle there, so at least I'll have some wheels."

Brooxie reached for a set of keys hanging on a corkboard. "Your truck is in good running condition. I've been cranking it twice a week and even drove it a couple of times. It needed new spark plugs, so I took care of that." He tossed the keys to Charlie. "I was plannin' to turn up the heat in your apartment tomorrow morning. It's probably a little chilly up there."

Charlie stuck the keys into his pocket. "After sleeping outdoors in the mountains of North Carolina, I can handle a little chill. Thanks for taking care of my truck, Brooxie. How much do I owe you for the spark plugs?"

"Shoot, it's on the house. The least I can do for someone serving our country. I gotta get back to this piece of junk my brother calls a car. I'm sure you have better things to do than watch me." Brooxie grinned and rolled back under the chassis.

Charlie took his time shaving and showering in hot water for a change. He splashed on a little English Leather cologne from the small bottle Grace had given him for Christmas last year. He'd had no use for it in the Army but wanted to look and smell his best for his girl.

He dressed in civvies for the first time in two months. His jeans had gotten loose in the waist but clung to his calves and thighs, and his shirt was almost too tight across the shoulders. All the PT had paid off.

By the time he showed up to surprise Gracie, the café was filling up with lunch regulars. There was no sign of her, but he could hear Miz Bonnie in the kitchen. He chose a stool at the counter and grabbed a menu to cover his face.

His back was to Ouida and Buddy when they sat down at their usual table. He heard Ouida whispering. "Who's that fella at the counter? He's not from around these parts."

"I don't know. Looka here. Bonnie's got pecan pie for dessert today. I'm ordering it first before it all gets gone."

As if on cue, Bonnie pushed through the swinging doors with a plate in each hand. Buddy waved furiously at her as she passed by their table. "Bonnie, save me a piece of the pecan pie!"

"Gotcha, Buddy. I hope you don't mind the wait. We're a little short-handed today. Gracie went to Thomaston to do a little Christmas shopping." She set the plates in front of two customers and scurried back into the kitchen.

Charlie's heart sank when he heard that Gracie wasn't there. Vern, who'd been flipping burgers, turned from the griddle. "What'll you have to drink, sir?" Then his eyes met Charlie's. "Well, I'll be, is it really you?"

Ouida, her sharp ears never missing anything, turned her gaze towards the counter just in time to see Charlie lay a shushing finger across his lips. "Charlie Callahan, what are you doin' home today? Gracie will be beside herself that she's not here." Ouida stood up. "I guess I get the first hug."

With that lopsided grin covering his face, Charlie obliged. "We got released a day early. I was going to surprise her."

On his customary stool by the cash register, Cooter Renfroe raised his voice. "Our soldier is home for Christmas." That was all it took for Charlie to be surrounded by well-wishers.

Even Buddy took a break from his lunch menu to stand up and pat Charlie on the back. "We sure have missed you around here. The Army's done muscled you up, boy!"

Ouida slapped Buddy on the arm. "He's not a boy anymore. He's a full- grown man!"

Arms full as she backed though the swinging doors, Bonnie still hadn't seen Charlie. "What's all the ruckus about out here?" Then she turned around. "You're home! You are a sight for sore eyes, Charlie Callahan!"

She quickly delivered the plates then hurried to give Charlie a hug. She stood back and studied him from his buzz cut to his trim waist. "You are one solid rock, aren't you?! Now sit down and I'll get you some lunch. We have meatloaf with mashed potatoes. How does that sound?"

Charlie grinned. "Anything you cook sounds wonderful, Miz Bonnie. A million times better than slop they served at the mess hall. What time will Gracie be home?"

"Oh my, oh my! Gracie should be back in a little while. She had a big surprise party planned for tomorrow evening. We can still have the party. Everybody in town knows you're coming home for Christmas." Bonnie smiled. "I guess the surprise will be on Gracie."

She scurried into the kitchen and returned with a huge helping of meatloaf accompanied by a pile of mashed potatoes and green beans. "Would you like a glass of sweet tea?"

Charlie dug into the food. "Miz Bonnie, I've dreamed of your sweet tea for weeks!"

By mid-afternoon, the café had emptied except for Ouida, who nursed a third cup of coffee and a fourth cigarette. Bonnie was busy prepping for the supper crowd, and Vern had taken a few hours off to do some Christmas shopping of his own.

Charlie was enjoying a second piece of Bonnie's pecan pie. "Miz Ouida, everybody's been asking about me. How are *y'all* doing?"

Ouida blew a smoke circle. "Don't you mean how is *Gracie* doing?"

"You always could see straight through the bull, Miz Ouida." Charlie finished the last of his sweet tea.

"That girl has certainly missed you, but she's also started to grow into herself."

"Whaddya mean, Miz Ouida?"

"She's learned to balance going to school, studying long hours, and working in the café. She's lost that teenage insecurity, Charlie. You'll see. She's blossoming into an intelligent, sophisticated young woman."

Charlie shook his head. "I hope she's not too sophisticated for this old country boy."

Ouida walked behind the counter and poured herself another cup of coffee. "Don't worry about that. You should see that girl's face light up when Cooter delivers a letter from you. She still carries a torch for you, Charlie. And by the way, you've matured quite a bit yourself. I can see it in the way you hold yourself, though you still have that mischief in those eyes. I hope you never lose the mischief."

Charlie beamed. "Me too." Just like old times, he gathered his dishes and carried them into the kitchen to wash.

He found Miz Bonnie busy mixing up her famous Mud Hens. "I'm baking these fresh especially for you, Charlie." She popped them into the oven. "Now onto supper. I'm serving your favorite—fried chicken." She pulled a large tray from the refrigerator.

"You need help cutting up the chicken?" Charlie didn't think about what he was saying until the words were out of his mouth.

Bonnie froze for a moment before pushing down the memory. "Umm, no. Vern and I got them cut up this morning after breakfast."

Since he'd opened the can of worms, Charlie figured he might as well continue down that path. "Any news about Beau Loosier's whereabouts?"

There was a slight tremor in Bonnie's hands as she battered the chicken. "The last report in the *Thomaston Times* was about two weeks ago. The Loosiers have offered a $10,000 reward for any information. The sheriff requested help from the GBI. They discovered that an old Ford car was reported missing from the A&P parking lot in Griffin on the same night Beau disappeared. Police found Beau's car parked in that same parking lot where the Ford was stolen. The owner of the missing car admitted that he kept a spare key in the glove compartment. That's about it."

Charlie took a deep breath. "How are you doing, Miz Bonnie?"

Bonnie was glad to change the subject. "We've been busy in the café. Ashley Miles works a few shifts during the busiest lunch days since Gracie isn't here to help. She misses you and so do I, Charlie."

Just then, the back door to the kitchen opened and in walked Grace. She was dressed in jeans and her soft blue sweater the color of her eyes, which grew to the size of saucers when she saw Charlie.

Charlie shot her his best lopsided grin. "Hi, Baby Girl. Long time, no see." He took three giant steps and pulled her into his arms.

Realizing she was in the way, Bonnie made an excuse. "I'll go see if Ouida is ready to settle up."

They held each other so tight that neither could barely breathe. Gracie was the first to pull away. She rubbed her hand across Charlie's stubbly head. "Fuzzy Wuzzy was a bear; Fuzzy Wuzzy had no hair." Then she burst into tears.

"What's wrong, Baby Girl!? Do I look that bad?"

Gracie hiccupped. "No. You look bigger and stronger and more confident. What about me?"

Charlie gave her a lustful once over. "Good enough to eat!"

"Oh Shug, I'm a mess. I wanted to be all made up and dressed in something spectacular when you arrived. And, and, I had all these plans to surprise you. I hope you aren't disappointed."

"Hush your fussing and kiss me." He pulled her close and kissed her until Gracie forgot why she'd been upset.

The day ended in Charlie's apartment. By then, Gracie had showered and done her hair, which hung in soft curls around her shoulders. She laid her head on Charlie's shoulder. "I hope you'll act surprised about the party we have planned for you tomorrow."

Charlie tucked a blonde strand of hair behind her ear. "I will, I promise. But I'm glad we have tonight to ourselves." His voice took a serious turn. "There's something I've been thinking about and need to tell you."

Gracie raised her head and looked into his eyes. "What's wrong, Charlie? Have they told you that you're going to Vietnam."

Charlie kissed her forehead. "No, I won't know my next assignment until I finish AIT. I just think you need these next two months while I'm away to be certain that you really want to spend the rest of your life with me."

Tears glistened in the corners of Gracie's eyes. "Of course, I want to spend my life with you, Charlie. I just don't want to be a widowed bride before I'm 20!"

Charlie lifted her chin and gazed into her eyes. "I understand your feelings and will respect them. But if I get posted somewhere other than Vietnam, I want us to be engaged before I ship out." He wiped a tear from Gracie's cheek. "But while I'm at AIT, I want you to feel footloose and fancy free."

"What do you mean by that, Charlie?"

"Baby Girl, you've never dated anyone but me. I know you must meet fellas when you go out with your new girlfriends. If you want to date one of those fellas, you should. I couldn't stand it if you ever regretted anything or felt like you settled for me."

"You are crazy, Charlie Callahan! I wouldn't call being in love with you settling. Don't you realize that you're the pick of the litter?" She giggled. "Enough ridiculous talk. This may be the only night we have alone. Let's not waste it."

Charlie folded her in his arms, picked her up, and carried her to his bed. The night was not wasted.

CHAPTER THIRTY-ONE

The week of Christmas flew by at record speed. Charlie and Gracie spent every waking moment together. Two days after Christmas, it was time for Charlie to head off to Fort Knox. Before daybreak, he and Gracie held each other next to Charlie's truck in Bonnie's driveway.

Charlie bade Bonnie farewell as she headed across the street to start breakfast at the café. Now the early morning sky began to turn pink with the sunrise. "It's time, Gracie."

Gracie clung to him. "No, no, no! Just a little longer." She sniffled as she tucked her head beneath his chin.

"Let me get one last look at my Baby Girl." He cupped his hands around her face. "I want to remember those crystal blue eyes and those gorgeous freckles across your nose. That's what I'll see whenever I get lonely for you."

The two kissed one last time then Charlie climbed into his truck. As he backed out of the driveway, he could see Gracie's lips quivering. She managed a smile and a small salute. Then she turned her back so she wouldn't have to watch his truck disappear.

Gracie spent more time sulking than helping in the café that morning. At least waiting tables kept her busy. Ouida and Buddy did their best to cheer her up, but Gracie was too forlorn to care.

After the breakfast crowd emptied, Bonnie shooed her back to the house. "Why don't you take a nap before lunch? You were up before I was this morning."

Grace trudged back to the house. Instead of sleeping, though, she spent the time writing a letter to Charlie. She ended it with a promise: "There'll never be anyone else for me. You are my one and only Shug."

Two days later Gracie had regained her usual upbeat disposition and was busy waiting tables at lunch. She'd just served Ouida and Buddy their Blue Plate special when she saw two familiar faces come through the door. "What are you two doing here?"

Bev Scroggins and Marcy Harper grabbed the last two stools at the counter. "Yinz have a great place here. The food smells delicious. Any chance I can get a cheesesteak?" Marcy grinned as Ouida turned a curious eye towards her.

"Miss Ouida, these are my friends from Tift." Gracie handed the girls menus. "Bev is the Thomaston softball player I told you about, and Marcy is from Pennsylvania."

Before Ouida could respond, Buddy interrupted. "What's a cheesesteak? Sounds like something I'd enjoy."

Vern turned around from the griddle. "Miss, I can make you a cheesesteak sandwich. We used to serve those in the Navy."

Marcy beamed. "And some fries on the side?" Vern got to work.

Bev studied the menu. "I'll have the burger and fries with a side of slaw. Is it homemade?"

"Of course, it is." Gracie wiped down the counter and delivered two glasses of water to her friends. "So, you never answered. What are y'all doing here?"

"I picked up Marcy at the airport this morning. We figured you could use some company now that your soldier boy is gone." Bev sipped her water. "How about some iced tea. Is it sweet?"

Gracie grinned for the first time in days. "Is there any other kind?"

Marcy watched as Vern expertly cut a thin piece of steak and allowed it to sizzle on the griddle. "Now that's what I'm talking about. I'll have some of that sweet tea, too. I couldn't get my mother to make it like yinz do."

Bev interrupted. "Whatcha doing on New Year's Eve, Gracie?"

Gracie shrugged. "I haven't even thought about it."

As Vern placed the cheesesteak sandwich on the counter, Marcy smiled in approval. "Gracie, you don't have to think about it. Bev and I have it all planned. We're going to Underground, and you're going with us."

Gracie handed Bev the ketchup bottle and sighed. "Not this time. I'd be an old stick in the mud. Besides I don't have anything to wear to Atlanta on New Year's Eve."

Ouida, who hadn't missed one word of the conversation, intervened. "We can fix that. I haven't bought your Christmas present yet, Gracie. I was waiting for you to have time to go with me to the French Shoppe in Thomaston to pick out something. They're having a huge after-Christmas sale."

Bev grinned. "Ha, there you go! Now you have no argument. My cousin Olivia is a nurse at Georgia Baptist. She and her friends are heading to Maggie Valley, North Carolina for a skiing trip, and she's offered to let me stay in her apartment on New Year's Eve. It's just a hop, skip, and a jump from Underground. So, we'll have a place to crash if we're, if we're...you know. If we're too tired to drive home."

Buddy just hooted. "Yep, it's always good to have a place to crash after a party in Atlanta."

"Who's going to Atlanta?" Bonnie pushed through the swinging doors with a pan of warm brownies to place in the display case.

"BonBon, these are my friends from Tift. You know, the ones I'm always telling you about—Bev and Marcy."

Bonnie slid the pan into the display case and wiped her hands. "I'm so happy to meet you girls, and you couldn't have stopped by at a better time. Gracie's had the mullygrubs ever since Charlie left. Vern, don't charge these two ladies. Lunch is on the house. Make sure y'all get one of these warm brownies, too."

Marcy grinned. "I'll take one for now and one to go, Miz MacGregor. And yinz cheesesteak's almost as good as back home."

"We'll have to make it a regular on our menu, then. And please call me Bonnie." She turned to Bev. "And you're from Thomaston, right Bev? Are you any kin to Estelle Scroggins?"

Bev smiled. "Yes ma'am, she's my great aunt."

"I thought you must be related. It's so nice to finally meet Gracie's friends. She talks about you two all the time, at least when she's not mooning over Charlie. I hope you gals can cheer her up."

Marcy interrupted. "We're taking her to Underground Atlanta for New Year's Eve. We have a place to stay and everything."

Bonnie raised her eyebrows until Bev explained. "My cousin Olivia has an apartment near Georgia Baptist. She'll be out of town and has given me the key. Olivia is my Aunt Estelle's granddaughter."

Bonnie looked relieved. "That sounds okay." Then she turned to Gracie, "Quit moping around here and go have some fun with your friends." And so, it was decided.

True to her word, the next morning after breakfast at the café, Ouida insisted on Gracie accompanying her to the French Shoppe. As she expertly parked her Cadillac in a spot on the Thomaston square, Ouida began her usual speech. "Now no worries about the price, Gracie. This is on me, and Buddy sent money for new shoes to match your outfit."

Gracie shrugged; she knew there was no sense in arguing with Ouida. However, after trying on several pieces from the sales rack, she hadn't found the right New Year's Eve look.

Ouida knocked on the dressing room door. "Try these two together." Through the small door opening, she handed Grace a pair of black velvet hip-hugging bell bottoms and a hot pink, long-sleeved blouse in a soft, creamy fabric.

Gracie had to admit that the fit was perfect, but Ouida couldn't get her to come out of the dressing room. "It's not on sale, Miss Ouida. I know BonBon would have a conniption if she saw the price tag."

Ouida rattled the handle on the door. "What Bonnie doesn't know won't hurt her. Now come on out and model for me."

Gracie opened the door to Ouida's oohs and aahs. "Honey, you were born to wear that. Those pants hug your hips just right, and that blouse is gorgeous! I have some costume jewelry that's all the rave right now. I can lend it to you." Ouida studied her once again. "What I wouldn't give to have your perfect figure."

"Oh, Miss Ouida, what are you talking about? You have a great figure!"

Ouida smiled and sighed. "A lot of good it does me."

By the time the two headed home, they'd added a pair of black strappy sandals with platform heels. "I hope I don't break my neck walking in these things. How can I ever thank you and Mr. Buddy?"

Ouida blew smoke out her half-opened window. "Honey, you have no idea what joy you bring to both Buddy and me. We've known you from the beginning when you were a skinny little thing with tangled curls. I thought we'd never get all those tangles out." They both laughed. "Just have a good time while you can, Gracie. Youth is so fleeting. Don't waste it."

"You sound just like Charlie."

"What do you mean, sweetie?"

A tear hit Gracie's blouse. "He suggested I date other people while he's away. He wants me to make sure I'm not settling for him. Can Charlie really believe that? There's no man on this earth I'd rather have."

"Charlie is wise beyond his years, Gracie. It's just like all those outfits you tried on at the French Shoppe. It took several tries before you found the right fit."

Gracie shook her head. "But Charlie and I are a perfect fit. You know that, Miss Ouida."

"Oh, my sweet girl. How do you know that for sure until you try a few others? I was young and naïve when I married. Jack was my first real boyfriend, and I was so ready to be out from under my parents' roof and their overbearing ways. It wasn't too long before I realized I'd made a huge mistake. Check out some other fish in the sea before you settle on the only one you've ever known."

The rest of their drive was silent as Gracie pondered Ouida's advice.

On New Year's Eve, Bev and Marcy arrived just in time for lunch at the café. While Thursday's special was pork chops, all three girls convinced Vern to grill up cheesesteak sandwiches for them.

"Gracie, do you think we're turning into Yankees?" Bev giggled as she took another bite.

Marcy answered for Grace. "I don't think yinz are in any danger of becoming Yankees. Not with those Southern drawls. Hurry up. We need to load up Bev's VW and get going."

"What's your hurry?" Grace dipped her last fry in some ketchup.

Marcy feigned a shocked look. "Do you know how long it's going to take us to do our hair and makeup? I want to be at Muhlenbrink's before it's so crowded that we can't find a seat. I heard on the radio that Piano Red would have the entire band there tonight. They call themselves Dr. Feelgood and the Union. We'll be dancing out of our shoes."

Her excitement was contagious. "I just hope I can *walk* in the shoes that Ouida and I bought in Thomaston."

Ouida sidled up beside the girls and stuck a twenty-dollar bill in Grace's pocket. "Have a cocktail on me, Gracie. There'll be a whole school of fish out there tonight. You girls just watch out for the sharks."

Marcy had been smart to suggest they arrive early. The apartment was small with only one bedroom and one bathroom. The girls took turns primping in the bathroom mirror.

Bev stepped out of the bedroom dressed in a red one-piece hotpants suit and white go-go boots. Marcy approved. "Wow, those huge earrings look so chic with your short hair! She turned to Gracie. "Let's put your hair in an updo with lots of fringe around your face."

Marcy was a magician with a comb and some hairspray. Standing behind Gracie and peering into the mirror, she grinned. "You could be Goldie Hawn's sister."

Gracie dressed quickly and added Ouida's long string of costume pearls and pearl drop earrings to finish her look. Bev stopped applying lipstick to study Gracie. "Girl, you're gonna turn some heads tonight."

Marcy had chosen a pair of paisley bell bottoms and matching blouse, with sleeves cinched at the elbows that then flowed out into bat wings. "My mom's a whiz with the sewing machine. She copied this outfit from a picture of Cher that I showed her." Her black platform boots made her two inches taller. "Easier to see all the men in the crowd," she laughed. "You gals ready?"

Bev pulled a note from her cousin's refrigerator. "Olivia suggested we take a taxi. Parking will be insane tonight. She says this company is very reasonable."

Gracie pulled Ouida's $20 from her evening bag. "My treat, then."

CHAPTER THIRTY-TWO

By the time the girls arrived, the bar at Muhlenbrink's was already three deep with thirsty patrons. The band was still setting up, and "Born to be Wild" by Steppenwolf blared from the jukebox.

Marcy moaned. "This is absolutely crazy! It'll take us an hour to get a drink. She scanned the crowd and spied someone waving. "Wait a minute. Is that the guy with the funny Aussie accent standing by that table in the corner?"

Gracie felt her ears burn, but she didn't move. Bev had to grab her by the arm. "Come on, Gracie. He's saved us a seat." She pushed Gracie through the crowd.

Hugh Lockett had not only safeguarded a table for them, but he'd also ordered drinks. "It's Tom Collins for you three Sheilas, isn't it?" He grinned at all three girls, but his eyes sparkled with delight at the sight of Grace.

She felt the heat rise in her neck. "How'd you know we'd be here?"

Hugh's brown eyes danced as he offered his infectious laugh. "I took a chance that you'd be back."

As Dr. Feelgood and the Union started up, two young men in yellow sweaters and navy Georgia Tech parkas stopped by the table. "You ladies want to dance?"

Bev took a huge swig of her cocktail and jumped up. "You betcha!"

Marcy eyed the taller guy who grinned back at her. "I dig your outfit. Come on, let's dance." And away they went.

Grace felt Hugh's gaze on her. "You look fabulous, Miss Grace! You are a good sort, you are."

She returned his gaze and smiled. "A good sort? I've never heard that before."

Hugh took a chug of his beer and then let out that glorious laugh. "It means that you are one pretty Sheila. Wanna dance?"

Before Grace could answer, he swept her onto the dance floor where they stayed for the band's entire set. By the time they returned to their table, they discovered Bev, Marcy, and their two new Tech friends had replenished their cocktails.

"Yinz having fun?" Marcy's words were slightly slurred, and Grace wondered how many Tom Collins she'd already had.

Bev giggled. "Looks like your Aussie friend knows how to dance. I saw y'all getting down out there."

Grace blushed. "It's really hot in here, isn't it?"

Hugh took her by the elbow. "Why don't we get some fresh air." With Grace hanging onto his arm, Hugh pushed his way through the crowd.

The night air had turned crisp and breezy. Gracie shivered. "Here, take my jacket." Before she could protest, Hugh had draped his sports coat around her shoulders. He was dressed in khakis and a button-down oxford shirt. He casually propped one foot against a lamp post.

Grace swallowed and tried to make small talk. "I like your boots. They're different from any I've ever seen."

He grinned once again showing his pearly white teeth. "You can't find boots like these in America. They're Blundstones made only in Tasmania since about 1870. Can't find khakis like these here either. They're called KingGees for King George. They're the tops."

"The tops of what?" Grace's blue eyes twinkled.

"That means the very best. KingGee made uniforms for Australian soldiers in World War II. My father still has his."

"Really? What did he do in the war?" Gracie snuggled underneath Hugh's jacket.

"He served as a medic in North Africa for two years. When the war ended, he returned to Australia and finished his medical studies at the Sydney University of Medicine. He had just started his practice when I came along in 1949." He smiled with those chocolate eyes.

Gracie smiled back. "So that's why you want to be a doctor. To follow in your father's footsteps?"

Hugh's eyes turned serious. "Let's just say that's what my father expects of me. If I had my druthers, I'd be in a rock band. That's one reason I wanted to participate in the exchange program in America. I'm not going home until I see the Allman Brothers in concert."

"You know they live in Macon, don't you? That's not far from my college. You'll have to check out their concert schedule."

"I already have. They'll be at the Macon City Auditorium in late February. I already have two tickets. Would you like to go with me?"

Grace hesitated. This man with the dark eyes and contagious smile mesmerized her. But she wasn't ready to agree to a date. Even though Ouida had advised her to check out the competition, it felt like such a betrayal to Charlie.

She was saved by her two very drunk friends with their Tech fellas in tow. "There you are! Did you know it's almost midnight?" Bev was wobbling in her boots.

Marcy wasn't in much better shape. She was holding onto her young man to keep from falling. "We're going to the Varsity. I think Bev and I need some grease to sober us up." She nodded towards the two guys. "Pete and Ricky are going to give us a ride home afterwards. Yinz want to go?"

The thought of greasy fries turned Gracie's stomach. "Um, not really. I'll catch a cab and see y'all at the apartment."

Bev eyed Hugh and snickered. "Yeah, I bet. There's a key under the mat."

Gracie blushed as they walked away. "Well, at least they're not driving. Maybe some chili dogs and fries will sober them up." She handed Hugh his jacket. "Now I need to find a taxi."

Hugh caught her arm gently. "My wagon is parked right down the street. What about a late breakfast and some coffee? There's a Waffle House on Clairmont not far from Emory. It stays open all night, so it's popular with us med students." He flashed that charming grin again.

While her head said no, her heart said yes. "I've never eaten at a Waffle House." She hesitated and then smiled. "Do you have a pair of oxen to pull that wagon?

"Not exactly. You'll see." Hugh offered his arm and led Gracie down the street to a Studebaker Wagonaire. "Here's my vehicle."

He opened the passenger door for Grace who couldn't control her giggles. "How did you ever end up with a station wagon?"

Hugh cranked the engine and shifted into reverse. "Now that's a good story. I came to Atlanta in late July to share an apartment with another bloke studying medicine here. Garry had finished his studies but was hanging around to do some touring before he returned Down Unda. He bought the wagon from a doctor with four kids and a fifth one on the way. The doctor's wife was insisting that they needed a bigger car."

"Is there really a bigger station wagon than this one?" Gracie's eyes sparkled with humor.

"Believe it or not, the Pontiac Estate dwarfs this old car. This one's a 1963, but Garry kept it in good running condition. We spent the rest of the summer on the road and went all the way up the east coast. The seats fold down and can sleep two people easily. We never had to pay for a motel room.

When Garry left in September, I took over the apartment lease and the car. I'll sell the wagon when I head home and mail Garry the profits."

"Sounds like a pretty good deal." Gracie rolled her eyes. "I haven't traveled much. You've seen more of the United States than I have."

"You need to get out more, little Sheila."

Fifteen minutes later, they were led to the only empty booth at the Waffle House on Clairmont. Grace was amazed at the breakfast menu. "I've never seen so many ways to have hash browns."

Hugh added sugar to his coffee. "Smothered and covered is my favorite, but I think I'll leave off the onions tonight," he said with grin.

Grace settled on scrambled eggs, crispy bacon, plain hash browns, and toast. "Playing it safe, I see." Hugh turned to their waitress, "I'll have fried eggs, snags, toast, with a side of chips."

The waitress wrinkled her forehead. "Sir, we don't serve chips, and I have no idea what snags are."

"Sorry miss, I meant sausage and French fries." He handed the bewildered waitress his menu as he grinned at Grace. "Sometimes I forget that I'm not in Australia."

Grace smiled back. "Tell me more about life as an Aussie." She stirred some cream into her coffee. "What was it like growing up there?"

For the next two hours, Hugh entertained Gracie with all things Australian. "You know, our summer is your winter. We actually spend Christmas at the beach. My family has a beach house at Gosford in New South Wales about two hours from Sydney. We'd spend two weeks there every December. I learned how to surf when I was eight years old."

Grace ordered a third cup of coffee and another plate of hash browns. "The only thing I know about surfing comes from songs by the Beach Boys. I'd love to ride a surfboard one day. The closest saltwater to me is the coast of Savannah. We do have lots of freshwater lakes and ponds for fishing. Did you fish much back home?"

"Oh yes! Night fishing was the best. My dad would take me out on the Hawkesbury River. There was an old shipwreck, the HMS Parramatta that's been scuttled there since 1934."

"What kind of fish did you catch?" Grace squirted catsup on her hashbrowns.

"Most of the time we'd catch hairtail fish. They're good to eat but ugly to look at. They're shaped like a snake and have sharp teeth."

Gracie's eyes grew wide. "Would they bite?"

Hugh tilted his head with that beautiful laugh of his. "Oh yes, that's why we'd use a torch to identify the fish and always had our Nulla Nulla nearby."

"A torch with fire? What's a Nulla Nulla?"

He laughed again. "A torch is what you Americans call a flashlight, and a Nulla Nulla is an aboriginal weapon that looks like a mallet."

Grace returned the laugh. "You Aussies have some funny words. What's the biggest fish you ever caught?"

"One night we took the big boat out on the Hawksbury River and towed a skiff behind it. We anchored the big boat and then took the skiff to get closer to shore. It wasn't long before my dad pulled up something too heavy to land in the skiff. He had to cut the line. It was an enormous Pike eel."

Gracie was enthralled. "What's a Pike eel?"

"A huge snakelike creature with a prehistoric head, almost like a dinosaur. This one was 14 feet long. It began circling our little skiff and thrashing its body. When my dad shone his torch on it, we could see its head on one side of the skiff and hear its tail beating the other side. Needless to say, we paddled back to the big boat as fast as we could."

Gracie's eyes were huge. "How creepy! I'd like to see one of those."

Hugh took her hand. "Perhaps you will one day." He cleared his throat. "Enough about me. Tell me about you and your family."

Grace saw sincere interest in his eyes, and so she began. "I'm adopted. My adoptive mother is Bonnie MacGregor, but I call her BonBon."

Hugh squeezed her hand. "Did you know your real parents?"

There was an easy comfort in the way Hugh asked her. Those brown eyes penetrated her blue ones with a tenderhearted intensity that melted Gracie.

The dam burst inside her, unleashing the story of her life, a story she'd never really shared in its entirety with anyone besides Charlie. She omitted the fact that her real mother was a prostitute and a junkie and chose not to revisit her terrifying ordeal with Beau Loosier. Instead, she regaled Hugh with stories of the amusing patrons of the café.

By the time she finished, the dark sky had evaporated into a soft sunrise. "You have lived an interesting life, Grace MacGregor!" Hugh hesitated for a moment. "So, are you and Charlie engaged?"

Grace swallowed at the mention of Charlie. "Um, no. Not yet. He wanted me to be absolutely sure before we, we…"

Hugh leaned across the table and brushed a loose strand of hair behind Gracie's ear. "So, it's not too late for me to change your mind?"

Grace felt herself nodding. "No, I guess it's not too late." The words slipped out before she could stop them. What was this feeling she had for Hugh? They were like two lonely souls who had collided unexpectedly.

They held hands as they walked to Hugh's car. He opened the door but stalled for a moment as his brown eyes met her blue ones. "I just realized it's 1971. Can I give you a New Year's kiss, Grace MacGregor?" Grace relaxed into his arms as her heart skipped a beat.

"Where in the Sam Hill have you been, Grace MacGregor?" Bev stood in her pajamas as she opened the apartment door. "Another 15 minutes and I was calling the Atlanta Police!"

"We went to the Waffle House for breakfast. We just kept talking, and time got away from me." Gracie quickly changed the subject. "Bev, your eyeballs look like road maps."

"Wait until you see Marcy's. Actually, we just got home a few minutes ago. I thought you of all people would be here getting your beauty rest. I wanna hear all about your night in about five hours. Right now, I'm hitting the bed. The couch is all yours." Bev stumbled back to the bedroom where Gracie could hear Marcy snoring.

Gracie stripped to her underwear and covered herself in an Afghan as she lay on the couch. She knew she needed to sleep, but her head was spinning. Who was this man who'd put her under his spell? She rationalized her feelings as a momentary infatuation with someone so different from any other man she knew. Even Charlie.

Her sweet, dependable, protective Charlie. He and Ouida had opened a real can of worms with their suggestions to date other people. Now that she'd taken their advice, there was no repacking that can.

She tried imagining the hurt in Charlie's green eyes if she told him. But instead, when she finally drifted off to sleep, it was Hugh's bright chocolate eyes that smiled back at her.

By mid-afternoon the three girls were on their way home. A few hours' sleep and a combination of Alka Seltzers and aspirin had somewhat revived Bev and Marcy.

"This bright sun is killing me. Gracie, I'm glad you're able to drive. I might vomit again if I got behind the wheel." Marcy sipped slowly on a bottle of Coke.

"No vomiting allowed in my car!" Bev interjected. "My mouth feels like a cotton ball. I could drink a gallon of water."

Gracie changed gears as they edged onto the interstate. "One day you two are going to learn to pace yourselves. I feel perfectly fine today."

Bev giggled. "Speaking of fine, that Aussie is one fine specimen of a man."

Marcy belched. "Oh, I feel better. Okay, spill the beans, Gracie."

Grace kept her eyes on the road. "There are no beans to spill. We had a nice breakfast at the Waffle House and some interesting conversation. That's all there was to it."

"I hope he paid the bill because that must've been a huge breakfast seeing y'all were there until daybreak." Bev winked at Marcy. "Come on, Gracie, what's he like?"

Gracie was about to burst. "This information does not leave the confines of this VW. Do you promise?"

"Hell yeah! I swear I'll never eat another cheesesteak if I ever repeat a single word." Marcy held her hand across her heart.

Bev agreed. "Your words will remain top secret. I was a Girl Scout, so Scout's honor!" She held up two fingers in a scout salute. "He is so dreamy. Those eyes make me swoon."

"His eyes are special, aren't they?" Gracie couldn't help herself. "They always seem to be amused by something."

Marcy hooted. "Amused at your beauty, I bet. Did he make a pass at you or invite you back to his apartment?"

"He did not invite me back to his apartment, but he did invite me to the Allman Brothers concert in February."

The girls chimed in simultaneously, "Are you going?"

Grace sighed. "I didn't give him an answer. I feel so guilty with Charlie off at Fort Bragg training for war, and me back here having fun."

"So. You did have fun!" Bev clapped her hands. "I knew if we could get you away from the café for a little while, you'd loosen up."

"I just hope I didn't loosen up too much. I let him kiss me."

Marcy shook her head. "Don't beat yourself up, Gracie. Everybody needs to kiss somebody on New Year's. I even let that Tech nerd kiss me. He tried to slip me the tongue, but I wasn't having any of that."

"Ewww!" Bev was disgusted. "No tongue for me either. Mine was a horrible dancer and wanted to talk about the amazing architecture in Atlanta. Who talks about architecture on a date?!"

Gracie was glad to change the subject. A few minutes later, Bev's cheek was resting on the passenger side's window as she snoozed, and Marcy started snoring loudly in the back seat. Grace giggled quietly as she wondered how Bev ever got any sleep with Marcy as her roommate.

CHAPTER THIRTY-THREE

After church the next day, Grace and Bonnie shared their usual Sunday lunch of soup and grilled cheese sandwiches. "I plan to do absolutely nothing this afternoon but read the Atlanta paper from cover to cover." Bonnie, already in her flowered duster and bed slippers, headed towards the couch. "Do you want a section, Gracie? I know you like to look at the book reviews."

Gracie started up the stairs to her room. "Actually, I need to return the jewelry Miss Ouida lent me. I think I'll drive over to her place and visit for a spell."

"Good, she'll enjoy the company. That woman doesn't know what to do with herself when the café is closed, and I think Buddy went to visit his cousin in Barnesville today."

When Grace returned from her room, Bonnie was stretched out on the couch sound asleep with the newspaper resting on the coffee table. She tiptoed through the kitchen and quietly closed the door behind her.

After cruising down the long driveway, Grace parked in front of Ouida's beautiful antebellum home. Before she'd even made it up the porch steps, Ouida flung open her front door. "Well, well, Gracie! How was your New Year Eve's celebration in Atlanta?"

Grace handed Ouida her jewelry. "Oh, Miss Ouida, it was wonderful and terrible." She burst into tears.

Ouida pulled her inside. "Whatever is wrong, sweetheart? Come on in the den. I have a fire going. This drafty old place gets so cold." She steered Gracie down the hallway to the back of the house and into a cozy room that was toasty warm. Ouida sat down on the sofa and patted the cushion beside her. "Come tell Ouida all your problems."

And Gracie did. "I can't stop thinking about his easy laugh and those intense brown eyes. What am I going to do, Miss Ouida?"

Ouida took a long draw on her cigarette, blew a smoke circle, and studied Grace. "Aren't you doing exactly what Charlie told you to do?"

Gracie sighed. "I know he told me to date other people. But Hugh isn't just someone to date. He's clever and handsome and worldly and so…so attentive when he listens to me. I've never known anyone like him, Miss Ouida."

"Of course, you haven't. He's from another part of the world. He's older and more mature than Charlie. He obviously has grown up in a wealthy home. Sweet girl, different can be so exciting." Ouida patted Gracie's hand. "I dare say that some of that shiny will wear off after a while. When it does, you can determine if this Hugh fellow is just what I think he is—a little fling."

Gracie relaxed her shoulders. "You think so, Miss Ouida?'

Ouida wrapped her arm around Gracie. "The only way to be certain is to let this little fling run its course. I have a feeling that by the time Charlie returns from AIT, you'll have things all figured out."

As Grace drove home, she reflected on Miss Ouida's advice. Maybe Hugh Lockett *was* just a fling. The phone was ringing as she walked in the back door, and she grabbed it before the noise woke up BonBon. "Hello?"

"So, my little Sheila made it home safely."

Gracie's heart leapt into her throat. She took a deep breath. "Yes, my friends were dragging, but I got them home in one piece."

"I should have given you my remedy for a hangover." Hugh chuckled.

His laughter eased the anxiety from Gracie. "And what would that be?"

"Hair of the dog, of course! Three ounces of gin, a squirt or two of freshly squeezed lemon juice, a couple dashes of Tabasco, and a slice of chili pepper."

Gracie giggled. "Sounds like that would eat away my stomach lining."

"Just tell Bev and Marcy to try it next time. I guarantee it'll take away that buggered feeling."

"Buggered?" Gracie giggled again.

"Aw, you know what I mean. They'll go from feeling hungover back to their tops." He hesitated as he changed gears. "Have you thought anymore about the Allman Brothers concert?"

Gracie had made up her mind to take Miss Ouida's advice. "Yes, I'd love to go." She wasn't so sure, though, that BonBon would approve. "Why don't you pick me up at Tift. It's on the way, and then you can drop me back there after the concert. I can stay with Bev and Marcy that night."

"That's the best! I'll ring you up a couple days before the concert so you can give me directions."

"Um, that's great. Call me between 5:00 and 7:00 PM." Gracie knew that BonBon would be knee deep with the supper crowd during that time.

"I'll do just that, my blue-eyed Sheila."

With school back in session the following week, Grace had little time to think about her decision to go out with Hugh. Rarely did a day go by that she didn't receive a letter from Charlie. He had hopes of getting leave soon but was still waiting to find out for sure. Grace always responded with a cheery letter in return even though she felt her words were sometimes forced.

The final Friday morning in February, Grace loaded an overnight bag into her car and then hurried to the café for a quick breakfast. Ouida, sipping coffee at the counter, winked at Grace. "I hear you're having a sleepover at Tift."

Gracie's face colored. "Just spending the weekend with Marcy and Bev at school. I, uh, have a big history project due next week and can use some extra time in the library."

Ouida lit a cigarette and grinned at Gracie. "Uh-huh." Through some kind of voodoo intuition, Ouida saw straight through Gracie's plan. "Remember that all work and no play will make Sunday Grace a dull gal."

Gracie's ears burned as she shoveled sugar into her coffee. She was glad when Buddy came to life. "I wish I could stay and listen to all this girl talk, but tax time is upon us." He pulled himself up from his chair. "Off to work I go."

Ouida laughed as Buddy went out the door. "I think he means off to work he waddles!"

Bonnie bumped through the swinging doors with two baskets of freshly baked biscuits. "Grace, I'm glad I caught you before you left. You forgot to tell me something."

Grace flinched. "What do you mean, BonBon?"

Bonnie pulled a twenty-dollar bill from her apron pocket. "Don't you need some money to eat on this weekend?"

"Oh yeah. I do." Grace stuffed the bill into the back pocket of her jeans. "Well, don't want to be late for my religion class. Dr. Bore Gore has a test scheduled."

Ouida hooted. "Is he the professor that can put an entire class to sleep in the first five minutes?"

Gracie relaxed as she snickered. "One in the same. I guess I won't see you again until Monday after class."

As Bonnie wiped down the counter, she gave Gracie a discerning eye. "And what about church on Sunday, young lady?"

Gracie moaned. "BonBon, they have services in the chapel on campus. I'll try to get there."

"Do more than try. Sunday is the Lord's Day, and the Lord has been good to you." She leaned over the counter and kissed Grace on the cheek. "I hope you have your peacoat. It's bitter out there today."

"I do, BonBon. See you Monday." Gracie stopped at the door. "Love you!"

Ouida couldn't help herself. "Take some time for a little fun, Gracie."

Grace wondered again if Ouida really knew her plans or was just guessing. Whatever the case, she felt a little guilty about not telling BonBon the complete truth. The guilt, however, evaporated the closer she got to Tift.

She'd packed her best bell bottom jeans and a soft peasant blouse to wear to the concert. It would be cold, but Bev had told her she could borrow her wool poncho.

In just a few hours, she'd be with Hugh headed to Macon. Her excitement outweighed any qualms she had as she pulled into campus. She shivered with the anticipation of a night with Hugh Lockett and the Allman Brothers.

"Stop fidgeting, Gracie, or I'll never get this hair braided." Marcy held three thick strands of Gracie's long, curly hair. "Bev, show me that picture of the French braid again. Lordy, girl, I've never seen so much hair on a head."

When Grace turned to study the model's picture in Bev's *Set and Style* magazine, Marcy tugged on her hair. "Sit still! I've almost got this."

"I'm sorry, Marcy. I'm just so nervous." Gracie picked up the hand mirror so she could study the French braid that curled around the crown of her head. The rest of her blonde locks hugged her shoulders softly. "Oh wow! It has a real hippie look. I love it, Marcy."

"Close your eyes, Gracie. Let's try some of this blue eyeshadow on your lids." Bev, in charge of makeup, brushed Gracie's closed lid. "Ok, now open," Bev ordered. "Yep, that makes your eyes look even bluer."

Just as Bev finished, the intercom buzzed. "Marcy, tell your friend Gracie that her date's here."

Gracie froze. "Do I look all right?"

"You look incredible! Hold still so we won't mess up your hair." Bev carefully pulled her blue wool poncho over Gracie's head.

Marcy handed her a slip of paper. "Here's the dorm hall's number. If you're past midnight, call and I'll sneak up and let you in. Yinz have a fabulous time, and tell Greg Allman hello for me."

Gracie's friends pushed her out the dorm room door. She closed her eyes for a moment, took a deep breath, and headed to the lobby.

Hugh had his back turned and was looking out the front door, so Gracie spotted him first. He was clad in his KingGees khakis but was wearing a paisley shirt and a fringed suede jacket.

When Grace cleared her throat, he turned around. Hugh looked her up and down with his smiling eyes. "Well, Grace MacGregor, you'll be the prettiest hippie chick at the concert." He put her arm in his. "Are you ready to go?"

The drive to Macon took less than an hour. Hugh impressed Grace with his knowledge about the Allman Brothers and their music. "Did you know that Gregg and his older brother Duane started their band in a garage? They called themselves the Escorts and then changed the name to the Allman Joys. Of course, now, they're known as The Allman Brothers Band. Duane Allman might be the finest guitarist of the 20th Century. Wait until you hear *Whipping Post*. It's the tops."

Gracie was fascinated. "You're like an Allman Brothers encyclopedia. Can you play any of their songs?"

"I'm working on *Midnight Rider*, but I've got a long way to go. Here we are." Hugh drove past several empty parking spots and pulled his car into a darkened area.

Gracie was confused. "Don't you want to get closer to the auditorium?"

"We're early, and I thought we'd have a little smoke." Hugh grinned as he pulled a plastic bag of pot and some rolling papers from his glove compartment.

Gracie felt her face flush. "Is that marijuana?"

"Bloody right, it is!" Hugh studied Gracie. "You've never gotten stoned, sweet Sheila?"

"I've never even smoked a cigarette." Gracie's voice shook slightly. "Isn't that stuff illegal?"

Hugh reared his head and laughed good-naturedly as he filled the square of paper with what looked like dried spices to Grace. "Only if you get caught." He rolled the paper tightly until it looked like a homemade cigarette. Then he punched in the cigarette lighter on the dash.

Although it was cold in the car, Gracie began to perspire under the wool poncho. "I think I'll stand outside the car while you smoke."

"Come on, little Sheila. Nobody listens to the Allman Brothers without being stoned."

He lit the cigarette and took a deep pull from it, then held the smoke in his mouth for several seconds before exhaling. "See, that's all you have to do. It's a lot healthier than alcohol, and you won't have a hangover in the morning."

Gracie hesitated. "Just try a little. I'll hold it for you." Hugh held the joint to her lips. Gracie closed her eyes and sucked on the cigarette. "Now hold the smoke in your lungs until I tell you to exhale." She followed Hugh's instructions.

When he finally told her to exhale, Gracie broke into a cough. "That is horrid!"

"I agree, it doesn't taste good, but wait until you see how it makes you feel. Come on, Gracie, take another couple of hits, and we'll be ready to groove with the music." Hugh put his arm around Gracie as she once again inhaled the joint.

Gracie didn't remember much about the concert. She floated above the band watching Duane Allman's fingers move with amazing dexterity across the strings of his guitar. Hugh's arms held her as they danced to *Sweet*

Melissa. For the first time in her life, she felt totally relaxed and free from all her worries, her fears, and her inhibitions.

Hugh started the car. "Aren't you glad we parked towards the back. Now we'll be one of the first ones out. Are you hungry?"

"Ravenous. How did you know?" Gracie snuggled up to Hugh as he pulled out of the parking lot.

Hugh laughed. "It's the pot. It gives you the munchies. There's a Shoney's not far from here. How does that sound?"

"Can I have fries and a hot fudge cake?" Gracie's speech was slow and deliberate.

After a satisfying meal at Shoney's, Grace could feel the fuzziness in her brain start to dissipate. "Oh no! What time is it? We need to get back to the dorm before midnight."

"Don't worry that pretty head of yours." Hugh checked his watch. "We have 45 minutes, and I can make it in less than that." He turned the key in the ignition, but the motor didn't even sputter.

"Do you think your battery is dead?" She'd learned that much about cars from Charlie.

Hugh tried the ignition again, but it was futile. "The bloody battery is less than a month old. I think it's the starter. Garry had some problems with it before he left. He was supposed to get a new one, but I guess he never did. Since it's been working fine up until now, I haven't thought about replacing it."

Gracie tried to hide her concern. "Where will you get a starter this time of night?"

Hugh's smile comforted her. "Let's go back inside. I can ask a local where the nearest auto parts store is, and you can call your friends back at the dorm and tell them you'll be late."

While Hugh talked to the manager, Grace pulled a dime from her pocket and headed to the pay phone in the back hallway. "Gracie, is it you?"

"Bev, were you sitting by the phone?"

Bev laughed. "I was heading back from the shower when it rang. Are you back in town?"

"Not exactly. We're stuck at the Shoney's in Macon. Hugh's car won't start. He's trying to find somewhere to get the part he needs."

"Honey, it's almost midnight in Macon, which is no better than being in Podunk. He ain't gonna find a thing open until the morning. You may be stuck there for the night."

Grace took an uneasy breath. "I guess you're right. What should I do?"

She could hear Bev sigh over the phone. "You're a big girl, Gracie. Make the most of it with your Aussie boyfriend. The only thing I remember from Mrs. Cavan's high school Latin class were the words, *Carpe Diem*."

"And what does that mean, Bev? I took Spanish in high school."

"Seize the day, Gracie. We have no idea what tomorrow may bring. Marcy and I are about to share a midnight snack of popcorn. We'll see you in the morning. Nighty night!" And the phone went dead.

Bev was right—it would be impossible to find a store open in the middle of the night in Macon. Gracie watched the last customer in the restaurant paying his ticket as a tired-looking waitress wiped down all the tables.

Hugh headed her way. He carried two cups of steaming liquid. "The bad news is the auto parts store doesn't open until 8 a.m. The good news is it's a half mile down the road." He handed Gracie a cup. "I hope you like hot cocoa."

Gracie took the warm cup from Hugh's hands. "Now what?"

"Don't look so glum, sweet Sheila. The manager has given his permission for us to stay parked here overnight. I can fold down the seats in the back. I have two sleeping bags back there." He took his hand and turned up Gracie's chin. "Didn't you tell me you'd always wanted to try camping."

"Well, at least we won't freeze to death. Let me run to the bathroom before they lock up." Grace handed Hugh her cocoa and headed into the ladies' room.

As she washed her hands, she studied herself in the mirror. *"I hope I don't have to pee again before Shoney's opens for breakfast,"* she thought as she wiped her hands dry. She squared her shoulders. *"Okay, Bev, I'm taking your advice. I'm off to seize the day, or in this case, the night!"*

By the time the manager turned off the lights in the restaurant, Hugh had reinvented the inside of the wagon. "I think it will be best if we use one sleeping bag for a bed and the other for some cover. It's going to get cold out here tonight."

Gracie was already shivering and kicking herself for not bringing her peacoat as BonBon had advised. She watched as Hugh set a case in the front seat. "What's that?"

"Just an old guitar I bought at a pawn shop on Stewart Avenue. I left my good one back in Australia. Kinda hard to travel that far toting a guitar. Your castle awaits you, Grace MacGregor."

He smiled as he helped Gracie into the back of the wagon. "I forgot I had a thermos under the seat. I got the manager to fill it up with the last of the hot cocoa. He was about to pour it out, so he gave it to me on the house."

Gracie held her half-empty cup out for Hugh to replenish. "I hope it makes me sleepy, but I'm actually wide awake." She eyed the guitar. "How about a lullaby to soothe me to sleep."

"Really? After hearing the Allman Brothers, you are in for a huge disappointment." Hugh climbed into the back of the wagon.

"Let me be the judge." The cocoa was helping Gracie relax. "Just one song, please."

Hugh opened the case and searched for a pick. "I always keep a couple in here." Once he found the pick, he strummed the strings, then stopped and expertly tuned them. He played a beautiful rendition of Dylan's *Blowin' in the Wind* as he sang in a warm deep voice.

When he finished, Gracie clapped. "You're really good, Hugh." She watched as his eyes looked downward and his face colored. "Play me another, please."

Hugh recovered quickly. "Okay. How about this one." He strummed a few chords, looked straight into Gracie's eyes, and sang. "If I were a carpenter and you were my lady, would you marry me anyway, would you have me baby?"

Gracie felt her ears burning. When Hugh finished, her eyes sparkled with admiration. "That was beautiful, Hugh."

He laid the guitar down and pulled Grace into his arms. She could hear Bev's words echoing in her mind: *"Seize the day, Gracie."* And so, she did.

Moments later, it seemed, she felt herself being softly shaken. "Grace, wake up. Your room service awaits." She opened her eyes to see Hugh holding a steaming cup of coffee.

Realizing she was still naked beneath the sleeping bag, she tucked it underneath her arms as Hugh handed her the coffee. "You're even prettier than you were last night." He grinned as Gracie once again blushed.

Hugh kissed her. "Now, get dressed before you freeze your bum off. I'm headed to the auto parts store. They open in 15 minutes. Go on in and order some breakfast. I'll be back in a while."

After dressing hurriedly, Grace shivered as she ducked into the ladies' room once again. She washed her face the best she could and then unraveled what was left of her braids. Her hair tumbled down into tousled curls.

She stared at herself in the mirror. *"You are a mess, Grace MacGregor, and you're in one helluva mess!"* she thought. After she exited the bathroom, she pocketed a peppermint from the jar beside the cash register.

She unwrapped it and popped it into her mouth. *"At least you won't have dragon breath."*

Grace was still studying the breakfast menu when Hugh slid into the booth. "I'm starving. Let's eat first, and then I'll get that starter installed. The fellow at the store was a good bloke. He loaned me a couple of tools I need. We can drop them off when I finish." His brown eyes were dancing with pleasure. "I could go for some pancakes."

Grace stared at this unusual man who had turned her life upside down. "Blueberry pancakes are my favorite," she said with a grin.

Long after they had devoured pancakes, the two were still sitting in the booth. Hugh took Grace's hand as his brown eyes turned serious. "Grace, I haven't been completely honest with you."

Grace's heart jumped, but she managed to nod. "Okay."

Hugh struggled for a moment. "Like you, I have someone back home. She's a good sort. We met several summers ago when her parents bought the place next to our beach house. She's halfway through her nursing studies in Sydney. Everybody back home expects us to marry, but I've been dragging my heels about getting properly engaged. She and I decided we should wait for me to return to Australia. She wanted me to have time for my great adventure."

"And you've had quite an experience, haven't you?" Grace managed a smile.

Hugh squeezed her hand. "Grace, would you consider moving to Australia? Our schools are always in need of teachers, and you'd make a fine one."

Grace shook her head. "I've got a scholarship at Tift, and I'm just getting started with my studies. Plus, I'd never leave BonBon or-or-or Charlie. They're my life here, and it's a good life."

She stared into Hugh's sad brown eyes. "You've had a grand adventure, Hugh Lockett, and I'm proud that I've been part of it."

The drive back to Tift was a quiet one. When Hugh parked in front of the dorm, he pulled Grace into his arms. She put on a brave smile. "You're going to be a bloody fine doctor one day, but I hope you never abandon your love of music."

Grace opened the car door, but Hugh grabbed her hand. "Wait. I want you to have something. He climbed out and pulled his battered guitar case from the back. "Keep it. Maybe I'll be back one day to play again for you."

Grace hugged the guitar case to her body. "Maybe so." But they both knew they'd never see each other again.

CHAPTER THIRTY-FOUR

Grace was thankful to be busy finishing papers and studying for finals the next two weeks. In his most recent letter, Charlie had written that he'd be delayed for at least another week as he completed some specialized training. While he didn't go into details about the kind of training, Gracie was relieved that she had time to let go of what could never be—and to recapture what she'd almost let slip through her fingers.

Once again Gracie chose to confide in Miss Ouida. Home early after her last final, she found Ouida sitting on her front porch enjoying the first truly warm day of spring.

Ouida grinned as Grace climbed her steps. "Did you ace all of your finals?"

Grace sank into a cushioned rocker. "I hope so."

Ouida lit a cigarette. "I don't hear any relief in that voice. Don't you have a couple of weeks off before spring quarter?"

Gracie shrugged as Ouida eyed her. "What's bothering you, child? Is it your Aussie fella?"

"That's over." Gracie sighed. "It just wasn't meant to be. We're from two different worlds, Miss Ouida, and...and I think I really love Charlie."

"Sounds like you're not absolutely sure about Charlie either." Ouida blew a smoke ring.

Tears collected in the corners of Gracie's eyes. "No, I am. I just pray Charlie's still sure about me after I tell him about my sordid romance with Hugh."

Ouida raised an eyebrow. "Sordid? Whatever do you mean by that?"

Ouida's question was all it took for Gracie to unload her guilt. "How will I ever tell Charlie that I've been unfaithful? It will break his heart."

Ouida patted her hand. "Sweet girl, you had a fling. It happens. But it will do you absolutely no good to share everything with Charlie. You're not married or even engaged as of yet. It's best to let sleeping dogs lie, honey."

"But I've always shared everything with Charlie. How can I deceive him?"

Ouida snuffed out her cigarette. "Sometimes we keep things from those we love because we know the revelation will hurt them too much. Every one of us has at least one secret we never share. This will be yours."

Since the café closed after lunch on Wednesdays, Grace knew she'd find Bonnie baking. The glorious aroma of chocolate hit her as soon as she opened the back door to the café's kitchen.

"Gracie, you're home!" Bonnie wiped her hands and hurried to give her a big hug. "A second quarter under your belt. How does it feel?"

Gracie laid her head on Bonnie's shoulder. "It feels good to be in this kitchen with nothing to do. Are those brownies I smell?"

Bonnie nodded. "They have a few more minutes in the oven. Wanna help me?"

Grace pulled an apron from the hook by the door. "I can't think of anything I'd rather do, BonBon."

"How about some mud hens?" Bonnie poured flour into the mixer. "I'll mix up the bottom layer while you stir up the topping. Do you remember the ingredients?"

"Butter, brown sugar, eggs, and pecans." Grace found the proper ingredients and began to blend them in a glass bowl.

After Bonnie poured the flour mixture into a large pan, Gracie added the brown sugar concoction. "I wish Charlie were here to have one of these mud hens. They're his favorite."

"Well, it won't be long before he's home." Bonnie tried to hide the excitement in her voice. She knew for a fact that Charlie was on his way. She'd read and reread the letter that arrived earlier in the week. In it, Charlie had asked for Gracie's hand in marriage. "Let's get this pan in the oven."

As they waited for the mud hens to bake, Gracie helped Bonnie clean up. Bonnie suddenly burst into laughter. "Do you remember the first time you sat at this worktable? You were such a scrawny little thing, and I let you eat as many biscuits as you wanted. I was amazed at the amount of milk you could drink!"

"I can still smell that first brownie you gave me from the display counter. It was the best thing I'd ever tasted." Gracie smiled as her thoughts returned to that rainy night so many years ago. "And your kitchen smelled so wonderful."

Bonnie grinned. "What did it smell like to you?"

"It smelled like home, BonBon." Gracie was happy to be back where she belonged.

Less than a block down the street, Brooxie Barnett was scrubbing the grease from his hands. He heard Charlie's truck before he saw it and opened the second garage door so that Charlie could pull in.

Brooxie smiled. "You're a sight for sore eyes, Charlie Callahan! Welcome home, soldier."

Charlie climbed out of the cab grinning. "It's nice to be home." He shook Brooxie's outheld hand. "Did you get my letter?"

"Yep. Come on back to my office so we can discuss it." Brooxie's tone was all businesslike as Charlie followed nervously behind him.

Brooxie sat at his well-worn swivel chair and pointed to a straight back one across from his desk. Charlie swallowed. "I'll understand if my request for a loan is too much to ask, Brooxie. You've already been so good to me, keeping my apartment available and all."

"Charlie, I won't give you the loan." Charlie's heart sank, but then Brooxie smiled. "Son, I've got something for you." He swiveled in his chair and leaned over to open a safe behind him.

Charlie watched curiously as he withdrew a small velvet box. Brooxie flipped the top open. Inside was a platinum band with an exquisite pear-shaped diamond.

"Charlie, this belonged to my grandmother. My mother gave it to me before she passed away. She had hopes that Flo and I would have a son one day and that I could give it to him for his bride."

Brooxie shifted in his chair. "Well, it just wasn't meant for Flo and me to have any kids." Then he looked Charlie in the eye. "Charlie, you're the closest thing to a son I'll ever have. I sure would be proud if you'd take this ring and put it on sweet little Gracie's finger."

Charlie was dumbfounded. "I'd be honored, Brooxie." Charlie took the box and held his hand out to shake Brooxie's again.

"Come here, son. I need more than a handshake." Brooxie encircled Charlie in a hearty hug. "Let's have a drink to celebrate!"

He didn't refuse as Brooxie poured two shots of Old Granddad whiskey. Charlie swallowed it down in one gulp. "Whew, that burns!"

Brooxie hooted as he poured a second shot. "This next one will be smoother, I promise."

CHAPTER THIRTY-FIVE

A hot shower and a cup of coffee revived Charlie from his long drive home and his celebratory shots with Brooxie. His hair had grown out enough to fall across his forehead. He splashed on some English Leather and took a final look in the mirror. "Dear Lord, I pray she says yes."

With the café closed on Wednesday evenings, BonBon decided to attend a prayer meeting. Gracie had begged off complaining she was too tired from exams.

Just after dark, Grace crawled under the covers with the library's only copy of *The Winds of War*. She was happy for the chance to read some fiction instead of a textbook.

She was just finishing the first chapter when the doorbell rang. *"Who in the world could that be?"* she wondered as she threw on a pair of shorts with the Tift College T-shirt she was already wearing. She headed down the stairs.

BonBon always left on the front porch light. It only took Grace a second to recognize that lopsided grin smiling at her through the windowpane. "Charlie!" She flung open the door. "You're home!"

Before she could say anything else, Charlie grabbed her in his arms and swung her around like a rag doll. "My beautiful baby girl! Have I ever missed you!"

"Stop, stop! You're making me dizzy!" Gracie giggled as Charlie set her down on her feet. "Look at you. Your hair has grown back, and you look taller. Are you taller?"

Charlie grinned. "You just make me feel ten feet tall." Then he tilted her chin and kissed her long and hard. When they let go to breathe, Charlie held her at arm's length. "Let me get a good look at you, Gracie."

Gracie covered her face with her hands. "I'm a mess, Shug. Why didn't you tell me you were coming? I haven't had a letter from you in over a week." She lay her head on his shoulder.

"I know, Baby Girl. I've been busy with some extra training."

She lifted her head with inquisitive eyes. "What kind? Was it jungle training?"

"Let's sit down, and I'll tell you all about it. Do you think I could have a sandwich? I haven't eaten since breakfast. I didn't want to waste time stopping on the road for lunch."

Gracie pulled him into the kitchen. "Sit down, and I'll make you something." She scurried around as she put together a ham sandwich and poured Charlie a glass of iced tea.

Charlie barely came up for air until he finished eating. "That was delicious. So much better than mess hall food. I'm looking forward to a few days' worth of Miz Bonnie's café cuisine."

"Only a few days? I thought soldiers got at least six weeks before they shipped out to Vietnam." Gracie's shoulders slumped as she refilled Charlie's tea glass.

Charlie grabbed her hand and squeezed. "Who said anything about Vietnam?"

Gracie's eyes lit up. "What? You're not going to Nam?"

"That's why I had to stay two extra weeks at Fort Knox. I received extended mechanical training for tanks. In a week, I head to Germany as an armor mechanic."

"Germany? Are you kidding me?" Gracie jumped up and pulled Charlie to his feet. They danced around the kitchen until they were both breathless.

Once they recovered, Charlie showed Gracie his papers. "I'll be a Private in the 4th Armor Division. It's a part of the 126th Maintenance Battalion. After a few months, I should be promoted to Private First Class."

Gracie put her hands on her hips. "And what exactly does all that mean?"

Charlie pulled her onto his lap. "It means, Baby Girl, that I'll work in Division Trains. That's Army talk for the motor pool. I'll be charged with maintaining armored tanks. My extra time at Fort Knox was for training to be a Track Vehicle Repairer."

Happy tears sparkled in Gracie's eyes. "My prayers have been answered."

"And I hope mine are about to be." Charlie reached into his pocket for the black velvet box, held it in one hand, and opened it with the other. "Sunday Grace MacGregor, will you marry me?"

For a moment, Gracie felt her heart in her throat. The ring was absolutely stunning. "Oh Charlie, it's…it's…it's…" and then she burst into tears.

Charlie held her as he laughed. "That wasn't exactly the answer I'd hoped for."

Gracie sobbed until her shoulders shook as Charlie rocked her in his arms. "Charlie, I have to tell you something first."

She hiccupped, blew her nose on a napkin, and then swallowed hard. "I went to the Allman Brothers concert and smoked pot."

Charlie looked amused more than anything. "Okay. How was the concert?"

"The music was great. The pot burned my lungs and tasted awful but made me feel like I was floating." Gracie hesitated.

Charlie laughed. "Yep, it did the same to me. We had a 24-hour leave a few weeks ago. I shared a joint with one of my bunkmates while we were in town. About two hours later, I was starving. It's okay, Gracie, neither of us has turned into a doper."

Grace grabbed his hands. "You don't understand, Charlie. I had a date with someone I'd met at Underground when I was with Bev and Marcy."

"Okay. So, I'm glad you took my advice."

Gracie started to explain, but Charlie pressed a finger to her lips. "You don't have to tell me about him. All I want to know is whether you still love me."

As soon as Charlie held her in his arms, Gracie had no doubts. "Yes! Yes! Yes! I love you, Charlie Callahan, and I will marry you."

The next morning, Gracie was up at the crack of dawn. She could barely wait for breakfast at the café. While BonBon had oohed and ahhed at the ring the night before, Gracie had sworn her to secrecy. She wanted to see who would be first to notice her left hand.

She poured Cooter Renfroe his coffee with her ring finger right under his nose, which he had stuck in the *Thomaston Times*. Then, she waved her hand in front of him. "Can I get you anything else, Mr. Cooter?" but he didn't take the bait. He just shook his head and kept reading.

A few minutes later Ouida walked in with Buddy Simpson close behind her. She took a seat at the counter while Buddy sidled up to his usual table and raised his squeaky voice. "Vern, put me an extra side of bacon on the griddle. I was so late getting home from Griffin last night I didn't have any supper."

Ouida laughed. "You mean you went without a meal, Buddy Simpson? Are pigs flying?" She lit her first cigarette of the day.

Buddy grunted. "Old Miz Bledsoe wanted me to look at every cancelled check she'd written in the past year. I thought I'd never get out of there. She offered me some dinner. She served me hash and stewed cabbage. It tasted more like dogfood with a side of boiled dandelions."

Grace smiled as she poured Buddy a cup of coffee, once again with her left hand. Buddy didn't react. He was too busy studying the breakfast menu even though he had it memorized. "Gracie, with the bacon, I'll have three eggs over easy, a large bowl of grits with extra butter, and three biscuits."

Gracie sighed while taking his order. As she headed back to the counter, Ouida grabbed her hand. "Grace MacGregor, what is that on your finger?" Ouida pulled her closer to study the ring. "My goodness, that is simply gorgeous." Then she grinned. "Who's the lucky fella?"

"I am!" At that very moment, Charlie, beaming from ear to ear, walked through the swinging kitchen doors. "She said yes, Miss Ouida." A plate of biscuits in one hand and a picnic basket in the other, Bonnie followed Charlie from the kitchen.

Ouida's eyes smiled with delight. "Charlie, where in the world did you come from?" Then she studied the ring again. "You definitely have good taste in jewelry."

Buddy ambled out of his chair to shake Charlie's hand. "Welcome home, soldier. Looks like congratulations are in order." He peered at Gracie's hand, which she was holding up for everyone to see. "I bet that set you back several months' pay, son."

Charlie shared a lopsided grin. "Actually, it's an antique from Brooxie's family. It was his grandmother's, and since he doesn't have a son, he wanted me to have it…for Gracie."

Cooter folded his paper. "Well, I'll be. Let me see that ring. You two are getting hitched. When's the wedding?"

Bonnie set the basket of biscuits by Buddy's plate. "Slow down, Cooter Renfroe. Let these two lovebirds enjoy their engagement."

She put an arm around Grace's shoulder as she handed the picnic basket to Charlie. "I packed all your favorites. You have this young lady for the entire week, Charlie Callahan." Then she untied Grace's apron. "Go have fun," and they did.

For the next week, the two were inseparable. They cruised the roads of Pike County in Charlie's truck every day, stopping at their favorite haunts. One day, they decided to go fishing at Flat Shoals Creek.

While they were sharing lunch on their favorite rock in the middle of the creek, they heard a large vehicle rumbling down the road. "Looka there, Grace. It's the bus from the Children's Home."

The two stood up and brushed the grass off their pants as they watched a group of children empty out of the bus. Then they heard a deep, jovial voice. "Okay girls, you grab all the picnic items. You fellas help me with the fishing poles and bait."

Charlie grinned. "It's Reverend Hogan!" He shouted up the hill. "Hi Rev, can I help you with anything?"

"Charlie Callahan? Is that you?" The Rev took up the rear as the kids spilled down the hill to the water. Charlie rushed over to shake his hand. "You are one fine specimen of a man, Charlie. I heard you'd joined the Army. Home on leave?"

"Yessir. I ship out to Germany in a few days. I'm gonna serve as a tank mechanic at Ansbach Army Air Base."

"I knew you'd make something out of yourself, Charlie!" Reverend Hogan smiled at Grace. "You're Grace MacGregor, aren't you? All grown up since the last time I saw you. And what are you doing these days?"

"Yessir, that's me. I'm studying education at Tift College." Then she held up her left hand. "Charlie and I just got engaged."

The Rev's eyes twinkled. "Well, isn't that something. You two make a fine couple." Then his eyes drifted to a little boy in a red shirt trying to bait his own hook. "Hold on, Jack. I'll help you."

Charlie held up his hand. "Let me help him, Rev. Brings back some fond memories." He grinned. "Now Jack, what you have to do is bring the hook to the worm, not the worm to the hook."

The Reverend chuckled and winked at Grace. "He'll make a fine father one day."

"Yes, he will, Reverend Hogan." Grace felt her heart blooming with a love that she knew would carry her through the long year without Charlie.

They spent their evenings making love in Charlie's apartment until Grace insisted that she had to go home. "I don't want BonBon worrying about what folks would think if I spent the night."

Early one morning, Grace cut roses from Bonnie's rosebushes in the backyard and wrapped the stems in a damp paper towel. Charlie was eating a stack of pancakes at the counter when she came into the café. "Morning, Baby Girl. What's with the flowers?"

Gracie laid them on the counter and poured herself a cup of coffee. "I thought you might want to visit your family at the cemetery before you shipped out."

Charlie covered her hand in his. It took him a moment to swallow the lump in his throat. "I'd like that, Gracie."

Later that morning, Gracie stood with Charlie at the gravesites of his entire family. Charlie laid the flowers on his granny's grave. "She took good care of me for as long as she could after my parents died. I was so hurt with her at first for leaving me at the Home, but I understand now." He enveloped Gracie in his arms. "It still seems weird being the only Callahan left."

Grace laid her head beneath his jaw. "Reverend Hogan told me that you'd make a fine father one day." She lifted her head and looked into his eyes. "You just come home safe, Charlie. Then you can make me a Callahan, and we can start our own family."

Late afternoon as Grace went home to get ready for their farewell dinner in Griffin, Charlie pulled into Ouida's driveway. He found her with a cigarette in one hand and a tall glass of some kind of frosty drink in the other.

"Charlie, where's your pretty sidekick? You two have been joined at the hip all week."

He grinned as he climbed the steps to her porch. "She's getting all gussied up for dinner at that new Italian place in Griffin." Charlie sat in the empty rocker. "And actually, I wanted a few minutes to talk with you, Miss Ouida."

Ouida raised an eyebrow as she lit a cigarette. "Okay. I'm all ears."

Charlie pulled an envelope from his shirt pocket and handed it to Ouida. She studied it. "This is addressed to Grace. Why are you giving it to me?"

He cleared his throat. "It's a letter I hope Gracie will never have to read. I need you to hold onto it in case something happens to me."

"Oh Charlie, you'll be safe in Germany." Ouida sighed. "But I'll keep it for you until you return."

"Miss Ouida, I need you to promise me that you'll only give this letter to Gracie under one condition."

She ground her cigarette into an ashtray. "And what is that condition?"

"The letter contains a secret that Miz Bonnie and I share. If both Miz Bonnie and I die, I want you to give it to Gracie."

"Oh my! I may outlive Bonnie, but I pray I'm long gone before you pass away." She studied Charlie's grave expression. "But I promise to put this letter in my safe and only give it to Gracie if such a tragedy befalls her."

Charlie stood up. "I knew I could count on you, Miss Ouida. Watch over my girl, please."

Ouida smiled. "She'll have the entire café watching over her, Charlie Callahan." She stood up as he did and hugged him. "You just take care of yourself and come home to your beautiful girl."

A few hours later, after they'd enjoyed dinner in Griffin, Charlie lay in bed with his arms wrapped around Gracie. "This has been the best week of my life, Baby Girl."

Grace snuggled against his bare shoulder. "Mine too. I'm going to miss you more than life, Charlie." She hesitated for a moment. "I have to ask you something."

"Shoot, Baby Girl."

"Do you think Beau Loosier is still alive?" She felt the muscles tense in Charlie's body.

He breathed deeply. "I don't know, Gracie, but I don't think he'll ever come back here again. There are too many people out to get him if he does." He pulled her closer. "You need to forget about him. You're safe here. I promise."

Gracie relaxed. "Okay. I guess you're right. It's been almost two years since he disappeared. I heard Mrs. Loosier has cancer and isn't doing well. Certainly, if Beau was alive, he'd come back to see his mother."

"You're probably right." Charlie pulled her face to his. "Now enough sad talk. I want this last night together to be perfect." He smiled wickedly at her. "And I know just how to make it one you will never forget."

An hour before daybreak, Gracie slipped back into her house. They'd decided that Brooxie would drive Charlie to the airport, and she didn't want Brooxie to know they'd slept together. She and Charlie had said their goodbyes as they held each other one last time. Gracie said she just couldn't watch him get on the plane. He was packed and ready to go when she left him. Gracie climbed into her own bed and prayed, "Keep him safe, Lord, and bring him back to me."

CHAPTER THIRTY-SIX

G racie was well into her second week of spring quarter before she received any word from Charlie. She'd already sent him a half dozen letters written on airmail stationery and scented with her perfume.

That afternoon, Gracie stopped in the café as usual when she got home from Tift. BonBon grinned as she pulled an airmail letter from her apron pocket. "Look what Cooter dropped off at lunch."

Gracie squealed, grabbed the letter, and scooted out the back door towards home, where she could read the letter in private. She waited until she was sitting on her bed to open it. When she did, a photo fell out.

She studied the picture of a soldier posing in front of a monstrous machine before she realized it was Charlie. He was clad in a heavy, Army-issued jacket and a green knit cap. He stood in front of a massive tank, the kind Gracie had only seen in World War II movies.

Charlie had scrawled a message on the back of the photo: "Ansbach Army Airfield, Germany, April 5, 1971." The letter had been mailed right after he'd arrived in Germany.

Dearest Gracie,

I'm officially a Private, First Class in the 4th Armor Division. Can you believe that I actually work on machines like the one in the picture? They're M60 tanks that weigh 50 tons!

As you can tell from my photo, it's still winter here, and there's snow on the ground. They say it'll start to thaw soon. I hope so. I'm freezing my butt off. I keep warm by thinking of that cute little butt of yours.

My quarters aren't too bad. I share a room with another mechanic in an eight-story brick dorm. My roommate is from Cincinnati. He calls me "Georgia" and teases me about how I'm so cold all the time.

I'm keeping count of the days before I see you again. As of today, I have 351 days left before you're back in my arms. Then we can start our lives together. You'll be a teacher, and I'll buy Brooxie's garage in no time.

So just hang on until I get back. You've always been the only girl I could ever love.

All my love to my Baby Girl,

Charlie

Gracie read the letter several times before sticking the photo in her jeans pocket. She knew everyone at the café would want to see it at supper.

Ever since Charlie shipped out and she started back to school, Grace had been overcome with fatigue. BonBon said it was the stress of missing Charlie and not hearing from him. Now that Grace knew he was okay, her body relaxed as she curled up on her bed and fell asleep.

At that very moment in Germany, Charlie had just hit the sack himself. The lights went out at 10 p.m., which was fine with him. He was always exhausted after working in the cold metal hangar all day. He'd received another letter from Gracie at mail call. He read it for the third time before he placed it under his pillow where he could make out the faint scent of her. He was fast asleep in no time.

Bright and early the next morning, he reported to the maintenance hangar for his duty shift. Chief Warrant Officer Strickland was already barking orders. "Move your asses, soldiers. We've got a fleet of tanks that need servicing. Private Callahan, I need your help with something else."

Charlie saluted. "Yes sir!"

While smoking was prohibited in the hangar, the chief always held an unlit cigar between his teeth and continually chewed on it throughout the day. He pulled it out of his mouth for a moment, spat some tobacco juice on the ground, and turned to Charlie. "Corporal Davis is still having trouble with the transmission on his tank. He's bringing it over now."

The chief spat again narrowly missing Charlie's boots. "Two of my mechanics have worked on it, but I've decided they don't know their asses from a hole in the wall. Let's see if you can prove to me why they didn't send you to Nam."

"Yes sir!" Charlie couldn't help but grin a little. So far, he'd been relegated to simple servicing of the huge machines. He was ready to demonstrate his mechanical know-how to his commander.

Rolling the cigar in his mouth, the chief nodded. "The tanker should be here any minute. I'm headed over to the medical building. Cut my damn hand on a rusty bolt this morning. I need a stitch or two and probably a tetanus shot." The chief spat again and looked down at the bloody bandage wrapped around his hand. "When he gets here, have Davis pull up behind that last tank, and get started on that faulty transmission."

Charlie saluted once more as Chief Strickland made his way out of the hangar. He heard the tank moving towards them before he saw it. The pavement rattled under its massive weight.

Davis, the driver of the tank, stopped and poked his head out of the cupola. "Where you want my old gal?"

Charlie chuckled. He'd learned that tank drivers shared a kind of love affair with their machines. "Follow me." Charlie stood in front of the last tank in a row of tanks as he directed Davis towards him. When the tank was close enough, Charlie gave him the stop sign.

As Davis put on the brakes, the machine's faulty transmission slipped, and the tank jerked forward. Before Charlie even realized what was happening, he was pinned between two tanks.

Chief Strickland had made it about halfway to the infirmary when he heard the screeching noise and cries of panic. Whipping around, his eyes grew wide. "Holy shit!" He shouted at two corporals heading into the infirmary. "We need medics at the maintenance hangar. On the double!"

Although he couldn't move, Charlie didn't grasp what was happening. He was still conscious when the chief arrived with two medics right behind him.

Charlie could hear Chief Strickland screaming to the tanker. "Don't back up! Don't back up!" Then the chief turned to Charlie. "Private Callahan, can you hear me?"

Charlie nodded. "What's wrong?" His voice was a whisper. He smiled weakly when he realized the chief had lost his cigar.

Chief Strickland looked at the medics who had been studying Charlie's injuries. One of them shook his head sadly. The chief had seen accidents like this before, but usually the victim was dead on impact. He turned back to Charlie. "You still with us, son?"

"Yessir. I don't feel anything. Are my legs broke? Am I gonna be okay?" Charlie's voice shook.

The chief never lied to his men and refused to start now. "I'm afraid it's bad, son. The pressure from the tanks is basically keeping you from bleeding out."

Charlie's body trembled involuntarily. "So, I'm gonna die?" he breathed in a weak whisper.

"When we pull the tanks apart, it'll be over, son. Is there anything I can do for you in the meantime?"

Tears ran down Charlie's cheeks. "Give my girl back home a message. Tell her that it's okay. She doesn't have to be afraid anymore. Beau can't hurt her."

Though Charlie's voice began to quiver, he wasn't finished. The chief grabbed a clipboard with paper and jotted down the rest. Then, Charlie's head slumped over as he lost consciousness.

One of the medics kept checking Charlie for a pulse. A few minutes later, he looked at the chief. "He's gone, sir."

Hands on his hips and shaking his head, Chief Strickland gave the order. "Back it up, Davis."

Saturday morning found Grace helping Bonnie in the café. "More coffee, Miss Ouida?" Grace smiled and began to pour before Ouida even answered.

Ouida eyed her curiously. "You certainly are the perky one today. You must have gotten a letter from your soldier."

"Two actually. The letters were dated the first week Charlie arrived in Germany. It's just taken them a while to get to me." She gazed out the window at a perfect spring day, and for the umpteenth time, pulled Charlie's snapshot from her back pocket. "I hope he's thawing out over there by now."

"Order up!" Vern was sliding eggs on a plate. Gracie sighed as she pocketed the photo and retrieved the food. With a warm plate in each hand, she threaded her way through the Saturday crowd of hungry patrons.

She heard the bell tinkle as the café door swung open. There were two grave looking men dressed in military uniforms. One of them looked directly at Grace. "Excuse me, ma'am. Do you know where we can find Grace MacGregor?"

For the next few moments, Grace's world turned into slow motion. She heard the plates hit the floor and a scream coming from somewhere. She didn't comprehend that the scream was her own.

Then Grace discovered that she was sitting upright in a chair. She felt a cool cloth on her face and heard the soft murmur of BonBon's voice. "Gracie, honey, can you hear me? Sweetheart, I'm right here. I won't let go of you."

Grace continued screaming as she collapsed into someone's arms. Buddy Sampson carried her limp body all the way to BonBon's house.

A while later Grace opened her eyes. It took her a few moments to realize she was in her own bed. She could see the moon shimmering behind her closed curtains and hear the muffled voice of Dr. Hunt in the hallway.

"The sedative should be wearing off by now, Miz Bonnie. If she's awake, maybe you can get her to drink something. She needs to stay hydrated."

Bonnie's reply was strained. "She's devastated, Doc. How will we ever get through this?"

Doc Hunt sighed as he patted Bonnie on her shoulder. "Like you've gotten through all the other difficulties you've ever faced, Miz Bonnie. You were a widow before you were 30. You run a successful business all on your own. Most importantly, you've fought like a warrior to make sure Grace could have the life she deserves. You've been a strong, independent woman as long as I've known you."

Bonnie began to weep. "I know I'll be okay, but what about Gracie? This may be too much for her."

"Now don't you sell Grace MacGregor short. Just think of all the hurdles she's conquered. She's always been a survivor, and with time and your love, your daughter will survive this tragic loss."

Grace listened as BonBon led Dr. Hunt down the stairs and said goodbye at the front door. Dr. Hunt was wrong. Grace did not want to survive without Charlie in this world. She'd rather die.

CHAPTER THIRTY-SEVEN

The Army took its precious time returning Charlie's remains to the States. The wait was agonizing for Grace. She wouldn't leave her room. She barely spoke. Bonnie watched Gracie revert to the frail, mute little girl who'd shown up at her café years before. She tempted Grace with all her favorite foods to no avail. When Grace did manage a few bites, she'd become so nauseated that she'd vomit it all back up.

Dr. Hunt encouraged Bonnie to make sure Grace stayed hydrated above all else. "Don't worry so much about the eating. She'll get hungry in time. I think the nausea is just a side effect of her grief."

When Charlie's body finally arrived, Bonnie recruited Bev and Marcy to coerce Grace into taking a shower. "Sweetheart, you'll never forgive yourself if you don't tell him goodbye. Your friends are here to help you get ready."

Bev and Marcy were standing just outside the bedroom door. Bev cleared her throat and tried to sound cheerful. "Hi, Gracie. Your wardrobe consultant and makeup artist have arrived."

Marcy piped in. "Vern is making us cheesesteaks for lunch. You don't want to miss that."

While Grace turned her back and rolled into a fetal position, the girls remained relentless. Somehow, they managed to get Grace to her feet and into the shower. Before Grace even registered what was happening, Marcy had her hair up in rollers while Bev took inventory of her closet.

Bev held up two dresses. "What about one of these? They're both pretty."

Marcy positioned Grace under the hair dryer and pointed to the blue dress. "That's the one. It's perfect with her blonde hair and blue eyes."

Grace didn't respond. She just sat quietly under the dryer as tears rolled down her cheeks. Her two friends sat on either side of her and held her hands.

An hour later, Marcy put the finishing touches on Grace's hair and makeup. Bev slipped off Grace's robe and helped her into her dress. "You were right, Marcy, this dress is perfect." Bev turned Grace towards the full-length mirror. "What do you think, Gracie?"

Grace stared at herself for a long moment as though she didn't recognize the girl staring back at her. Then she began to crumple. "I can't. I just can't."

Just as Marcy and Bev got her in a chair, the bedroom door opened. It was Miss Ouida. "Hi girls. You look lovely, Gracie. Your friends did a fantastic job."

Ouida smiled at Bev and Marcy, who both shrugged their shoulders. "Why don't you two run on over to the café and have some lunch. I'll stay here with Gracie." A look of relief spread over their faces as they headed out of Grace's bedroom.

Ouida sat down on the edge of the bed and took Grace's hands in hers. "Sweetheart, I know your heart feels fractured in pieces, and I understand why you want to hide in your room. When we're faced with death, especially an untimely one, we want to run the other way."

Grace sobbed. "It's my fault, Miss Ouida. That's why he's dead. God's punishing me."

"Whatever do you mean, Gracie?" Ouida handed her a tissue. "Now blow your nose, honey, and talk to me."

Grace obeyed and blew her nose as if she were a little girl again. Then she hung her head and whispered. "I cheated on him, Miss Ouida. I'm no better than my whore of a mother. I'm just like her."

Ouida's arms surrounded Grace. "Honey, you are nothing like your blood mother. Your real mother is downstairs worried sick about you." She lifted Grace's chin. "You are a MacGregor through and through. Don't you ever believe otherwise."

Grace's bottom lip quivered. "If I hadn't cheated on Charlie, he'd still be alive."

Ouida grabbed her hands tightly. "First of all, you did not cheat on Charlie. As I remember it, he wanted you to play the field while he was gone. And secondly, God doesn't work that way. If He did, honey, I'd be burning in Hell."

Gracie sniffled a giggle. Then she gathered what little strength she had deep within her. "Will you help me get downstairs, Miss Ouida? I don't think I'm strong enough on my own."

"Sweet Gracie, you have an entire family here. We'll be your strength." As they made their way across the alley and into the café, Grace understood what Ouida meant. Even though the café was closed, there were people milling all around inside.

Buddy was the first to stand up. "There's our girl. How're you feeling? Take my chair, sweetheart."

Brooxie and Chief Bushy were drinking coffee at the counter. At first glance, Gracie didn't recognize her high school softball coach. Miss Hughes, dressed in a simple navy sheath, smiled lovingly at Grace. "I'm so very sorry, Gracie."

BonBon took Grace by the hand. "I've got you a little lunch, honey. You need some nourishment." She guided Grace through the swinging doors and into the kitchen. The counters were crammed with dishes covered in foil. "Everybody has been by with food. I guess I'll have to serve some of this in the café. We certainly can't eat it all."

She led Grace to her usual stool at the stainless table. "I thought just the two of us could have some lunch. I know you're not ready for a big meal, so I made a batch of fresh biscuits." She halved a warm biscuit on Grace's plate and added some butter and jam. "That's the first thing you ever ate in this kitchen."

Grace put on a brave smile. "It smells as delicious as it did that first day." Mother and daughter sat quietly as they ate.

The funeral was a complete blur to Grace. She tried to concentrate on Reverend Hogan's eulogy and take in all the beautiful flowers surrounding the pulpit. But all she could see was the flag-draped coffin holding her precious Charlie, his body too mangled for viewing.

The next thing she remembered was the cemetery with people standing all around. She smelled the newly turned earth that would be Charlie's resting place. She was so tired and weak. When the first spade of dirt hit Charlie's coffin, she squeezed BonBon's hand. "Can we go now?"

As they headed back to the car, she caught a glimpse of Brooxie standing under a tree away from the crowd of mourners. Her heart ached as she watched this always sturdy and self-assured man sobbing uncontrollably.

CHAPTER THIRTY-EIGHT

The following Monday morning, Grace sat at the café's counter nursing a cup of coffee and picking at her bacon and eggs. She'd missed a week of school and was ready to go back. It certainly would be better than wasting away in the house.

Bonnie stopped on her way to the kitchen and leaned over Grace's shoulder. "Honey, you must eat something. You can't go to classes all day on an empty stomach."

Obediently, Grace forced down a mouthful. Within minutes, though, she felt the food coming back up and dashed to the bathroom off the kitchen.

Bonnie stood outside the door with a cool, wet cloth. "Here, honey." She studied Grace as she wiped her mouth. "Are you sure you're ready to go back to school?"

"Yes, I'm sure. I don't want to have to repeat this quarter, and I'm already a week behind." Her eyes were determined.

Bonnie gave in. "Okay, honey. But I've made you an appointment with Dr. Hunt on Wednesday afternoon at 4." She pulled Grace close to her. "Drive safely."

Gracie remained in BonBon's arms for a few extra moments. It was the one place she felt truly safe these days.

Two days later, Grace sat on the examining table in Dr. Hunt's office as he studied her chart. "Miss Grace, you've dropped five pounds since you were here for your annual checkup in the fall. That's five pounds too many."

He looked up at her. "I know you're still grieving, but we need to boost that appetite. Are you eating any better?"

Grace grimaced. "I'm trying, but just about everything I eat, with the exception of BonBon's biscuits, wants to come back up."

Dr. Hunt rubbed his chin. "I'm going to order some blood work today. It will take a few days to get the results. Until then, you enjoy all the biscuits you can eat." He smiled and sent Grace on her way.

Since the café was closed on Wednesday afternoons, Grace headed straight home. BonBon had left a note reminding Grace that she was getting her hair done and added that she'd left some mail on Grace's bed.

With plenty of makeup classwork still to complete, Grace relished the silence. As she plopped her books on her bed, she found an official looking letter on her pillow. It was an airmail envelope with an APO return address.

Could it be a final letter from Charlie? Even as her eyes began to tear up, she had her doubts. The handwriting wasn't Charlie's, and she'd already received a letter on the day he was buried. That letter had been dated the day before he died.

The letter she held in her hands now was just one page written in an unfamiliar scrawl:

Dear Miss MacGregor,

As Pvt. Charles Callahan's commanding officer, I was present at his tragic death. I want you to know that he died courageously.

Pvt. Callahan's last words were about you. After he passed away, I wrote down his words so I could deliver them to you as he requested. These were Pvt. Callahan's last words:

"Give my girl back home a message. Tell her that it's okay. She doesn't have to be afraid anymore. Beau can't hurt her. Don't quit living just because I'm not there. You go on and be the finest teacher in the state of Georgia. You'll always be my Baby Girl."

Grace read and reread Charlie's last words until she had memorized them. It was just like her Charlie to be taking care of her even during his last moments on earth.

While she didn't understand what he meant about Beau Loosier, a sense of peace fell over her. She folded the letter and placed it in a miniature cedar chest that held all of Charlie's other letters. As she slid the chest under her bed, it bumped into a cardboard box.

Grace withdrew the larger box to study its contents. The container held the mementos of her childhood all the way through high school. She had forgotten that she'd also stored all of Charlie's memories in the box.

Charlie had only one picture of him with his family before their house burned to the ground. In it his mother was holding the baby and his father had Charlie lifted atop his shoulders. Grace could tell by their smiles that they had been a loving, happy family. His father's hair hung across his forehead, and he shared Charlie's lopsided grin.

Grace ran her fingers across the photo and mumbled. "I guess you were glad to see him when he got to Heaven."

Charlie had given all his school pictures and Boy Scout paraphernalia to Grace for safekeeping. She lined the items up by year and actually giggled to see the transformation of Charlie from a little boy to an awkward adolescent to a handsome young man.

Her favorite picture was one of the two of them dressed in formal wear for Grace's senior prom. While Grace was looking at the camera, Charlie's eyes shone on her. His loving gaze made her heart ache.

Grace's hand fell upon a folder of essays from her senior British literature class with Miz Runelle Meeks. The class had been her favorite. Grace thumbed through the papers until her fingers landed on her last essay that year.

Miz Meeks had devoted the last week of class to the poetry of William Wordsworth. Their final assignment had been to choose one of his poems and write an analysis of it.

Grace smiled to herself at the cover sheet sporting an A+, a score typically unheard of in Miz Meeks' class. Grace's teacher had added a comment next to the grade: "Your study shows insight with a maturity beyond your years. Bravo!"

Deciding against Wordsworth's popular poem about daffodils, Grace had instead chosen *Ode: Intimations of Immortality*. In this poem, Wordsworth compares youth to the beauty of nature and discusses how we often mourn the loss of youth as we grow older. Miz Meeks had pointed out that the final stanza of the poem was often considered a poem of its own, referred to as *Splendour in the Grass*.

In her paper, Grace chose to focus on that last stanza:

Though nothing can bring back the hour
Of splendour in the grass, of glory in the flower?
We will grieve not, rather find
Strength in what remains behind...
In the soothing thoughts that spring
Out of human suffering,
In the faith that looks through death,
In years that bring the philosophic mind.

She had forgotten what she had written until she studied her comments:

"While some may view this poem as a study of aging, Wordsworth's words could also be a commentary on losing someone dear. Even when we lose the person with whom we shared the 'splendour of the grass' and 'the glory of the flower,' we still retain the memories of those special moments. We may suffer our loss, but we can always return in memory to those 'soothing thoughts' if we possess 'the faith that looks through death.'"

Grace closed the folder and returned to the photos that held all her memories of Charlie. As she studied his loving gaze, she made a promise. "Okay, Charlie Callahan, I'll keep living, but I'll never forget you. And I have the faith to believe that one day I'll see you again." She packed up the box and turned her eyes towards the living.

⚜

A few days later, Grace sat once again in an exam room waiting on Dr. Hunt, who had received her lab results. When he entered the room, the doctor's demeanor seemed more detached than usual. "Grace, do you know the date of your last period?"

She blushed and then shrugged. "I'm not sure with everything that's happened. I do remember having a period right before Christmas, but after that, I can't recall. I've never been really regular, um, since my accident a few years back."

Dr. Hunt cleared his throat as he took her pulse. "How's the nausea? Any better?"

Grace nodded. "Actually, it is. Well, I'm still nauseated early in the day but seem to feel better as the day goes on."

Dr. Hunt took her hand. "That's because you're almost through your first trimester."

"First what?" Grace's eyes grew big. "What does that mean?"

"Grace, you're pregnant."

Grace went limp. "Pregnant? But how?"

"I doubt I need to explain how that happens, Grace. Let me listen to your heart."

Even though the stethoscope was cold against her chest, Grace remained speechless. Then she burst into tears. "What am I going to do? BonBon will kill me!"

Doc Hunt patted her shoulder. "There, there. I seriously doubt that will be Miz Bonnie's reaction." He smiled kindly. "But I think you need to decide on an obstetrician. You can see Dr. Mincey in Thomaston. He's excellent."

"NO! Not in Thomaston! BonBon has so many friends there." She knew BonBon would be mortified with shame if all of Thomaston knew about her condition.

"That's fine." Doc Hunt scribbled something on notepad. "There's a new obstetrics practice in Griffin. I've heard good things about them." He tore off the piece of paper with the phone number and address of the practice and handed it to Grace. "You shouldn't waste any time getting in to see them."

Grace held the piece of paper like a hot potato as Doc Hunt wrote something else on a prescription pad. "Also, I want you to start on these vitamins today. They should help your appetite and put some weight back on you. Since you're at the end of your first trimester, your nausea should improve greatly in the next few weeks."

Doc patted her again on her shoulder. As he headed towards the door, he turned back. "And Grace, don't wait to tell Miz Bonnie. You're going to need her help. Once she recovers from the surprise, I wager she'll be quite supportive."

Since BonBon would be busy preparing for Friday evening's supper crowd, Grace drove out the Concord Highway. If anyone could give her perspective on what to do, it was Miss Ouida.

As she pulled up the long drive, Grace could see Miss Ouida in her usual spot on the front porch. She was enjoying what she called her afternoon toddy. Grace wondered if she would mind sharing.

"Sweet Gracie, how wonderful to see you out and about on this beautiful afternoon. I was just having a cool cocktail. Can I offer you something?" Ouida stopped with the niceties long enough to notice that Grace was trembling from head to toe.

Ouida met her at the bottom step. "What's wrong, honey. Are you sick?"

Grace shook her head. "Not exactly. I'm pregnant." She hadn't intended to blurt it out. The words sounded so alien to her ears. She looked at Miss Ouida for a reaction.

Ouida took in a deep breath. "I think I need a cigarette. Come sit down, child."

"I think you need to come up with a better nickname for me, Miss Ouida. I don't want to be known as a child having a child." Gracie slumped in the other rocker. "How will I ever tell BonBon?" She hung her head. "I told you I was no better than my whore mother." Tears splashed on her blouse.

Ouida handed her the napkin she was holding beneath her cocktail glass and then took two long drags on her cigarette. She raised an eyebrow as she studied Grace. "I've always wanted a child. Did you know that, Gracie? A child is one of God's finest miracles. I realize the timing isn't always right for the Lord's miracle, at least in our way of thinking. But I also know that God's plan is perfect even if it takes us a spell to figure that out."

Grace stared at her. "Miss Ouida, I didn't realize you were so religious."

Ouida laughed. "Honey, I guess I'm more spiritual than religious. I've lived long enough to be witness to some miracles, and I know they were the work of the Lord's hand."

Grace was intrigued. "What miracles have you witnessed?"

"I'll tell you my favorite one. A dear friend once told me that her deepest regret was never having a child. God must have been listening because one day He left a child practically on my friend's doorstep."

"You're talking about BonBon and me, aren't you?"

Ouida blew a smoke ring and smiled. "About the only thing better than a child is a grandchild."

Grace sighed as she touched her stomach. "With Charlie gone, this child will be fatherless."

"Gracie, you are so wrong! Since Bonnie adopted you, have you ever felt bereft of a father or a mother? All you need to do is look around the café every morning. There's Buddy and Cooter and Vern. And then there's Brooxie, who thought of Charlie as a son. He'd give up his whiskey for a grandchild. Not to mention Bonnie and me. Just like we did with you, we'll circle the wagons around this baby."

For the first time since Doc Hunter had given Gracie the news, she smiled. "I'm going to have Charlie's baby! A part of him will always be with me." She grabbed Ouida's hand. "I don't want to tell BonBon until after I see the obstetrician. Will you keep my secret, Miss Ouida?"

Before she answered, Ouida's mind hovered over the secret she was already harboring for Charlie. She lit another cigarette. "My lips are sealed, Gracie."

Dr. Bishop at Griffin Obstetrics confirmed what Doc Hunt had already told Grace. "Yes, you are a good three months pregnant. I put your due date in late September. I want you to continue the vitamins he prescribed...and *eat*, young lady! I expect to see at least a two-pound weight gain when you return next month."

When Grace scheduled her next appointment at the checkout desk, the secretary handed her a bill. "Now honey, this is due in full before you deliver. Tell your husband that you can pay a little each month."

At the mention of a husband, Grace's face colored. She emptied her wallet of her entire savings, which totaled $20. "I'll get started on that monthly payment now." The secretary amended the balance and returned the bill to Grace.

She waited until she was in the car before she looked at the balance. Somewhere, somehow, she would need to come up with $350 before her due date. "Okay, Lord, I'm going to need one of your miracles."

At home that evening, Grace watched as the lights went out in the café. Her eyes followed BonBon as she crossed through the alley and under the streetlights to their house. She was sitting at the kitchen table pretending to study when BonBon walked in.

"Whew, my feet are aching." BonBon slipped out of her shoes and sat down at the table. "Did you eat the supper I sent over by Vern?"

Gracie smiled. "I cleaned my plate. I probably would have eaten another pork chop if there had been one."

"I'm so glad my girl is getting her appetite back. How was your day? I was so busy when you stopped by after school, I hardly saw you."

"I had a good day." Gracie picked up her ink pen. "Just need to finish this paper before I go to bed." She swallowed, quickly losing her nerve to share the news with BonBon.

"I think I'll make me a cup of hot cocoa to help me sleep." BonBon headed to the stove in her stockinged feet. "You want some?"

"Yes, that would be good, BonBon. Thanks." Gracie tried to concentrate on her paper, but her heart was pounding with something—either dread or excitement.

She waited for BonBon to sit down with their cocoa. "Give it a minute to cool, honey." BonBon looked up just in time to catch a glimpse of worry in Grace's furrowed brow and blue eyes. "What's wrong, sweetie?"

Just spit it out, she told herself. "I'm three months pregnant. You're going to be a grandmother in September."

The kitchen grew painfully silent. Grace studied the shock on BonBon's face. "I know it's bad timing, BonBon. I know you're disappointed."

BonBon held her hand up to stop Grace. Then she took a slow, deep breath. "You're having Charlie's baby?" She studied Grace from head to toe.

There was another brief silence. Then BonBon's eyes began to sparkle. "Do you know how much I resented that Oscar didn't give me a child before he left me? At least then I would have a part of him with me."

Gracie's voice was timid. "So, you're okay with having an unwed pregnant daughter? Aren't you worried about what people will say?"

BonBon stood up and threw her arms around Gracie. "I'm delighted! And I don't give-give a rat's ass what anybody else has to say!"

Gracie burst into laughter. "Did you just say 'rat's ass'? I don't know whether to be shocked or impressed!" They fell into each other's arms as they both laughed through tears.

The two sat at the kitchen table until after midnight plotting and planning life with a baby in the MacGregor household. "BonBon, the only other people who know are Dr. Hunt and Miss Ouida. Let's keep it that way until I start showing."

BonBon agreed. "That's a smart idea. The two of us need time to get used to the idea before we spring it on everyone." Her heart was brimming with an excited anticipation like she'd never felt. "Now you need to get to bed, little Mama."

When she finally climbed into bed, Grace whispered a prayer. "Dear Lord, I guess BonBon's reaction would count as your first miracle. I'm gonna trust in You to take care of all the other stuff." She fell into the soundest sleep she'd had since Charlie died.

。◆。

Ouida had been right about Grace's café family circling the wagons around her. Grace spent early September waddling from table to table as she served coffee to the regulars. She'd taken all the classes she could over the summer quarter knowing she would miss the fall session.

At Cooter's suggestion, Vern had set a "Guess the Date" fruit jar by the cash register. For a dollar, customers could wager on the birthdate of Grace's baby. The jar was brimming with cash, which would be a gift for Grace and the baby.

One bright sunny morning in late September, the sign on the café's door was still turned to "Closed" when Cooter arrived. Buddy was right behind him, but neither complained. As a matter of fact, Buddy gave a hoot. "September 25! That was my bet. I win!"

Cooter sighed. "Shoot, we should have wagered on whether she would have a girl or a boy."

"It's a girl!" Ouida walked down the sidewalk grinning and carrying a huge pink bow. "Born at 4:05 a.m. I just left Griffin Hospital. Mama and baby are doing fine."

As Ouida tied the bow to the café's front door, Buddy sighed. "I can pick up some breakfast in Thomaston, I guess. But what will I do about supper tonight?"

"All you ever think about is how you're gonna get fed!" Ouida sighed. "Don't worry, Bonnie will open for supper at 5. I'm going to take the evening shift with Grace and the baby at the hospital."

The café was teeming with customers that evening. Though exhausted from a long, sleepless night, Bonnie beamed as she served her patrons. Vern posted a huge sign above the griddle that read, "Little Miss Bonnie Kaye MacGregor, Born September 25, 1971, 6 lbs. 14 oz."

Not a single soul had one unkind word about Grace and her new daughter. Instead, they were already arguing over who would get to hold the baby first.

Two days later, when Bonnie pulled into her driveway with Grace and baby Bonnie Kaye in tow, there was a band of well-wishers waiting. Brooxie opened the passenger door. His eyes sparkled as he studied the pink bundle Grace was holding. "She's a beauty!" His voice quivered. "Charlie would be so proud."

Before mama and baby could make it inside, everyone oohed and aahed as they each got a personal peek at the tiny creature. Buddy was the first to notice the baby's hair. "Is she a little carrot top? Must be some redheads on Charlie's side of the family."

Ouida punched Buddy in the arm and whispered. "Hush. It could be someone on Grace's side. She doesn't need to worry about that. This baby is a MacGregor!"

As she walked up the front steps, Grace pretended she hadn't over-heard Buddy's remarks. While her heart harbored suspicions about the baby's red hair, she'd already made up her mind that she would never share the possibility that someone besides Charlie was the baby's father. No one ever needed to know.

PART FOUR

CHAPTER THIRTY-NINE

The next few years were a whirlwind of bottles and diapers then baby food and training pants. Without the help of Gracie's makeshift café family, she would never have finished her education.

"Come on, BK. One more bite of eggs for BonBon." After realizing that the name "Bonnie Kaye" was a mouthful, Buddy Simpson had christened the child with the nickname of BK, and it stuck.

BonBon was sitting in the café's kitchen while she helped BK with her breakfast. The child insisted on using the spoon by herself even though much of the egg landed on her shirt instead of in her mouth.

When Grace, a cup of coffee in her hand, hurried into the kitchen, BK looked up with a milky grin. "I eat all by myself, Mama."

Grace's heart bubbled with love as she leaned over and kissed her daughter atop her red curls. "I'm so proud of you, BK!" She turned to BonBon. "I'm sorry I have to take off early. It's my turn for morning bus duty." Grace was now a first-grade teacher at Pike County Elementary School.

"Don't worry about us, honey. You know I'm always up early anyway to start the biscuits."

BK chimed in. "I help make biscuits, BonBon. Okay?" Her vocabulary seemed to grow overnight. Grace credited it to BK's being surrounded by adults so much.

By the time Bonnie turned over the sign to "Open," the biscuits were in the oven and little BK was covered in flour. "Come here, sweetheart, and let me clean you up." Bonnie wiped the child's face and hands with a warm washcloth.

BK slid off her stool. "I see Misser Vern now." She scampered through the swinging doors to visit with Vern at the griddle. "Bacon, please."

Vern smiled as he handed the child a piece of bacon. "Just for you, BK." She giggled as she took the bacon, an act that had become a daily ritual. "Thank you, Misser Vern."

Moments later the bell on the front door jingled. "BonBon, it's Misser Cooder!" The child struggled with pronouncing her "t's," but it just made her more endearing.

Cooter smiled as he approached his usual stool at the counter. "How are you today, Miss BK?" He leaned over to shake her hand. "Wanna practice our snapping?"

Cooter was teaching BK to snap her fingers. So far, she had not been successful, but she kept trying. "Mine don' make noise like you."

"Just keep at it, sweetheart." Cooter winked at her as Vern poured him a cup of coffee.

"Aun' Ouida here!" BK ran to the front door before Ouida even opened it.

"There's my redheaded Angel Pie!" The child hugged Ouida's skirt. Ouida laughed as she squeezed the little girl tightly. "You want to get a new book at the library today?"

BK's big brown eyes sparkled with excitement as she nodded her head. Once a week while Bonnie was busy in the café, Ouida and the little girl would walk to the library for children's story time and then pick out a new book for BK to bring home.

Buddy Sampson wasn't far behind Ouida. As he waddled into the café, BK ran to him. "Good morning, Uncle Buddy. When we go ride in your big car again and ged ice queem?"

"How about tomorrow?" He tousled the child's curly locks. "Ask Aunt Ouida if she'll ride to Thomaston with us."

BK's round questioning eyes turned to Ouida. "You go, Aun' Ouida? We get ice queem with cuwy top."

The entire café, now filling up with patrons, giggled at BK's precious pronunciations. As Bonnie threaded through the tables pouring coffee for customers along the way, she nodded at BK. "Honey, go in the kitchen and ride your scooter."

BK poked out her lip. "I stay with Aun' Ouida." Bonnie gave the child a gentle but serious look.

Ouida, though dying to light a cigarette, never smoked in front of BK. "Mind your BonBon, honey. We'll go to the library in a while." Obediently, BK scampered into the kitchen. Ouida lit her cigarette as soon as the coast was clear. "Thank goodness! I'm about to have a nicotine fit."

Smothering his biscuits in syrup, Buddy chimed in. "Maybe it'd be a good time for you to give up those cancer sticks."

Ouida blew smoke his way. "I will when you give up all that butter and syrup!" She hooted. "Of course, that'll never happen."

Bonnie returned to the kitchen to start her vegetables for the Blue Plate dinner special. "Watch out, honey!" BK rolled around the kitchen on the same scooter that had once belonged to Grace. "You're about to get too big for that scooter, aren't you?"

"Uncle Bwoosie gonna gid me a new one!" As if on cue, Brooxie tapped on the back door and then stuck his head in. "Bonnie, it's just me."

BK squealed in delight. "Uncle Bwoosie, Uncle Bwoosie!" Of all her café family, Brooxie Barnett was BK's favorite. She slid off her little scooter and ran to him.

Brooxie scooped the child up in his arms and swung her around. "How's my favorite redhead in the whole world?" The normally gruff, often irreverent Brooxie Barnett became a different man with BK, whose unconditional love for him softened his edges. With the precious little girl, he became a cuddly big bear.

BK patted Brooxie's scruffy face. "Chief Bushy have the kiddies now?"

"Not yet, sweetheart. But you get to choose the first kitty for your own as soon as it's born." He set the child down on a stool at the table and turned to Bonnie. "I rotated the tires and put new spark plugs in your car. I went ahead and pulled it into your driveway, Miz Bonnie." He handed her the keys to her car.

"Thanks so much. What do I owe you, Brooxie?"

Brooxie shook his head. "It's on the house, Miz Bonnie." When she began to protest, Brooxie held up his hand. "Okay, maybe just one favor. Could I take BK out to my cousin's farm in Barnesville this Sunday? His sow just had piglets, and I know she'd love to see them and all the other animals."

BK, eyes glistening with excitement, listened intently. "Can I go, BonBon? I jus' love aminals."

Both Brooxie and BonBon laughed. "As long as your mama says it's okay, but you'll have to take a nap after church before you go to the farm." Nap time had become a battle with the child. Oftentimes, when Bonnie or Gracie would peek in on her, BK would have book, which she was pretending to read to her stuffed bunny. BonBon made the bunny when the child was a baby. Although the bunny was ragged after being washed and mended countless times, it remained BK's favorite companion.

"I pwomise me and Bunny will do a good nap!" She turned to Brooxie. "Can I hold a pigley, Uncle Bwoosie?"

"Of course, you can hold a piglet, sweet girl." Brooxie gave the child a big hug before he left.

"Honestly, that man is worse than anybody for spoiling you rotten!" BonBon muttered as she poured water over her peas to cook.

BK tugged at her grandmother's apron. "Uncle Bwoosie love me the bess."

When BK turned five, she was delighted to start kindergarten. She got to ride to school with her mother each morning. During their drive to school, BK entertained Gracie by singing along with whatever was playing on the radio. The child had an uncanny ear for music and could not only remember the lyrics but also sing them in tune.

"I believe you'll be a famous musician someday, BK. Would you like that?"

BK gazed at her mother with serious eyes. "No, I'm gonna be a mechanic like Uncle Brooxie." The child had become adept at handing Brooxie the right tool when he worked on a car at the garage. She'd come home with grease on her hands and a contented smile on her face.

Grace never discouraged her. "You'd make a fine mechanic, BK. Just remember that you can be anything you want to be as long as you're willing to work hard."

Usually, Ouida picked up the child when kindergarten ended at noon each day. Bonnie was always up to her eyeballs with the lunch crowd at that time, and Grace's school day didn't end until 4.

Ouida enjoyed her afternoon drive with BK, who always had a story to share. Yesterday, it had been, "Wally Jones had to stand in the corner for picking his nose and eating his boogers."

"That sounds disgusting, BK!" Ouida tried not to giggle.

But on this particular day, BK didn't scamper out to Ouida's car as usual. Instead, she trudged along dragging her little red book satchel behind her. When she got into the car, she didn't return Ouida's greeting. "Whatever is wrong, sweet BK? Did you have a bad day?"

Tears started to trickle down her usually cheerful face. "Miss Ouida, do I have a daddy?" While Ouida considered her answer, the child continued. "Ellie Cato said I don't have a daddy. Is she right?"

Ouida sighed and longed for a cigarette. "Honey, you do have a daddy."

BK sniffled. "Where is he? Is my daddy the soldier in the picture on Mama's dresser? She's never told me anything about him."

Ouida treaded water as she searched for an answer. "Sweetheart, I think that's something you need to ask your mama."

The remainder of the ride back to the café was quiet. BK grabbed her satchel and shuffled into the back door of the café's kitchen. Bonnie had her lunch waiting on the stainless table. "How was school, sweetie?"

BK just shrugged as she picked up her peanut butter and jelly sandwich. Bonnie looked at Ouida with questioning eyes. Ouida raised one eyebrow. "I think I'll take a seat in the café. I'm famished."

Once the lunch crowd had dispersed, Ouida followed Bonnie into the kitchen. They discovered BK clutching her tattered bunny as she lay sound asleep on the little cot Bonnie kept in the back closet of the kitchen.

"Well, that's the first time in forever that she hasn't complained about taking a nap." Bonnie looked at Ouida for answers. "Did she tell you what upset her today?"

Ouida sighed. "One of the little girls in her class teased BK about having no daddy. When she got in my car, she was crying. She asked me about the picture of Charlie on Gracie's dresser."

"I'm not surprised. I knew this was bound to happen when BK started school." Bonnie poured each of them a cup of coffee and sat down at the table. "I've encouraged Gracie to tell Bonnie Kaye about her daddy, but Gracie argues that the child is too young."

"Innocence seems so fleeting these days." Ouida stirred some sugar in her coffee. "I know talking about Charlie is difficult for Gracie, but I don't think she can stall any longer."

"I agree, Ouida. The child shouldn't receive her information from outsiders. I'll have a talk with Grace when she gets home." And she did.

After BK's bath that night, Gracie stood behind her brushing out her tangled curls. "Ouch, Mama! That hurts."

Grace put the brush down. "Is there something else hurting you tonight, sweet one?"

BK hung her head. "Ellie Cato says I'm the only one in class without a daddy." Brown eyes brimming with tears, she stared at her mother in the mirror. "Why don't I have a daddy like everybody else?"

Grace took a deep breath as she offered BK a tissue. "You have a daddy. Would you like to hear about him?" BK's eyes grew big as she nodded. "Let's go into my bedroom, and I'll tell you about your daddy."

BK followed her mother into the bedroom and climbed up on her bed. Her cat Bingo jumped up beside her. Although Grace usually forbade the cat to be on her bed, she smiled and let it go. She opened a drawer and withdrew the small cedar box that held Charlie's letters and the snapshots taken during their years together.

Before Grace could gather her thoughts, BK pointed at the framed photo on the dresser. "That's my daddy, isn't it? Was he a soldier?"

Grace was glad for the ice breaker. "Yes, that's your daddy, and he served in the Army." She handed BK the framed photograph. "This was taken when he was stationed at Fort Bragg for training." Grace studied her daughter as she gazed at Charlie's lopsided grin.

"They cut off all his hair when he first went into the Army. Let me show you some of my favorite pictures of him." She opened the small chest and pulled out the photos of the two of them during their high school years. BK stared at the one of Grace in her blue prom dress, Charlie gazing at her instead of the camera.

"You look like a fairy princess, Mama!" BK studied Charlie's face. "Was he your prince?"

Grace's voice quivered. "Yes, he was my very own Prince Charming."

"Just like in Cinderella." BK was intrigued. "Who was your Fairy Godmother?"

"I had two Fairy Godmothers. First was BonBon. She adopted me when I was younger than you are now."

"What does 'adopt' mean?" BK's brown eyes sparkled with questions.

"BonBon loved me so much that she wanted me to be hers after my real mama went to Heaven."

Grace's answer seemed to mollify BK. "Then who is your other Fairy Godmother?"

"Your Aunt Ouida. She used to take me shopping for pretty clothes and to the beauty shop to get my hair done." Grace pointed to the photo in BK's hands. "As a matter of fact, your Aunt Ouida and Uncle Buddy took me to Rich's in downtown Atlanta to buy that dress."

"Did you ride the Pink Pig?" Buddy and Ouida had taken BK to see Rich's big Christmas tree and ride the Pink Pig the previous December.

Grace giggled. "I was too big for the Pink Pig by then."

BK's eyes turned solemn. "Why isn't Charlie here now like Ellie Cato's daddy?" A lump in her throat prevented Grace from answering. Instead, tears rolled down her cheeks. "Why are you crying, Mama?" BK reached out and patted away her mother's tears.

Grace tried again. "Your daddy went to Germany to work on big Army tanks when you were already in my tummy. There was a terrible accident, and your daddy died."

Too smart for her years, BK sighed. "So, my daddy died before I was even born? And that's why you're sad?"

"Yes, honey. That's why I'm sad." Grace cleared her throat. "But your daddy watches over you and me from Heaven. Do you understand?"

"Of course, I do! He's an angel, like BonBon taught me in Sunday school." BK picked up a tiny box snuggled inside the cedar one. "What's in here?"

Grace's heart skipped a beat as she opened the ring box. "Your daddy gave this to me before he went to Germany. It was his promise to marry me when he returned."

"Why don't you wear it now, Mama?"

Grace brushed a stray red curl from her daughter's face. She didn't have the heart to explain that she had betrayed Charlie and didn't feel worthy of the ring. "I'm saving it for you to wear when you grow up. I think your daddy would like that."

BK ran a finger over the ring and replaced it in the box. Then she yawned. "Okay, Mama."

Grace lifted her precious child into her arms and carried her to her own bed. Bingo jumped up right beside BK. "Watch over her, Lord. She's all I have to call my own."

CHAPTER FORTY

1987

Sixteen-year-old Bonnie Kaye MacGregor stood in front of the bath-room mirror as she fiddled with her curly hair. "Mama, did you buy anymore hairspray?"

Gracie, dressed in a suit and heels, poked her head in the door. "Under the sink, BK. You better hurry. You promised to help BonBon with the supper crowd tonight." She stared at her pretty daughter. "You need a little help with that ponytail?"

"Yes, please." BK handed her mother the brush. "Sometimes I wish my hair wasn't so red and so curly."

Gracie expertly threaded the thick, curly hair through an elastic band. "Hush your mouth! Do you know how many women would kill for your hair?" She grinned at her daughter in the mirror. "Not to mention those huge brown eyes."

BK MacGregor was no longer a little freckle-faced child full of mis-chief. She had matured into a stunning young woman with a feisty, dimpled smile. She had a natural gift for anything musical. As Grace studied her daughter, she was amazed at BK's metamorphosis into womanhood.

BK nodded in satisfaction with the ponytail. Then she turned to face Grace with those dramatic caramel eyes. "Have you given any more thought to the guitar lessons, Mama? I talked to Mr. Holloway, and he said he had an opening on Tuesday nights. It wouldn't interfere with my piano or voice lessons."

For the last six months, mother and daughter had argued about guitar lessons. Grace was furious with herself for not getting rid of Hugh's old guitar that she'd hidden in the attic so many years ago. She shuddered at the memory of the day her daughter emerged from the attic with the long-forgotten instrument in her hands.

BonBon had sent the child up the attic ladder to dig through an old cedar chest filled with BK's great-grandmother's wardrobe. She was searching for Roaring 20s attire to wear in her role as Jo Stockton, the female lead in the Griffin Community Theater's production of *Funny Face*.

On that fateful day, BK stood clad in a flapper dress that reeked of moth balls, holding the dusty guitar. "Mama, look what I found! It was behind that old cedar chest." Since then, she'd been campaigning for lessons.

"I don't have time to debate with you about that right now, Bonnie Kaye." Grace's rare use of her daughter's full name signaled her exasperation. "I have two committee meetings before the school board meeting tonight." For the past five years, Grace had served as principal of Pike Elementary School. "Get yourself over to the café. We'll have this discussion later."

Grace hurried down the stairs before BK had time for a rebuttal. As she drove to the school, Grace's mind struggled with the thought of that long-ago weekend she'd spent with Hugh Lockett. As her daughter grew older, there was no doubt in Grace's mind that she was the child of the handsome Australian. Bonnie Kaye not only had his hair and brown eyes but also his sharp sense of humor and his gift for music.

Pulling into the school parking lot, Grace shrugged away the memories to focus on the meetings ahead. Only 36 herself, Grace was the youngest person and first woman to hold the position of principal in Pike County. She loved her job and served relentlessly as a champion for the children, the faculty, the parents, and the building itself.

The one thing missing in Grace's life was a man. Still a stunner in her own right, she'd never been interested in a serious relationship. Her excuse for not dating was always the same: "I'm too busy for a social life."

BonBon was continually fussing at her. "You just make yourself too busy. You need to have someone other than BK and me in your life. Before long, your daughter will be gone, and I'll be dead." She'd succeeded only in getting a giggle out of Grace.

The truth was that Grace felt undeserving of a man. Wasn't being alone God's punishment for her? Besides, she doubted any man could ever compare to her Charlie. She still missed his lopsided grin and sometimes berated herself that Charlie's smile didn't belong to BK. She picked up her briefcase, squared her shoulders, and headed into the school.

Back at the café, business was brusque for a Tuesday night. As she carried dirty dishes through the swinging door, BK almost bumped into her grandmother. "BonBon, if you'd stop serving your chicken and dumplings as the Blue Plate special, we'd get a break."

"And then what would I do? Sit around and knit all day?" BonBon smiled at her granddaughter, who grinned back.

"You're not the typical granny, thank goodness!"

BK started scrubbing dishes as BonBon patted her on the behind. "And don't call me a granny!" While she was nearing 70, Bonnie MacGregor was as spry as someone half her age. Her hair was completely gray, but her step was still brisk. She would never admit that the long days on her feet had begun to take their toll.

Those feet still hit the floor every morning before daybreak. By the time Cooter Renfro, still the café's first customer each day, came through the door, Bonnie had baked three batches of biscuits and started on whatever her evening special would be.

Although newly retired from the US Postal Service, Cooter's breakfast hour remained the same. Nowadays, he would often tarry on his usual stool at the counter long after the breakfast crowd left for their perspective places of business. He rarely returned for the evening meal as his wife, Miz Fannie Mae, was a pretty good cook.

On this evening, BK scooted back and forth from the kitchen to the dining room with an agility that came from years of helping in the café. She was surprised to see Mr. Cooter at the counter. He was holding up the afternoon edition of *The Thomaston Times*. "Did y'all see this?"

Ouida, jumpy from a week without cigarettes, almost fell off her stool. "Do you have to shout, Cooter Renfroe? Nothing's that important unless they've declared World War III."

BK stopped long enough to smile at Ouida. She whispered in her ear as she poured Ouida another glass of tea. "I'm so proud of you, Miss Ouida. You've made it seven days without smoking. How do you feel?"

Ouida raised an eyebrow at BK and grimaced. "Miserable. How about some more sugar for this tea, honey?" The she turned to Cooter. "So, what's the news?"

Cooter never tired of an audience. "Says here that this drought's done caused the lake out at Camp Thunder to drop ten feet. Some Boy Scouts were out there yesterday fishing and saw the bumper of a car sticking out of the lake. Turns out it's an old Ford with a skeleton in it. They've called in the GBI to investigate."

That news sent a wave of murmurs across the café—except for Buddy Simpson, who never stopped eating. Bonnie, who had just walked in from the kitchen, caught the tail end of the conversation. Her face lost all its color. "Have they identified the body?"

Cooter looked back down at the paper. "Paper says that there's nothing left of the body but bones. The GBI hopes to make an identification through dental records. That vehicle must've been on the bottom of the lake for years."

As Bonnie headed back to the kitchen, her legs almost gave way. BK grabbed her by the arm. "BonBon, you alright?"

Bonnie patted her granddaughter's arm. "I'm fine, honey. The dining room is thinning out now. Vern and I can close up. Why don't you run along and get your homework done."

Bonnie was already in bed by the time Grace arrived home. She found BK at the piano playing a tune she'd never heard. "Hi, sweetie. Is that one of yours?"

"Just something I'm working on. Did you hear they found a body in the lake at Camp Thunder?"

Grace sat down on the couch. "A body? Do they know who it is?"

BK proceeded to share the story in detail. "I think the news upset BonBon. She would've fainted if I hadn't caught her. When she got home, she went straight to bed. We didn't even share our usual cup of hot cocoa."

"Oh dear, I hope she's not getting sick again. That bronchitis she had last winter really set her back." Grace leaned over and hugged her daughter. "Why don't you give the piano a rest so you won't disturb BonBon. It's almost time for you to go to bed, anyway."

"Have you thought anymore about the guitar lessons? I can pay for half of them with my babysitting money." When BK wanted something, she could be relentlessly persistent.

Grace sighed. She'd finally worn her down. "You have to pay for strings and picks and any other accessories. And the minute your grades start to fall, the guitar is history." BK squealed. "Shhh! Don't disturb your grandmother! She needs her rest."

BK danced a quiet little jig. "Thanks, Mama. I promise I'll keep my grades up." Grace pointed at the math book on the kitchen table, and BK hung her head. "Including Algebra II, which I detest because I'll never use it a day in my life!"

⚜

Two weeks later, Sheriff Riggins sat at the café's counter for a mid-morning cup of coffee and a slice of Bonnie's apple pie. The café was empty except for Leon Smith from the *Thomaston Times* who sat beside him. "Is it a good time for that interview, Sheriff?"

"As good as any." The sheriff added some cream to his coffee. "Whaddya want to know?"

Leon removed a small leather notebook and a pen from his pocket. "Let's start with the findings from the dental records. Did the GBI get a match?"

"As we expected, the records match Beau Loosier. He went missing about 17 years ago. Do you remember him?"

Leon nodded. "Yes. He was the son of Talmadge and Louvenia Loosier. They've both passed away, haven't they?"

"Yep. Louvenia lost her battle with cancer a few years ago. Talmadge passed away last summer. He spent most of his money searching for his son. I hate to speak ill of the dead, but that money was wasted on Beau Loosier. That boy stayed in some kind of trouble from the time he was 12. I don't reckon we'll ever know all the evil he did in this community."

Leon scribbled away for a minute and then looked up. "Where will his remains be buried?"

"In a plot by his parents. There won't be a funeral. I doubt anybody would come if there was one." The sheriff looked up. "Miz Bonnie, can I have a refill on that coffee?"

For a brief moment, Bonnie stood immovable behind the counter. Her hands shook as she poured the sheriff some more coffee.

As soon as the two men left, she locked the café's door and turned the sign over from "Open" to "Closed." With Vern running errands, the kitchen was quiet. Bonnie laid her head on the stainless table and sobbed.

CHAPTER FORTY-ONE

1989

"BK, I hope that's everything. I can't fit another thing in this trunk." Brooxie grunted as he shoved a heavy laundry bag between two boxes. "Are you taking the kitchen sink too, honey?" He grinned as he pulled a handkerchief from his back pocket and wiped his face.

"That's everything but my guitar. I can put it next to me in the passenger seat." BK gave Brooxie a hug despite his sweaty shirt. "How can I ever thank all of you for my graduation gift?" After BK's high school graduation that June, Brooxie, Ouida, and Buddy had surprised her with a candy apple red Mustang. While it wasn't the newest model, Brooxie had spent hours tinkering with it to make sure the car was in perfect running condition.

Grace wrapped her arm around her daughter's shoulder. "You can thank all of us by behaving yourself in that big city."

"Aww Mama, Nashville's not that big. Besides I'll be too busy studying to get into any trouble." She kissed Grace on the cheek. No one had been surprised when BK received a full music scholarship to Belmont College.

Ouida, smokeless for two years now, never seemed to know what to do with her hands. She brushed an errant curl from BK's forehead. "You just be careful of those cowboys in Nashville's honkytonks."

BK hugged Ouida and giggled. "The only time I'll step foot in one of those places will be to sing, I promise."

Buddy patted BK on the back. "Nashville's supposed to have some of the best barbeque in the country." He sighed. "With this diet Doc Hunt's got me on, I don't reckon I'll ever get to eat any." While he was still quite portly, Buddy had lost over a hundred pounds in the past two years after Dr. Hunt said his heart was a ticking time bomb.

BK gave Buddy a peck on the cheek. "I'm so proud of you, Mr. Buddy. You keep at it—and stay away from BonBon's biscuits and gravy."

Bonnie stood under the only shade tree in their front yard. Her eyes brimmed with tears. "Come give your BonBon some sugar before you leave, sweet girl."

BK threw her arms around her grandmother and squeezed her. "BonBon, you need to start eating Mr. Buddy's biscuits and gravy. You're nothing but skin and bones!"

"I'll do my best, honey. Now you go set the world on fire and make me proud!" Tears running down her cheeks, Bonnie hugged her granddaughter tightly.

Climbing into the front seat, BK felt a lump in her throat. "I'm going to miss y'all so much."

Grace choked back tears. "Call me when you get to your dorm, honey." She leaned in for one last kiss on her daughter's cheek. "I'm so proud of you. Go make your dreams come true."

Once BK was settled in at Belmont, Grace was glad that school was back in session. There was always a meeting or a parent conference or a student to counsel. It kept her too busy to worry over her daughter.

As of late, Grace's biggest concern was BonBon. She'd taken a downward spiral in the last months. Although he could find no physical reason for Bonnie's weight loss, Doc Hunt had encouraged BonBon to turn over the café to Vern or hire a manager, but BonBon was stubborn.

Every morning, before she left for school at daybreak, Grace first stopped by the café where she'd find BonBon pulling warm biscuits from the oven. They'd sit in the café's kitchen together and enjoy their first cups of coffee before the doors opened.

One morning Grace noticed her mother's hands shaking as she poured coffee. "BonBon, why don't we take a little trip during my fall break? We could drive up to Nashville and visit BK. The autumn leaves should be gorgeous in the mountains."

Bonnie just sighed. "Oh honey, I can't leave the café for that long. Nobody can make my biscuits. And Charlie will be expecting a batch of my mud hens when he gets home."

"Charlie? He's been gone for years, BonBon." Grace's voice was tinged with concern.

"Oh, I know that! I just meant he always enjoyed my mud hens. I do miss that boy."

Grace's voice caught for a moment. "So do I, BonBon. So do I." She gathered her purse and briefcase and pecked her mother on the cheek. "It's Wednesday. I want you to get some rest as soon as the lunch crowd leaves."

Bonnie just waved her off. "Stop worrying about me, Gracie. I'm fine." But Bonnie wasn't fine.

A week later Grace missed breakfast with BonBon so she could get to the office and finish some state-required paperwork before the school day began. Later that morning, Grace visited a class of third graders who had made dioramas about their favorite books. When her walkie talkie beeped, she slipped out in the hall to answer it.

"Miss Mac, sorry to bother you, but there's a phone call I think you need to take." The voice belonged to Grace's secretary, Faye Johnson.

Faye was adept at managing problems in the office and rarely disturbed Grace when she was visiting classrooms—so Grace knew it was important. "I'm on my way, Faye."

The phone call was from Vern, whose voice shook with distress. "There's something wrong with Miz Bonnie. You need to get over here." He hung up before Grace could ask any questions.

Grace sped the three miles to the café. She found the front door locked and the "Closed" sign showing. That was odd since it was almost time for the lunch crowd to trickle in.

She hurried to the back of the café and went into the kitchen. Vern was pacing and wringing his hands. "What's wrong, Vern?"

Vern wouldn't look Grace in the eye. "Uh, it's Miz Bonnie. She ain't right, Miss Gracie."

"What do you mean? Where is she?" Grace's voice shook with concern as Vern pointed to the dining room.

Grace rushed through the swinging door. Bonnie stood frying bacon on the griddle. No wonder Vern was embarrassed. BonBon was dressed in nothing but her bra and panties.

"BonBon, what are you doing?" Grace removed her jacket to cover Bonnie, whose arms seemed to have grown thinner overnight.

Bonnie didn't look up. "I'm getting this bacon fried for BLTs. That's the lunch special. Oscar just brought by the remainder of this season's tomatoes." She smiled at an empty stool as she set the plate of bacon on the counter. "Now Oscar, I know how you love bacon, but let's save some for the customers."

Although her eyes grew wide with concern, Grace quickly transitioned into principal mode and spoke to her mother like she was addressing a kindergartener. "Why don't we get you some better clothes to put on? That bacon grease might spatter all over you."

She guided Bonnie into the kitchen where Vern averted his eyes. "Can you take care of the lunch crowd, Vern? I'm going to get BonBon over to see Dr. Hunt." Vern nodded in assent.

As they walked over to the house, Grace noticed for the first time that BonBon shuffled her feet as though she couldn't pick them up correctly. *How long has she been shuffling*, Grace wondered. She silently chastised herself for not paying closer attention to the changes in her mother.

When Dr. Hunt finished his examination of Bonnie, he ordered some bloodwork. "Miz Bonnie, the nurse will be in to take some blood. You just sit tight while Gracie and I have a conversation." He nodded to Gracie who followed him to his office.

"What's wrong with her, Doc? She's so thin and she's shuffling her feet and she didn't remember to get dressed this morning. Then she was talking to her late husband Oscar. Is she seeing ghosts?" Grace was close to tears.

Dr. Hunt took a moment to study Bonnie's file. He cleared his throat. "I think Miz Bonnie is suffering from some kind of dementia."

"Dementia? Is she crazy? What can we do?" Grace became unglued.

"Slow down, Gracie. As best I can tell, Miz Bonnie has no real physical ailments to explain the weight loss and the shuffling. Along with her forgetting to dress properly and the hallucinations, I think she is in the early stages of brain disease."

Grace began to cry. Dr. Hunt handed her a tissue. "I'm concerned about the tremor in her hands and her legs, too. Have you noticed Miz Bonnie demonstrating any other confusion as of late?"

Grace blew her nose and tried to recollect unusual behavior in Bonnie. "Not long ago she told me she wanted to make mud hens for Charlie when he got home. I thought it was just a slip of the tongue."

"I'm not an expert in brain disease. I think you should take Miz Bonnie to see a neurologist at Emory in Atlanta." Dr. Hunt scribbled something on a prescription pad. "Here's the name of a doctor who specializes in dementia."

Grace's hand shook as she took the paper. "In the meantime, what can I do to help her?"

"She doesn't need to be left alone, especially in the café. She could forget that she turned on the griddle and start a fire." Dr. Hunt studied Grace.

"I know this is a shock, but I also know that you have the capacity to take care of Miz Bonnie. She has friends all over this county. Let them help you."

After the appointment, Bonnie insisted on heading back to the café. "Vern has no idea how to make my chicken and dumplings!" She seemed like her old self again, but Grace took the rest of the day off to be with her.

Ouida was surprised to see Grace bringing out plates from the kitchen. "Are you moonlighting these days?" She smiled at Gracie, whose eyes sparkled with tears. "What's wrong, honey?"

As Grace handed Ouida her plate, she whispered in her ear. "I can't talk right now. I need a meeting with you, Buddy, and Brooxie. Since tomorrow is Saturday, can you set it up with everyone? But not here."

Although she raised an eyebrow, Ouida refrained from asking any questions. "Of course! Brooxie closes up at noon on Saturdays. How about my house tomorrow after lunch?"

Grace nodded. While the café was busy with its usual Friday evening crowd, Grace observed that BonBon appeared normal. She did notice that BonBon's hands shook when she poured anything. As the night wore on, she could see BonBon grow much slower in her movements. She wished she'd been more observant sooner.

Staying after closing time to wash dishes, Grace watched BonBon shuffle to a stool in the kitchen. "I'm slap worn out! I don't know why I'm tired all the time." BonBon laid her head on the table and fell into a deep sleep.

Grace wondered how many times BonBon had slept in this kitchen when Grace thought she was at home in bed. She was sick with guilt. She ran her fingers through BonBon's unkempt gray hair and whispered. "From now on, I'll take better care of you."

Dr. Anders, the Emory neurologist Doc Hunt had recommended, was much younger than Grace had expected. His friendly, comfortable demeanor had a calming effect on Bonnie, who had complained the entire drive to Atlanta that all of this was nonsense.

In his examination room, the doctor drew a clock and asked Bonnie to fill in the numbers. While her hands shook, she was able to complete the assignment correctly.

She struggled, however, when Dr. Anders gave her a list of words to repeat. "This is all so silly! Can I go home now?" Bonnie looked exhausted.

Dr. Anders smiled. "I think that's enough silliness for one day, Miz MacGregor. The nurse is going to come in and take some blood, and then your daughter can get you home." He patted Bonnie kindly on the shoulder and motioned Grace to follow him.

In his office Dr. Anders handed Grace a thin pamphlet. Grace studied it. "What's Lewy body dementia? Is that what my mother has?"

"In my best estimation, it is. The disease is caused by protein deposits called Lewy bodies that attach to nerves in the brain. This pamphlet is based on the latest report on the disease. Just three years ago, there was a consensus of doctors and scientists about how to diagnose the disease."

Grace wanted more answers. "What are the symptoms? Does my mother have all of them?"

Dr. Anders gave her the truth. "The sad truth about LBD is that it often presents as a combination of both Alzheimer's and Parkinson's. I'm afraid your mother demonstrates symptoms from both those diseases. The only way we can be certain is to conduct a biopsy of the brain, which is only done postmortem."

"Oh, dear God! How can this be happening? Isn't she too young?"

"We are discovering that LBD often affects patients at an earlier age than Alzheimer's. I'm sorry to paint such a glum picture for you."

Grace nodded. "No, I want the truth. What kind of treatment is there?"

Dr. Anders pulled out his prescription pad. "I'll prescribe something for the tremors and something else that should calm down Mrs. MacGregor's hallucinations." He looked up at Grace and smiled. "Besides that, let Miz

Bonnie stay as active as she can. The one good aspect of this type of dementia is that the patients usually continue to recognize all the people they love."

"I can do that, Dr. Anders." Grace swallowed. "Please tell me if you can—how long does she have?"

Dr. Anders shrugged. "I think her condition is more progressed than originally diagnosed by Dr. Hunt. I believe Miz Bonnie has been struggling for at least two years now."

Grace's tears began to fall. "I've been too involved in my own world to notice."

"Don't beat yourself up. Symptoms are very subtle at first." Dr. Anders smiled kindly. "Miz Bonnie has a minimum of two years and, perhaps, a maximum of five."

Bonnie slept the entire ride home, giving Grace the chance to absorb the heartbreaking diagnosis. She couldn't fathom a life without her BonBon, the woman who rescued her from a loveless life and showered her with unconditional love.

By the time they were back in Zebulon, Grace had a plan. She would make certain that the last years of her BonBon's life were filled with the same devotion that BonBon had always given her.

CHAPTER FORTY-TWO

1991

As Grace entered the café kitchen late one afternoon, a delightfully familiar aroma filled the air. "I think I finally mastered your mama's recipe, Gracie!" Ashley Myles Bennett grinned at Grace and handed her a small plate bearing one of BonBon's famous mud hens.

Grace's mouth watered as she took a bite of the still-warm treat. She savored the deliciousness for a moment and then grinned. "I agree, Ashley. These are as good as BonBon's."

Two years had passed since Bonnie's diagnosis. While her disease had been a roller coaster journey of good and bad days, Grace was thankful that she still had her mother with her.

When Grace offered Vern and Ashley a contract that would enable them to purchase the café after BonBon died, they both jumped at the offer. For decades Vern had been a permanent fixture at the griddle, and Ashley had dreamed of owning the café since her waitressing years.

Ashley began working full-time in the kitchen, first helping Bonnie prepare meals and then, in the last few months, doing all the preparation herself. Grace's only stipulation for the purchase of the café was that the new owners retain the name, Bonnie Mac's Café.

"Hold your horses, Miz Bonnie. We're almost there." The back door to the café opened as Lisa Leonard, clad in scrubs, wheeled Bonnie through in a wheelchair. When Grace realized she needed a caregiver for her mother, Doc Hunt recommended Lisa, who had worked as a skilled nursing assistant for years at the Upson County Hospital.

Lisa had been a godsend, living full-time at the house and catering to Bonnie's every need. "She's having a good day, Miss Gracie. But she's hungry." They always fed Bonnie before the supper crowd began to arrive at the café.

"I smell my mud hens. Come on, Oscar, let's have some." Everyone had grown accustomed to hearing Bonnie speak to her long dead husband. He was her constant companion and seemed to bring her peace, so nobody tried to convince her otherwise.

Lisa was already tying a bib around Bonnie. "Let's have some real food first, Miz Bonnie." Ashley handed her a plate on cue. "Look at that country fried steak and gravy. I know how you love those mashed potatoes, too." Lisa patiently cut the steak into tiny pieces and fed them to Bonnie.

Grace always made an effort to have supper with her mother. "BonBon, guess who'll be home next month?" Even though Bonnie's eyes seemed to stare into another dimension, Grace continued. "Bonnie Kaye's coming home. She's been writing songs for all the country stars and performing at the Bluebird Café in Nashville. I bet she'll sing some of her originals for you when she gets here."

Bonnie suddenly acknowledged Grace and smiled. "Bonnie Kaye is going to sing for me and Oscar? That's nice." Then she turned to Lisa. "I want a mud hen."

Bonnie was always ready for something sweet these days. Lisa and Gracie grinned at each other. At least Bonnie remembered what the dessert was tonight. Dr. Anders, the neurologist, had explained that Bonnie's memory was like a huge spiral with the memories on the outer loops being the newest ones. Those outer loops faded quickly for Bonnie, but closer into the inner spiral, the older the memories were. Those were the memories that Bonnie seemed to retain.

As supper patrons began to arrive, the kitchen got busier. Ouida pushed through the swinging doors. "Oh good! I wanted to tell Bonnie good night before she went to bed." She leaned over the wheelchair and smiled at Bonnie. "You look beautiful, Bonnie. Hazel did a wonderful job on your hair yesterday. And I like that pink lipstick on you."

Ouida gave Lisa some time off each week when she took Bonnie to the beauty shop and out to lunch. She and Buddy also insisted on getting Bonnie to her various doctor appointments so that she could go early in the morning when she was at her best and when Grace had to be at work.

Bonnie smiled at Ouida. "Oscar likes my hair, too." Ouida patted Bonnie on her shoulder. As if a light had been switched to its off position, Bonnie suddenly withdrew from reality. Her eyes grew vacant as she began to nod off.

Lisa gently wiped Bonnie's mouth with a napkin. "Let's get you to bed, Miz Bonnie." She headed out the door pushing the wheelchair.

Almost overnight, Bonnie stopped eating. No matter what delicious temptation Lisa or Gracie offered, she refused it. Bonnie grew too weak to get out of bed and started to sleep most of the time.

When Gracie told BK that BonBon's time was drawing near, BK canceled her upcoming set at the Bluebird Café and hurried home. She sat by BonBon's bed for hours at a time playing her guitar and singing her repertoire of songs.

One long day when BonBon had barely stirred, both Grace and BK sat by her side. BonBon suddenly opened her eyes and looked at them with clear eyes. "My beautiful girls. I want to go with Oscar, now." Those were the last words she ever uttered.

Half of Upson County and nearly all of Pike County crowded the Methodist Church for Mrs. Bonnie MacGregor's funeral. Grace delivered BonBon's eulogy with an elegance and confidence that belied her broken heart.

"Most of you know that I was adopted by Bonnie when I was a little girl. From the very first time she held me in her arms, I knew I would always be loved. And love me she did. She suffered with me through every valley and celebrated with me on every mountaintop. She taught me how to work hard, how to love unconditionally, and how to always rely on Jesus."

BK was too emotional to sing one of her original songs. They had all been so special to BonBon. Instead, she chose Brad Paisley and Dolly Parton's moving ballad "When I Get Where I'm Going." BK's guitar came to life in her hands as she sang the poignant lyrics:

When I get where I'm going
There'll be only happy tears
I will shed the sins and struggles
I have carried all these years.
And I'll leave my heart wide open
I will love and have no fear.
When I get where I'm going
Don't cry for me down here.

⚜

Two weeks after Bonnie's funeral, Buddy and Ouida drove BK to the Atlanta airport for her flight back to Nashville. Since Grace was busy with Christmas activities at school, BK and her mother had said their goodbyes early that morning.

Grace, tears glistening in her eyes, had embraced her daughter tightly. "I'll be home for Christmas in two weeks, Mama." BK studied her mother intently. "Will you be okay until then?"

Grace stood straighter and offered a weak smile. "Of course, I'll be just fine. The kindergarteners have a Christmas tea for their parents today. Then the rest of my week is jammed with various concerts and art shows by the other grades. I won't come up for air until school lets out for the holidays."

While Grace rarely acknowledged her own grief, BK had discovered her in the café's kitchen the night before. Grace was weeping into BonBon's favorite apron.

On the way to the airport, BK turned to Ouida. "Please promise me you'll check on Mama every day. She's too thin. She hasn't eaten a proper meal since BonBon took sick two years okay." BK's voice shook with concern.

"Between Ashley and me, we'll get her fattened back up. I wish I could give her some of the pounds I've gained since I quit smoking." Ouida was no longer stick thin, but the extra weight had softened her and made her even more attractive.

Buddy chimed in. "Don't look at me, Ouida Clarkston! Since Doc Hunt put me on that diet, I can see my feet for the first time in years."

Ouida laughed at Buddy and then turned back to BK. "Honey, don't you worry about your mama. I'll be watching over her." Ouida's thoughts drifted to the letter she had hidden in her purse. How many years had she guarded Charlie's secret? She knew the time had come to share whatever was in Charlie's letter with Gracie.

The December day had turned to dusk by the time Buddy dropped Ouida off to pick up her car in the alley behind the café. Although the café was closed since it was Wednesday, Ouida saw lights under the kitchen door.

Ouida tried the handle to the back door and found it was unlocked. "Gracie, you in here?"

She found Gracie drinking a cup of tea at the stainless kitchen table. "I remember the first time I sat at this table, Miss Ouida. I loved the way it smelled in here and the sound of BonBon's sweet voice. She let me help her make biscuits. I was covered in flour by the time BonBon put them in the oven. I figured she was going to slap me for getting dirty because that had always been my blood mama's punishment for me when I made a mess. Instead, BonBon just grinned and wiped my hands and face with a warm, damp towel. When the biscuits came out of the oven, I'd never smelled anything so wonderful. BonBon opened a steaming biscuit and slathered it with butter and strawberry jam. It was the best thing I'd ever put in my mouth. I was always hungry back then. I guess I was so malnourished that I couldn't get enough to eat. Now I can hardly stand to put a bite of anything in my mouth." Grace choked back tears.

"Sweet Gracie, grief can do strange things to us. I've been craving a cigarette for days now; I think the smell reminds me of sitting at the counter while Bonnie scurried around the café." Ouida grabbed Grace's hand and squeezed it. "Let's make a pact: I promise not to smoke if you promise to eat!"

Grace giggled. "Okay. There are some biscuits in the fridge that Ashley made up for tomorrow. Why don't we pop a pan of them in the oven?"

After a plate of warm biscuits and several cups of tea, Grace's shoulders relaxed for the first time in weeks. "There's nothing better than comfort food to heal the blues."

Ouida smiled and cleared her throat as she pulled the faded envelope from her purse and held it up for Grace to see. "Gracie, I've been keeping a secret from you. This letter is from Charlie. He gave it to me just before he left for Germany and made me swear that I would only share it with you if both he and Bonnie were gone." She sighed. "I often wished I had not made that promise, and I always hoped that I would be gone long before Charlie. Of course, life doesn't always give us our druthers. I kept the first part of my promise for all these years by holding onto this letter. Now it's time for me to complete that promise by giving it to you." She handed Grace the envelope, patted her cheek, and left.

Grace poured herself another cup of tea and sat at the table studying her name printed on the envelope. She recognized Charlie's handwriting immediately but couldn't bring herself to open the envelope. Instead, she closed her eyes and prayed. "Lord, whatever this letter contains, give me the strength to endure its message."

A sense of calm enveloped Grace. She felt as though Charlie's hand rested on one of her shoulders and BonBon's on the other. She took a deep breath and then tore open the seal.

The letter inside was only one page. After all the years, she still recognized Charlie's unique scrawl.

Dearest Gracie,

If Miss Ouida kept her promise and you are reading this, I guess both Miz Bonnie and I are in Heaven. Please try to understand that what we did was to protect you, and I truly believe that, if necessary, Miz Bonnie and I would do the same thing again. I need to tell you what really happened to Beau Loosier...

Grace's hands shook as she studied the contents of the letter. She reread it several times before the truth began to sink into her heart. "My sweet protectors," she whispered to herself as she returned the letter to its envelope. That night, for the first time since BonBon's death, Gracie slept like a baby.

The following Saturday, Grace, with Ouida Clarkston by her side, was accompanied by Sheriff Riggins to the law office of Derwood Brownlee. The venerable judge, whose practice had been in business for almost 50 years, was now known as Colonel Brownlee. He and Sheriff Riggins had become good friends over many years of shared cases.

The sheriff's appearance had changed little since Grace's first dealings with him when she was just a child. His temples were gray, and although his shoulders were slightly stooped, he still appeared fit. The rumor around Pike County was that the sheriff planned to retire after this term. Everyone hoped that his eldest son Frank, who served as his deputy, would run for office.

Grace twisted her hands in her lap as Colonel Brownlee read Charlie's letter aloud for the sheriff to hear. When he finished, the Colonel folded the letter and handed it back to Grace.

As Sheriff Riggins shook his head and sighed, Grace shivered. "What do I need to do to make this right, Colonel Brownlee?"

The sheriff was the first to break the uncomfortable silence. "It seems to me there's nothing to do, Gracie. All the involved parties, both victims and perpetrators, are dead." Sheriff Riggins grunted. "I figure Beau Loosier was the perpetrator, and Miz Bonnie and Charlie were just defending themselves and you." He turned to face Derwood Brownlee. "Would you agree, Colonel?"

The colonel removed his reading glasses and rubbed his eyes. Then his gaze softened. "Gracie, I agree with the sheriff. There's no one here to charge and no one here to defend. We need to let the dead rest. Let's consider this case closed."

When Grace returned to the house, she took the letter and buried it beneath all of Charlie's other letters. It would be a long time before she shared all her secrets with her daughter.

EPILOGUE

2008

After her near fatal stabbing at school, Grace was transported to the ER at Upson County Hospital. Once the doctors there saw the extent of Grace's internal injuries, she was airlifted to Grady, the best trauma hospital in the state.

When BK's plane landed at the Atlanta airport, her mother was already undergoing surgery. Buddy Simpson waited at the gate for her. "Come on, honey. I'll get you there as fast as I can."

There would be a series of surgeries over the next two weeks to repair Grace's intestines. The surgeon insisted that she be kept sedated until all the surgeries were complete.

A hematologist on staff was called in to review Gracie's bloodwork. He stopped by with Gracie's records early one morning while BK and Ouida sat by her bed. "I'm Dr. Sievert. I have some concerns about your mother's B-12 levels. Has she complained of feeling weak or fatigued?"

BK shook her head and turned to Ouida who considered the question. "She has seemed tired as of late, but the end of the school year is always a busy time for her."

Dr. Sievert raised his eyebrows. "Any signs of memory loss or confusion?"

"I don't live with her anymore, but she's always on top of her game when we talk." BK found his questions disturbing. "Do you think she has Alzheimer's?"

"No, nothing like that." Dr. Sievert offered a comforting smile. "She does have pernicious anemia, which is caused by a lack of B-12 in her blood. It can present with some of the same symptoms as dementia. We'll start her on an IV to get the B-12 to where it should be and hopefully, reduce any symptoms she may have been experiencing. Once she's released from the hospital, I can prescribe some high-dosage vitamins to keep her B-12 from falling so low again."

For the next couple of weeks, BK rarely left her mother's side. After the second surgery, Ouida showed up with a picnic basket of food from the café. "I figured you're tired of this hospital food, so I got Ashley and Vern to pack up some of your favorites."

BK didn't realize how ravenous she was until she smelled the familiar aroma of biscuits and fried chicken. A chicken leg in one hand and a biscuit in the other, she smiled through her exhausted eyes. "You're a lifesaver, Miss Ouida. They just took Mama down for another set of X-rays, but Dr. Gower said that the bowel resection looks good."

Ouida handed BK a plastic cup of sweet tea. "That's wonderful news. Oh, I almost forgot." She pulled a manila envelope from her oversized purse. "Faye Johnson, your mama's secretary, said she found this envelope on Gracie's desk when she was allowed back in the office. Since it has your name on it, we figured your mama meant for you to have it. Buddy and I are going to do a little shopping at Lenox Mall, but we'll be back tomorrow." She placed her hand on Grace's shoulder. "Is there anything we can get you, honey?"

"I'm good now that I've had some decent food. Mama will be awhile with the X-ray, so I'm going to work on a new song that's been simmering inside me. I'm glad I brought my guitar."

As Ouida left, BK fingered the clasp on the envelope addressed to her. The bold printed letters belonged to her mama. Had she meant to put it in the mail but never got the chance?

Inside, there was a stack of legal papers including her mama's life insurance policy and the deed to her house. Although she found all the papers somewhat disconcerting, BK was even more confused when she located a thumb drive at the bottom of the envelope.

She opened her laptop and inserted the drive. There was only one document on the drive entitled, "Letter to Bonnie Kaye." BK was in no way prepared for the letter's contents.

Dearest Bonnie Kaye,

If you're reading this, I'm probably gone. You may never forgive me for taking my life, but I could not bear having you watch me wither away like BonBon did. I guess that ultimately, I do not have the courage to face the long, slow torture that she endured.

I also could not summon the courage to tell you some secrets I have been hiding from you all your life. Instead, I swam in an abyss of sorrow and deception that I hid within myself. I cannot meet my Maker without making things right with you, so here's my story...

Before she could read further, BK was interrupted as a nurse rolled her mama back into the room. "Dr. Gower will be by in the morning to give you the results of the latest X-ray." Another nurse appeared to assist with moving Grace to her bed and reattaching her IV bag.

BK didn't relax until the nurses left and she could return to the letter on her screen. Grace's story was a long one, and BK found herself overwhelmed with conflicting emotions as she arrived at each new revelation.

While BK knew her mama was adopted, Grace had never shared anything about her life before BonBon had become her legal mother. BK's throat ached with pity as she read about her mama's life as a little girl, barely surviving in an apartment with her drug-addicted prostitute mother. Tears of anger and relief choked BK as she discovered that Grace had been abandoned at the café. She reached over and patted her mama's pale cheek as she whispered. "Thank God that horrible woman did one right thing when she left you with BonBon."

BK had never heard of Beau Loosier. Her emotions vacillated between terror and anger as she read about Beau's vicious attack on her mother when she was barely 13. While she was mortified, she couldn't help but be impressed to discover that Beau met his justified demise at the hands of her grandmother. She whispered to the ceiling, "I always knew you were a tough cookie, BonBon."

Although Grace kept a photo of Charlie on her dresser, she had never again talked about him to BK since she came home from kindergarten that day with questions. BK received most of her information about her daddy from BonBon, who always ended with, "Those two were meant for each other. I guess that's why your mama never found another man." BK realized now that Charlie had been her mama's protector. She wondered if Grace had ever felt totally unafraid since Charlie died.

It was the graveyard shift for the nursing staff by the time BK arrived at Grace's final admission. BK's real father was most likely a doctor and a musician and lived in Australia. She shook with rage as tears streaked her face. "How could you keep this from me, Mama? How could you?" Her voice fell on the deaf ears of her sedated mother.

Light from the hallway streaked through the room as someone opened the door. "Is everything okay in here, honey?" A nurse BK had yet to meet strolled to Grace's bed and checked her IV.

BK swallowed her tears. "Um, yes. I just woke up from a nightmare." Her explanation was not far from the truth.

Several days later Ouida sat with BK waiting for Grace to return from her fourth and final surgery. BK had spilled all her mother's surprises to Ouida. "How could Mama lie to me all these years?"

For the first time in quite a while, Ouida wished for a cigarette. "Sweet girl, your mama didn't lie. She just withheld information."

BK lost her struggle to remain calm as tears streaked her cheeks. "No matter the semantics, she kept secrets from me. Why would she do that?"

Ouida wrapped her arm around BK's shoulder. "Love."

"Doesn't sound like love to me." BK hung her head in defeat.

"Sweetheart, love in all its power is often misunderstood. Your BonBon's love rescued Gracie from a hopeless situation. Both Charlie and Bonnie's love, at the potential cost of their own freedom, kept Gracie from ever again being hurt by Beau Loosier. Gracie's love for Charlie kept her from revealing your biological father to any of us. My love for Grace kept me from sharing Charlie's letter until after both he and Bonnie were gone. And Gracie's love for you controlled her decisions, however misguided those decisions may have been."

BK's eyes were filled with unresolved questions. "What kind of love does such a thing?"

"Don't you see her reason for the deceptions, BK? Your mama loved you too much to destroy you with the truth."

⸙

"Mama, Mama, can you hear me? I know I felt her hand move, Miss Ouida. Did you see it move?" BK squeezed her mother's hand, and for the second time, she felt a slight movement from Grace. "Get the nurse! Get the nurse! I think she's waking up!"

While Ouida hurried down the hall to find a nurse, BK kept talking. "Mama, can you hear me? Mama, you're going to be okay." This time BK felt a stronger squeeze, and then for the first time in two weeks, Grace's eyes flickered open.

"Thank God, she's awake!" BK turned to the nurse as she entered the room with Ouida right behind her. "Her eyes are open, Miss Ouida!"

For a few moments, everything was fuzzy. Then Grace's vision cleared. "Can I have some water?" she whispered weakly. BK placed a straw in her mother's mouth to let her sip.

As Grace's focus grew stronger, she became agitated. "Why am I here? I'm supposed to be in Heaven."

BK exhaled with relief. "No, Mama. You're at Grady Hospital. You've had a difficult time, but you're all right."

Dr. Gower, the surgeon who had been caring for Grace, entered her room smiling. "Well, look who's awake." He shined a flashlight into Grace's eyes and took her pulse. "Mrs. MacGregor, welcome back to the living." He turned to BK. "Her vitals are good, and the stitches in her abdomen are healing well. Dr. Sievert still wants her on B-12 intravenously for a few more days. Then we can talk about her going home."

BK threw her arms around Dr. Gower. "Thank you for saving her." The doctor smiled and nodded his head as he left. BK turned all her attention to her mother. "Did you ever give us a scare, Mama!" She offered Grace some more water.

Ouida hugged BK and smiled down at Gracie. "Buddy's in the waiting area. I know you two have lots to talk about, so we'll head home to Zebulon and give everybody the good news." She slipped out before BK could even thank her.

Gracie drifted off to sleep for a while, but BK never left her side. When she woke up again, the sun was going down. BK was strumming some chords on her guitar. Grace tried to wrap her brain around what was happening. Her eyes filled with tears as she studied her daughter. "I was supposed to die. I have BonBon's disease."

"No! You do not!" BK squeezed her mother's hand. "The doctor said your symptoms were the result of something called pernicious anemia. When they did bloodwork for your first surgery, they discovered that your B-12 was non-existent. Dr. Sievert, the hematologist, said the anemia sometimes has the same symptoms as dementia."

BK plumped her mother's pillow so she could sit up. "Here, Mama, drink some more water. You need to get your strength back so you can go home. I'm tired of this hospital room."

Grace took a few sips. "How long have I been here? The last thing I remember is the pain in my belly." She touched her abdomen, which was covered in bandages."

"You were stabbed by a crazed maniac on drugs. The sheriff caught him. Do you remember any of that?"

"Weston Turner's father. He didn't have clearance to get his son, and I was stalling until Faye could get the authorities there." A movie-like image of the knife tearing into her belly drifted across Grace's mind. She shivered. "Did he get to little Weston?"

BK pulled a blanket over her mother. "No. The sheriff said you probably saved Weston and his mother's life. You're a hero, Mama."

Moments later Grace's eyes closed as she drifted back to sleep. BK kissed her on her forehead. Then she wandered towards the nurse's station. "I think I'll get some coffee while my mama's resting. I'll be back soon."

The nurse on duty smiled. "Honey, you take your time. You've barely left this place in two weeks. Your mama's in good hands."

When Grace opened her eyes again, the morning sun was streaming through the blinds. BK snuggled under a blanket on a recliner beside the bed. How beautiful and peaceful her daughter looked as she slept. *"Was I willing to give this child up just so I didn't have to suffer?"* she questioned herself. Her heart pounded at the thought of what she'd almost accomplished.

Grace watched as her daughter stirred, opened her eyes, and yawned. She lifted her arms up and stretched the way she'd done since she was a child.

"Good morning, Mama. You look so much better." Her brown eyes shone with a soft contentment.

"I feel much better, BK." Grace suddenly spied the manila envelope that she'd intended to drop off at the lawyer's office before she'd been interrupted.

She gasped. "So, I guess you read my letter."

BK straightened up and brushed her red curls out of her eyes, which were glistening with tears. "Your secretary sent it to me by Miss Ouida. Since the envelope was addressed to me, Mrs. Jones thought it was probably important."

"Poor Ouida. Always the bearer of bad news." Gracie sighed. "I thought I'd be gone before you learned all my secrets." Tears trickled down her face. "I'm so sorry, Bonnie Kaye. There were so many times I almost told you about your real daddy, but I just couldn't find the words."

BK climbed up in the bed beside her mother. "It's okay, Mama. I was angry at first—but these past few days sitting with you and begging God to save you, my heart softened. I'm just glad I didn't lose you."

Grace squeezed her daughter's hand. "Would you like to hear about your daddy?"

Six months later, Grace MacGregor sat on the edge of a boat as it rocked gently on the warm, turquoise waters off Key Largo. Fully recovered, newly retired, and at the urging of her therapist, Grace had finally decided to take a vacation. She'd rented a little bungalow in Key Largo for six months with the intention of exploring all the Florida Keys. Today was her final free diving lesson with her guide.

Ron Bennett, known as "Froggy" throughout Key Largo, was a retired Navy Seal. He'd settled in the Keys and bought a charter boat a few years back. While his clients were usually fishermen, when Grace showed up at his small office on the dock, Ron was smitten almost immediately.

Grace, now sporting a short, blonde pixie cut and a lovely tan, had asked if he offered free diving lessons. Ron grinned. "It's not my usual gig, but I've got the gear—and I think I can accommodate you." The two spent days on the water and evenings at a nearby waterside joint that served locals the best grilled grouper in Florida.

Over the course of Grace's lessons, she and Ron's friendship blossomed into something deeper. His quick wit reminded her of a certain Aussie she once knew, but his lopsided grin, so much like Charlie's, tugged at her heartstrings.

"Let me help you with that sunscreen." As Ron rubbed the lotion into Grace's back, she shivered with delight. "You look sexy in that swimsuit." He pulled her to him and kissed her.

Grace felt almost surreal whenever Ron kissed her. She'd never planned for romance in her life again. She still felt sometimes as if she didn't deserve love, even though Dr. Bates, her therapist, had helped Grace to see that she was deserving. Grace still knew she'd disappointed God and her daughter in so many ways. Life had dragged her down so often that she felt as though she lived underwater. Maybe that's why she'd wanted to learn to free dive.

She pushed Ron away playfully and smiled. "I paid for one more lesson, Froggy. Am I going to get it?"

Ron started the motor. "Our free diving spot today is six miles out and 25- feet deep. So, you'll get to practice holding your breath and using the surface dive I taught you. You think you're ready?"

"I've had a good teacher, so let's do this!" Gracie tucked her bangs under a Braves baseball cap as the boat gathered speed.

Thirty minutes later, Ron began to ease up on the motor as he maneuvered the boat until it was parallel to a buoy. "We can tie up here. There's something underwater here I want to show you. It's the statue you've been asking me about. Gear up, pretty lady."

"You mean Christ of the Abyss? That statue?" Grace's voice filled with excitement. She'd read about the statue and had told Ron when she first signed up for lessons that she wanted to see it. She'd felt as though she'd been living in an abyss for so many years with all her secrets. Now that she was rid of the secrets, she was ready to face her Christ of the Abyss.

Ron offered his lopsided grin as an answer. "Yep. This is your final test. If you can dive 25 feet, you'll see something marvelous."

Grace obediently donned her flippers and secured her snorkel mask. The two jumped in the water together. Ron offered instructions. "Remember what you learned about a surface dive: move your arms in a semi-circle and kick your feet. When we get close to the site, I'll signal for you to take a deep breath and push downward. As we get deeper, you'll start to feel pressure on your ears. Remember to hold your nose and force air into your nasal passages to equalize the pressure."

Her mouthpiece already in place, Grace just nodded. Ron put in his mouthpiece. Grace obediently moved her arms and kicked across the surface of the water. As they reached the dive point, Ron held up three fingers then dropped one finger at a time. When the last one dropped, they both took tremendous breaths and dove downward.

The statue came into sight almost immediately. Grace was so enthralled that she didn't think about her breath. Her heart almost exploded with joy at what she saw. The hands of Christ were lifting upward as though He was holding someone above the water.

When the two resurfaced, Grace gasped for air. "It wasn't at all what I was expecting."

Ron was mystified. "What do you mean?"

"I was never sinking into an abyss. The Lord's been holding me up all this time."

Over 9,000 miles away, on the other side of the world, BK MacGregor wrestled a tattered guitar case from the storage bin of the airplane that had just landed in Sydney. It was the last leg of her journey to Australia.

Someone tapped BK on the shoulder. "Excuse me, can I be of assistance? A little Sheila like you shouldn't have to struggle that way."

Bonnie grinned at the handsome Australian's accent. "Thanks for your help."

The fellow handed her the guitar case. "So, you're a musician. Looks like this case has seen better days. Is it an antique?"

"As a matter of fact, it is. I'm here to return this guitar to its rightful owner."

ACKNOWLEDGEMENTS

There would be no story without those who offered their expertise and contributed their true-life tidbits, which became the fodder for this book. While my acknowledgements may be brief in length, my gratitude is immeasurable to the following people:

- Dan Colwell, my go-to Pike County native for confiding in me about every interesting personality and unique setting in and around Zebulon, Georgia.

- Miller Fowler for sharing her vivid experiences of life growing up in the Georgia Baptist Children's Home in Hapeville, Georgia.

- Faye Bridges for offering details of her late husband Dick Bridges' early years of law practice in Zebulon, Georgia.

- Russ Head for painting a picture of a country doctor through the life of his father Dr. Doug Head.

- Marilyn Harris for sharing her memories as a Pennsylvania transplant attending Tift College.

- Jimmy and Kay Parrott for giving me the grand tour of Boy Scout Camp Thunder and for always buying my lunch when I visit Thomaston, Georgia.

- Truett Mallory for providing colorful tales of the legendary Midnight Myra.

- Beverly Crum for offering her heartwarming details of her career as a Physical Education teacher.

- Cherry Rayfield for explaining ladies' softball leagues in the 1960's.

- Mark Johnson for recounting the first day of Army basic training during the Vietnam War and for contributing his vast knowledge of "muscle cars" from the 1960's and 1970's.

- Rob Bell for describing in layman's terms the mechanics of Army tanks and the history of US bases in Germany in the 1970's.

- Garry Patrick for regaling me with descriptions of life "down under."

- Connie Bryant and Karen Davis for reading this story piece by piece and offering both technical and content feedback.

- Kim Dickerson for inspiring me to be my physical best through her yoga and core classes and for helping me look my best with her makeup magic.

- Anne Armstrong and Denise Shawver for keeping my muscles pumped for that much needed oxygen to my brain.

- Chris Curry and Karen Lacey for allowing the storefront of A Novel Experience Bookstore to grace the cover of this book.

- Rachael Weaver for her unfailing and remarkable talent to get the perfect cover shot.

- Jana Miller for her artistry in designing a cover that sings with personality.

- The members of the Lit Fits Book Club whose love of reading motivated me to keep writing.

- Lisa Loftin and the Women of Faith Sunday School for encouraging me throughout this journey.

- Janet Gilbert for listening to all my writing woes and convincing me that cheesecake is good for the soul.

- Shelley Martin for offering her IT knowledge to someone who doesn't know the difference in upload or download.

- Holly Wasson for utilizing her marketing finesse to obtain creative outlets for sharing my story.

- Amy Bell for ensuring that every single word counts and for discovering all the errors which this long-retired English teacher missed.

- Peggy Dumas Hollis for contributing precious memories about our grandmother, and most of all, for baring her soul to me.